Earthburst

Dennis Royer

Other books by Dennis Royer

Perry County Mysteries:

Catamount
Treasures
Night of the Walrus
Dancing Bear

Information at: **www.dennisroyer.com**

This book is dedicated to all of you, my readers, who have supported my novels during the past decade. Your encouragement is what keeps me writing. Thanks to my beta readers including my wife, Beth, and Don, George, Jane, Allen, Deb, and Jay.

Chapter 1

The President of the United States was the most powerful man in the world, but even the presidency wasn't enough power for R.A. Kall.

Standing on the dais at the Smithsonian Institution Air and Space Museum, Kall scanned the multitude of faces, all of them appearing eager to hear his words. His wide smile disguised the contempt he felt toward the assembled throng. He waved to them, the Washington press corps, wealthy political donors, leaders of industry, his party apparatchik, and other members of Congress. Puppets he had deftly manipulated since the time he accepted his first political office as local school director all the way through his meteoric ascendancy to the highest office in the free world. After today's Congressional vote approving funding for the final phase of his Earthburst project, Kall no longer needed them. His lifelong ambition had been set in motion…

…And the countdown clock had started ticking.

Kall's political adversary, Senator Winston Halbert, glared at him from the crowd. Halbert had made his feelings clear to Kall how he wanted to share in the spotlight, felt it was owed him since the bill wouldn't have passed without his deciding vote. He had hailed its passage as a bi-partisan effort.

A load of crap, Kall knew.

There was nothing bi-partisan about Halbert. Kall had beaten him by playing hardball. By illegally using the F.B.I. as his very own private secret police, Kall had found out about Halbert's relationship with a mistress, a relationship unbeknown to his wife and constituents back in Vermont. An envelope filled with compromising photographs conveniently slid under the senator's office door immediately converted Halbert's opposition toward Earthburst into complete support.

The senator had gotten the message. Nobody messed with R.A. Kall.

On the other hand, snubbing Halbert may have been a political miscalculation. Kall still needed the man. He was the best fit for a newly created cabinet position. No problem. He'd invite the senator to the White House for a tête à tête. He would mend damaged fences. Now that Kall understood Halbert's weakness, he knew exactly how to get what he needed from the man.

The lights dimmed and a hush fell over the crowd. Flash bulbs popped as the museum's curator, Dr. Nika Cho, approached the podium.

Kall beamed, this time his smile genuine and with delight, at the diminutive Amerasian beauty, who also happened to be the First Lady. He had met Nika at a ZPG rally when they were both university students. Engaging her in conversation, Kall discovered that she was not only beautiful, but also intelligent, charming, and witty. He was instantly smitten with her, and she with him. Perfect kindred spirits, both of them possessing the determination that they would transform the world, make it better. Life hadn't been easy back then living hand-to-mouth, but Nika had stuck with him through the lean years when they had shared an idea which had blossomed into a dream.

Nika stood on a step stool and tapped the microphone. "Good evening, ladies and gentlemen. Welcome to today's signing ceremony." She paused as technicians compensated for feedback in the sound system. She blew into the microphone before continuing. "Can everyone hear me?"

"We hear you," several people responded from the far end of the hall.

Nika waved at those people in acknowledgment. "Wonderful." She shifted her gaze toward Kall. "When my husband and I came to Washington we shared a common vision, a vision to improve the lives not just for those of us fortunate enough to live in this great country, but for everyone sharing the planet with us, all of humanity. As a scientist, I advanced our vision among the scientific community while R.A. shepherded this vital project through the Washington bureaucracy."

She spoke in a more serious tone. "It's been an arduous struggle, but as the old cliché goes, nothing worth fighting for is easy. America's image has become tarnished in recent years. The rest of the world is weary of our imperialistic ambitions and our military posturing. The Earthburst project is finally something we can give back to the world, something peaceful and benevolent;

something to make us once again proud to be Americans."

Nika paused, her cheeks dimpling when she smiled. "Sorry, folks, I didn't mean to sound like a politician. I'll leave that for my husband."

A wave of polite guffaws sounded from the crowd.

"I might as well get him over here to the podium. Ladies and gentlemen, it is my honor to introduce you to the man with the vision and the courage to fight for Earthburst. The man who will make it official today by signing this bill into law. I give you my husband, the President of the United States, R.A. Kall."

Kall kissed Nika on the lips and the crowd roared their approval and applauded. His spirits soared. Utopian societies had been tried many times throughout history and all of them had failed. The men behind those movements just didn't have enough conviction, courage, and intelligence to pull it off. This time it would be different.

Kall raised his arms and gestured for the crowd to calm their applause. He forced a smile for the cameras and began his speech. Teleprompters flashed the words for him to read, but he didn't need them. These words of victory he had dreamed of speaking long ago.

"My fellow Americans," he said and pointed at the ceiling. "All of the aircraft you see suspended above us, the Wright Flyer, the Sputnik, the Mercury capsule, and the rest, represent technology that has been directed outward, beyond our world. The Earthburst web of satellites re-shifts our focus earthward, toward improving the quality of life for all mankind.

"How so, you may ask?

"Imagine a lost child separated from his mother in a crowded city or God forbid abducted. With a touch of a button, that child's mother could instantly activate an unobtrusive homing beacon, implanted subcutaneously in her child at birth. A beacon that would lead the mother to her lost child while simultaneously alerting the police.

"Or consider the possibility of a soldier wounded in battle and a doctor half a world away being able to monitor that soldier's vital signs and advise his comrades on how to perform an emergency medical procedure.

"Picture a citizen from any third world country victimized by a natural disaster being able to communicate their status in real time to a regional relief agency.

"These are but a few examples."

Kall paused to ponder the real reason behind Earthburst, the truth he dared not mention to this crowd.

Tapping the podium with his finger, Kall went on, "You are all aware of the current telecom shortcomings, too many isolated areas with poor signal reception, lack of worldwide network reliability, and satellite phones that only the wealthy can afford.

"The Earthburst web of geosynchronous satellites guarantees high speed, portable, next generation communications over every square inch of planet Earth. This bill authorizing activation of the new planetary grid ensures ubiquitous communications at low cost for those industrialized nations that can afford it and at no cost for those nations that cannot.

"I realize that giving away U.S. taxpayer dollars is anathema to the conservative block, but a wise man once wrote, 'cast your bread upon the waters, and it will be returned to you many fold.' After years of bullying our neighbors, it's high time for America to spread her largess among the nations. Earthburst is a gift to all mankind, a sign of our nation's goodwill. As my wife, Nika, already mentioned, this gift represents an offering that will once again make us proud by reasserting America's moral authority."

Always looking for a way to zing his adversaries and to use their arguments against them, Kall pounded the podium with the edge of his fist. "And asserting moral authority, my fellow Americans, is a basic principle of our conservative opponents, is it not?"

This statement brought scattered nervous chuckles from the crowd and murmuring. It was after all a mixed audience spanning the entire political spectrum. No matter, Kall possessed the panache to rally them all. He raised his arms and shouted. "We all win."

He repeated. "We all win."

Like a Baptist preacher, he gestured with his arms and shouted one more time, "We all win."

The crowd erupted into thunderous applause. Kall paused to savor the moment, then picked up a gold pen to sign his name to the bill. With a stroke of that pen, R.A. Kall affirmed his destiny as president for life, and he rejoiced in the knowledge that in just a few months Washington D.C. would be an ash heap, and the United States of America in its present form would no longer exist.

Chapter 2

Cooper Stover mashed his straw hat tight to his head after having almost lost it to a gust of wind. The breeze carried a chilly bite, typical of a March morning in northern Pennsylvania, but it felt refreshing as he labored behind his horse drawn plow.

The calendar had changed from winter to spring only a few days ago, but the sun's rays were already strong enough to threaten Cooper's fair complexion. Despite his straw hat, his skin would soon bloom with freckles, as it did every year, making him look like a little boy instead of an 18-year-old man.

Cooper slapped the reins across his horse's back and dug the point of his father's plow into the dirt. He didn't mind tilling the ground, breathing in the sweet aroma of moist, rich soil, yet a dissatisfaction stirred his soul. For the world was large, and he had never once set foot outside of Tioga County.

He daydreamed of visiting the ocean to witness the awesome power of crashing waves and to marvel at its vastness. Cooper longed to experience that which had inspired the great poets such as Hugo, Kilmer, and Whitman. He recalled a favorite passage from Robert Frost's, *Once by the Ocean*:

"There would be more than ocean-water broken
Before God's last Put out the light was spoken."

And he realized with sadness that he may never enjoy the simple privilege of finding out for himself about the allure of the sea. While working, Cooper dwelled on his regrets. According to the ordnung or rules of his church, he was free to leave for a period of time to test his faith, to decide if he wanted to be baptized Amish or become part of worldly society.

His friends, Liam and Andrew, had moved into a Philadelphia apartment and offered Cooper a place to stay, but he wasn't sure about city life with people living stacked atop one another, their unceasing noise, and blatantly decadent lifestyle.

At the edge of the field, Cooper turned his horse and started back the way he had come, turning a new row of soil. Back and forth. Back and forth. Good work. Honest work, his father had drilled into him; except he recalled Andrew's reasoning. "How can you know what you really want in life if you don't first experience what the English have to offer?"

The answer lay with his sense of duty as an only child, an unusual circumstance since the Amish faith encouraged large families. Although they didn't speak of it, Cooper sensed his parents had wanted more children, but it was Gottes Wille that their family would remain small. A few years earlier, his mother bore a stillborn infant, a little girl. His father had been sickly for many years with a bad heart. It fell to Cooper to do all of the heavy work around the farm. He couldn't abandon his parents under those circumstances.

As a result, Cooper limited his rumspringa or period of running around to attending Sunday evening hymn sings. He considered many of the maidels he had met at those gatherings to be pretty, desirable even, but he hadn't found one yet with whom he could develop a romantic attachment. The situation being, once formal courtship began, members of his congregation assumed it would end in both parties becoming baptized and then ultimately wed.

Better not to trifle with a maidel unless he really meant it.

Cooper had urges, though, and wondered if he would eventually marry just to satisfy his desires instead of marrying for love. He suspected that many families within his faith started out that way, and that seemed wrong, sad even. He often wondered if that is what had happened between his own mother and father. They weren't very affectionate toward one another. Had they married out of need instead of love? If so, could that perhaps explain why God had withheld his blessing of children?

A glint of reflected sun flashed in Cooper's eyes interrupting his thoughts. "Whoa," he said and pulled back on the reins. Cooper watched a red car jetting up Cove Road and felt a thumping in his chest probably caused by one of those powerful radios with the big, rear mounted speakers the English kids favored.

During their rumspringa, many Amish youth bought vehicles. Seeing this one prodded a yearning within Cooper to give it a try. Maybe when Liam and Andrew visited the next time, he'd ask them to let him drive their truck.

The red car flew past. Although Cooper knew very little about cars, this one looked old fashioned to him. Cove Road curved slightly near the end of his father's property line. This car moved too fast and would never make it around the curve. He removed his straw hat, waved it in the air, and hollered, "Slow down."

Tires squealed and a cloud of dirt exploded into the air. Cooper abandoned his horse and plow and sprinted toward the curve wondering what he would do if someone were seriously injured, silently praying that nobody was.

He found the car nose down in a gully on the outside radius of the curve. As Cooper neared, the driver gunned the engine spinning the wheels forward, then in reverse, but the frame balanced on the berm of the road with both rear wheels off the ground.

The thumping music stopped when the driver killed the ignition and kicked the door open. Katie Hunt, daughter of Dr. Hunt, who lived in the last house at the back end of the valley spilled out of the passenger compartment and onto the ground. Why had she driven so fast? Since Cove Road was the only way in and out of Wineberry Hollow, she should've been familiar enough with the curve to slow down.

Katie got up from the ground, brushed herself off, and began to kick at the car. "No good piece of crap," she yelled, "Now I have another reason to hate you, you pathetic rust bucket."

Cooper called out to her. "Are you hurt?"

She spun around and gawked at him. "Didn't see you standing there. You speak Spanish?"

Such a strange response. Was she in shock? "No, I do not speak Spanish."

"Good, then this isn't going to burn your delicate Amish ears." She began kicking again at the driver's door and yelled at the car as if it were some living thing. "Tu madre es una puta."

"Please stop yelling, Katie. I asked if you were hurt."

She glared at him. "How do you know my name, Amish?"

He pointed a thumb over his shoulder at the house. "Your father attended my mother during her pregnancy." He left out how his sister had been stillborn. "You came with him. We played games together while Mother was in labor."

She cocked her head. "Oh, yeah. Dominoes wasn't it?"

It pleased him that she had remembered. "I'm Cooper Stover,

Coop to you."

"That was ages ago."

"Six years. You sure you're not hurt?"

She put her hands on her hips. "Duh, am I bleeding? Do I *look* like I'm hurt?"

Coop had been looking. And he liked what he saw. No longer the bean pole she had been back then, Katie's body had blossomed. Her low slung black denim jeans accented the curves of her hips. The V-neck sweater she wore revealed far more than he would ever see from the maidels. He recalled from their previous meeting six years ago that the two of them were the same age.

Coop's arousal and resulting embarrassment painted his face cherry red. Cursed complexion. He didn't know what to say and blurted, "Your hair. It's black now."

"No shit, Sherlock. It's good to know that they teach you the primary colors in that Amish school of yours."

He cleared his throat. "What I mean is, you used to have golden brown hair. Why'd you change it?"

Katie relaxed and waved an arm. "My natural color bored me. I was a blonde last semester, now I'm raven. When the weather turns nicer I'm thinking about going red."

"Say, it's Wednesday. Shouldn't you be in school?"

Katie's hands shot back to her hips. "What are you, the freaking principal? I decided to ditch today."

"Ditch?"

"Yeah, you know, ditch, hook out, skip, flee the scene, go AWOL, play hooky. What do you Amish call it?"

"Truant?"

"Well, there you go."

"Why are you truant?"

"You're awfully nosy, but if you must know, the guy I've been dating, Stan, pissed me off."

"You're truant because your boyfriend upset you?"

"I don't want to talk about it."

"You frightened me, Katie. You shouldn't drive so fast."

"Now you sound like my Dad." Katie looked at her car. "Crap, speaking of Dad, he's going to kill me."

"Punish you, maybe, but he won't kill you."

"Whatever." She pulled a cell phone from her purse.

"What are you doing?"

"Calling triple A. I'm obviously going to need a tow."

"Wait," Coop said. "Let me take a look."

He walked around the car, examining it. "I don't know much about cars, but I'm familiar with motors. We have generators and diesel powered equipment around the farm. I don't see any fluid leaks, and it doesn't appear as if your vehicle suffered any damage. This is quite a sturdy car."

"That's exactly why Dad said he bought it for me. He tells me that he's gonna get me something nicer once I get some more driving experience, maybe for graduation. This thing is so ancient that I'm embarrassed to drive it to school." Katie gave the car another kick then flexed her foot having stung her toe. "I mean, this is the 21st century. What father buys their kid a 1981 Buick Skylark?"

"You could ride the school bus instead."

"No way. The only thing more embarrassing than driving this piece of crap to school would be taking the bus."

"The car may still work. I'll get Bonnie. She should be able to pull it back onto the road. With luck, your papa will never know you crashed."

"Who's Bonnie?"

"My plow horse. I'll be right back. Stay here."

"Does it look like I'm going anywhere?"

Cooper hurried back into the field and found Bonnie resting exactly where he had left her. He unhitched the horse from the plow and led the beast to the car. He eyed Katie sitting on the ground, legs pulled up, resting her chin on her knees. She certainly had grown into a pretty young lady, full of spirit.

Despite Katie's unladylike speech, it dawned on Coop how easy and natural it had been having a conversation with her, different from the maidels at the Sunday hymn sings where he always felt awkward and could never find the right words.

"It's been like five minutes, what took you so long?" Katie smiled. "Just teasing."

Coop noticed that she trembled. "Are you cold?"

She cleared her throat. "No. It's catching up with me now. I could've killed myself. That asshole, Stan, isn't worth it."

"You want me to walk you to my house? Mother can make you

some hot tea."

"Thanks, Coop, but I'll be alright."

He wrapped a length of bull rope around the rear axle and secured it to the horse's harness. After some coaxing, Bonnie stepped forward and pulled the car from the gully.

With all four wheels back on the road, Coop freed the rope and patted Bonnie on the rump, shooing the horse back into the field. Bonnie was an old, contented beast and wouldn't wander far.

Katie remained seated on the ground looking at him.

"Start it up," he said. "See if it'll run."

Katie got up and brushed off her backside. "Listen, Coop, I'm sorry for being such a snot. I didn't mean to offend you in any way."

He opened the car door for her. "You didn't."

She slid into the seat. "Unlike Stan, you are a gentleman. Thank you."

A perfect smile with perfect teeth. She should smile more. Leaning on the edge of the car door, Coop looked down at her and enjoyed the close up view provided by her V-neck sweater.

The engine turned over on the first try. Katie gunned the motor a few times to make sure. She met his gaze. "Thanks, Coop. You're a life saver. I don't know how I can repay you."

"You could let me call on you." The words escaped Coop's lips on impulse. His face grew hot, and he figured he displayed an even deeper shade of red than before. What had he been thinking? This girl was English.

"Holy shit," Katie said. "Did you just ask me out?"

When he opened his mouth, all that came out was a squawk.

She grimaced. "Are you out of your freaking mind?"

Coop expected to be rejected, but not this harshly. He grew indignant. "You're the one who asked how you could repay me."

"When someone says I don't know how I can repay you, that's just an expression. You're supposed to reply with 'think nothing of it,' or 'you would've done the same for me,' or 'fuhgeddaboudit,' or any number of other canned responses. Besides, wouldn't you get into trouble, maybe even shunned?"

"I'm in rumspringa. The rules are relaxed." Coop removed his straw hat and raked a hand through his hair. "Katie, would you really be so embarrassed to be seen with me?"

"Hell, yes, I wouldn't be caught dead sitting in some buggy wearing a long black dress and a bonnet over my hair."

Coop laughed. "Katie, I would never expect you to do that. That's not exactly what I had in mind."

She furrowed her brow. "What did you have in mind…exactly?"

"How about I come visit you at your home? With your papa there, of course. We'll talk. I'll bring the dominoes. Maybe we can play a game or two."

Katie closed her eyes. When she opened them, she said, "That would be the most boring date in the world. I mean, with my dad there and us playing dominoes? Come on, we're not children anymore."

Coop's heart sank.

Katie muttered something to herself that Coop couldn't make out. She looked him over. "Moving on with my life so soon after a breakup would certainly teach Stan a lesson, but going out with an Amish dude would be all the way over the edge and into the abyss."

She looked Coop in the eye. "God, I should have my head examined. Okay, I'll go out with you, but here are the rules."

Rules? He didn't know English girls came with rules.

"I'm gonna pick you up Friday evening. I assume that you don't own a car and don't drive?"

"I don't. Where will you drive us?"

"Dinner, and if that goes well, maybe a movie."

"Katie, please understand. That would be strange to me. I've never been to a movie."

"That settles it. I'm taking you to a teen slasher horror flick. If you want to dip your toes into the water, might as well go all the way."

"What?"

"Never mind. Next, dude, you gotta do something about your wardrobe. Blue shirt, black trousers, and black suspenders aren't going to cut it. If you expect me to get gussied up for you, then I expect you to wear something a bit more hip. And you'll have to lose the straw hat."

Why would he want to misplace his hat?

"What other clothes do you have?" she asked.

"Other than these, I have my for-gut clothes. They're dressier."

Katie rolled her eyes. "You're about the same height as my father except you're built a lot more solid than he is. I'll bring you something of his to wear."

Coop felt ill at ease. "There's no need for us to do anything fancy. All I really want is to spend time with you."

"Look, I can't even pretend to understand what your life is like, and I know a date with a bona fide English girl is way outside of your comfort zone. Believe me, going out with you is way out of my comfort zone, too. This will be like going out with someone from Mars. That's why I think we should do it, but listen, you and I both know this is a lark, right?"

"A lark?"

"I mean I'm not promising anything more than just one date." She took a breath and exhaled. "I can't believe I'm going through with this. Somebody pinch me awake and tell me that I'm dreaming."

"You aren't going to ditch, are you?"

She giggled. "How could I? Your family doesn't even own a phone. I won't be able to call it off."

He pretended to wipe perspiration from his brow. "Whew, that's a good thing."

Katie dropped the transmission into gear. "See you Friday, and don't you bail on me, either."

Coop watched the tail lights of her old Buick Skylark. Long after she disappeared from view around the corner, he could still feel the thump, thump of her radio in his chest.

Or was it his pounding heart?

Chapter 3

President R.A. Kall stood in the White House Rose Garden admiring the high flying cirrus clouds painted vermilion by the setting sun. A beautiful March evening and perfect ending to a momentous day. Yesterday, he had signed the final phase of Earthburst into law, and today Congress had just released funding.

He glanced at the envelope in his hands, the results of his background investigation into Senator Halbert. The sound of footsteps against the walkway alerted Kall that his visitor had arrived. An aide ushered the dour faced senator into the Rose Garden. Kall believed Halbert to be the man he was looking for, but first he had to peel away the legislator's self-righteous façade.

Kall stuffed the envelope into the vest pocket of his blazer and shook hands with Halbert. Then he made eye contact with the Secret Service detachment. "Give us some privacy, please."

The men walked out of earshot but stayed within eye contact.

With a bowed head and feigning humility, Kall mumbled, "Senator Halbert, I'm glad you could come so that I could personally apologize for yesterday's affront."

Halbert's voice took on a growling tone. "After voting your way, I earned the publicity. You stabbed me in the back by snubbing me. My party has branded me a turncoat. My approval ratings back home are plummeting."

"I'll find a way to make it up to you."

The senator made a clucking sound with his tongue. "Don't play me for a fool. You have the reputation for kicking your political enemies while they're down. You and I have nothing in common, and let me be clear about this, I don't like you personally, nor do I approve of your socialist agenda."

Halbert's vehemence surprised Kall. Sure, the man was upset, but this seemed over the top. "Have I done something to offend you?"

The senator waved his hand in a dismissive manner. "Your entire presidency offends me, especially your heavy handedness. You are a tyrant, sir, who demands unconditional submission to an agenda I find repugnant."

Kall felt his temperature rise. "Get over it. I won the election. Twice, I might add, both times in a landslide. I have a mandate from the American people."

"Give me a break. You're a political hack who pandered to the voters and ascended to the presidency under a nebulous, undefined, pretext of 'change.'"

"Really, senator, that sounds like a loser's sour grapes, accusing me of pandering."

"Yes, pandering. By promising to fix things for the common working American and pledging justice to those victimized by so-called corporate greed. You're just a snake oil salesman pedaling passion inspiring platitudes which sound rosy but mean nothing."

It was all Kall could do to remain civil. He took a calming breath. "Is it my fault that voters are duped by the same old recycled slogans, or are you just jealous at my effectiveness in using them? And how dare you accuse me of lacking substance. I've accomplished more in my seven years than your party has accomplished in generations. I've implemented sweeping health care reform, a government takeover of the financial markets, and unprecedented environmental regulation over the private sector, not to mention the Earthburst project."

Halbert snorted. "All of which would not have been possible without your playing the race card."

Kall felt as if he had just been slapped. "What the hell is that supposed to mean?"

"I stand by what I just said. My party leaders have been completely emasculated by your political correctness police. Anytime we oppose anything you want, your minions in the liberal media paint us as being racist. You brandish racism like a fist. Don't deny that your being African-American plays a big part in your success."

Those words had to be a calculation, Kall realized. Halbert was no fool. He was just trying to get a rise out of him in an attempt to gain the upper hand. Suddenly, he admired Halbert for being so ballsy. The man just might work out. "I'm not going to dignify your statement with a response, and quite frankly, I'm disappointed. That kind of talk is beneath you."

"Your policies have divided this country, maybe irreparably so."

"Don't be so melodramatic."

"I'm not. People have a visceral reaction to you unlike I've ever seen."

Kall needed to get Halbert settled down so that he could get to the real reason he sent for him. In a submissive gesture, he held out both of his hands, palms up. "All right. I'll admit it. I had to play a bit rough to get you Republicans to approve sending the remaining 8 of Earthburst's 48 satellites into orbit. I couldn't unilaterally authorize a NASA rocket launch." At least not yet. "This is nothing new in politics. We all play the game. It's only natural that liberals will worship me for my political acumen and conservatives are going to despise me."

"We despise you, and we fear you," Halbert said. "Instead of engaging us in political debate, you destroy people who stand in your way. Like meddling into their personal affairs. Like taking covert photos in their bedrooms and threatening to expose their secret lives which, by the way, is none of your business."

Kall admitted to himself that he enjoyed this verbal sparring. "My dear senator, I'm sure I have no idea what you are talking about."

"Bullshit."

Kall reached into his blazer pocket and pulled out a pack of smokes. "A while ago, you said that we have nothing in common. You're wrong about that. We both crave power and possess a strong will to survive."

"That's impossible politically. When you survive, I go down, and vice versa."

"I'm not talking about politics right now. I'm talking about life."

In a pause that followed, Halbert relaxed. "Why am I here?"

Kall extended the pack of cigarettes. "Smoke?"

The senator shook his head.

"Nika constantly reminds me how filthy this habit is." Kall lit his cigarette and led Halbert to a gurgling bronze fountain in the shape of an angel holding a harp. He sat on a white marble bench and motioned for Halbert to take a seat beside him.

Halbert brushed the bench with his hand before sitting.

Kall took a deep drag from his cigarette and said, "I like it here. The fountain's background noise masks private conversations, and we're away from the Oval Office's recording devices."

He took another drag. "It's a nice spring evening. Spring is my favorite season. A time for renewal. Did you ever wish you could renew, start over in life, do things differently?"

"I'm sure you didn't call me here to discuss philosophy."

Kall leaned back and crossed his legs. He needed to make Halbert more comfortable, get him to let down his guard. "Indulge me, Winston. May I call you Winston?"

"I prefer just plain Win."

"Alright, Win, let's set aside our differences for a moment and act like two normal guys having a conversation. I'll repeat my question. Did you ever wish you could start over?"

The senator shrugged. "No. I am who I am because of my life experiences. My parents raised me to be self-reliant, charitable, and respectful. I believe in the Christian core values they instilled within me. It's an honorable way of life."

"Is that so?" Kall took another puff. He just couldn't resist saying it. "Do those Christian core values include cheating on your wife?"

Halbert sprang from his seat and shook a finger. "You rotten son-of-a-bitch. I figured you to be the bastard behind those pictures. How dare you lecture to me about morality. How many millions of innocent souls do you allow to be murdered every year under the guise of a woman's right to choose?"

Kall didn't need to dwell on the topic. He had made his point. The senator was a hypocrite. Despite his sanctimonious image, Halbert was as vulnerable to sexual seduction as any other man. Now, he just needed to get Halbert to open his mind a little wider. "I'm sorry, Win. My words were uncalled for. Please forgive me, and give me another chance to explain. Sit down, I think you're going to be interested in what I need to tell you."

The senator trembled, red faced. "Look, about my infidelity. I've made mistakes, done things that I regret. That's between me and God. All of us are sinners. Even you. Especially you."

"I can't argue that." Kall patted the bench beside him. "Please, I have a confession to make."

Halbert sat.

Kall figured his words would get the senator's attention. "You do indeed have me pegged. I am a liar. This country isn't enlightened enough yet to elect an atheist president, so my affiliation with the A.M.E. church and all of my religious observances are just for show. A political calculation."

Halbert grunted. "No surprise there."

"And it's no surprise to me that you're such a religious man, so I need your help with a religious question." Kall crushed out his spent cigarette butt under foot. He looked Halbert in the eye. "The Bible tells us that God destroyed man during the flood, because he regretted the evil things that men did. He wanted to start over. If it happened once, do you think God would see fit to destroy us again?"

Halbert leaned away and gave Kall a sidelong glance. "I'm no clergyman, so I'm not qualified to answer your question."

In other words, the senator didn't know the Bible from Hustler magazine. "Hear me out. Seven billion people live on Earth, certainly more than in Noah's time, and the world has to be many magnitudes worse off than it was back then. What's God waiting for?"

"I don't presume to know the will of God."

Which meant that Halbert didn't have a clue. One thing for sure, Kall wasn't about to leave such an important decision to some fickle deity. "What if I were to tell you that God has provided me with the means for humankind to start over?"

"I'd say you were deranged."

Kall chuckled. "That's also what Noah's critics said about him."

Halbert sneered. "Noah was a man of God. You just admitted to being an atheist."

"So true. You've pegged me again."

"Get to the point. What is it that you really want from me?"

Kall uncrossed his legs and sat erect. "I'm going to remake this country. Start it anew from scratch. I want you to be part of my team, Win. I need you."

Senator Halbert's jaw dropped. "You really *are* insane."

"I'm also serious."

"Okay, I'll play along with your notion. What could you possibly want from me? Why are you telling me this? I'm a political enemy."

"What I propose transcends politics. I need a person with your business background, your specific private sector skill set."

A glint appeared in Halbert's eye. "Go on."

Kall pulled the report on Halbert from his inside pocket, opened it, and glanced at the pages. "I've studied your life, Win. It says here you're a self-made multimillionaire who started as a bag boy in a local grocery store at the age of 15. You worked your way up to become grocery store manager at 22 and president of the chain at 29. You left the company at 33 and started a wholesale food distribution network that's now the largest in Vermont. Such an achievement demands cunning and fortitude. On top of that, you managed to convince the people of Vermont to elect you as their senator. I'm impressed."

Halbert's lips turned up. "Yeah, that is quite a record, especially since I had the benefit of only a high school education. I do have one correction for you, though. My company's the largest in all of New England when you consider the volume we handle, not just Vermont."

He had definitely stroked Halbert's ego, made him receptive. Kall stood and looked down on the senator. Time to go for the close. "Win, I'm about to reorganize the United States government, and I want you to fill my new cabinet position, Minister of Logistics. I can think of nobody more qualified."

Halbert got up and stood eye to eye with the president. "This is a joke."

"I assure you, it's no joke."

"Half the people of this country hate you. They won't stand for it, your remaking the country in your own image."

"The people will never see it coming. It'll be all over in an instant. Afterwards, I'll replace our current inefficient form of government with a smooth running, benevolent hegemony. With me as hegemon, of course." He touched Halbert's arm. "Me and my team."

"That's trashing the Constitution." Halbert paused and his face paled. "My god, you're proposing mass destruction, aren't you?"

Kall met Halbert's gaze but said nothing.

The senator took a step backward. "Not only are you insane, you're also a psychopath. What about the rest of the world? If you incapacitate us as a nation, we'll be invaded. China, Russia, and the Muslim nations will all be clamoring to get a piece of us."

"Win, you're not thinking big enough."

Halbert gasped. "Are you telling me that you have the power to take down the entire planet? With no fear of retaliation?"

The president tried a reassuring smile. "I'm about to reboot the entire human race. Join us. There's room for you and your immediate family in our plans."

"Who is *us*?"

"Say yes, and I'll tell you more."

"I suppose if I say no, I'll not see another sunrise."

Kall laughed. "Nothing quite so dramatic. If you share this private conversation with anyone else, they'll just think you're a kook. You'll be ruined." He paused and for emphasis, frowned. "On the other hand, if you say yes, there will be no turning back.

After you learn our plan, betrayal will indeed result in a swift death to you and your entire family." He reached over and straightened the senator's necktie. "So, what's it going to be? Can I count you in?"

Chapter 4

Bathed and freshly shaven, Cooper Stover pulled on a clean white shirt and black trousers and joined his family in the parlor. His mother sat in an old wooden rocking chair preoccupied with sewing. His father sat at a desk looking over some bills.

Coop sat on the wide ledge of a window sill and looked outside checking the sky. Enough light remained from the setting sun for him to distinguish the barn but not the distant pond. Katie had agreed to come for him shortly after sundown which meant she would soon be here. His heart beat faster in anticipation of seeing her again, and also from the anxiety over the strangeness of it all.

He caught fleeting glances from his parents. Other than the song Mother hummed, the room remained eerily quiet.

His father broke the silence. "It's not too late for you to put an end to this foolishness. When the girl comes for you, just send her away."

Coop had grown frustrated defending himself. He had discussed his feelings with them several times, but his mother and father remained united in their disapproval. Fighting hard to maintain a normal, respectful tone, he said, "What of my friends Liam and Andrew? Nobody judges what they do during rumspringa. In far away Philadelphia, you must know that they also spend time with English girls. Katie is no stranger to us. She's Dr. Hunt's daughter. The Hunts are a good family, good neighbors."

Coop's mother rested her sewing on her lap and looked up. "Not a day goes by that Liam and Andrew's mothers don't pray for them, as I pray for you now."

"Nothing good can come of your seeing this girl," his father added.

"Isn't the whole point of rumspringa for me to experience the ways of the outsiders, to learn to make my own decisions?"

"One need not put a hand into the fire to know that it will burn," his mother said.

Headlights shined through the window along with the rumble of a car's engine.

They all got up and stared at the door. It struck Coop as silly, all of them standing there frozen in position, as if helplessly waiting for some demon to invade their home. Coop opened the door after hearing a timid knock.

Katie wore a knee length, black wool coat. She stood stiff and wide eyed, arms clutched around herself, shivering from the cold.

Coop leaned toward her within an inch of her ear. She smelled like lilacs. "Don't be frightened," he whispered. Then he stepped back and in a normal tone said, "Please, come in."

Like stone statues, his parents eyed her.

"Hello Mr. Stover, Mrs. Stover," Katie said.

Coop's mother uttered a feeble, "Good evening." His father just grunted and dipped his head.

After a long pause, Coop cleared his throat. "We should be going."

Mr. Stover glared at Coop. "I'll expect you home early. You'll have a long day tomorrow finishing up with the spring plowing."

Coop placed his hand on the small of Katie's back and led her out the door. After they climbed into the car and shut the doors, Katie let out a long sigh. "What the f…udge was that icy reception all about?"

"They don't approve," Coop told her.

"No shit. Talk about hostile vibes. Now I know what guys feel like when they pick up their dates."

"They're upset with me, not you."

"They're more than upset. You still want to do this, Coop?"

"Yes. More than anything."

Katie started the car. "Then let's make tracks." She pulled from the driveway onto Cove Road and headed toward the township road at the end of Wineberry Hollow.

"I'm happy you didn't ditch," Coop said.

Katie giggled. "I must confess that I did have second thoughts. You up for pizza?"

"I like pizza with sausage and extra cheese."

"A new place just opened in Wellsboro. Cecil's. Supposed to be pretty good." She pointed a thumb over her shoulder. "There's a gym bag in the back seat with some of my dad's clothes that I picked out for you."

"What? Do you want me to change clothes in the car? In front of you?"

"Amish boys wear underwear, don't they?"

His face flushed. "Of course we do."

"Then don't be so modest. You'll be covered up. Go on, climb into the back seat and change out of those Sunday-go-to-meetings. Besides, it's dark. I won't see anything, and I promise not to peek in the rearview mirror."

Coop's embarrassment gave way to a daring sensation, a feeling like stealing a slice of pecan pie when his mother wasn't looking. He crawled into the back seat and rummaged through the gym bag.

Sitting out of view directly behind the high headrest of Katie's seat, he yanked off his trousers and then quickly slipped into the ones belonging to Dr. Hunt, thinking irrational thoughts while doing so. What if at that moment, Katie crashed the car and they were both killed. What would his parents think finding him dead in Katie's car and wearing no trousers?

The material felt soft against his skin. Khakis, he believed they were called. Being used to buttons over the fly, he struggled with the zipper. The trouser legs were long enough, but the waist hung loose. He'd have to cinch up the belt. Next Coop tried on the shirt.

"Everything okay back there?" Katie asked.

"Your father's shirt is too tight. It won't button."

"I was afraid of that. You have a broader chest than Dad, more muscular arms, too. You'll have to improvise."

"How?"

"Put your own shirt back on. Dad's denim jacket is too big for him, so it should fit you perfectly. Wear the jacket over your shirt and whatever you do, don't take it off. That white shirt doesn't go well with those khakis."

"What did your father say about my wearing his clothes?"

"He doesn't know I borrowed them, and since I do the laundry, he'll never know."

Coop rejoined her in the front seat.

"How do those clothes make you feel?" Katie asked.

"Different," Coop said, "in a good way."

"Oh yeah, why?"

"Because you seem to like me better this way."

She giggled.

He asked, "I'm curious. What are *you* wearing under that long coat?"

"Cooper Stover, are you having dirty thoughts?"

Did he say something wrong? Why did she react that way? Before he could ask, Katie started talking.

"I actually thought about wearing a skimpy dress to give you a real thrill, but it's too cold for that. I'm wearing the same black jeans you saw me in when I crashed the car the other day, but don't worry, I washed them. Oh, and a red, midriff blouse."

Coop scratched his head. "What's midriff?"

She reached over and gave him a playful punch in the arm. "It means you get to see my belly button, dude."

"Why did you punch me?"

Katie clucked. "It was just an emphatic gesture, you know, like an exclamation point at the end of a sentence. Or you might call it a love tap."

A love tap. Coop liked the sound of that. "Okay then, dude," he said and punched her in the shoulder.

The car swerved over the centerline. Katie shrieked and pulled at the steering wheel until the car settled properly in the right lane. She shouted, "What the hell, Coop? That hurt."

Coop pressed his back against the passenger door. "I'm sorry. I just wanted to give you a love tap back."

"God, you are so naïve. Look, Coop, girls can give love taps to guys, but guys never hit girls. You got that?"

"I didn't mean to hurt you."

"Don't worry about it. Just don't do it again."

Coop's heart thundered in his chest. Maybe this had been a mistake. He just didn't know how to act around the English, didn't understand their strange ways. How was he expected to know the rules surrounding love taps? Hanging his head, he said, "I feel like a fish out of water."

Katie laughed which made him feel a little better. At least she wasn't angry with him anymore. "We'll just go with the flow, Coop. I expect you to make some mistakes, but you'll learn from them. I won't let you get in over your head."

Go with the flow? In over your head? Were her references because of what he had said about being a fish out of water? He wished she would speak hoch English instead of using slang.

"Wanna listen to some tunes?" she asked.

"Does it have to be so loud, like when you crashed your car?"

"Hell, yeah. The louder the better." She fiddled with some portable device which Coop assumed was what some English kids called an iPod and plugged it into the dashboard. "And I know exactly the right song to fit the occasion, even if it is an oldie."

Music exploded from the speakers, assaulting Coop's hearing like he was sitting in the middle of a thunder storm. He tensed and covered his ears. Bass notes thundered in his chest like a battering ram.

Katie held the steering wheel with one hand. With her other hand, she slapped the dashboard in time with the music. She reached over and gave him another love tap. "Lighten up, Coop. Live in the moment."

Coop lowered his hands from his ears.

"Sing along with the chorus. Don't be bashful."

How could he? He didn't know the words.

Katie screamed out the lyrics along with the music. She looked at him and laughed.

Watching her laugh made Coop happy. Katie was so full of life. He smiled, and then he laughed. It started small, but soon became uncontrollable, way down deep, soulful laughter like he never experienced before. As if someone opened the barn door and all the animals were stampeding. Coop felt wonderful, lighter than air, audacious, and dare he even think it?

Immortal.

The music transformed him. He didn't understand how, nor did he care. The utter joy of it, he hoped would never end. Sitting alongside Katie and letting go of his inhibitions, Coop took up the chorus right on cue with her. The two of them belted it out:

"Tramps like us, baby we were born to run."

Chapter 5

"This way, sir. The president is already aboard and waiting for you."

Senator Halbert followed the secret service agent to the Sikorski Sea King helicopter waiting on the south lawn of the White House.

Having already powered up, the machine's engines roared. Halbert covered both ears. Whirling rotors kicked up dust, stinging his face.

A man in a dress blue uniform helped him up the stairs and into the cabin. "Welcome to Marine One, Senator Halbert."

Halbert spotted President Kall waving him over, pointing to the seat beside him. An attendant buckled Halbert in and slipped a set of headphones with an attached microphone over his head.

Relieved by the relative silence provided by the noise damping headphone, Halbert relaxed.

A disembodied voice emanating from the ear cup announced that they were cleared for takeoff, and Halbert felt a sinking sensation in his stomach as the aircraft lifted from the ground.

The next voice Halbert heard was the president's. "Beautiful sight, the lights from the city." He pointed out the window. "I wonder how much of it will remain a year from now."

Halbert watched as the White House and great buildings surrounding the Washington Mall slipped from view and felt a tinge of nausea. He wasn't sure if it was from the sudden take-off or from Kall's words.

After being asked by the president to participate in the Earthburst project, Halbert quickly calculated that it would be in his best interest to say yes. If Kall did indeed have the will and the power to carry off a reboot of the human race as he put it, he definitely wanted to find out all he could about it. He believed that Kall possessed the megalomaniacal ego to attempt such a plan, and although he had no direct evidence, Halbert knew the president had orchestrated the plot to blackmail him into voting for the Earthburst authorization bill.

He winced after recalling the damning photos. Had Lenore been in on it from the beginning? After all, it had been awfully easy for him, a middle-aged balding man with a soft middle to seduce a beautiful 22-year-old intern. Nevertheless, he figured Lenore would remain his paramour as long as he continued to spend money on her. The Georgetown apartment, her clothing allowance, and the Porsche he had bought her would keep any woman happy. At the very least, it should've insured her silence. Then again politics being such a dirty business, he was a fool not to have smelled the trap. Lenore was so beautiful, so willing, so young.

Even now, he longed for her.

If he were a liberal Democrat representing some godless big city district, keeping a mistress would probably have been a resume enhancer, but as a conservative Republican who wore his religion on his sleeve, Halbert's constituents held him to a higher standard.

He had been backed into a corner. Desperate to keep his wife and the voters from finding out, Halbert had to play along. If he didn't agree with what the president was about to reveal, he could possibly turn it around and use it as leverage against his political foes, get out of the mess he found himself in. Kall wasn't the only person in Washington who could play dirty.

The city lights below became more widely scattered. "Looks like we're heading north."

"Does that surprise you?" Kall asked.

"I assumed we were heading for the command center in the Virginia mountains."

"Not a large enough facility for what I have planned. We're going to Site R."

Halbert recalled the moniker. Site R, also known as Raven Rock, was the nation's alternate joint communications center in the event that Washington D.C. was destroyed or otherwise taken out of play. Most people knew the site by its more common name: The Underground Pentagon.

Located near the Maryland / Pennsylvania border, the flight lasted less than half an hour before the aircraft touched down. They waited until the engines powered off before exiting.

Halbert walked alongside President Kall as agents escorted the two men through an opening in the side of the mountain which one of them referred to as Northwest Portal One. The portal resembled a tunnel opening with several vault-like doors that Halbert assumed could seal the entrance and probably withstand a direct nuclear strike.

"This reminds me of Cheyenne Mountain in Colorado Springs," Halbert said.

"The entrances may look the same," Kall said, "but Cheyenne Mountain is nothing compared to this facility."

Halbert hadn't worn an overcoat and hugged himself against a cold, damp draft.

They boarded a tram piloted by an unsmiling female soldier wearing fatigues. She drove them deeper into the mountain and stopped in front of a double door marked Room 32. The doors slid open with a whoosh, and Halbert felt a puff of warm air against his face. He was happy to get out of the damp weather.

On the other side of the door stood the First Lady. "Welcome to Raven Rock, Senator Halbert. Please, come in."

The agents remained outside while Halbert and the president entered.

They walked into a living room furnished with a sofa and two lounges. A large flat screen TV hung on the wall opposite the sofa and an oversized, glass coffee table lay between the sofa and the TV display.

Halbert glanced around and noticed a fully furnished kitchen and a long hallway. What lay back there? Bedrooms? Some high tech office?

President Kall said, "Since I don't believe the two of you have been formally introduced, Senator Winston Halbert, this is my wife, Dr. Nika Cho, Curator of the Smithsonian Institution. Nika, this is Senator Halbert."

Nika and Halbert shook hands and exchanged greetings.

"Please, sit," Nika instructed. "Can I get you something to drink?"

President Kall sat in one of the lounges, Halbert at one end of the sofa. Ordinarily he'd ask for a cocktail. Under the circumstances, he thought it best to keep his mind free from fog. "Perhaps some tea?"

"Excellent," she said. "I was about to make myself a pot of African bush tea."

"I'll have the same," Kall said.

Nika filled a tea kettle with water from the tap and set it on a burner. Then she took a seat on the sofa beside Halbert. She spoke. "R.A. has told me a great deal about your accomplishments and logistical skills."

Halbert had never heard anyone refer to the president by his initials. Is that really what she called him? "Yes, I've done well in the private sector."

"How did you manage to build New England's most successful food distribution network starting from nothing?"

He sat up straight in his seat. "Hard work. I served my customers better than my competitors." Halbert had often related his life story during various motivational seminars. Nika held his gaze and seemed to hang on his every word as he related his rise from store clerk to magnate.

Nika rested her arm on the back of the sofa extending it toward him. She swiveled in her seat so that both knees pointed at him. "You control 40% of the food supply for all of the New England states. The impact of your next largest competitor is marginal at best. What would happen if you suddenly ceased operations?"

With that question, it struck Halbert that the First Lady already knew all about him. She wasn't really interested in hearing what he had to say and had gotten him to talk just to puff up his ego. What did she really want him to say, and why was President Kall sitting there saying nothing, studying him?

Halbert tugged at his shirt collar. "If my company ceased operations and nobody stepped in to fill the void, I'd say a lot of people would starve."

"You feed the people of New England. They are completely dependent on you." Nika grinned. "You hold their lives in your hands."

"I never thought about it that way."

"It's no oversimplification. You're the most powerful person in the northeast United States. Maybe even more powerful than my husband."

Halbert laughed. "Is this your scheme? Is this what Earthburst is all about, starving people into submission?"

"The scope of Earthburst is far more comprehensive than just controlling the food supply," President Kall said, "although that's a very effective means of maintaining power. It's been used throughout history and even in the present. Think of Somalia, Haiti, even China. The rulers in those countries have figured out that if you keep your people starving, if you keep them in a daily struggle to obtain meager supplies of food, then they have neither the time nor the energy to consider insurrection."

The tea kettle whistled. Nika stood. "Let me get that."

Halbert sat in silence considering the implications of what Kall had just said.

Nika returned with a tray on which sat a teapot, three china tea cups on saucers, a glass jar containing honey, and a plate of cookies. She placed the tray on the coffee table and poured for all of them. She added a teaspoon of honey to her own cup. Making a hand gesture toward the arrangement, she said, "Please."

Kall picked up a cup and sipped. "Delicious. Outstanding as usual, Nika."

"Thank you."

Halbert sipped. He preferred regular black tea to the exotic varieties. "Very good. I believe we were discussing the food supply?"

Nika glanced at President Kall who answered some unspoken question with a barely perceptible nod.

She set her tea cup on the saucer. "This country's founding fathers envisioned a citizen legislature where men would serve in Washington for a term or two and then return to their civilian businesses and lives. An altruistic vision which no longer reflects present day reality. Today, congress has only one goal in mind: to get reelected, to hold on to power. Do you consider that to be a selfish motive?"

Halbert took another sip of tea wondering how she wanted him to respond. What game were they playing? He set the cup down. "Yes and no."

She laughed. "Spoken like a true politician."

"Allow me to explain. As a matter of fact, my main goal is to get reelected, because I sincerely believe that nobody else is in a position to serve the interests of the people of Vermont better than I can. My vision remains intact and in complete agreement with the philosophy of the founding fathers."

Kall rolled his eyes. "Give me a break. Are you saying that you would willingly step down if someone better than you came along?"

Halbert shrugged. "Nobody is better than I am, but ultimately it's for the people in my state to decide."

"What?" Kall asked, his mouth agape. "You would actually trust the people with a decision like that, yokels who have no concept of running a country? Apathetic, ambivalent, ignorant voters? C'mon, Win, you've worked too damn hard to become a senator to allow your fate to rest in their hands."

Why didn't Kall just tell him what was on his mind. Halbert

grew tired of the dance. "I suppose it would be easier, and I could get a lot more done if I didn't have to spend half my time campaigning. It would be more productive if the people just elected me as senator for life."

"Now we're getting somewhere," Kall said. "That's what Earthburst is really all about. Permanent, irrevocable power."

"The people aren't that ignorant, and they're not starving. They'll revolt."

President Kall narrowed his eyes and lowered the pitch of his voice. "Not after I get through with them." After an uncomfortable silence, Kall sat back and smiled. In a normal tone, he said, "You conservatives are a dying breed. You fight a hopeless war. The forward thinkers of my party set in motion years ago the mechanism to control the masses, to make them completely dependent on government. From Roosevelt's New Deal to Johnson's Great Society to my pledge to end corporate greed, we've successfully pitted the disadvantaged against the so-called wealthy."

Halbert groaned. "Every one of those programs you just mentioned has ended in failure."

Kall scoffed. "Failure? Says who?"

Halbert pressed an index finger into his palm. "You liberals have bankrupted this country, financially and morally. You're African-American, Mr. President. Can't you see how programs like the Great Society have destroyed the black family. Instead of lifting up young black men and helping them to become self-reliant, you've made them irrelevant by means of welfare. In essence, you're saying it's okay for men to abandon their families, that the government will take care of their children. Father's don't have to worry about their responsibilities."

The president smirked. "Blacks vote 90% Democrat in every election. I'd call those programs a resounding success."

Staring into his teacup, Halbert wished now that he had asked for something stronger.

"Look, Win," the president said, "it's all very simple. You buy the people's loyalty by giving them a little bit of what they want. Not too much so that they prosper. Just enough for them to survive, like those starving people we spoke of. It keeps them coming back to you for more. If the people question the pittance we hand out, there are plenty of villains to blame like obstructionist Republicans, corporate greed, the religious right, or angry white men to name a few. If you give them just enough, they quit trying to make it on their own. The moment that happens, you own them."

Halbert sighed. "It's amazing to me that the majority of the people don't understand how your party plays them for fools."

Kall sneered. "They understand. They just don't give a damn as long as we send them a government check every month or grant amnesty to their illegal cousins or give them free needles to shoot up with or provide free health care or allow them to marry their gay partners. Do I have to go on and on?"

Halbert sat back against the soft sofa cushions. He wasn't going to be able to convince Kall that a dependent citizenry led to self-loathing and the inevitable moral debauchery which had resulted in the demise of every major civilization throughout history. The man was too far gone, too drunk with power.

He looked at Nika. "Don't take this the wrong way, the tea is fine, but do you have any liquor around here? Maybe a gin and tonic."

The first lady removed his tea cup. "Coming right up."

"Make that two," Kall said.

While she made their drinks, Kall said, "Despite all that I've told you, there's one major flaw in the liberal quest for power. The United States of America is still too wealthy. It'll take at least another twenty years to tear this country down to the level where the overwhelming majority are dependent on Washington."

He looked Halbert in the eye. "I'm not willing to wait another twenty years. It's my destiny to become president for life, America's final president. I have the intelligence and wherewithal to create a new socialist utopia and the means to make it happen. Me and my loyal advisors. People like Nika who will serve as my Minister of Culture, keeping a watchful eye over what the people read and write about us. People like you who will serve as my Minister of Logistics overseeing the distribution of food, supplies, medicine, everything essential for the well being of our citizenry."

Nika handed the two men their cocktails.

Halbert controlled the urge to down the entire glass in one gulp. "You just told me you had the means to make it happen. My guess is that it has something to do with the Earthburst satellites?"

Nika powered on the flat panel monitor. It displayed a map of the Earth. Superimposed on the map were the locations of the 48 Earthburst satellites. Forty green dots and eight white outlines.

"The remaining eight will be launched into orbit next month," Nika said. "Thanks to your vote the communications mesh will finally be complete. Two satellites providing coverage to each time zone located half way between the equator and each of the poles."

Halbert saw what appeared to be a countdown clock in the upper right corner of the screen. "What's that?"

"The number of days until detonation," she said matter-of-factly. "On June 21. That's 82 days, 7 hours, and 25 minutes from now."

The skin on Halbert's arms and legs stiffened with goosebumps. This time he didn't hesitate and gulped his drink.

Kall picked up the remote control unit and pointed it at the monitor. A map of the continental United States freckled by red dots replaced the world map. "What you see here are our domestic enclaves. Enough equipment, supplies, and personnel will be located in each of these enclaves to begin anew."

Halbert sat on the sofa, feeling weighted down. Was this really happening? Was the President of the United States sitting in this room casually discussing the destruction of civilization? "Enclaves? I don't understand. If you're planning on nuking the planet, won't that destroy everything?"

Kall's eyes widened. "Are you insane? Who said anything about nuking the planet?"

"But…" He pointed to the countdown clock on the display. "How then?"

"That's classified for now, but you'll find out soon enough. Win, don't misunderstand my intentions. The Earth wouldn't be much of a utopia if it could no longer sustain life. Sure, we're going to lose the cities. As long as our enclaves thrive, we'll come out the other side just fine."

Halbert didn't know what to say and waited for the president to continue.

"The problem currently facing us," Kall said, "is the Earth has far too many people."

Nika spoke. "I have a Ph.D. in history and another in

anthropology. This planet cannot sustain its current seven billion people. The population needs culled. Only then will the populace be more controllable. In times of cataclysm, people are conditioned to turn to their leaders. If we leave them with nothing, then we will become everything to them."

Culled. The word echoed in Halbert's mind. "And just how many people do you intend to murder?"

"We intend to murder nobody," Kall said. "Nature will take care of that for us. To answer your question, though, our experts estimate the die off in this country to be in the range of 96%. Worldwide, around 99%."

"Seven billion trimmed to maybe 70 million, guaranteeing humanity's sustainability with sufficient numbers for a diverse gene pool," Nika said matter-of-factly. "A chance for a new beginning."

"And that's Project Earthburst in a nutshell," Kall said.

The drink glass in Halbert's hand trembled. He set it down. "Are the leaders of the rest of the world on board?"

Kall burst with laughter. "God, no, can you even imagine the U.N. General Assembly debating this?"

"Who else knows?"

The president waved a finger. "I'm afraid that'll have to remain classified. Instead, I can tell you how many. About 300 people in the world know what you know now, and only I know the identity of all 300."

Halbert didn't know how to respond or what to think. He sat there, numb.

"You haven't screamed yet or run from the room," Kall said. "Can I take that as a sign that you're favorably digesting what we've told you?"

Halbert looked the president in the eye. "Digest this? I'm still wondering if this is some kind of political trick. Some kind of set up?"

Nika leaned over from her position on the sofa and touched Halbert's arm. "My husband has just revealed to you a plan that if it became known would result in his impeachment and charges of treason. It is he who is reaching out to you, putting his trust in you. If this is a setup, who has more to lose? You or him?"

Kall spoke next. "Remember that conversation we had in the

Rose Garden about Noah and how God killed everyone on Earth except for Noah and his family? I'm no biblical scholar, yet I seem to recall the reasoning behind that act had to do with humanity's wickedness. During that time period, the people were idolaters, corrupt, self-serving, sexually perverted, filled with greed."

He waved his arm in a grand gesture. "What do you see in the world, Win? Does that sound familiar?"

"History repeats itself," Nika said.

"You dare cast yourself in the role of God?" Halbert asked.

"No, I cast myself in the role of Noah," Kall answered, "and I can anticipate what you're going to say next. That God spoke to Noah. No, I haven't heard voices. God hasn't overtly spoken to me, but he did allow me to become president. I admit that I am no saint, but neither was Noah. Even the Bible makes note of his public drunkenness. God used him as a tool to serve a purpose. You believe in God's will, don't you?"

"Yes," Halbert said, but after what had just been revealed to him, he wasn't sure if he believed in anything anymore.

"Can you consider the possibility that the real purpose behind Earthburst is God's will?"

Halbert stared at the empty drink glass sitting on the coffee table. He could use a refill. "I…I don't know."

Kall continued. "Let me help you wrap your mind around the concept. It's quite simple. If you believe that God exists, then you have to believe that if He allows a cataclysm to occur the magnitude of what I am proposing, then it has to be His will. If it weren't His will, then God most certainly would intervene."

Logical. What the president just said made sense. Sort of.

Kall walked over to Halbert and placed a hand on his shoulder. "You have nothing to lose by committing to Earthburst."

Nothing but my soul, Halbert considered. But maybe it *was* God's will. "You can guarantee the safety of my family?"

The president pointed to the display. "You get to choose which enclave to send them to. Each enclave will be stocked with enough food and supplies to last many years all guarded by the military."

"The military? Will they remain loyal if their families are at risk?"

"That solution is already in place," Kall said. "Someone else's worry."

Halbert studied the map. "Your enclaves. How are you going to stock them? How are you going to move everyone around at the appropriate time?"

"As Minister of Logistics, that task falls to you. Are you up to the challenge?"

Halbert stood and walked over to the display. He studied the location of the 104 enclaves, their disbursement and location relative to Interstate highways, waterways, airports, and military installations. "Difficult, given the short time frame. Difficult, but doable."

He turned to face the president and Nika Cho. "Would it be possible for me to select a personal staff, a small number, maybe three or four other people?"

Nika glanced at the president.

Kall shook his head. "We have our own vetting process. I'll provide you with your manpower. If it's Lenore you're thinking of, I consider her as a member of your family. You will, of course, say nothing to her about any of this just as you will say nothing to your wife and other family members. Just get them to one of the enclaves before…" He nodded at the countdown clock.

Nika added, "Perhaps it would be in your best interest to direct Miss Lenore to a different enclave from your wife."

That much was a given.

"And you'll be doing a lot of traveling between the enclaves, both before and after detonation," Kall said. "You'll have sufficient opportunities to spend time with them wherever they may be located."

Halbert swallowed. "Thank you, Mr. President."

Kall approached the senator and extended a hand. "Welcome aboard, Win."

Chapter 6

Cecil's Pizza was set among other small restaurants and family owned shops in Wellsboro's downtown area. Serving as the gateway to Pennsylvania's Grand Canyon, the quaint tourist town with its gas-lit streets struck Coop as odd. Many of the English looked down on the Amish lifestyle, yet here they considered old-fashioned ways to be appealing and even paid to experience a ride in a horse drawn carriage.

They picked a table by the window, but when Katie removed her wool coat, Coop decided that he'd rather look at her than out the window. The long sleeved, red knit blouse Katie wore covered her up to the neck, but her stomach was exposed. Midriff, she had called it, and the curves of her hips were clearly visible above the belt line of her tight fitting black jeans.

When the waitress came, they both asked for water and Coop ordered a large pizza.

After she left, Katie asked, "What do you think of our date so far?"

Dressed in Amish garb, he had grown used to people's stares. Now that he wore Katie's father's clothing nobody gave him a second glance. It was as if he were invisible, just another face among a sea of people. "I feel free."

"That's a good thing, right?"

"It's wonderful. Liberating."

"You make it sound like you've been a prisoner. I guess I don't get it. What's it like growing up Amish? I mean I only know what I see, how the Amish dress, how they don't use modern technology, and how they only go to school up to the eighth grade, but what's it really like for you? Give me the inside scoop."

It warmed him, her taking such an interest in him. "Mostly it's good. Despite what you might consider to be a plain life, we are born, live, and die surrounded by family and friends who care about us. It gives us a sense of security being part of a congregation and community and how well we watch over one another."

Katie tilted her head, "But you just said that now you feel free and liberated. Sounds to me like you're conflicted."

How could he explain it to her? "The Amish life is a good life, Katie, but it's not an easy one. I'm fascinated by the world and the people in it, but I know that I'll never be able to experience it. I've never even been as far as Williamsport. Yes, I would like to see more of the world, but I don't want to live in those other places. I just want to visit them."

"Don't you people travel, take vacations?"

"It's not so simple, me having to do all of the work around the farm."

"That's really sad, Coop. Tragic."

"I would like to see the ocean. I've dreamed of it. It's hard for me to imagine water so vast that you can't see the other side."

"Yeah," Katie said, "It makes a person feel small, humbled."

The waitress delivered their order. Katie didn't object when Coop devoured more than his share of the pizza. It was one of the most pleasant meals he ever had.

Coop wiped his mouth with a napkin. "Your turn. I want to know everything about you."

She snickered. "There's not much to tell. What you see is what you get. I play loud music, curse a little, and despite my crashing the car the other day, I usually don't take a lot of risks."

Coop leaned forward over the table. "Come on, Katie. There's more to you than that."

She tapped the tabletop with her fingers. "Okay. Dad and I moved to Wineberry Hollow after he got out of the Army. Let's see, I was 8 at the time. I'm graduating from high school in the spring, and then I plan on studying to be a doctor. Like Dad."

Katie sucked at her water through a straw. "Anything else you want to know?"

"You haven't mentioned your mama."

Katie's smile disappeared. She glanced at the tabletop, but only for an instant before looking up. "Mom is gone. Dad raised me by himself. Overly protects me at times."

"Does he spoil you?"

"Duh, he bought me an ancient Buick Skylark. I wanted something new and sporty."

"Sounds to me like he's a good father. He loves you."

She stared out the window. "I know that. No matter what I do, he's always there for me. Keeps me safe. Dad's my hero."

Coop wanted to know what had happened to Katie's mother but sensed something deeper lay there that she wasn't comfortable expressing. Instead, he wondered about her plans to become a doctor. "Do you want to be a doctor because that's what your father does? Do you feel obligated to follow in his footsteps? For instance, my father inherited the farm from his father. I come from a long line of farmers and am also a farmer."

Her eyes widened. "No, it's not that way at all. Dad was a medic in the Army. After he was discharged, he had all kinds of offers to join private medical practices, mostly in the cities. Instead, he wanted to serve a rural area, so we moved to Wineberry Hollow seeing as how the nearest medical center is an hour away by car. He built his office at our house to keep it convenient for all you country folk. He's also the only doctor I know who still makes house calls."

Coop scratched his head. "So why *do* you want to be a doctor?"

Katie clicked her tongue. "Don't be so impatient. I'm getting to that part."

He sat back in his chair. "Okay, I'll shut up."

"I work with Dad part time and have been learning as much as I can from him. At first, I just helped with small stuff like keeping kids like you occupied playing dominoes while Dad treated your parents' ailments."

Coop faked like he was surprised. "Aha, that's why you came to keep me company when my mother was having her troubles."

"I do bookwork for Dad and sterilize his instruments. Sometimes he lets me watch while he does sutures, debrides wounds, and delivers babies, with patient consent, of course. Dad says I've probably had as much emergency first aid training as any paramedic he's worked with."

"Katie, that's amazing."

"When I see someone hurting, Coop, when I see pain in a patient's eyes, it makes me ache when Dad can't help them. But nothing is more rewarding than seeing a person's eyes when the pain goes away, the gratitude. That's what calls me to become a doctor, being able to take away people's pain."

Katie's sincerity and resolve moved him. "You're not a girl. You're an angel."

"Nuh uh, not hardly," she said with a grin that reminded him of what she looked like when he had first laid eyes on her six years ago.

Her expression turned serious after checking her watch. "Time's a wastin'. We need to go if we're gonna catch that movie."

Coop didn't want to sit in silence in some movie theater and not be able to talk to her. "We passed a roller skating rink outside of town. Let's do that instead."

Katie applauded. "You're learning. Girls like it when guys take charge during a date."

* * *

"You ever do this before?" Katie asked as they laced up their skates.

"We ice skate on the pond all the time, but I've never been on wheels."

"The concept's pretty much the same. I gotta warn you though, I'm not good at it. Weak ankles." She stood and took a few tentative steps heading for the rail along the wall.

Coop stood and gave it a try. It surprised him to find it easier than ice skating. He skated a few circuits around the floor and caught up to Katie who had only made it half way around.

"Sorry, Coop, told you I wasn't good at this."

After a few more circuits, the music slowed and the lights dimmed. Coop caught up to her. "What's happening?"

"Couples only." She offered him her hand. "Don't pull me too fast."

Her hand felt soft and warm in his. They didn't talk as he led her around the rink. Katie worked hard to keep her balance. Every once in a while she would glance at him and smile, warming him inside, and to Coop, the song ended too soon.

"I need to sit," she said. "Pull me to the snack bar."

After finding an empty horseshoe shaped booth, Coop offered to buy her a soda.

"Plain water will be fine."

Coop purchased two plastic water bottles and slid into the booth beside her, taking the liberty of closing the gap between them so that their legs touched. He couldn't hold back a grin when she didn't object or try to move away. They sat that way in comfortable silence watching other people and occasionally stealing glances at each other.

He was about to ask if she wanted to skate again when a young man wearing a football jersey slid into the booth on the other side of Katie. "Wuzup, sweets?"

Still touching, Coop felt Katie's body stiffen. "What are you doing here?"

"Thought that was your rust bucket parked out front."

A sense of dread welled up within Coop.

"What do you want?" she asked.

The young man ignored her and raised an eyebrow at Coop.

"I'm Stan. Who are you?"

Katie answered for him in a tone clearly meant to be unfriendly. "A friend."

Meeting Coop's gaze with a cold stare, Stan said, "You don't go to our school. What's your name?"

Coop shrank in his seat. He had been brought up as a pacifist, his Amish culture including a code of nonresistance to the point of not even defending oneself from physical attack. He recalled the scriptural admonishment, *Recompense to no man evil for evil.* If Stan decided to cause trouble, he was supposed to just sit there and take it leaving things to Gottes Wille.

A great weight clamped his stomach. Why now, in this moment of happiness, had God put this obstacle in his path? Perhaps that was the answer. In Katie's presence he had gone too far, forgotten his demut or humility and had become arrogant by wearing the clothes of an English man. Simply put, he was sinning. Perhaps this was God's warning to him.

"Go home, Stan," Katie said, "or at least go away. You and I are done."

"You and I are done," Stan repeated in a soprano voice, mocking Katie. "You seemed to enjoy my company well enough in my back seat."

Katie narrowed her eyes. "In your dreams, asshole." Then she softened and looked at Coop. "Don't believe the crap he's spewing. He and I never did anything."

Stan laughed and pointed a thumb in Coop's direction. "What, you mean you're saving yourself for him? A scared rabbit who can't even talk? This mutey is so afraid he won't even tell me his name."

Coop felt despondent at his inability to act. As his mother had warned, he had put his hand into the fire and was now suffering burns.

"C'mon Katie, what did I do to get your panties in such a twist?"

"Don't even go there. When you and I first started dating I warned you about my zero tolerance for drugs. You crossed a line."

"Aw, c'mon, you're treating me like some kind of a street junkie." Stan slid around the horseshoe seat until he sat on the other side of Katie, squeezing her between himself and Coop. "Why don't you tell your mutey friend to take a hike and come with me?" He took her by the wrist and began to tug.

Katie struggled and started slapping at his hand. She raised her voice, "Let go of me."

Coop just watched them, unable to act, humiliated.

Stan met Coop's gaze and narrowed his eyes. A silent challenge. He tugged Katie harder. "You're coming with me."

"Like hell I am," she yelled.

Coop's anger swelled. He wanted to strangle this intruder with his bare hands, but he had promised his papa that he would bring no dishonor on the family. What would happen if he came to Katie's assistance and seriously injured this English boy? Then again, how could he allow him to drag Katie away against her will? How could he live with himself if he allowed that? Which was the greater evil, dishonoring one's family and faith or allowing someone innocent to be brutalized?

Unable to reconcile his conflicting emotions, Coop just sat there and looked at his lap.

"Hey," the snack bar attendant called from the counter, "everything all right over there?"

"This asshole is bothering me," Katie shrieked.

The attendant stepped from behind the counter and removed his apron. An average man in his forties, he approached the booth with a confident swagger. In an even tone, he looked at Stan and said, "Let her go, kid."

Stan released his hold on Katie, smirked, and held his hands in the air.

"Get outta here," the attendant told him.

He slid around and stepped from the booth. Stan leaned toward Coop and sneered. "Another time, mutey." He pointed his index finger, making the sign of a gun and poked Coop's forehead.

"I'm not gonna to tell you again," the attendant warned.

Stan snickered and exited the building.

The attendant turned to Katie. "You okay?"

She rubbed her wrist. "I'll be fine."

"Stupid kids," he grumbled and returned to the snack bar.

The look Katie gave Coop tore at his heart. He wished she would've shown anger at his inaction. Instead, the shake of her head, her quivering jaw, and downcast eyes displayed disappointment, hurt, and betrayal.

"Take me home," Coop said, near tears over his devastating humiliation.

*   *   *

During the drive home, Katie played no music, and they sat in silence. Finally, in a scornful voice she said, "What kind of a man are you, anyway? You have a real yellow streak, don't you? From now on, I'm going to call you Chicken Coop."

He blurted, "Katie, I am not a coward."

"You could've fooled me."

"My faith forbids the use of violence…"

"… Don't you dare hide behind your faith. Stan was hurting me and you just sat there. You Amish are like a colony of ants always helping one another, barn raisings and such. Do you expect me to believe that if someone attacked a member of your congregation that you would simply turn away?"

"Yes."

"Bullshit."

Coop rarely felt ashamed about being Amish, but in that moment, if he had the ability to do so, he would shrink away and die. Things had been going so well with Katie. He really liked her, and now he felt utterly humiliated. "I'm sorry to have disappointed you."

"Look, I know you're supposed to turn the other cheek and all, but couldn't you have at least said something to Stan? Even if it was just bluster. That snack bar dude was old, but he was able to kick Stan out without getting physical. My god, Chicken Coop, all that physical labor in the fields has made you as strong as an ox. You're built like a linebacker and could probably tie Stan into a pretzel. Why didn't you just stand up and point at the door? I know him. He would've backed down."

"That's not something I would've known." He paused. "Katie, I would never have let him take you away against your will."

"He almost did," she shouted.

They rode in silence for a minute before Katie said, "I'm not some totally helpless female and would've fought Stan like a wildcat before allowing him to drag me through the door. I can take care of myself to a point, but a girl does like to feel at least a little secure with the guy she's with. Someone to back her up. I wouldn't expect you take a bullet for me or anything like that, but Stan really hurt my wrist."

"I'm sorry," he repeated, the irony being that he would take a bullet for her. His faith would allow that, because it wouldn't result in his perpetrating violence. No use explaining that to Katie. She wasn't in the mood to listen to the finer details of Amish faith.

"I need to tell you something," Katie said. "At dinner you said that you wanted to know everything about me. And you asked about my mother. The truth is, I barely remember her. She died when I was 5. She was murdered."

Coop's breath caught. "Murdered?"

"Mom worked as a pharmacist at the barracks hospital where my dad was stationed. One night after everyone left, she stayed behind to do inventory. A junkie broke in and pulled a gun. Demanded drugs. He ended up killing her."

"That's terrible."

"That's why I'm so radical about drug abuse and the reason why I dumped Stan. When he and I first started dating, I loved all of the attention he showed me. He reminded me of Dad. Protective, you know? Not a coward like you. When I think back on it, though, I should've seen the signs. He wasn't protective, but possessive and controlling."

"You deserve better than him."

"Someone like you, I suppose? No thanks. I don't want no Chicken Coop."

Cut to the core, Katie had hurt his feelings to the point of tears. After a few moments, he pulled himself together and glanced her way. The dashboard lights reflected from her face. Katie's lips formed a straight line.

She gripped the steering wheel and shot a glance in his direction. "Don't look at me like that."

He had already blown it with her. Coop decided he had nothing to lose by being truthful. "Katie, I've never felt about a girl the way I feel about you."

She banged her fist on the steering wheel. "You certainly didn't show it tonight. Haven't you heard a word I said?"

"Despite the ugliness that occurred tonight, I really enjoy your company."

She burst into laughter. "Go figure."

Coop didn't understand. "Are you laughing at me?"

"I'm laughing at the ridiculousness of this situation, because you actually mean what you say. You're not just using some line to score with me. Oh, god, this is too much."

She had loosened up, dropped her guard. Dare he push his luck? "I want you to give me another chance."

Katie snorted. "Not even if you were the last eligible bachelor on Earth. I'll never get past what happened tonight."

Coop fumbled to find the right words to reach her. "Even if I promise to never again allow anyone to bother you?"

Katie groaned. "Get a grip on reality. Not only are you Chicken Coop, but from the start I told you that we're from two different worlds, remember? Face the facts, in your world, at 18 you're looking to get married. In my world, at 18, I'm just fretting about my next bio exam. Marriage isn't even on my radar. I told you that I want to be a doctor. That means I won't even be done with school until I'm like 30."

He could think of no comeback to what she had just said, all of it being true. Neither of them spoke again until Katie turned onto Cove Road.

"Hey, Chicken Coop, we're almost home," Katie said. "You should probably change back into your Sunday-go-to-meetings."

Nothing she said could depress him more. Coop slipped into the back seat and changed. He climbed back into the front seat as Katie pulled into his driveway.

"Wow, your house is pitch black. Makes me paranoid. You sure your mom and dad aren't in there giving us the evil eye?"

"They're sound asleep." He paused. "Katie, I'll never forget tonight, and I'll never forget you. Someday you'll be a great healer. I just know it to be true."

Katie touched her chest. "Don't try to be nice to me. I'm really angry right now, more so with myself for agreeing to go out with you. I should've known how absurd it would be."

Coop swallowed hard. "I don't want the night to end like this. Can we at least be friends?"

"Yeah, we have that much, but don't expect more from me. Get out of my car, Chicken Coop."

He got out and waved as Katie turned onto Cove Road. She

pointed her old Buick toward home and drove away.

"Good bye, Katie," he said.

Chapter 7

Stanley Cox fired up his Jeep Cherokee and drove east on U.S. Route 6 through Wellsboro. He had wanted to wait outside the skating rink for Katie and her mutie friend. He would've enjoyed beating the blank expression from the mutie's face and making Katie pay for breaking it off with him.

Who was this new guy anyway? He didn't go to their school and wasn't a familiar face from around the area. An out-of-towner maybe? Granted, the mutie was built like a weightlifter, but Stan had seen the fear in his eyes when he had played rough with Katie. The coward wouldn't stand up to him.

He imagined what the mutie would look like after a few quick jabs to the face. Whap, and he'd flatten Mutie's nose with a satisfying crunch of cartilage. Whap, and Mutie's front teeth would crack from their sockets. Whap, and he'd break Mutie's jaw bone.

All in good time. It could wait until later, and Stan definitely looked forward to that occasion.

Tonight he had a bigger fish to fry, a chance to escape life in his freaking, boring home town. At least Wellsboro had a few bars and some action, but life in his rural home town of Wynot was too much to bear.

Stan had been average his entire life. He got Bs and Cs at Wynot High School making him an average student. He played second string on the high school football team making him an average player with average skills. He lived in an average sized house with his parents who earned average wages. He drove an average SUV and had average friends.

He hated being plain vanilla average. There had to be more to life than the numbing sameness of daily life in a small town.

Last summer, Stan had found the answer: dealing drugs.

He had smoked pot and popped pills since he was 12. Getting high provided a temporary escape, but this summer, Stan figured out that dealing instead of using led to a greater high, a regular trifecta of *unaverage* living: the adrenaline rush that came from breaking the law and doing business with gangsters, the boost to his self-esteem, and the money, oh yeah, the money. Stan would soon be pulling down way more than his old man could ever dream of.

But he was smart about how he spent his money, or rather his lack of spending. He knew not to call attention to himself, didn't want his parents or guidance counselors at school to ask questions about how he was able to afford the lifestyle of a rich kid. Quitting school would be out of the question. It would separate him from most of his customer base. Might as well take advantage of the situation, fly under the radar, be an average student, and graduate on time in the spring.

Stan stashed his cash and took no small measure of pride in the discipline that took for an 18-year-old. In less than a year, he had squirreled away nearly 20 large in various hiding places.

Tonight was all about setting himself up after graduation, taking the next step.

A few miles east of Wellsboro, Stan turned north onto U.S. 15, his destination, Corning, New York. His supplier, a biker chick who called herself Rhoda Dendron, agreed to meet with him at midnight.

Stan checked the clock and figured he had plenty of time. Maybe he should've waited a while longer at the rink. Scared as he was, Mutie would've probably wanted to take Katie home right away. Stan pondered that. It was Katie's old heap that he had spotted in the rink's parking lot. Why would they have taken her car?

Two possible answers. Either Mutie's car was even older and crappier than Katie's, something Stan doubted, or else Katie drove. What self-respecting high school jock would ride shotgun on a date? Stan's lack of respect for Mutie dropped even lower.

He banged his fist on the steering wheel. "What is it that she sees in that dork?"

Stan's infatuation with Katie began when second semester started. He had noticed her before, but the two of them never had classes together. They met in tech ed, specifically wood shop. Katie told him that she took the class as an elective, a diversion from her core courses and as a creative outlet.

He could read between the lines. Wood shop was beneath her. She was just slumming.

Stan had figured out high school girls. Make 'em laugh and make 'em feel good about themselves, and they become putty in your hands.

Katie had been just as easy as the rest. He acted goofy around her and wasn't afraid to make an occasional ass out of himself. She soaked up the attention he showered on her. Stan made her feel good by asking for advice, little things like what color stain would look best on his wood project.

She drove like a maniac and loved loud music, a self-proclaimed wild child. The thing that iced it for him, his wood project had been a set of speaker boxes for Katie's old car. He had mounted a radical set of woofers in those boxes.

"You spent a whole marking period making those cabinets, and you're giving them to me?" Katie had said it with such elation that Stan knew she had been sincere.

Thinking back, he could still see the way her face glowed as he wired those speakers to the MP3 input jack beneath her dashboard. She was a hot babe, and she made him hot. Turned out she was just a tease. She didn't go as far as he wanted her to. She never did.

The two of them lasted two months until their big fight.

Like most brainiacs, Katie was a loner and didn't have much of a posse, nobody to warn her about his dealing. She had made known her negative feelings about drugs, so he was careful about keeping his secret from her.

"Katie may be smart," Stan mumbled while driving, "but she has no street smarts. All that time we dated, and she never suspected."

It all came crashing down Wednesday morning. While the two of them walked down the hall holding hands, a stoner approached them asking to buy some weed. The stoner had looked Katie in the eye and told her how lucky she was to be dating a dude who had the best damn smoke this side of the Mississippi.

And that ended that.

"Too bad. One or two more dates and I know I could've had you. You were wearing down." She would've been his greatest conquest. Unlike the rest of the girls he had dated, Katie Hunt had class.

"You may be done with me, but I'm not done with you yet. Wild child, my ass. You're nothing but a poser." Two months of frustration while fantasizing what she would be like. All for nothing. Except now he didn't have to concern himself with being such a gentleman. Next time, he wouldn't let her just say no.

* * *

Stan found the address where Rhoda Dendron had setup the meet and parked across the road so that he had a view of the front door. He checked the clock on the dashboard, fifteen minutes 'til midnight. Stan shut off the engine.

The small brick house located in an older, suburban neighborhood seemed deserted. Other than a porch light illuminating the front door, he could see no sign of anybody in the house.

Was this the right place? Stan flipped on the Cherokee's dome light and double-checked the address he had written down. Yeah, this was the place. Rhoda usually met him in tavern parking lots. He had never been here before and wondered why she would change the way she did things.

Changes like this made Stan nervous.

Stan kept his eye on the house. At exactly midnight, he still could see no sign of life. Was this some sort of setup? What happened if he knocked on the door waking some John Q. Citizen who might be frightened enough to dial 9-1-1? What could he say, that he had made a mistake? Sorry, wrong address, go back to bed. That wouldn't fly.

Drug dealing and trust didn't go together, but this meeting was too important to Stan's plans. He had to risk it. He swallowed and reached for the door handle.

A beam of light shining through the passenger side window focused on Stan's face and blinded him. He shielded his eyes with his hands. Damn, a cop, or maybe some nosy neighborhood watch patrol.

"Are you going to let me in or what?"

Stan recognized the voice. Rhoda. He took a breath. She had scared the crap out of him.

Pressing the electric lock, Stan said, "It's open."

Rhoda slid her skinny butt into the front seat, her face expressionless. She wore jeans and a black leather jacket. When they first met, Stan had figured her to be around the same age as his mother. Tonight she looked older.

Stan heard the rear door open and someone getting into the car directly behind him. "What the hell?"

"Eyes forward. I decided to bring back up tonight," Rhoda said. She nodded to the person in the back seat. "Say hi to Stan."

"Hello, Stan." The voice was deep and masculine. Stan's heartbeat thumped all the way up into his ears. He pictured himself being garroted from behind with piano wire.

"Say hi to my brother, Philo."

"You're kidding me." Stan hated that his voice quavered. "Rhoda Dendron and Philo Dendron. What parents would name both their kids after flowers?"

Rhoda shrugged and held her palms face up. "Yeah, I guess that would be cruel. Okay, you must know that those aren't our real names, and Philo isn't really my brother, and that isn't our house over there, but let's play pretend."

Her words didn't make Stan feel any more comfortable. Despite the chill air that spilled into the car when the pretend Dendron siblings let themselves in, he felt a bead of sweat trail from his left armpit. "Look, Rhoda, you were never afraid to meet with me before. Why the change?"

Rhoda chuckled. "I'm not afraid of you, Stan. I just brought backup in case you brought backup."

"Why would I do something like that? I'm no freaking narc."

Rhoda chuckled again. "We live in treacherous times, right Philo?"

Philo remained silent which frightened Stan even more.

Rhoda crossed her legs. "Let's get down to business. Other than product, what is it that you want from me?"

"I'll be done with high school in the spring. I'm ready to move up in the organization."

"Yeah, that's what you told me on the phone. I want to know how you think I can help you with that."

"I'm moving a lot of your product, so I thought maybe you could arrange a promotion for me."

Rhoda laughed. "A promotion? You hear that, Philo? This kid's got real ambition, doesn't he?"

Philo said nothing.

Rhoda's voice took on a serious tone. "That's not how this business works, Stan. If you want to grow your income, you need to setup your own network of dealers. I'll supply you with all the product you need."

"No way. I only trust myself."

Rhoda pulled a pack of smokes from her jacket and lit up. She didn't pass the pack around. "You're a smart kid, not trusting anybody. Neither do I. That's why I brought Philo with me tonight. That's why I'll never tell you the name of my supplier, if that's what you had in mind."

She pulled open the ashtray in Stan's console and flicked ashes. "I'm not stupid. I get it what you mean by wanting a promotion. You want to come off the street, right? Maybe work on the inside? The only way that's going to happen is when someone in our up line invites you in. You'll never be able to solicit them. You'll never even know who they are. I'm the only face you will ever see in the organization."

Stan coughed from Rhoda's cigarette smoke which filled the passenger compartment. "How do I receive one of those invitations?"

"Simple," Rhoda said. "You have to get noticed."

"How do I get noticed?"

"Again, simple. You sell lots and lots and lots of product. Make a name for yourself. You gotta pay your dues, kid. There are no shortcuts." Rhoda took another puff from her cigarette. "Anything else you wanna know?"

Stan mentally calculated how much he had bought from Rhoda during the past year. He had worked his butt off, taken risks, and made her a bundle of cash. He couldn't do much better in the sparsely populated area where he lived. Twenty grand wasn't a bad cut for a high school senior dealing drugs on the side, but that amount was laughable compared to what he wanted. He was desperate to be in Rhoda's position selling directly to established dealers instead of end users.

An idea formed in Stan's head. "Guess I have some more dues to pay."

Rhoda stubbed out her cigarette in the ashtray. "Watch your back and in a few years, who knows?"

"Who knows?" Philo echoed from the back seat.

Rhoda wiggled her fingers. "I believe you have something for me?"

Stan reached into his shirt pocket and pulled out a wad of bills. He passed the wad to Rhoda. She licked her fingers and counted.

"A pleasure as always," she said and opened the door.

"Hey, where's my stuff?"

"Right here." Philo's arm appeared between the front seat headrests. In his hand, he held a plastic garbage bag. He dropped the bag onto the passenger seat after Rhoda got out. Stan heard the back door slam shut and looked in his side view mirror.

Rhoda and Philo vanished into the darkness as quickly and quietly as they had come.

Stan closed his eyes and sighed. His fear of Philo gave way to disappointment. No way did he want to accept being just an average dealer among thousands of other average dealers. He had expected more, and he was through with being average. Rhoda's words echoed in his mind. "You have to get noticed. Make a name for yourself."

Other than working his butt off for a middleman like Rhoda, Stan knew of only one other way to "get noticed."

He could muscle his way to the top.

What was it that Rhoda had said? "We live in treacherous times."

"Yeah," Stan mumbled. "Treacherous times."

Chapter 8

Cooper stroked the heifer's ear. The animal pressed its muzzle against Coop's chest.

"When did you teach it to do that trick?" his father asked.

"No trick. That's just Clarice's way of asking me to rub her forehead." Coop obliged the beast by scratching a white spot just above its brow.

His father shook a finger. "I warned you about naming the farm creatures. They are food, not pets."

"I know that," Coop said, feeling anger well up within him. Why did his papa always criticize? The two glared at each other.

"Good." His father handed Cooper the lead rope, pulled the pin in the gate, and swung open the door. "That means you won't have any trouble walking it over to the Wetzels."

Coop had been fixing a well pump, a task his father insisted he complete before dark. Coop realized the change in chores was punishment for his disrespect. Papa leaned forward and walked away wearing a scowl. Coop couldn't remember the last time he had seen the man smile.

Coop glanced into the heifer's soft brown eyes and sighed. He had raised Clarice from a calf, and it tug at his gut to see her go. Being the one to take her to the butcher was punishment harsher than his father imagined, yet Cooper understood the way of things, the necessity. He thought of the food that filled his belly, his leather boots, his horse tack, and the many things an animal like Clarice provided. Still, it saddened him.

"C'mon, Clarice, not much daylight left," Coop said and tugged at the rope. He led her down their driveway and onto Cove Road.

The Wetzel family lived on the other side of the road about a quarter mile west, easy walking distance for both man and heifer. The family operated the only butcher shop in Wineberry Hollow.

As they walked up the Wetzel's dirt lane, Coop wondered how he could get someone's attention. He didn't see a place to pen up or tie Clarice, so he approached the door of the converted barn that now served as the butchery and shouted, "Hello. Anybody home?"

A tall boy peered out from an aluminum screen door which looked out of place on the rustic exterior of the old barn. "Hello, Cooper."

"Hi Sammy, you already home from school?"

The boy pushed the screen door open and greeted Cooper with a wide smile. "Just got home. I'm just about done with my bow. Want to see it?"

Coop regarded Sammy, a 12-year-old English kid, like a little brother. Sammy enjoyed hanging around Coop, and Coop indulged him. Last week when Coop had visited, Sammy showed him the self-bow he started constructing, a skill the boy had picked up from a local Boy's Club campout. "Sure, I want to see it. Let me settle up with your father first."

Mr. Wetzel came out of the barn and joined them. He wiped his hands on a rag before shaking Cooper's hand. He gave Clarice a quick glance. "Thought Amos was gonna bring her. How's he doing?"

"My father is doing well enough, but he wanted me to bring Clarice, I mean the heifer instead."

Mr. Wetzel rubbed his hand over the animal's hide. "Nice size for a two-year-old."

"I've been feeding her corn."

Mr. Wetzel raised an eyebrow. "Is Amos agreeable to the same deal as last year? I get to keep a hind quarter for my services?"

"Yes, that is what father expected." A lot of business took place among neighbors of Wineberry Hollow using barter or by trading favors.

Mr. Wetzel held out his hand and Coop handed over the lead. Mr. Wetzel led the cow around the corner of the building out of sight. The pang in his gut intensified. His father had been right. Why had he made a pet of the animal, treated it as a friend?

"My bow's on the back porch," Sammy said. "Let's check it out."

"Sure." Thankful for the distraction. Coop followed the boy to the house.

They climbed the three steps onto the covered porch where Sammy lifted the bow off a picnic table. The youngster grinned, his ruddy complexion almost a perfect match to his hair. He presented the bow to Coop. "What d'ya think?"

Coop sighted along the ash stave, impressed that Sammy had the persistence to stick with the task. Most English kids would've been too impatient. "Looks good to me."

"It's not quite done." Sammy took the bow from Coop and ran his thumb over a spot. "I'll have to shave some more heart wood from this lower limb. It's slightly thicker and won't draw straight if I don't."

"Ach, yes Sammy. I can see where you mean."

"I'm gonna use real sinew from the butcher shop as my bow string."

"Are you going to use poplar saplings as arrows?" Coop asked. "That's about the straightest wood around these parts."

"Not yet." Sammy reached into a bag and pulled out a perfectly straight rod. "Dad had some old dowels. I'll try them first."

Coop took one and felt the pointed tip with his finger. "How did you get such a perfect point?"

"I stuck the dowel in Dad's electric pencil sharpener."

"Where are you going to find one of those in the woods when you need one?"

Sammy shrugged his shoulders.

Coop pulled a pocket knife from his pocket and unfolded the small blade. "A point's not hard to carve. Give me one of those dowels." Coop shaved the end until it was nearly as perfect as the arrow Sammy had showed him.

"Nice," Sammy said. "Coop, how come you know so much?"

"I don't know nearly as much as I should in the way of book learning, but I learned how to live without the convenience of electricity."

"That must be hard, I mean living without electricity."

"Sometimes it is." Coop thought about his friends Liam and Andrew enjoying the wonders of living in a modern world. He wished he could join them to experience it. "But I have confidence that I can do just about anything for myself without relying on electric power."

Sammy's eyes widened. "When you get all that meat back from my dad, what are you going to do with it? You don't have a freezer."

Coop stroked his chin. "Hmm, I guess we'll have to eat everything all at once."

The bewildered expression on Sammy's face amused Coop, the way the young man's mouth hung agape. "Just fooling. When the meat is ready, we'll share it among the other families in our congregation. In another few weeks, someone else will butcher one of their cows and share it with us. That way none of us needs to keep an electric freezer."

Sammy imitated Coop by stroking his own chin. "That makes sense."

"We do have an icebox. That keeps our share of the meat cold enough to last for a week or two. The bologna your dad makes for us keeps a lot longer than that, and I make jerky, too, which will last all summer if I hang it in the root cellar."

"Geez, Coop, you must live the same way people did a hundred years ago."

Coop pondered that statement. Was it easier on his ancestors a hundred years ago, the rest of the world being more or less at the same technological level? Did the current Amish way of life really afford them a closer relationship to God, or were they deluding themselves? He looked into the sky and noticed the dwindling twilight. "I should start home."

As they walked around to the front of the house, Coop saw a pickup truck that hadn't been there before. Mr. Wetzel emerged from the shop carrying a cardboard box loaded with meat to the waiting vehicle. Two men followed also carrying boxes.

The older of the two men spoke, "Half a beef is a lot of meat. You think we'll get it all in the freezer, son?"

"I dunno," the other muttered.

Something about this second person struck Coop as familiar, his voice and demeanor. After glancing at him, Coop recognized him as being Katie's ex-boyfriend, Stan. His heart sped up. At the rink, Coop had been dressed in English clothes instead of Amish garb so he hoped Stan couldn't identify him. Coop tilted the brim of his straw hat in Stan's direction to hide his face.

Mr. Wetzel spotted them. "Sammy, give me a hand with Mr. Cox's order. There are six more boxes inside."

"Sure, Dad," he said, then to Coop, "Want to help?"

Coop hesitated. He desperately wanted to escape, but saying no would probably call more attention to himself than helping. "Okay."

Mr. Wetzel engaged Stan's father in conversation while Coop and Sammy made three trips between the shop and the truck loading the rest of the boxes. As much as he could, Coop kept his back turned to Stan. Stan kept his hands stuffed into his front jacket pockets and stared at the ground. He made no attempt to help.

After setting the last box onto the truck bed, Coop secured the rear lift gate. He didn't realize that Stan had approached, so when Coop took a step back, he bumped into him.

"You blind or something?" Stan asked.

Coop kept his gaze cast to the ground. "Sorry."

"Next time watch where you're going."

Coop's heart pounded. "Sorry."

"Is that all you can say? Sorry?"

"Stop back soon," Sammy said. Coop wasn't sure if Sammy was speaking to him or to the Cox men, so he decided not to respond. He just wanted to get away.

The dusk-to-dawn light at the front of the shop snapped on. Coop winced and turned to leave.

"Hey," Stan called as Coop walked away at a brisk pace. "Do I know you?"

Coop kept walking. "I have to go."

While putting distance between himself and the butcher shop, Coop heard Stan's father ask, "That young man is mighty peculiar, isn't he?"

Stan snorted, "He's Amish, ain't he? They're all strange."

Chapter 9

Dr. Stewart Hunt double checked the lab results, knowing that looking at them again wouldn't change the outcome. Delivering devastating news to a parent about their young child was the most unpleasant duty of being a doctor.

Patients often complained about doctors being cold and clinical with awful bedside manner. What people didn't realize was that medical practitioners were only too human and had to maintain an emotional distance to preserve their sanity. Still, when it came to little kids, it was difficult to wall off one's emotions.

Stu picked up his office phone and pressed the button for the outer office.

His daughter answered. "Hey, Dad, what's up?"

"Katie, are the Fooses here yet?"

"Yup." She paused. "Dad, I'm just about done with today's billing and the Fooses are your last patients. Is it okay if I go to my room and study after I finish up?"

The Fooses' 3-year-old son was too young to understand the diagnosis, but old enough to be frightened by his parents' reaction. "I'd like you to keep little Lucas out there with you, but send in his parents."

"Oh," Katie said. He detected sadness in her voice.

Stu had hired his daughter as a receptionist and to help with billing and coding when she turned 16. She knew what the medical codes meant, and by the tone of her voice she probably understood why he had asked her to baby sit Lucas.

Grace and Timothy Foose entered his office, a young Amish couple in their early twenties, Timothy fingered his hat with downcast eyes while Grace loosened her bonnet. The bulge in her belly reminded Stu that their second child would soon be due.

Stu motioned toward the sofa. "Please, sit."

The young couple exchanged glances and did as he asked.

Through experience, Stu knew that revealing a bad diagnosis to patients overwhelmed their emotions and kept them from hearing anything said after that. He had learned it was always better to begin the education process first.

Sitting on the edge of his desk, he faced the couple and cleared his throat. "As you know, the food we eat provides fuel for our bodies. It's what makes our muscles work. Deprived of fuel, we become tired and moody and have trouble concentrating."

"I don't understand," Timothy said. He glanced at his wife. "The boy eats well and has a hearty appetite. We don't feed him junk. He eats good food, vegetables from our garden, eggs from our chickens."

"Yet Lucas is always so tired," Grace said, "and the other day when I couldn't get him to wake up, I was so scared and didn't know what to do."

"Listen to me," Stu said. "You are not bad parents and you have done nothing wrong. Our bodies need a chemical called insulin to carry this fuel into the muscles. For reasons that we don't fully understand, sometimes our body's immune system attacks the cells which produce insulin. When that happens muscles and organs don't get the nourishment they need to function."

Timothy mumbled, "Are you saying that our son is diabetic?"

"I'm sorry to say that's the case. Lucas's condition is called Diabetes mellitus type 1."

"How can this be?" Timothy said, anger in his tone. "Nobody in either of our families has this condition. Isn't it supposed to be hereditary?"

Grace wrapped her hand around her husband's forearm. "What are we supposed to do? Will our unborn child also be diabetic?"

Stu raised a hand, signaling for their attention. "I'll answer all your questions, but first I need both of you to focus on Lucas."

He spent the next several minutes explaining how Lucas would probably be on insulin replacement therapy for the rest of his life, how he would need to be monitored several times a day, stressing the importance of managing the disease, warning them how neglect could lead to heart troubles, stroke, coma, and death.

Stu knew the young Amish couple had no health insurance, that it was contrary to their ordnung. He had already decided that he wasn't going to charge them for this office visit, but also was concerned they probably wouldn't be able to afford Lucas's treatment long-term. "You're going to have to speak with your church aid group about this. Please ask them to contact me about the details."

After exhausting their questions, Stu presented them with a book on diabetes and showed them out.

He watched from the waiting room window as they climbed aboard their buggy and drove away. Katie stood at his side and leaned against him. Stu put an arm around her.

"Poor Lucas," she said.

"It'll be a life changing event for the entire family."

"I wasn't much older than Lucas when Mom died. I can relate to life changing events at that age and how difficult it's going to be for him."

As Katie grew into an adult, she looked more and more like her mother. Even her mannerisms, the way she tilted her head when concentrating, the way she rolled her eyes when frustrated. Stu's heart still ached for Kay, and her senseless murder still angered him. "Practicing medicine is mostly about life changing events, and helping your patients through them, births, deaths, chronic illnesses."

"Cures, too, Dad. Cures can be life changing. That's why I want to be a doctor."

Kay's unceasing optimism had been the quality Stu admired most about his wife. Another characteristic passed on to their daughter. "Yes, cures, too, sweetheart."

A cloud of dust rising above the trees indicated that a vehicle approached traveling down off the mountain. Stu recognized Sheila Cunningham's maroon Chevy Avalanche. Sheila was a home builder by trade, a rare occupation for a woman.

"I saw Mrs. Cunningham drive up the mountain about the same time the Fooses got here," Katie said. "Her passenger was a black guy."

Another rarity. Only one black family lived in the hollow, the Doaks family.

Stu's property lay at the end of the paved portion of Cove Road at the back end of Wineberry Hollow. Sheila owned mountain ground above him and had bulldozed a dirt lane into the mountainside. At the upper end of that dirt lane, she had built a bi-level log home.

Sheila parked her vehicle. She and her passenger emerged. Sheila pointed up the mountain as if explaining something. She spotted them watching from the window and waved.

"Aw shit, this is awkward," Katie said. "They probably think we're being nosy. I guess we're busted, huh?"

Stu felt the discomfort, too. As a matter of fact, they *had* been nosy. "Grab your jacket. Let's see what the lady wants. And watch your language."

Stu and Katie met Sheila and her passenger in the front yard. She opened her arms inviting Stu for a hug. Despite her reputation as a hard nosed business woman, she was also a hugger.

"Haven't seen you out and about much," she said as Stu wrapped his arms around her.

"You know how it is in the wintertime," Stu said while extricating himself from her embrace. "People tend to hole up."

Sheila hugged Katie. "Child, you're growing up so fast. What are you now, 17?"

"Eighteen," Katie corrected her.

"Oh my, Stu, you'll soon have every boy in the county beating at your door."

"They already are, Sheila."

Katie's cheeks turned rosy.

The man standing beside Sheila cleared his throat.

"Forgive my manners," Sheila said. "This is Mr. Declan Orr. Mr. Orr, this is Dr. Stewart Hunt and his daughter, Katie."

Dr. Hunt extended his hand, "Call me Stu."

"Pleased to meet you, sir," Orr said in a strong voice. He stood erect and took Stu's hand. The handshake was firm, and while shaking Orr maintained eye contact. He backed away, fluid like a cat and extended his hand toward Katie. "Miss Hunt."

Stu noticed how he gripped Katie's hand gentler and how he inclined his head toward her in a slight bow. Despite the chill March air, Orr wore only a flannel shirt as if the cold didn't bother him. He could also see that the man didn't have an ounce of fat on his body and looked to be in great physical shape.

Sheila spoke. "Mr. Orr is giving serious consideration to buying the new log home I built in the woods. You might soon be next door neighbors."

"Don't put the cart before the horse, Ma'am," Orr said. "I haven't given you the green light yet."

Something about the man's speech, his demeanor, and the way he moved remind Stu of his past. "Mr. Orr, if you don't mind my asking, are you military?"

The man raised an eyebrow and met Stu's gaze. "Mr. Orr is my father, sir. Call me Declan, and that's affirmative. I'm Army. A newly retired Sergeant Major. How'd you know?"

"Well, Declan, since you're no longer in the Army, drop the sir and call me Stu. I know because I'm also ex-Army. A medic. Retired ten years ago."

"Hooah!" Declan exclaimed.

"I guess it takes one to know one," Sheila said.

"I've seen my last patient of the day. Can I interest the two of you in a drink?"

"Love to," Sheila said quickly and gave a sidelong glance to Declan. "That is, if Mr. Orr can spare the time."

"I appreciate the offer, but the missus and my kids are expecting me for supper, and it's a long drive back to where they're staying in Wellsboro. If you don't mind, Stu, I'd like to give you a call later tonight to talk about the neighborhood. Get your opinion on things. Can I have your number?"

"Certainly." Stu patted down his pockets. "Damn if I don't have a business card on me." He looked at Katie. "Sweetheart, can you run inside and get a card for Mr. Orr."

"No need." Declan tapped the side of his head with his index finger. "Just tell me and I'll remember."

This man was no ordinary soldier. Stu recited his telephone number.

They climbed back into Sheila's car. She rolled down her window. "Stu, I'd really like a rain check on that drink."

"Sure, stop by anytime."

She smiled. "I'll do that."

They walked back inside the house. Katie looked his way. "You want some tea? Before hitting the books, I'm gonna make a pot to take to my room."

"I'd like a cup."

While Katie put the teapot on the stove, Stu rifled through the day's mail.

"Dad?"

He looked up and found Katie slouching against the kitchen counter. "What, sweetheart?"

"Sheila Cunningham likes you. You know that, right?"

Since Sheila's divorce, Stu had noticed a change in the woman's attitude toward him but thought it was his imagination. "You think so?"

"Isn't it obvious?"

"I don't know, Katie. Sheila's kids are grown and now that Hank's left her, I guess she's lonely. She'll talk with anyone. I don't think her interest in me is romantic."

Katie pulled a chair from the dinette and sat. She wore a puzzled expression.

Stu sat in the chair beside her. "What's bothering you?"

She frowned. "I stopped seeing Stan, but we only went out a few times. The Cunninghams were married forever. They seemed happy. They had it all, a nice place, a good family. Why would they divorce?"

Crossing his arms, Stu said, "Let's back up a minute. I noticed that Stan hasn't come around lately, but I thought maybe he just lost interest. Am I to understand that you were the one who broke it off?"

"Uh, huh."

"Come on, Katie, I'm your father. Tell me. Was he inappropriate with you in any way?"

"No, it's nothing like that. Actually, I'm the one who lost interest."

Stu knew that Katie didn't tell him everything about her personal life or about the friends she hung out with, nor did he expect her to. As a young adult, he respected that she needed some space and mostly trusted her judgment. She was well educated as to life's dangers and risks. On this one issue, though, he demanded complete transparency and felt the need to press her. "You'd tell me, right? If some boy acted less than gentlemanly with you?"

Katie leaned in and touched her head to his shoulder. "Of course I would, and you shouldn't worry so much."

Stu chuckled. "No can do. You're my daughter, my baby. I have years worth of worry ahead of me. Besides, being of the male species, I know what boys think about."

"About you being one of the male species. Even though Mrs. Cunningham does man's work, she's definitely feminine. I mean she's got a great figure for her age. You should call her."

"For her age? Gee, thanks, Katie. I think she's a year or so younger than I am. And you just heard me tell Sheila that she could stop by anytime."

"That's not the same as you calling her."

What was really going on inside his daughter's head? He decided to remain silent and wait for her to speak.

Katie broke eye contact and looked at the tabletop. "It's okay with me. I wouldn't see it as you betraying Mom, and I know that no other woman would ever come between you and me. I'm old enough to understand that, Dad. I get it. It's been 13 years since Mom died, and I want you to be happy."

Stu leaned in from his chair and hugged her. "Seems my baby is becoming more of an adult every day."

The phone rang.

Katie jumped from her chair. "I'll get it."

Stu watched her pick up the phone. The caller spoke, because Katie didn't say anything. Her smile turned to a frown. Finally she said, "Where are you calling from?" A moment passed and she said, "We'll be right over."

After hanging up, she grabbed her coat. "That was Cooper Stover calling from a neighbor's house."

"The Amish family?"

"Yes, Dad, please hurry. Cooper thinks that his father is having another heart attack."

Chapter 10

Cooper Stover burst from the farmhouse as Stu got out of his car. The young man extended a hand, his face flush. "Thank you for coming so quickly."

Stu shook Cooper's hand. "Where's your father?"

"Lying down in bed upstairs."

Katie got out from the passenger side of the car carrying a satchel holding medical instruments.

Cooper glanced at the ground. "Hello, Katie."

"Hiya, Coop."

Coop? Stu wondered why Katie presumed to use such a nickname. Then again, it wouldn't be that unusual for them to know each other through casual contact.

He turned his attention to the matter at hand. "Take me to your father."

Cooper led the way to his father's room. Mr. Stover lay there, clutching his left shoulder with his right hand and panting. Mrs. Stover knelt at his side wiping her husband's forehead. "Mrs. Stover, you need to step away so I can examine your husband."

She said nothing but did as he asked.

Stu removed the stethoscope from his satchel. "Mr. Stover, how are you feeling right now?"

The man's words came out ragged. "Can't...breathe."

During the past few years, Stu had been treating Mr. Stover for his bad heart. Not wanting to take any chances, during the short drive to the Stover's farm he had asked Katie to dial 9-1-1 from her cell phone to summon an ambulance. He knew, though, that the closest EMTs in the small town of Wynot would take a good 20 minutes to get there, big disadvantage to living in an isolated rural area.

"Mr. Stover, have you been taking the nitroglycerine tablets I prescribed for you?"

The man nodded.

"How long since you took the last one?"

Mr. Stover's gaze shifted to the night stand. The vial of pills sat beneath a kerosene lamp. "Maybe half-an-hour ago," he said in a weak voice. He coughed and suddenly stopped breathing.

"Damn it," Stu uttered. He turned to the others. "Everybody listen to me and do exactly as I say. Mrs. Stover, go downstairs. Katie, run to the car and get my portable AED. Hurry."

He turned his attention to Cooper. "Help me move your father off this bed and onto the floor. Grab his legs."

Stu took the man under his arms while Cooper grasped his father's ankles. They laid him gently on the hard floor.

Katie returned and handed him the AED.

Stu powered up the unit. "Both of you step out of the room, but don't go far. I might need you."

"I'll be right outside the door," Cooper said.

Stu laid the contacts on the man's chest and the machine fired.

He listened with his stethoscope and heard a faint thumping, but Mr. Stover's breathing was shallow and sporadic. He yelled at the door. "Katie, get the oxygen tank from the car. Cooper, help her. It's heavy."

Stu turned his attention back to Mr. Stover. Until the EMTs arrived, the best he could do would be to give Mr. Stover a shot of Heparin.

He finished giving the shot as Katie and Cooper returned with the apparatus. Stu checked Mr. Stover's breathing. Still shallow, but more regular now. Dr. Hunt lifted the man's head and slipped a mask over his nose and mouth. He turned a valve to start the flow of oxygen.

Through the stethoscope, he could hear a more regular heartbeat.

He looked up into Cooper's eyes. "Son, your father is stabilized. I'm going to stay by his side and monitor him until the EMTs get here. Go get your mother."

When he returned with Mrs. Stover, Stu told them what to expect, a trip to the hospital for a more specific diagnosis and treatment. He stressed that Mr. Stover was only stabilized and not yet out of danger.

When the ambulance finally arrived, Stu briefed the attending personnel. He told them he would telephone Mr. Stover's cardiologist with a report of his actions.

"I want to ride along," Mrs. Stover said. She had been stoic throughout and hadn't lost her composure. Now she was insistent.

One of the attendants said, "I'm sorry, Ma'am, I can't let you ride in the ambulance, but I'm sure one of the volunteers will take you to the hospital." He asked around and found someone willing to do so.

"I should come, too," Cooper said.

"No," Mrs. Stover told him. "Stay home and mind things."

Stu watched as the ambulance and other vehicles pulled away.

"Thank you, Dr. Hunt," Cooper said. "You saved my father's life."

"I hope so, son."

Katie gave Cooper a sympathetic hug. Dr. Hunt was proud of

his daughter. She was a good kid with a big heart.

"Do you need anything?" she asked.

Cooper stared at his shoes. "I'll be fine."

Was the young man bashful or just humble?

During the short ride home, Katie leaned back and rested the back of her head against the headrest. "How long might Mrs. Stover be at the hospital?"

Stu shrugged. "It's hard to say. She'll have to rely on someone to go get her when she's ready to come home."

"If she's not home by tomorrow evening, I'll bring dinner for Cooper."

"Oh?"

"On the way home from school, I'll make a side trip to Wellsboro and pick up a pizza. Coop likes pizza."

"How do you know that?"

Katie stared at him, mouth agape, "Dad, everybody likes pizza, even Amish."

They arrived home to a ringing telephone. Stu picked up hoping that no other emergencies would intrude on his evening.

"Stu, this is Declan Orr."

"Ah, yes." He remembered that the man had wanted to call.

Katie stared at him, her head cocked.

"Hang on," he said. Then to Katie, "It's for me, sweetheart."

"I'll be in my room studying." She walked away.

"Go ahead, Declan."

"I'll get to the point. I'm serious about buying that property from Mrs. Cunningham and being a fellow Army man, I can trust you not to BS me. Will my family and I be welcome in the neighborhood?"

"I can't guarantee you paradise, but I can say that Wineberry Hollow is a wholesome place. A mix of Amish and whites and one black family, the Doaks's. We all seem to get along."

"I'm not expecting paradise. I'll settle for wholesome."

"You can tell me it's none of my business, Declan, but what attracts an ex-Sergeant Major to this laid back part of the world?"

"You said it yourself, Stu. Wholesomeness. I spent my youth in Detroit city. God only knows how I managed to graduate high school in the middle of that cesspool. As a young black man, I had no future, could find no job. The Army became my way out.

Luckily, I had a knack for soldiering.

"I want my kids to have options. No way will I raise them in some concrete jungle. My oldest boy, Jamal, just turned 15. A formative age, but I'm not telling you anything you don't already know having a teen daughter."

Stu chuckled. "Katie considers herself a bit of a rebel." He glanced in the direction of her room to make sure she wasn't within earshot and lowered his voice. "Truth is, she's straight as an arrow. I have to scold her occasionally for driving too fast, playing her music too loud, and for cussing. But Katie's a gem. I'm the luckiest Dad in the world."

"I hear you," Declan said, "and I want to be able to say the same thing about my kids."

"How many children do you have?"

"My wife, Chelsey, and I have 3. Jamal is 15, Nate is 12, and Keisha is 10."

"Oh man, you're going to have your hands full."

"That's my main reason for leaving the Army. I need to spend time with those kids. Keep 'em on the straight and narrow."

"Laudable. Where were you stationed?"

"Fort Benning, Georgia, 4th Ranger Battalion."

"You're a Ranger?"

"More. I'm a Ranger's best friend and worst nightmare, an instructor."

"You trained Rangers?"

"Affirmative."

"I thought there was something special about you, Declan."

"Not special. I bleed red the same as you do, Stu."

"You're too modest."

Declan laughed. "Anyway, that's behind me now. I plan to live on my Army pension and maybe do some security consulting work."

"I'll be pleased to have you as a neighbor. Call me when you get a move-in date. Katie and I will give you a hand."

"Appreciate it."

After ending the call, Stu plopped into his favorite easy chair and eyed the pile of medical journals on his reading pile. Although way behind, tonight he was bone tired. A frantic day. One thing after another. Picking up the remote, he switched on the TV and found a basketball game. The Sixers, losing as usual.

He leaned back in the recliner and closed his eyes.

Jarred awake by the ringing phone, he glanced at his watch. 11:35. Stu jumped off the recliner and went for the phone, wanting to get to it before the infernal ringing woke Katie. Being a school night, she needed her sleep.

"Hello?"

"Dr. Hunt?"

"Speaking."

"This is Ruth Stover at the hospital. Please forgive me for bothering you, but I didn't know who else to call."

"No problem, Ruth, how's Mr. Stover?"

Her voice broke. She sobbed. "The Lord has taken him."

Chapter 11

Cooper stood with his mother at the entrance of the family barn. The strength of the April sun had broken winter's grip providing a mild Saturday with temperatures in the 60s. He focused on the procession of carriages trailing from both directions on Cove Road. His neighbor, Joseph Hutmaker, directed them to pull their horses into the adjacent meadow. If Papa were still alive, he would be cross about all the wheel ruts. Joseph motioned the arriving automobiles to park in the stone driveway.

Technically, the property now belonged to Mother, but Coop understood the responsibility for running the farm would fall squarely on his shoulders, a job he wasn't sure he wanted. For Mother's sake, what was he to do?

They had laid his father to rest in the graveyard earlier in the day. Friends and neighbors had been invited to come share a meal with him and his mother. The house was too small to accommodate all of the expected guests, so Coop and Joseph had cleared an area in the barn.

First to greet them were his friends Liam and Andrew. They had driven in from Philadelphia and had come to the barn in a carriage instead of their truck. Out of respect, they had changed out of English clothes into traditional Amish garb.

His mother shook the young men's hands. She maintained a stoic expression, but Coop had heard her crying last night behind her closed bedroom door. She was only 38, as was his father. Too young for a father to die. Too young for his mother to be widowed.

Coop contemplated his guilt feelings. He had shed no tears and wasn't sure if he would really miss his papa. What was wrong with him? Didn't all children mourn the loss of their parents?

He greeted Liam and Andrew. "I'm glad you came, and I hope you forgive me, this interruption of your rumspringa."

"You've interrupted nothing," Liam said.

Andrew simply laid a hand on Coop's shoulder and then moved on.

The English lady who built homes stood next in line. Coop couldn't remember her name until his mother greeted her as Mrs. Cunningham. None of their English friends had attended the funeral services as it would've been considered an intrusion, but his mother passed the word throughout Wineberry Hollow that everyone would be welcome at this more informal gathering.

Coop agreed with his mother. Why should religious differences prevent neighbors from being friends? His papa had been well-known among both Amish and English.

Mr. Wetzel, the butcher, and his wife approached wearing serious faces. They expressed their condolences. His friend, Sammy, shook Coop's hand and asked, "How'ya holding up?"

He'd be fine, Coop thought, after all of these people finally left. Although they were well meaning, he felt uncomfortable, all of them feeling sorry for him. Coop answered Sammy. "Okay, thank you for asking."

"Stop by sometime. I made lots of progress on my bow."

Mr. Wetzel clamped his hand onto the boy's shoulder. "That's not an appropriate comment at this time."

"It's okay, Mr. Wetzel." Coop winked at Sammy. "I'll try to visit soon."

As the Wetzels walked past and into the barn, Sammy looked over his shoulder and grinned. Seeing the youngster's carefree expression brightened Coop's mood.

The Kroh family came next. Theirs was the first farm near the entrance to Wineberry Hollow. Coop couldn't remember for sure how many children Elam and Ruth had, but it was one of the largest families in the area. Today, eight heads trailed behind Elam and Ruth and Ruth held an infant in her arms.

Coop knew the Krohs fairly well because their son, Stephen, was his age and had attended school with him. Smaller than most of the other boys and a stutterer, Stephen had endured a lot of teasing, much of it from Coop.

"I'm s-s-s-sorry," Stephen said while shaking Coop's hand.

His friend was trying so hard to be supportive that Coop felt guilt-ridden over having tormented him as a youth. Coop clasped his hand and pulled him closer. "Thank you for coming. It means a lot to me, and I'm the one who is sorry."

From Stephen's puzzled expression, Coop knew he didn't understand. Typical for the man, he had always been good-natured about the ribbings and never held it against anyone. "We'll talk later," Coop said before Stephen moved on.

Most of the visitors greeting them passed in a blur. As time went on, Coop tired of hearing the same thing over and over again: "Sorry for your loss," and his automatic response, "Thank you for your concern." It wasn't because he felt ungrateful, but his emotions were spent. He had grown numb.

Some of the visitors, however, had made an impression. Vicky Clark, an English neighbor, and part-time nurse for Dr. Hunt offered to help Mother with household chores.

A black family, Fred Doaks and his wife Caroline, came to express their condolences. Fred was a farrier and wheelwright by trade. He did a lot of business with the Amish.

The line finally ended. He and Mother were about to take a seat when Dr. Hunt drove up. They waited to sit until the doctor had a chance to greet them.

The man's posture drooped when he stood in front of them. "Ruth, I did the best I could. Sometimes we just don't know why."

Mother mustered a smile. "Because of what you did, I was able to talk with Amos a little while at the hospital. Without you, I wouldn't have had those final precious moments." She took his hand in both of hers. "Thank you, Dr. Hunt."

The doctor nodded, shook Coop's hand, and moved on.

A group of friends in their congregation, Coop didn't know who, had made several large platters of ham sandwiches which they now passed around. Coop sat with his mother on the bench beside Vicky Clark.

Coop spoke with as many people as he could but found it an

effort to concentrate. He remembered how on Sunday afternoons after church, while Mother prepared lunch, he would often rest in his bed and nap, drifting in and out of sleep, catching snippets of conversation between his parents, hearing but not fully understanding what they were talking about.

This felt like one of those times. The same sense of detachment.

In time, the visitors began to leave. They had lives to get back to, chores, obligations. He'd have to bring wood in tonight for the woodstove and put in the chickens. A good thing. With work to be done, he wouldn't have much time to ponder his feelings. It would be a normal evening for him, just like any other evening.

Coop walked among the gathering, thanking his friends again for coming. He poured a glass of water and took a seat on an abandoned bench.

Liam and Andrew slid onto the bench, one on either side of him. "Are you okay?" Andrew asked.

"I guess."

Liam pointed at his water. "Want something stronger than that? I hid a bottle under the seat of our buggy."

During their last visit, Coop and his two friends had shared a bottle of Jim Beam Bourbon while hiding in the barn's hayloft. They had laughed, and it had made Coop forget about life's monotony for a few hours. It had also made it terribly difficult for him to get up for church the following morning.

Liam's offer tempted him. He could use a few hours of forgetting. "Thanks for wanting to cheer me up, but tonight's not a good time."

"What are you going to do, Coop?" Andrew asked. "With your papa gone, you're even more tied to this place."

Andrew's implication was clear. Coop would never be able to get away. "I'll always have the Sunday Hymn sings to look forward to."

Andrew groaned. "There are a lot of other pretty girls in the world beyond our pool of available maidels."

Liam's eyes grew large, and he gawked at the threshold to the barn. "Speaking of pretty girls."

Coop glanced in the direction Liam looked and saw Katie standing there. She scanned the faces in the barn and settled on Coop's gaze. She walked over.

Katie wore the same black wool coat that she had on their date, but it hung open revealing a black dress hemmed at her knee. The black shoes she wore had raised heels which showed off the curves of her legs.

He hadn't thought much about Katie during the numbness surrounding his father's death, but now that she walked his way, Coop felt a weight lift from his chest, and he was suddenly able to breathe easier, as if a ray of warm sun had pierced his gray veil.

Coop and his two friends stood. He introduced them to Katie.

"Appears that the hymn sings have changed since I last attended," Liam mumbled.

Katie cocked her head and looked at him.

"He's just making a joke," Coop explained.

Andrew cleared his throat. "Come on, Liam. See you later, Coop."

They hurried away leaving Coop and Katie facing each other.

Coop's mother and a few remaining ladies cleaned up.

Katie stuffed her hands into her coat pockets. "I would've come sooner, but I just got back from visiting the university. Then when I passed here on the way home, I was going to stop but wasn't dressed appropriately, you know, for the occasion. Dad had just gotten home before I did and told me that I still had time to visit, so I changed clothes and scooted back. Sheesh, I hope you don't think it rude of me, my coming late."

Coop didn't understand about her visiting a university, but it didn't matter. She could've said anything. Just listening to her talk lifted his spirits. "I can think of no occasion where I would consider your visit to be rude, no matter how late you might come." He motioned to the bench. "Sit with me."

After they sat, Katie said, "Listen, Coop, I want to apologize for being so harsh with you. I was really upset, because of the way you really disappointed me. After what's happened to your father, it all seems so trivial."

Coop studied her eyes. "After our date, I thought I'd never see you again. I wonder if my papa would appreciate the irony that although he didn't approve of our seeing each other, it was because of him that I've been able see you again twice more in the past two weeks."

Katie said, "Yeah, he's probably rolling over in his…" She put a hand to her mouth and her cheeks reddened. "Oh, crap, I'm so sorry. That's really insensitive of me. God, sometimes, I'm so stupid."

"But it is funny," Coop said, "and probably true."

Katie pressed her lips together in a straight line, but then the corners of her mouth turned up. "You're so bad." She poked him in the arm.

What had she called that before? A love tap.

Katie's smile faded and she looked down. "Remember on our date when I told you how I ache when dad can't help someone? That's how I feel now. I ache. Dad really tried to save your father."

"Gottes Wille."

"I envy you, your faith, despite the fact that it sometimes seems misguided."

I envy you, your freedom, he thought of saying. What came out of his mouth instead was the thought that had bothered him all day. The truth that left him feeling so guilty. "Katie, I'm not sure that I loved Papa."

She looked up and met his gaze but said nothing.

Coop wondered why had he just blurted his innermost thoughts to her? After all, she had only come to visit him to express her condolences. Why was she so easy to talk to? What was it about her?

When Katie looked away, Coop went on, "It's not that I hated him or anything like that. I respected my papa, and I'm grateful to him for my upbringing. He was a strict man but never abusive, always fair. Yet, there were times when I resented him, when he tried to make decisions for me, to run my life."

Katie touched his hand but then pulled it away. "I'm no shrink, but in psych class we learned about what I believe you're experiencing. It's called survivor's guilt."

In the background, Coop heard the scraping of bench legs against the floor as the ladies began moving them out of the barn. He spoke softly. "I don't think it's guilt. More like anger. I'm a prisoner, Katie."

"Only in your own mind, Coop."

It relieved him, her not calling him Chicken Coop. "You don't understand."

Katie stomped her foot. Not hard. Just enough to snap him out of his thoughts. "Cooper Stover, look at me."

It was easy for him to do that, drink in the sweetness of her face, stare into her golden brown eyes.

"Don't tell me that I don't understand. You're 18 and a young adult, just like me. You have choices, just like me."

"Oh, so now I'm a young adult. You once told me that I was a Martian."

Her lips quivered as if suppressing a smile. "That's because you chose a life that's different from mine, the operative word being *chose*. We all have choices."

Coop groaned. "That's easy for you to say."

"Bullshit. Don't insult me. I love my father, but I've had to grow up without a mom. It would've been easy for me to pity myself, to become self-destructive, to drink, do drugs, to sleep around. You talk about your Amish lifestyle? Well, us English kids are under a lot of peer pressure. It's damn hard to stay focused, so don't tell me that I can't understand what you're going through or that my life is somehow less complex than yours. Don't even go there."

He took a breath. "What am I going to do, Katie?"

She softened her tone. "First of all, don't be so hard on yourself. Give yourself time. I mean, you just lost your father. When your head clears, you'll be able to think it through. You'll figure out what's best for you."

"I wish I had your confidence."

Katie sighed. "I'm no expert on you, Cooper Stover, but I think you'll make the right choices."

How was it that her words were exactly what he needed to hear? How was it that she knew exactly what to say to him? "Too bad it was only that one time we went out."

She gave him a sidelong glance. "I should go."

"You don't have to."

She stood and buttoned her coat. "Yeah, I should. Your mom needs you."

He would see Mother everyday. When would he see Katie again? "At least let me walk you to your car."

"Okay. Sure."

They walked together in silence, and when they got to Katie's car he held the door for her. She started to climb in but hesitated.

"Coop, I don't understand your sudden fixation on me. I think I've made myself clear that I'm not interested."

"Didn't you just tell me that my life is no different from yours and that it's all about choices? I could choose not to be a Martian. For you, I could do that."

Her eyes became large as if she just saw a ghost. "The other night proved otherwise. Besides, I wouldn't want you to change your faith on account of me."

"Maybe I should consider it."

"If you keep talking like that, then we can't be friends anymore."

"I take it back," he said quickly.

She smiled, but it was a different kind of smile, a sad one. "You're such a guy, Coop. You'll say anything right now."

He raised his right hand. "Katie Hunt, I swear to you that I won't do anything stupid on account of you. I'm Amish, so it's not possible for me to break this oath." But he also knew that "being stupid" was open to interpretation and left him a wide latitude.

"I don't know about you, Coop."

"Katie, please?"

She sighed. "You're going to persist, aren't you?"

"You said it yourself, I'm such a guy."

"Okay, okay, but we can't date. At least not like we did the other week." She raked a hand through her hair. "I suppose if you showed up someday at my house with the dominoes, we could play a few games."

"With your papa there, of course."

Katie rolled her eyes. "Do you really want my father to be there?"

"No, not really."

"Didn't think so," she said and climbed into her car. Coop shut the door for her.

Katie powered up the engine and drove away.

Coop's emotions swirled. The warm glow he felt during his time with Katie subsided, and the reality of his papa's passing crashed down on him when he entered the house.

Mother had been looking out the window, watching them. She untied her bonnet and sat at the kitchen table. "I want to talk with you, son."

Coop pulled a chair and sat beside her. "Katie and me, it's not what you think it is."

His mother's gaze was soft, kind. "Gottes Wille you are now a man. This burden of being head-of-household is difficult, even more so for an unmarried 18-year-old man. To ease this burden, you need to have someone to confide in, someone you feel comfortable with. Your papa had me."

"And I also have you."

She shook her head, and used a napkin to wipe her eyes. "During rumspringa, it's customary for parents to pretend as if we do not see, do not hear, but while cleaning the barn, I listened in on your conversation with Dr. Hunt's daughter. Please forgive me this transgression."

Maybe she had listened in, but Coop was sure she hadn't heard it when he said he might not have loved Papa. "You need not ask my forgiveness over such a little thing."

His mother raised a hand, cutting him off. "Cooper, you have never confided in me the way I heard you open up to Dr. Hunt's daughter, and the counsel she offered came from her heart. She cares for you, and she displayed remarkable kindness by listening. You really like this English girl, don't you?"

Coop stared at the tops of his shoes. He wouldn't lie. "I wish you would call her by name, Katie, and yes, I like her more than I should, but you need not worry. She doesn't feel that way about me."

She hesitated as if thoughtfully considering his words and said, "I'm not so sure about that."

"At best we have a strained friendship."

"Katie is a young lady, and you make her feel special by chasing after her. She isn't going to discourage you. Even if she feels neutral toward you."

"Mother, she has made it clear that we have no future together."

"Then, Cooper, Katie truly is your friend. She sees what you do not, and she selflessly puts your interest above her own, not wanting to hurt you."

Except she *had* hurt him, calling him Chicken Coop. "She is so exceptional."

His mother's lips curled up into a sad smile. "I understand. Dr. Hunt and Katie fought valiantly to save your father. With no hesitation, they came when we called. Our anguish is their anguish. The genuine depth of their caring, I daresay is not often seen even among the Amish. Dr. Hunt has dedicated his life to helping the people in this area to the point of forsaking a more lucrative practice elsewhere. We thank God for the two of them. They are a gift."

She sighed. "I've always liked Dr. Hunt. Your father liked him, too. What we feared is what has happened. Katie is uncommonly pretty, and the way she dresses and makes herself up coupled with her innate goodness and the allure of her worldliness makes her enticing. Cooper, our maidels cannot compete with a girl like that. Your Papa and I knew you would fall for her and tried to save you from the pain you now experience."

The truth of her words hurt his heart. "What am I going to do?"

"Even if you were to leave the faith, what chance would you have? Katie is a pretty girl now, but in a few years she is going to mature into an even more beautiful woman, a highly sought after prize. Katie is going to be a doctor like her father. Think of those with whom she will be associating. You are my son, so this is hard for me to say, but consider your chances against handsome, intelligent, highly-educated, wealthy English men. Be honest with yourself."

It's something Coop had not thought about. He only had an eighth grade education and knew nothing of the world. He realized with a profound sadness that for the rest of his days he was doomed to live as a simple farmer. Looking his mother in the eye, he said, "I know only one thing for certain. I will always be your son. I will provide for you as best I can."

He closed his eyes and pictured Katie. "As to any future friendship with Katie, that is Gottes Wille."

Chapter 12

Captain Douglas Sloat sat at the front of the Army bus directly behind the driver, a chubby corporal. The vinyl covered bench seat smelled of dried sweat and squeaked every time he shifted position. He could hardly complain, in fact he was damn glad to be there. Sloat's platoon sat on the benches behind him. Most of them slept. A few stared at the scenery as it whooshed by their windows.

Four hours ago, he and his men had arrived at Pennsylvania's Fort Indiantown Gap after a fourteen month deployment to the Middle East. It had been a long time since they could let down their guard and relax. No worries about improvised explosive devices. No concern about snipers. No suicide bombers.

By the grace of God they were finally back in the States, a cause for celebration if there ever was one. But the young men he led harbored no desire for festivities today, opting instead to enjoy the blessed oblivion that could only come from a deep sleep, safe and far from the horrors of battle.

Sloat's own eyelids grew heavy. He fought the urge to doze and tapped the driver on the shoulder. "How much longer?"

"Almost there, sir," the driver said never taking his eyes from the road. "Five minutes at most."

"Home," he muttered, but even as the word left his lips Sloat knew that wasn't exactly true. His home was Idaho, not Pennsylvania, and this return to stateside wasn't the end of their tour. His platoon had been redeployed under President Kall's domestic security initiative, their assignment, one of the new bases simply known as E38, the military acronym for Enclave number 38 of 104.

"Where exactly is this place," Sloat asked the driver.

"The enclave is located just north of the Pennsylvania community of West Milton," the driver explained. "I've been told the location for E38 was chosen due to its proximity to Interstate 80 and U.S. 15. Its area of responsibility includes the northern tier of Pennsylvania and parts of southern New York state."

Captain Sloat leaned back in his seat. He had heard the controversy surrounding the government buying up huge swaths of land all around the country to build enclaves. Conservative politicians howled about President Kall abusing his authority, extorting landowners under the threat of eminent domain and paying pennies on the dollar for prime farmland.

The president answered his critics by claiming that all landowners had been compensated according to fair market value and that the land being purchased was mainly unproductive, low value farmland. Besides, the enclaves would represent a boon to the local economies providing thousands of jobs.

Sloat recalled the day Kall announced his domestic security

initiative. After years of irresponsible deficit spending by previous administrations, it was time to rethink America's military presence in the world, Kall had said. The United States could no longer afford to be the world's policeman and other countries had grown weary of America's imperialism.

He would bring the troops home. All of them. Implement a strong defensive position to protect the homeland. Secure the borders. America first, the rest of the world be damned. They didn't want us, so let them stand on their own. And woe be it to any country or terrorist group with the temerity to attack the American people on their own home soil, the veiled accusation being that anyone in opposition to the domestic security initiative was being unpatriotic.

Sloat followed his orders and wanted to trust his commander-in-chief, but privately, he questioned the president's agenda. What about the lives lost in the Middle East? Pulling out would result in a return to chaos, the loss of life counting for nothing. And what about the country's dependence on foreign oil? Wasn't anyone concerned about that anymore? Surely, Kall's advisors had considered these things. Surely, they knew what they were doing.

The bus lurched as it slowed and turned off the main highway onto an access road. Most of the men woke and looked around. They began to murmur.

Lieutenant Jack "Halfjack" Kettering, Sloat's second in command poked him in the rib. "Get a load of that, captain."

A shiny, new chain link fence extended as far as Sloat could see, ten feet high and topped with razor wire. Every hundred feet or so, signs hung from the fence reading:

U.S. MILITARY INSTALLATION
COUNTER MEASURES IN-PLACE
DANGER - KEEP OUT
DO NOT APPROACH FENCE

"Counter measures. I like the sound of that. It's about time domestic military installations beefed up their security," Halfjack muttered. "Damned Bin Laden wannabees are everywhere."

Sloat regarded the man. During their many firefights, Sloat had been happy to have Halfjack on his side, a dependable officer who could be counted on. His fault was a gung-ho attitude, the kind of man who subscribed to the philosophy of kill them all and let God sort out the mess. The lieutenant had trouble switching off, exercising good judgment, and controlling his bigotry. He was the type of guy with a temper who would not do well in civilian life.

He wondered how Kettering had acquired his moniker, Halfjack. Despite the implied pejorative of being half of anything, Kettering liked the nickname and preferred to be called Lieutenant Halfjack instead of Lieutenant Kettering. He even went to the extreme of sometimes having the nickname printed on his official uniform patch.

Another issue Sloat had with his second stemmed from the fact that Halfjack thought himself better educated and more knowledgeable than his superiors. Sloat often had to reign the man in and remind him who was in command. During those occasions, Halfjack sulked and overflowed with resentment.

In other words, despite Lieutenant Halfjack's dependability in combat, Sloat regarded the man as somewhat of an asshole. Women thought so, too. He conducted himself in a boorish manner and showed them no respect. How had this man ever made it through OCS?

The bus stopped at a security checkpoint manned by a half-dozen rifle toting guards. One of them saluted, opened the gate, and allowed the bus to enter. To the left, Sloat observed heavy equipment being used to construct what appeared to be a road.

The driver answered Sloat's unasked question. "The enclave's new runway. Long enough to accommodate heavy transports."

They crested a rise, and in the distance, Sloat saw what appeared to be a small city newly sprouted from the soil. New buildings, tens of them. Some looked like high rise dormitory style barracks, others like offices, and other structures resembled hangars or warehouses.

Halfjack quipped, "Didn't expect the place to be this plush. Where do they keep the women?"

"Stand down, lieutenant. We'll find out soon enough," Sloat answered him.

The driver referred to a note on his clipboard and turned onto a side road. "Says here that I'm to drop you at Sheridan Hall. That's where your platoon will be billeted, the headquarters for Green

Company."

"Does Sheridan Hall house the entire company?" Sloat asked.

"Affirmative. Each dormitory holds about 200 men."

"How many dorms are there?"

"Between 20 and 30."

Sloat did the math in his head. "That's up to 6,000 soldiers, a small division."

"When you count families and civilian staff, this enclave has the capacity to house up to 15,000. You and the lieutenant will eventually be assigned private bungalows in the bachelor officer's quarters. You'll be briefed on all the particulars."

It really was a small city. Could all of the enclaves be this large? If so, they could handle a total population in the hundreds of thousands.

Halfjack spouted, "We'll be getting our own BOQ? Hot damn, that'll be a welcome change from sleeping in the sand with this smelly bunch."

Sloat motioned with his eyes toward the enlisted men and spoke softly, "Dampen your enthusiasm, lieutenant. No need to rub their noses in it."

Anger flashed across Halfjack's face, but he quickly adjusted to a neutral expression. "You want to live in the common barracks with them? Go ahead, captain. I paid my dues. I'm better and expect to be treated better."

"Enough," Sloat spoke in the sternest tone he could muster.

The driver pulled the bus under the canopy of a green block building and announced, "Sheridan Hall." He saluted the captain. "It's been a pleasure, sir. I hope you enjoy your new assignment."

Before Sloat could respond, a colonel stepped onto the bus. Sloat snapped to attention, saluted, and called out, "Officer on board." He heard the men behind him jump to their feet.

The colonel saluted and then extended a hand to Sloat. "Welcome captain, I'm Colonel Muncie."

Sloat shook Muncie's hand. "The pleasure is mine, sir."

Another man stepped onto the bus. Colonel Muncie said, "This is Sergeant Adams. He's going to show you and your men to your quarters. I understand you had a long trip and could use some sleep."

"That's a fact, sir," Sloat said.

"Speak for yourself, captain," Halfjack said. "Time enough to sleep when I'm dead. Where can I find the officer's club? I got a lot of partying to catch up with."

Colonel Muncie glanced at Halfjack then checked his watch. "Get some rest, men. That's an order. We'll meet tomorrow at 0800 for an orientation. There's a lot you'll need to know."

* * *

Sheridan Hall impressed Captain Sloat. Laid out like a university dormitory, the small rooms held two men each. Each wing had a common bath and shower. An all purpose room located on the ground floor could be configured for conferences or building-wide events. The next morning, Sloat's men mustered in this room and Colonel Muncie joined them at exactly 0800.

"At ease," the colonel told them.

The men in Sloat's platoon sat around a half dozen conference tables facing the colonel. From the wall hung two large maps, one of the Eastern United States, the other of Enclave 38. Sloat thought it curious in this digital age that they would be referring to old fashioned pull down wall maps.

"I trust all of you found the accommodations satisfactory?" Colonel Muncie asked.

"Luxurious," Sloat said.

The rest of the men grunted their assent.

Lieutenant Halfjack blurted, "Yeah, swell. When do I get my assignment to the BOQ?"

Muncie ignored the man and walked to the maps. "This orientation is going to answer some of your questions, and it's going to cause you to have more questions, many of which I'll not be able to answer. The clock is ticking and things beyond our control are in motion, so listen up and pay attention."

The colonel picked up an old style wooden pointer. "As you know, the current administration has adopted an isolationist political policy. The role of the U.S. military has shifted from one of protecting foreign national interests to one of securing the homeland."

He tapped the map of the Eastern United States and drew an imaginary circle around the top of the state. "The most efficient means of accomplishing the new policy is to adopt a military model based on feudalism. The system of enclaves has been evenly distributed throughout the country as geographic safe havens in the event of attack. Each enclave has been designed to be self-sufficient, self-sustaining, and autonomous. Our enclave, number 38, is assigned to protect the northern tier of Pennsylvania roughly above the 40.5 parallel."

Sloat scratched his head. Protect the northern tier from whom? Was command aware of some threat that they weren't openly sharing with the public?

Colonel Muncie walked to the map of Enclave 38 and used the wooden pointer while he spoke. "At the center of the enclave is the command center complex housing administrative offices, communications, and executive offices. Immediately adjacent is the enclave's new high-tech medical center. Those buildings are ringed by dormitories and civilian housing. The enclave has its own shopping center, entertainment complex, and several places of worship."

He tapped the upper right corner of the map. "Within the fence we have many square miles of an agricultural complex where we grow our own food, raise livestock, and operate a dairy. As I said, we are totally self-sufficient."

The colonel pointed at the bottom of the map. "You probably noticed the new airstrip on the way in. We also have a state-of-the-art power plant operating on a combination of solar, geo-thermal, and biodiesel technology." He snorted. "Clean enough energy to make any tree hugger proud."

He opened a large cardboard box setting atop one of the tables and began passing out binders. "This is your manual. It'll detail everything that goes on here." When he finished passing out the binders, the colonel put his hands on his hips and looked out over the men. "Any questions?"

Captain Sloat raised his hand and asked the question that had been on his mind ever since he learned of the new initiative. "Sir, my men and I are battle hardened professional warriors always eager to mix it up and kick enemy ass. What, exactly, are we supposed to do here? Who, exactly, is the enemy?"

One corner of Colonel Muncie's lips turned up and his eye twinkled. "Our enemy is whoever our commander-in-chief tells us it is. Don't worry, men, your soldiering skills won't become rusty, and you're also going to gain additional experience to add to your resumes. You'll be assigned wherever you're needed within the enclave and rotate through a variety of tasks. Your platoon will split into squads. Besides patrolling the countryside outside the fence, you'll also take part in protecting the enclave, working on the farms, attending to the civilians, and I promise that all of you will get an opportunity to milk cows."

"Hooah!" One of the soldiers exclaimed.

From the back, a soldier stood and asked, "Sir, you mentioned civilians. Who are they and what are they doing at this facility?"

"Good question, soldier. E38 is home to contractors, specialists, consultants, technical experts, civilian employees, their families, and a handful of politicians."

As the colonel continued to answer questions, Captain Sloat became lost in thought, trying to figure out why his instincts screamed how this seemed all wrong. First, the administration's new isolationist policies ran counter to civilization's evolution into a global economy, then the recall of all military personnel, and now high tech enclaves populated by soldiers, experts, and politicians.

A chill ran up Sloat's spine. He gripped the edge of the table to steady himself. "Concentration camps," he mouthed inaudibly. Only in reverse. Society's elite were being clustered together for some unknown purpose. Which made everyone outside the fence, the rest of the U.S. citizens and all of the other nations of the world…the enemy.

Chapter 13

Thank God, Stu thought as he grabbed the last box inside the moving van. His back ached. Helping the Orrs move in reminded Stu how out of shape he was. Declan and his older son, Jamal, did most of the heavy lifting while he and Katie had helped Declan's wife, Chelsey, unload clothing and kitchen ware. He set the box on the dining room table and let out a moan.

"What's wrong, Daddy," Katie asked between gulps of water. Although rosy faced from the effort, she seemed to be holding her own.

"Just a little stiff. Nothing that a hot shower can't take care of." Tomorrow he'd need the BenGay for sure. He grabbed a paper towel and wiped perspiration from his brow.

"Mighty kind of the two of you to help," Chelsey said and handed him a bottle of water.

Stu twisted the top off the bottle and gulped the icy liquid. "I enjoy a good workout. It's something I could use more of."

Declan strutted into the dining room whistling a tune. Although he had labored all morning, the man appeared as if he just enjoyed a walk in the park. "Hey, babe." He kissed his wife on the cheek.

Where Declan was tall and angular built, Chelsey was petite, maybe five four, with pronounced curves, their chocolate colored skin a near perfect match. During the course of their conversations, Declan revealed he was 44, the same age as Stu. He figured Chelsey to be a few years younger, but not by much.

Jamal entered carrying a sealed plastic bucket. "Yo, this one ain't tagged. Where's it go?"

"Set that on my workbench in the garage," Declan said.

Jamal wheeled around and left them with no further word. At 15, the young man looked a near perfect copy of his father, although not as filled out yet. He hadn't said much all day and Stu thought him to be distant, if not a little unfriendly. Most unusual was his reaction when introduced to Katie. He didn't give her a second glance and acted as if she wasn't there. Jamal showed zero interest in her.

Not that that was a bad thing.

The Orrs only daughter, 10-year-old Keisha, acted completely opposite to her older brother. With her wide eyes, ebullient personality, and picket fence smile, she had already hijacked Katie, taken her hand and led her away giggling to the backyard.

Their other child, 12-year-old Nathaniel, made himself busy by unboxing and hooking up a computer. He had quizzed Stu all morning about various Internet options and wanted his opinion about the best ISP in the area. Obviously the nerd of the family.

"Nice kids," Stu commented.

Chelsey sighed. "We try. It's hard on them being military brats and us always moving around."

Declan sidled up beside his wife and reached an arm around her. "Not anymore. Here, at last, we have a home. A place to settle down and raise them right." He eyed Stu. "What did you call it? Wholesome, I believe?"

Stu tipped his water bottle in their direction. "Wineberry Hollow isn't perfect, but it's as close to *Little House on the Prairie* as you can find."

Declan noticed the water bottle in Stu's hand. "What are you doing with that?" He stepped to the refrigerator and pulled out two bottles of beer. He glanced at Chelsey. "Want one, babe?"

Chelsey waved a hand. "Better not. Gotta make up the beds. I have the feeling we'll all sleep soundly tonight." She left the kitchen.

"I know I will," Stu said as he took the offered beer and twisted off the top. He took a long pull.

Declan tipped his bottle. "Ah, now that's what I'm talking about."

"Yeah." Stu held back a belch.

"Thanks again for helping," Declan said. "I'm happy to have found this place and having you as a neighbor helped seal the deal."

"You kidding me? It's my good luck to have an Army Ranger living next door. Adds some class to this neighborhood."

Declan grinned. "C'mon, I have something to show you."

Stu followed the man outside to a large covered trailer. He first noticed it earlier in the day when he and Katie arrived but figured that it had already been unloaded. Did this mean they weren't done yet? Was this another full trailer to unload? He sure hoped not.

Declan unlocked the trailer's double rear doors and opened them. "Check this out." He pulled a set of ramps from a side compartment and locked them in place on the deck of the trailer. Then he disappeared inside.

His curiosity having gotten the better of him, Stu peaked inside. "Wow."

Keisha chased Katie around the yard and both girls ran over after hearing the rumble of an engine coming from inside the trailer.

"What's going on, Daddy?" Katie asked.

"Tag, you're it." Keisha squealed and ran off.

Jamal appeared from the corner of the house and scolded his little sister. "Let her be."

"She's not bothering me," Katie said.

Jamal walked over and stood beside Katie, arms folded across his chest. Keisha wormed her way in between Jamal and Katie.

Declan backed a car from the trailer and gunned the engine before shutting off the ignition. He climbed out wearing a wide smile. "Other than my wife and kids, this is my pride and joy. 66 Mustang convertible."

"God, it's even older than my piece of shit car," Katie muttered.

"Mind your manners," Stu snapped.

Declan laughed. "Young lady, it 'pears as if you have no eye for the classics."

Stu walked around the car admiring the perfect white paint job and red vinyl interior. Pefection. Right down to the "289" emblems on the front fenders. "Stock engine?"

"Affirmative. The 4 barrel carburetor with 225 horsepower. Not very powerful by today's standards, but it's not for racing. Just a show car."

"It's a beaut," Stu said. "Can we go for a ride sometime?"

"Count on it."

"Tag, you're it," Katie said to Keisha. She stuck out her tongue. "Caught you daydreaming, didn't I?"

Keisha squealed and resumed her chase of Katie.

Declan glanced at Jamal. "You have that space cleared out in the garage yet?"

Jamal grunted and walked away.

"I get the feeling he doesn't like me," Stu said.

"One of the reasons I had to quit the Army," Declan said. "Jamal makes friends, gets close to people, then we end up moving. Had to leave a girlfriend behind this time. Now, he's reluctant to get close to anyone. He's anxious about fitting in."

That explained a lot. "I'll be honest with you. There aren't many black kids in the Wynot school system."

"He'll make friends. We also left behind drugs and gangs. He needs this environment."

Stu wondered if Declan remembered what it was like to be 15. It wasn't going to be easy for the poor kid. An idea flashed into his head. "Remember how I told you about the Doaks family? The other black family here in Wineberry Hollow. They have kids. Might help if Jamal got to know them."

"Outstanding idea."

"I'll call you later with their phone number. Fred Doaks is our local farrier and wheelwright. Does a lot of business with the Amish."

"Chelsey wants to throw a getting-to-know-you party to meet the neighbors. I'll be sure to invite them. Can you suggest any other neighbors we should add to the guest list?"

"Sure," Stu said. He ticked off some names in his head before speaking. "You already know Sheila Cunningham who lives across the street from Katie and me. Then there's Vicky Clark, the nurse who works for me part-time. She lives at the other end of the hollow. I can think of a few Amish families who would probably come. They mostly keep to themselves but usually welcome an opportunity to get to know new neighbors."

"That would be outstanding." Declan stroked his chin. "Although I'd have to mind my language around them."

"And don't forget to invite Katie and me."

Declan raised an eyebrow. "I'll consider it, but there's no room for riff raff." He grinned.

Chelsey yelled at the them from the front door. "Come inside, guys. I have sandwiches."

"Sounds good to me," Stu said. After washing his hands, Stu noticed that their middle son, Nate, had moved on from hooking up the computer and was now in the living room busy plugging cables into the back of a flat screen TV. He winked at the boy. "You hungry?"

"Not for sandwiches. I wish Mom would've called out for pizza."

"You'd wait a long time," Stu said. "Nobody delivers anything way out here except for the U.S. Mail."

Nate ignored Stu and pressed the button on the remote. The display flashed to life.

Nate pumped his fist. "Yes."

Declan joined them in the living room and glowered at Nate. "Turn that TV off and get in the dining room."

Stu hoped the ex-sergeant major would never look at *him* that way. He imagined how intimidating Declan could be to a young soldier.

Nate pointed the remote at the TV. Before he could press the power button, Declan said, "Hold up, son."

They looked at the TV screen and saw President Kall adjusting the microphone on a podium. Declan spoke. "I always get nervous when that man holds an unannounced news conference. Makes me wonder what mess we're about to find ourselves in."

"My fellow Americans," Kall said. "I'm here to announce that the recall of all U.S. military personnel is now essentially completed. Other than a small contingent of Marines guarding our embassies abroad, all armed forces have been redeployed to domestic enclaves. Not since the founding of this great nation have the combined armed forces been concentrated exclusively within our own borders."

President Kall paused and leaned forward over the podium. "Our sons and daughters are safely home. In commemoration of this achievement I'm issuing an executive order establishing a new national holiday. Armed Forces Homecoming Day will take place June 21 every year, beginning this year."

"Can he do that?" Stu asked.

"If nobody stops him, he can," Declan answered.

The president continued, "Additionally, to kick off the new holiday for this year, I'm also offering to spouses, children, and other dependents of military personnel the opportunity to visit their brave soldiers on site at their respective enclaves at government expense. I'm authorizing transportation vouchers which are to be honored by all airlines, bus companies, railroads, and gas stations."

Stu gasped. "How the hell are the taxpayers supposed to pay for that?"

President Kall shook his finger at the camera. "I'm also issuing an executive order that no employee of any business is to lose their job for taking advantage of this order, and in the spirit of patriotism, I urge all businesses to compensate those employees as if they had worked their normally scheduled hours during this holiday."

"I've seen enough." Declan took the remote from his son and powered off the television. "This is another reason I had to get out. It isn't the same Army I joined, not the same mission I signed up for."

"Is it even the same country?" Stu asked.

Declan just shook his head.

Stu remembered his own experiences in the Army. "Don't you think it's just the yo-yo effect of politics? You know how

Democrat administrations typically gut the military to feed their pet social programs. I know it's frustrating as hell, but the next Republican president will build the military back up."

"You've been out for awhile," Declan said. "This goes beyond the yo-yo. Big changes, repositioning of personnel and assets with no logical explanation. My instinct tells me those enclaves have to do with something big that's about to go down. Too few people know what really goes on in there. I have no clue, nor can I speculate. I just know that I needed to get out. Out and far away. Before it's too late."

Hearing these words from an elite Army Ranger sent chills up Stu's spine. "Sounds like you have no confidence in our commander-in-chief."

"Damn right I have no confidence."

Why was Declan so unnerved? Stu thought it best to change the subject. "Let's get those sandwiches Chelsey promised us."

"Sorry for barking at you like that, Stu."

"No problem."

"I'm expert at sizing up people. It's part of my training. In the field, we sometimes have a split second to make life and death decisions, to determine if a stranger is a threat or not. I've never met the current occupant of the White House, but I've seen him perform often."

Stu wondered at his choice of words. "Perform?"

"Some time ago, a team I led wandered into a god-forsaken Middle Eastern desert village. Found a kid doubled over on the side of the road, a boy, probably no older than my Nathan, crying, holding his stomach, like someone had kicked him in the gut.

"That kid had a cold stare, made every hair on the back of my neck stand straight out. Before I had a chance to shout a warning, one of my team members walked up to the kid. The last thing that soldier saw were the explosive charges strapped to the kid's chest. That man was a good friend of mine. Saved my bacon more than once.

"Everything that R.A. Kall says and does is a calculated performance. Just like that kid's calculated performance."

As a medic, Stu had seen mangled men. He couldn't imagine seeing a friend killed by an IED. Still, he wondered how Declan could project a wartime horror onto the President of the United

States. Maybe it had been wise for Declan to leave the Army, to preserve his sanity. "Sorry about your friend, Declan."

"Lost a lot of good men in that damn sandbox." Declan shook his head. "Anyway, in speaking about the commander-in-chief, I'm sure something isn't right with that brother. I can sense it."

Stu wanted to say something to lighten Declan's mood. "Nobody that's a politician is right in the head."

Declan looked Stu in the eye. "You don't understand. He's broken. He's…pathological."

Chapter 14

Perspiration ran down Coop's back. He wished he could take off his shirt and work bare chested like English men were free to do, but his faith forbade it. Although it was only the beginning of June, it felt like mid-August.

He sat on a stool in his front lawn in the shade of an oak tree. A cardboard box holding chains for his gas powered chain saw sat on the ground beside him. It made no sense to Coop how the ordnung or laws of his church permitted the use of this tool while forbidding the possession of an automobile. On the other hand, he was grateful. With the many chores that had fallen on his shoulders since the death of his father, he had gotten behind on his wood cutting. Coop couldn't imagine the trouble he and his family would be in if he were forced to fell trees by hand.

On a day like today it would be easy to forget the bite of winter's chill, but the family woodpile had been severely depleted last season. He needed to hike into their woods at the foot of North Mountain and look for dead trees to cut. Since Coop had gotten such a late start, green trees wouldn't be suitable for burning next winter. Green wood needed to dry for at least a year.

With the seed now in the ground and growing, he had a couple weeks to cut and split wood before the next cutting of hay.

Coop grabbed one of the chains from the box and filed sharp edges onto the worn metal teeth. Like most farm work, this chore was tedious but necessary. He looked up only to watch the occasional automobile or buggy passing by. He would wave at just about everyone as Coop knew most of the people who lived in Wineberry Hollow.

He watched Katie's old car approach. She honked the horn after spotting him and slowed down. Having already driven past the driveway, she stopped, backed up, and pulled in.

Coop stood and straightened his shirt. He wiped his hands on his trousers.

Katie powered off her car and got out. "Hi, Coop."

She wore a beige tee shirt and purple shorts. Coop's eyes settled on her legs, and he felt his face flush after allowing his gaze to linger too long. Her hair was fashioned into a pony tail. Coop hadn't seen Katie since his papa's funeral in April. She looked even prettier than he remembered.

"Ditching school again?" he asked.

"No, silly, it's the last week of school, you know, finals week. We're allowed to leave after taking our exams."

"Oh." He couldn't think of anything else to say.

"I graduate at the end of the week, finally."

"Congratualtions."

Katie sat on the rear bumper of her old car and leaned forward resting her hands on her knees. "Am I keeping you from your work?"

It didn't matter how busy Coop might be, he would happily set aside all his chores to visit with Katie. "No, I have some time."

She looked him in the eye. "How have you been getting along, you know, since your father's passing?"

It ate at Coop's conscience how he only missed his papa because of the extra hand he provided around the farm. In fact, Coop enjoyed the freedom from being out from under his father's domination. He hadn't told anyone else about his feelings. Maybe he could confide again in Katie. She had obviously stopped by with a purpose. For now, he decided to answer truthfully, but without exposing his deeper thoughts. "I have to do the work of two men now."

Katie sighed. "I'm sorry to hear that. Do you get any help from your church?"

"Ach yes, our neighbors pitch in when they can."

The wooden screen door slapped against its frame. Mother walked off the porch followed by his little cousin, Hattie.

"Hello, Mrs. Stover," Katie said.

Mother glanced between the two of them but said nothing.

"I know you," Hattie said. "Your name is Katie."

Katie winked at Coop. "I know you, too, from seeing you around the hollow. Your name is Matilda."

"It's Hattie," the little girl corrected her.

Katie approached the girl and gave her a hug. "I knew that. Just checking to see if you remembered. What are you doing here?"

"Helping my Auntie Ruth with the laundry. I'm getting old enough to do laundry all by myself. Never mix whites and colors. In the fall, I'll be in the first grade."

Katie said. "Is that so? In the fall I get to start my first year of university." She looked at Coop's mother. "I can't wait to get high school over with."

"Don't wish the time away, young lady. Someday you'll wish you had it back." Mrs. Stover smiled ruefully. "I remember how I felt at your age. Your perspective changes as you grow older."

"Hattie speaks English very well. I thought you didn't teach it to your youngsters until they started school?"

"She's a precocious child," Mrs. Stover said, "learned it all on her own by listening and then imitating."

After clearing her throat, Katie said, "When I drove by, I noticed Coop working out front. I stopped to find out how he...how all of you are getting by."

"That's kind of you. It's been difficult, but we're managing, right Cooper?"

He figured how Mother might be misinterpreting Katie's motives for stopping. Like maybe this wasn't the visit of a friend who just happened to be driving by, like maybe Katie was encouraging something more. If only that were true. "It is thoughtful for Katie to check on us."

Mrs. Stover motioned with her arm. "Come inside and have lunch."

Katie glanced at Coop. "I wouldn't be intruding, would I?"

Was this an attempt by Mother to determine if anything might be going on between the two of them? It didn't matter. No way did Coop want Katie to leave. "Please join us."

At the table, Coop offered a blessing and they shared a platter of chicken salad sandwiches. The topics of conversation remained light, the weather, Katie's schooling, the work needing done around the farm, and Mother asked about Dr. Hunt who, according to Katie, was doing just fine. Despite the non-controversial nature of their conversation, Coop sensed tension. Katie and Mother acted too formal, unnatural, as if weighing every utterance before speaking.

The banter between his little cousin and Katie was much easier, friendly. Too friendly. In the middle of dessert – shoo fly pie – Hattie belted out, "My cousin likes you."

Mother raised an eyebrow.

After an uncomfortable moment of silence, Katie smiled. "I'll bet Cooper likes all the girls."

That made Hattie giggle and Coop felt relieved when his cousin didn't pursue the conversation further.

Katie pushed back from the table. "Thanks for lunch, Mrs. Stover. Everything was delicious, especially the shoo fly pie."

Coop stood and walked Katie to the door.

"Be sure to greet your father for us," Mrs. Stover said.

"I will."

"Katie," Mrs. Stover called before the two of them walked out. "You're welcome to stop by anytime."

Notwithstanding the earlier strained conversation between the two women, Cooper sensed sincerity in his mother's statement. Had Katie passed some sort of test?

Katie replied with a simple, "Thank you."

Coop wondered if Katie might have been put off by anything Mother had said. He studied her closely but saw no indication on her face, just a shy smile. After they got to her Buick, she said, "So, your secret is out."

"What secret?"

"You like me."

"Yeah, but it's no secret. You already knew that."

Her expression hardened. "Don't like me, Coop. It's a waste of your time."

"So why then did you stop by to see me?"

Katie crossed her arms in front of her chest. "Don't read anything into my visit other than friendly concern."

Was she speaking the truth? No better way to find out than trying to ask her a personal question. "You seeing anyone yet? I mean after Stan."

She glanced at the ground before meeting Coop's eyes. He

expected her to tell him it was none of his business.

"I went to the prom with a guy from my chem class. We went out a time or two after that. He's nice, but nothing's going to come of it. I'm not ready for a romantic attachment with anyone."

Katie paused. "How about you?"

Coop shook his head. "There's nobody, and with Papa gone, I have more responsibility than I can handle. I have no time to go courting."

"No time to stop by with your dominoes?" she asked, then quickly added, "not as a date or courtship, just to visit."

Her words warmed Coop, that she recalled such a small detail from their previous conversation. "For you, Katie, I'd make the time."

"Did you meet the new neighbors yet?"

"What new neighbors?"

"The Orrs. They moved into the place Sheila Cunningham built on the mountain, you know, right above where Dad and I live."

"I haven't been to your end of the hollow in a long time. I don't recall meeting anyone with that name."

Katie laughed. "Trust me, you would've remembered them. They're having a party to get to know the neighbors. The Orrs are asking Dad and I for suggestions on who to invite. I'll see to it you get an invitation. Bring your mom and Hattie."

"When is it?"

"June 20, a Saturday."

Only a couple weeks away. It would give Coop something to anticipate. Lately, he hadn't had much in his life to look forward to. He wondered, though, if he would have to compete with anyone else for Katie's attention. "Will I know anyone there?"

"Duh, you'll know me."

"Does that mean I get to spend time with you?"

Katie rolled her eyes. "You're supposed to meet and spend time with the Orrs. I told you that it's a getting to know your neighbor party."

"You're my neighbor. How about I get to know you?"

"God, Coop, I didn't realize Amish men were such shameless flirts."

"I may be Amish, but never forget that I'm a man, too."

"Obviously." She gave him a sidelong glance. "Seriously,

Coop, we'll see each other at the party. Just don't forget that other people will want to talk with you, too. And understand how serious I am about not expecting anything more from me than friendship."

He raised his hand. "I promise to behave."

Katie walked to her car. "I'll believe that when pigs fly." She climbed in and started her engine.

Coop watched, unable to erase the smile from his face or the warmth he felt inside.

Katie waved as she pulled away then stopped at the end of the driveway. She rolled down her window. "You know, there will be plenty of other activities at that party."

Coop felt his eyebrows knit together. "What do you mean?"

"Leave the dominoes home. Save that for when you visit with me," she said, "at some other time."

Chapter 15

Stan patted the front pouch of his hoodie and felt the comforting lump. He had taken the revolver from his father who kept it in a shoebox on the top shelf of his bedroom closet. Stan would be keeping late hours tonight, latitude his parents allowed him on weekends. The same thing couldn't be said about the revolver. His parents would definitely freak out if they knew he had the weapon. No worries, though. Stan would return it to the shoebox in the morning and his parents would be none the wiser.

His heart raced as he pulled the gun from his pocket. Just holding it made him feel powerful. He inspected its shiny nickel finish as it lay in the palm of his hand. Stan disengaged the cylinder and checked to make sure that each chamber held a round. He wished it were more potent than a .22 but figured it would do. He didn't plan on shooting Rhoda Dendron, just intimidating her.

Stan was supposed to meet Rhoda at *Hell Bent For Leather*, a biker bar outside the college town of Mansfield. At 18, Stan wasn't legally able to visit bars, but nobody ever questioned him when he asked for Rhoda. She dealt drugs at biker bars, Stan figured, because Rhoda felt secure in her element. Nobody would mess with her inside those doors where she was considered family.

That's why Stan waited outside.

A floodlight illuminating the entrance made it easy for Stan to spy on the patrons coming and going. He had parked in a dark corner of the lot, his black Cherokee nearly invisible. Stan hunched down in the seat, his eyes peering out over the dashboard at the front door. Rhoda had rode in on her Harley a half-hour ago and had disappeared inside.

Stan checked his watch. Fifteen minutes past their scheduled meeting time of 10:30. He knew that fidgety and impatient Rhoda wouldn't wait much longer. She never could sit still. Sure enough, a few minutes later, Rhoda exited the bar, cigarette dangling between her lips, a scowl on her face.

Rhoda threw the cigarette on the ground and fussed with her hair before slipping a shiny black helmet onto her head. She mounted the Harley and started it up, gunning the throttle.

Stan switched on the Cherokee's ignition but waited until Rhoda pulled from the lot before turning on his headlights. Rhoda had driven in a direction away from town which worried him. The roads opened up in that direction, and it would be easy for him to lose sight of her if she goosed her bike. His Cherokee was no match for her Harley.

Pulling from the parking lot, Stan could see the red glow from her tail light. He followed, keeping a good distance between them. Rhoda maintained a leisurely pace which left Stan feeling confident that she hadn't suspected anything. He followed her for about 10 miles until she drove into the parking lot of an adult video store.

Stan drove past about a quarter mile and doubled back.

The store's parking lot was too open. No place for Stan to park in the shadows and hide. He spotted an abandoned gas station diagonally across the street and pulled in, driving around the side of the building where he wouldn't be seen from the video store. He got out of the Cherokee, leaned against the wall, and watched.

At exactly midnight, the last car pulled from the parking lot and the neon "open" sign went dark. Closing time? If so, why hadn't Rhoda left? Her Harley remained the only vehicle parked in the lot.

Stan had hoped to follow her to her supplier, the next person in the organization's upline. After he found out who that person was, Stan intended to make a pitch to try and squeeze Rhoda out. He didn't expect her to stop at this place. What the hell was she doing? Making her own adult video with the owner of the store? Could it be possible that she lived here? Lights still glowed from the store.

At 12:30, Stan decided he had waited long enough. Hardly any traffic traveled the road this time of night which made it easy for him to sneak across the street in the dark. He walked around back to scout out the place, and there he found a Dodge pickup.

Rhoda was inside with someone else. Maybe more than one someone else.

He approached the back door and used some pages from a discarded newspaper to unscrew the light bulb which was too hot for his bare fingers.

Stan tried the door knob and to his surprise found it unlocked. Rhoda couldn't possibly live here. As paranoid as she was, the door would be bolted tight. He eased it open and stepped inside. A glow shone from a hallway probably leading to the store.

He shuffled his feet, careful not to kick anything or trip and headed for the hallway. Along the way he checked again for the revolver in his hoodie pouch. Despite the reassuring feel of the gun's cold metal frame, Stan's heart raced from the adrenaline rush, his breathing heavier than normal.

The end of the hall opened into the store. The glow he had seen earlier came from a TV. Rhoda sat on a sofa facing away from him. She was watching *Saturday Night Live*. Stan couldn't see anyone else in the room.

Stan pulled the gun from his hoodie and held it in front of him. His hand shook. Making his voice sound low and threatening, he said, "Don't turn around."

His words had the opposite effect on Rhoda. She screamed, leapt from the sofa, and spun around in a crouch. "What the hell is this," she yelled but then stiffened when she saw the gun pointed at her.

Startled, Stan took a step back. "Damn it, Rhoda, can't you follow simple instructions?"

Rhoda's eyes widened when she recognized him. Her voice cracked. "Stan, what are you doing here?"

Seeing her fear gave Stan more confidence. He turned the revolver sideways gangsta style and marched up to her. He pressed the end of the barrel against Rhoda's forehead. She squeezed shut her eyes.

"Who belongs to the Dodge pickup parked out back?"

Rhoda opened her eyes. Her lips quivered, but she said nothing.

Stan pulled back on the hammer, cocking the revolver. "I asked you a question, bitch."

"Philo," she blurted, "this is his place. Please, Stan, lower the gun."

Stan realized how much of a turn on this was for him, her fear. He wished it was Katie Hunt instead of Rhoda. If he got away with this, he decided to take a similar run at Katie sometime real soon. Stan growled at Rhoda, actually growled like a dog, trying to coax more fear out of her.

She sighed and squeaked in a little girl's voice. "Please, Stan."

"Where is Philo?"

"Out on a drug run."

"If that's true then why is his truck still parked here?"

"He took his chopper. Look, Stan, I expect him back any minute."

He suspected she was lying, but even if Philo was due back, Stan sensed a connection between the two of them. Philo wouldn't attempt anything heroic as long as he held a gun to Rhoda's head. "Give me the name of your contact."

Rhoda raised an eyebrow. "You know I can't do that. He'll kill me, then he'll kill you."

Stan pressed the barrel harder against her forehead. "He might or he might not, but if you don't tell me, I'll kill you right now."

"Think about what you're doing, Stan. You're just a scared kid."

Stan didn't like Rhoda's defiant display. Apparently, the shock of his intrusion had worn off. He wanted the fear to return to her face and cracked her alongside the head with the gun.

Rhoda whimpered and crumbled to the ground.

Stan pointed his gun at her face and chuckled. Who knew this could be such a turn on?

She raised a hand shielding her face. "He goes by the name of Toss. I don't know his real name, I swear it."

Rhoda grabbed the arm of the sofa and pulled herself up. Blood trickled between her fingers as Rhoda pressed her hand to her head.

Careful to keep an eye on the front of the store, he wanted to see if headlights turned into the lot. It wouldn't do to have an unexpected visitor. "Where can I find this guy named Toss?"

"I'll take you to him."

That idea made Stan nervous. He wanted to meet Toss at a time of his own choosing and after some careful planning. "No. Tell me where I can find him."

She hesitated.

"I'll give you to the count of three." Stan pressed the barrel against Rhoda's head. He wouldn't shoot her, because she wasn't any good to him dead. He needed Toss's address. Still, what could it hurt to bluff? "One… two…"

"Wait," she said. "I'll tell you, just relax, okay?"

"So tell me already."

"Remember the address I gave you the night Philo and I met up with you in Corning? Toss's hangout isn't far from there. That's why it was so convenient for us. We got our stuff from him that night, drove down the street, and did your deal."

Stan believed her. What she said made sense. "Where exactly is his hangout?"

"*Racks and Pinions*, a gentlemen's club. He owns the joint and also uses it as a front to deal."

Stan knew the place. He had driven by it many times but being underage never ventured in. "How do I know you're telling me the truth?"

"You're holding a gun to my head, Stan. I get it. You're serious, and I know what'll happen to me if I lie to you. You found me once; you can find me again."

"You're a smart woman. Remember that."

"Stan, can you please point that gun away from my face?"

"Shut up." He needed a moment to think. Stan suspected that she was telling him the truth, but how could he really know for sure? He came up with an idea.

"I'm going to tie you up and gag you. We'll wait for Philo to return. If what he says agrees with what you just told me, I'll be on my way." It wasn't convenient to tie her to the sofa, but her spied a swivel chair with slats that he could tie her to. He took a step back and lowered the gun, relaxing his finger on the trigger. "Stand up."

Rhoda did as he asked and faced him, hands at her side. Her expression looked more calm now. This wouldn't do. He liked it better when she was scared. Before he could do anything, she said,

"If that's your plan then I might as well tell you. Philo isn't coming."

Heat rose into Stan's face. The bitch had lied to him. What else had she told him that was untrue?

Rhoda continued. "Philo isn't coming, because he's in jail. I arrested him. Stan, I'm an undercover DEA agent."

Stan blinked. The palm of his hand holding the gun started to perspire. What she just said blindsided him. In his moment of inattentiveness, Rhoda produced a badge from her back pocket. She held it out in front of her.

"Stan, you got the drop on me. That's my bad, but I don't think you've ever done anything like this before. What you did tonight, what you're doing now is just an impulsive mistake." She held out her hand. "Give me your gun."

"What?" Stan couldn't wrap his mind around what she had just said. He raised the gun, pointing it again at her face. "You mean you're a freaking cop?"

"Easy," she said.

The perspiration from his palm caused Stan to lose his grip on the gun. He adjusted his hold, but squeezed the trigger a bit too tight. The gun popped and jumped in his hand. Surprised, he looked at the revolver.

What just happened?

Probably scared the crap out of the cop.

He glanced up and saw a font of bodily fluid gluing from a hole in Rhoda's head where her left eye used to be. In the background, he noticed the spray of blood on the wall and TV screen.

Stan lowered his arm and let the gun fall from his grasp onto the floor. Rhoda stood in-place, a blank expression on her face before folding at the waist and collapsing to the floor.

"Holy shit," Stan mumbled.

He stood and gazed at the hole in Rhoda's head. Her lifeless right eye, the one that wasn't ruined by the bullet, stared back at him.

Stan wondered why he wasn't scared out of his mind? His heart which previously pounded in his chest now seemed steady. He breathed easily. "Whoa." The moment of exhilaration soon passed, and he started to think.

What did he touch? The gun and the back door knob. He picked up his father's revolver and returned it to the pouch of his hoodie. Pitch dark outside. Nobody had seen him either here or at *Hell Bent for Leather*. Nobody would know. He was going to get away with murder.

The badge which Rhoda held out for him to look at lay at his feet. He picked it up and shouted a triumphant, "Yes." If Rhoda had told him the truth about Toss and where to find him, Stan realized that the badge might be his ticket to the big league.

He glanced at his watch. 12:45. He would have plenty of time to drive to Corning to visit *Racks and Pinions*. The place probably didn't close until 2:00 AM.

* * *

With an air of confidence and holding his head high, Stan Cox strutted through the front door of *Racks and Pinions*. Loud music, a thick haze of tobacco smoke, and the smell of stale beer assaulted his senses. He also caught a whiff of weed. Striding into the lounge, Stan saw two naked girls dancing on the bar. One of them wrapped herself around a pole and smiled at him. She was really hot, but he didn't have time to stare. He had another mission to accomplish. Stan approached the bartender, but before he could speak, he felt a hand clamp onto his shoulder.

Stan swiveled and found himself staring into the chest of a giant ape of a man. He looked up into the big man's scowling mug. The man's head was shaved bald. He reminded Stan of Vin Diesel. Obviously, he was the club's bouncer, yet despite his apish physique, Stan detected keen intelligence behind the man's green eyes.

"I'm gonna need to see some ID." The ape man's booming voice sounded loud and clear above the blaring dance music.

"I'm not here for the girls or the booze. I'm here to see Toss."

The bouncer grabbed Stan by the back of the neck and marched him to the door. "Hold up," Stan yelled, "he's gonna want to see me. This is important."

The bouncer opened the door and shoved Stan out. "Don't even try to come back in here, or I'll bust you up good." The man turned and walked back into the club.

Before the door closed, Stan yelled, "His dealer, Rhoda Dendron, is a DEA agent. This place is going to be raided. There's a warrant out for Toss's arrest." Stan didn't say exactly when those things would happen. From what Rhoda had told him, Stan knew it was only a matter of time, and once the cops discovered Rhoda's corpse, it would definitely happen sooner rather than later.

The big man did an about face. Stan could've swore that his eyes glowed with fire. His confidence shriveled as the bouncer approached. Stan backpedaled and pulled Rhoda's badge from the pouch of his hoodie, opened it for the man to see, and said, "I can back up what I just told you."

The bouncer ripped the badge from Stan's hand and examined it. "Okay, kid, spill it."

Stan didn't know how hard he could push this guy, and he was in a precarious position, but he decided to go all in. He inhaled. "What I have to say is for Toss's ears only, and with all due respect, mister, I don't know you."

The bouncer looked down his nose at Stan studying him. He held out a hand.

Stan understood at once what the bouncer wanted, and he handed over his revolver.

The ape man's hand was so huge, that when his fingers closed around the revolver, the gun disappeared. He grunted and continued to eye him.

"That's all I have." If Stan even thought about lying, he'd wither under the big man's gaze. "I swear."

The bouncer looked Stan over, measuring him. Apparently convinced that Stan spoke the truth, he said, "When we go inside, walk straight to the door on the left side of the bar. I'll follow behind."

Stan did exactly as the man said. When they walked through the door, the man grabbed Stan again by the back of the neck and guided him through another doorway into a side room. The man closed the door behind him and directed Stan to a leather chair.

"Sit."

After taking his seat, Stan examined his surroundings. The room was an office, and he sat in one of four visitor's chairs. He noticed an oversized cherry desk in front of him. Behind the desk sat an equally oversized executive chair padded with tan leather. The carpeting matched the color of the leather and thick beige padding lined the walls. Sound proofing. Was it to keep the loud music out, or was it to keep patrons from overhearing what went on inside? Things like screaming and gunshots.

The bouncer took a seat in the executive chair and folded his arms across his chest. He glared at Stan.

Suddenly, it made sense how a bouncer would have the nickname Toss. "You?" Stan asked.

Toss dropped the ID badge on the desktop. "How'd you get that?"

"I took it from Rhoda Dendron." Stan sat up straight in his chair. "After I shot her in the head."

Toss reacted by unfolding his arms and resting them on the desk. He leaned forward and locked his gaze with Stan's. "Kid, who the hell are you?"

"Stan Cox, one of Rhoda's dealers. Tonight I was supposed to meet with Rhoda to do a deal. I waited for her in the parking lot of *Hell Bent For Leather* in Mansfield. You know the place?"

Toss nodded.

"Anyway, I screwed up and got there an hour early. While waiting for Rhoda in the parking lot, I saw her come out of the place with a guy in a suit. The guy had cop written all over him. I stood her up over the deal and followed her to find out what was up. We ended up at an adult video store off of U.S. 15. I busted in and confronted her. We were alone, and she tried to arrest me. I got the better of it."

Stan paused and waited for Toss to react. Was the big man buying this slight departure from the truth?

Toss picked up the ID badge and studied it. "That's one hell of a story, Stan. You playing straight with me?"

Stan liked that Toss had started calling him Stan instead of kid. "You can check it out. Her corpse is likely still there. I just did her a little over an hour ago."

"How'd you get her to give me up?"

"Before I offed the bitch, I made her tell me about you."

"Why?"

"To warn you, of course."

"Why would you want to do that?"

Stan leaned forward trying his best to portray confidence. "To prove my loyalty."

Toss tilted his head. "I'll have to ask you again, Stan. Why?

What did you expect to get out of warning me?"

"Simple. I want Rhoda's job. I want her network of dealers."

The big man leaned back in his chair and regarded Stan. Had he made a mistake? Was he asking for too much?

Toss asked, "How old are you?"

"Eighteen."

"Jesus."

Stan's heartbeat picked up. "Look, man, I did this for you. I didn't have to come here."

Toss bellowed, his laughter reminding Stan of a baritone Santa Claus. "Indeed, you didn't." He got out of his chair and sat on the corner of his desk. "Let me get this straight. You had the balls to uncover and take out a DEA agent and then even bigger balls to come see me afterward in the hopes of landing a job as a mid-level drug dealer?"

Stan looked the man in the eye. "Yeah, that's about it."

"Never in my life have I seen such cheek, and believe me, Stan, I've been around."

Stan wasn't sure if his meaning was good or bad and decided to keep his mouth shut.

Toss wagged a finger under Stan's nose. "You had better believe that I'm going to check out your story. Then I'm gonna check out your life, the lives of your parents, and the lives of your friends. I'm going to find out everything about you, Stan, leaving no stone unturned. If you're lying to me or aren't who you say you are, you won't live to see 19."

The big man pulled his finger from under Stan's nose and smiled. "On the other hand, if you're being straight with me, and somehow I believe that you are, by god, what you did tonight is the stuff of legend. If there existed a gangsta hall of fame, you'd be in it."

"Does that mean I get Rhoda's old job?"

Toss leaned back and looked down at Stan, an incredulous look on his face. "Hell, no. That would be a waste."

Stan wondered if he misunderstood. Didn't Toss just praise him? What could be the problem?

"You're going places, Stan, maybe all the way to the top."

"The top?"

"There are some people in New York City who are going to

want to meet you. Maybe even people from Bogota."

Jackpot.

Chapter 16

Coop held the reins of the family buggy. Mother and Hattie sat on either side of him. The family buggy horse, Tony, clip clopped his hooves against the pavement of Cove Road. The sound relaxed Coop, making him drowsy, but the four mile trip didn't take long. Conditions weren't exactly ideal for an outdoor gathering. A passing cold front brought rain that morning. Although the storm had passed, the sky looked to be gloomy for the rest of the day. They packed jackets in the back of the buggy in case the evening became too chilly.

Katie had raved to the Orrs about his mother's shoo fly pie, so the new neighbors sent word requesting a few for the dessert table. His mother packed the pies inside a basket.

The gravel driveway leading up the mountain to the Orr's new home wasn't suitable for buggies, and there was no place among the trees to pasture horses. Consequently, Dr. Hunt opened his meadow for use by his Amish neighbors.

Coop steered the buggy into the pasture and waved to the Foose family. They had already unhitched their horse and were climbing into Sheila Cunningham's Chevy Avalanche.

Mrs. Cunningham had agreed ahead of time to shuttle Amish guests up to the house. "I'll be right back for you," she called out.

"Take your time," Coop said.

While unhitching Tony, he recognized other buggies belonging to the Hutmakers and the Krohs. "Mother, I don't believe we will feel out of place. Many of our church friends are here."

When Mrs. Cunningham returned for the next shuttle run, they climbed into her vehicle. During the short trip from the meadow to the house, Mrs. Cunningham didn't have much to say except for once again expressing her condolences over the family's loss.

The first thing Coop noticed after getting out of the vehicle was the aroma of hot dogs cooking over a charcoal grill. He carried the basket of pies while his mother took Hattie by the hand. Coop led them to the grill where a large man with dark chocolate colored skin was busy with the frankfurters.

"Good day," Coop said, "My name is Cooper Stover. This is my mother, Ruth, and my cousin, Hattie."

The man wiped his hands on his apron and shook with Coop. "Declan Orr," he said. "I'm pleased to meet you folks. My wife, Chelsey, is inside making ice tea. My two boys are around here someplace, and here comes my little girl."

A girl wearing a broad smile ran to her father's side. "I'm Keisha."

After introducing themselves, Keisha turned to Hattie and asked, "You want to swing with me? Daddy tied an old tire to a tree out back."

"Okay." Hattie ran off with Keisha, the two of them disappearing out of sight around the house.

Mother pointed to the basket Coop carried. "We brought pies for dessert."

Mr. Orr pointed a fork in the direction of the house. "Check with Chelsey. I'm not sure what her arrangements are for dessert."

Coop followed Mother into the house which teemed with people. He recognized just about everyone as neighbors in Wineberry Hollow and knew most of them by name. They found Chelsey Orr, introduced themselves, and Coop set the basket on the table.

Chelsey had been in the process of peeling potatoes. Mother joined in. "Let me help you with that."

Stephen Kroh, Coop's former classmate with the stuttering problem, waved an arm for Coop to join him. Feeling a bit overwhelmed, Coop welcomed the opportunity to talk with someone he knew well. The two of them greeted each other and walked into the living room where they found some kids huddled around a TV screen playing a video game.

"That black kid is N…Nate," Stephen said. "He lives here. That's his g…game. Did you ever see anything like that before?"

Coop watched as two girls moved sticks in their hands. The TV screen showed cows racing around a track and jumping hurdles. Coop shook his head. "I don't see much use in something like that. We have too many farm chores."

Stephen shrugged his shoulders.

"Let's go outside," Coop suggested. It was too close for him in the house.

They walked around the house and Coop checked on Hattie. She was tossing around a beach ball with Lucas Foose. Little Lucas, Coop remembered, was recently diagnosed with diabetes. He made a mental note to ask Lucas's folks how he was doing.

Vicki Clark, Dr. Hunt's part-time nurse greeted them. She began a conversation with Stephen about one of his brothers who had apparently sprained an ankle after stepping into a groundhog hole.

While they spoke, Coop drifted away to find something to drink.

He heard Katie's voice. "Over here, Coop." She waved at him from an outbuilding that looked like a shed. Just like when Coop saw her last, Katie was dressed in shorts, tee shirt, and hair in a pony tail.

Feeling his mood brighten, Coop walked over.

Katie introduced him to Jamal, the Orr's oldest son. Jamal shook Coop's hand with little enthusiasm and had trouble looking Coop in the eye.

"Can you help Jamal carry this picnic table to the front of the house?" Katie asked. "I tried, but it's too heavy for me."

Coop grunted under the weight. Made of hickory, it felt like it might weigh 200 lbs. The solid table was constructed with the benches attached. "Where to?"

"I got the front end. Just follow me," Jamal said.

They carried the table to a spot midway between the front door and the grill. Jamal stopped and set his end of the ground. Coop let go of his end and asked, "Here?"

Jamal walked away. Under his breath, he said, "I set it down, didn't I?"

Coop turned to Katie. "He doesn't seem very friendly."

"Jamal's having trouble adjusting. You remember what it was like being 15, all the angst."

"Geez, Katie that was only three years ago. And I still have a lot of angst."

Katie ran a hand through her pony tail. "It takes Jamal a while to warm up to strangers, but he's okay after he gets to know you."

Coop gave her a good up and down look. "How have you been?"

"Fine. Been working in Dad's office doing medical coding and being his receptionist. Get all your wood cut?"

"Yes, got most of it dragged down to the house, too. Still have some splitting to do, though." He paused. "It's good to see you, Katie."

"Thanks." She sounded noncommittal. "We have about an hour before supper. Want to play badminton?"

Coop was fairly good at the game so he figured he wouldn't be too embarrassed. Besides, it would be a fun way to pass the time. "I'll play if you don't beat me too badly."

She gave him a love tap in the shoulder. "Cooper Stover, I play to win. No mercy."

"You're on."

They had to wait until two boys finished a game. That suited Coop, giving him a chance to chat some more with Katie. When the boys finally finished, they invited Coop and Katie to play doubles. They agreed and played until Keisha ran up to them yelling, "Burgers are done. Time to eat."

Katie left Coop to eat with her father. Coop joined up with Mother and Hattie. There weren't many places to sit, so Coop and his family claimed one of the porch steps and ate with their plates in their laps.

Coop liked Mr. Orr's hotdogs and ate three of them. Everyone raved about Mother's shoo fly pie. She promised to give Chelsey Orr the recipe.

As people finished up, they began milling around again. Before anyone could stray too far, Declan stood and asked for everyone's attention.

He stood in the midst of the gathering and spoke. "On behalf of me and my family, I want to thank all of you for coming to our party. I've had an opportunity to speak with everyone, and to a person, you've all made me and my family feel welcome. We're glad to be your neighbors."

"Of course we're making you feel welcome," someone shouted. "We'll welcome the chance to eat your food and drink your beer anytime."

That comment drew laughter from the crowd. Declan continued. "Look, I've traveled the world as a soldier, seen some nasty shit." He paused. "Pardon my language. My point being I've seen just about every kind of horror imaginable."

Declan grew more animated, waving his arms and hands for emphasis. "Nations against other nations, families against other families, Muslims against Christians, hell even Muslims against other Muslims. We have politicians who for personal gain continue to pit one group of people against another, separate us into groups: blacks, whites, Latinos, pro-this, and anti-that."

Cooper looked around at the crowd. He thought Mr. Orr would probably make a good deacon, the way he commanded everyone's attention.

Declan continued to speak. "When I retired from the Army and decided to leave the Rangers, my commanding officer asked me why I would want to throw away my career while still in my prime. You know what I said to him?"

Other than Grace Foose's infant who Coop could hear crying from inside the house, nobody made a sound.

"I asked him, what happened to my America? Why do politicians want us to fight each other instead of our common enemies? Is that why the president is recalling all of the armed forces? What happened to the pioneer spirit of fending for oneself and family, of neighbor helping neighbor? How have politicians gotten away with seducing our countrymen with handouts and then making veiled threats about how the handouts could disappear if the other party gets into office?

"My CO sat back in his chair and said he couldn't answer my questions, that those decisions were made by personnel above his pay grade. Then he went on to say that I was naïve, that my version of America only existed in my own mind."

Declan took a breath. "Look at us. Have you ever seen a more diverse group of people? I see white people, black people, Amish people, farmers, a doctor, a builder, a butcher. We're not perfect, we're still human and have our disagreements, but what I *don't* see is hate or intolerance. Look at the way you all live, helping one another, not by providing hand outs, but by working together."

"Folks," he went on to say, "America doesn't just exist in my own mind. It exists right here in Wineberry Hollow, and I'm damn proud to be a part of your community."

The crowd applauded. Dr. Hunt shook Declan's hand. Coop heard that Mr. Orr had been some kind of elite soldier, and after listening to that short speech, he understood how he would be able to inspire the men under his command. Mr. Orr was a true leader, and as far as Coop could tell, there was nothing phony about him.

The crowd began to disperse, some to grab more food, some to visit with each other. The kids went back to playing.

Coop felt a tap on his shoulder. He turned and found Sammy Wetzel. "Finished my bow. It shoots those dowel rods pretty good. Want to see it?"

"You have it here?" Coop asked.

"In the backseat of the car. I figured you'd be here so I could show it to you."

He followed Sammy to the car parked along the driveway. Sammy reached in, pulled the bow from the back seat, and handed it to Cooper.

The bow felt well balanced in Coop's hand, a big difference from when he had handled it before. "Nice job. Stop by the farm sometime soon so we can shoot it."

"Waste of time," Jamal Orr muttered as he walked by carrying a bag of garbage to a nearby burn barrel. He snickered. "Won't do no good against someone with a Glock."

"What's wrong with him?" Sammy asked.

"I don't know. Don't worry about it," Coop said.

Mr. Orr followed shortly thereafter carrying more garbage bound for the burn barrel. "What do you have there, son?" He set the bags down and Coop handed over the bow.

"I make bows. Sort of a hobby of mine." Sammy's voice was tentative as if unsure of the man's reaction.

"You made this all by yourself?"

"Yes, sir. That's my third one. Dad helped me with the first two, but I did this one alone."

"Impressive. You bring any arrows?"

Sammy glanced at Coop before turning his attention back to Mr. Orr. "Yes, I have some in the car, but don't worry, I'm not going to get them out. Just wanted to show it to Coop."

Mr. Orr's eyes twinkled. "Aw, come on, let's give it a try. I'll setup a straw bale in the backyard."

Sammy beamed. "If you say so, sir."

Jamal walked by during his return trip. Mr. Orr motioned him over. "Check out what this young man made."

Jamal kept walking. "Already seen it."

Coop and Sammy followed Mr. Orr into the backyard. Sammy's father, Sam Wetzel, stood with them.

"Your son has an interesting hobby," Mr Orr said.

"Two summers ago when Sammy was 10, he attended a workshop during a boy's club campout," Mr. Wetzel said. "The instructor taught primitive bow making. Thought it might be a phase he was going through, but Sammy's been passionate about it ever since."

Mr. Orr pointed to the straw bale set against the tree line and looked at Sammy. "Light 'er up, son."

Sammy pulled one of the dowels from his quiver. "I haven't mastered arrow making yet. These are dowels that I jerry rigged into arrows."

Mr. Orr's eyes widened. "That's using your imagination, son. Great improvisational skills. You'd make a good Army Ranger."

Sammy nocked the arrow, drew back, and let it fly into the straw bale.

"Impressive," Mr. Orr commented. "What's the draw weight on that bow?"

"Only about 45 to 50 pounds. I'm not so sure about my tillering skills and am afraid the stave might break. Besides, I'm not strong enough yet to pull much more than 50 pounds."

Coop was happy for young Sammy and all the attention he was getting, but he discretely walked away to check on his mother and Hattie. He found them in the house. Mother held hands with a sleepy looking Hattie while she conversed with Caroline Doaks, the farrier's wife.

"I suppose we should soon be going," Mother said.

Like on so many other occasions when Coop enjoyed himself, the time always passed too quickly. He would've liked to stay longer, but understood that his mother and cousin were tired. "I'll find Mrs. Cunningham to see if she can shuttle us back down to the meadow."

Katie popped into view from a neighboring room. "There you are, Coop. I've been looking all over for you."

"And I'm glad you found me so I can say goodbye. We need to leave."

Katie looked down and said, "Oh."

"What's wrong?" Mother asked.

Katie didn't say anything for a few moments. Then she took a deep breath and let it all gush out. "Some of the kids found a couple of Mr. Orr's old army tents in the shed. They asked him if they could set them up and camp out tonight. Mr. Orr agreed and even promised to build a campfire, but he said that he wanted somebody older to watch over the kids so they wouldn't get into trouble. I volunteered to stay with the girls in their tent. We asked Jamal if he wanted to chaperone the boys, but you know how Jamal has such an attitude. He wants nothing to do with it. So, Coop, I was wondering if you'd want the job?"

Surprised, Coop stared at her. "You and me and children?"

"Uh huh. You'd be watching Nate Orr, your archery friend Sammy, Trace Hullman, Kyle Murfree, and Greg Yost."

"I don't know those last 3 children you mentioned."

"They're just typical boys, Coop, Trace is 10 and Kyle and Greg are 9. In my tent will be Keisha, Sadie Doaks, Carly Munson, Siobhan McMurphy, and Lila Kent. Keisha is the oldest at 10 and all the rest of the girls are 8."

Spending quality time like this with Katie was something Coop could only dream of. Of course, he was eager to accept her offer, but would Mother approve? He exchanged glances with her. "I don't know, Katie."

"C'mon, Coop, it should be fun."

"I think you should do it," Mother said, "it would be good for you."

Coop's jaw hung agape. Did his mother really just say that?

"Katie, may I have a few words in private with my son, please?"

"Sure. I'll see you outside, Coop."

They watched her walk away.

Coop spoke first. "The night of father's funeral you tried to make me see how impossible it would be for me to pursue this girl. Why is it that you now encourage me?"

Mother told Hattie to use the bathroom before the trip home. After Hattie scurried off, in a stern voice she said, "Don't get the wrong idea. I am not encouraging you to pursue Katie."

"Then I don't understand your intentions."

Her voice softened. "Cooper, I know that life hasn't been fair to you. You have always been the only son to work our farm, and now that Amos is gone, it is an even heavier burden for you. You speak often about your friends Liam and Andrew and their rumspringa with a longing in your eye. Because you are so tied down, it is not possible for you to experience what they now experience, but an overnight stay with these English children can be instructional. I don't want you to completely deny yourself your reasonable desires, and something like this is reasonable."

Coop kissed Mother on the cheek. "Someday, too, I would like to see the ocean. It has always been a dream of mine."

"Then you should go, maybe after the harvest."

"Thank you, Mother. I'll take you and Hattie home and return with the buggy."

"You stay here. I'm perfectly capable of handling the buggy and hitching Tony. I'm sure that Katie or someone else can bring you home tomorrow morning."

After Mother and Hattie departed, Coop found Katie, and together they helped the kids setup the tents. While doing so, he pondered what Mother had told him. She definitely didn't want him to see Katie as someone other than a friend or neighbor. In his head, Coop understood the logic. But he couldn't think about Katie as only a friend. He couldn't deny his feelings for her.

Chapter 17

Stu grabbed a stick and skewered two marshmallows. He held them over the campfire that Declan had built for the kids. The sun had just set, and the gloomy canopy of clouds that had dominated the earlier hours of the day finally dissipated as the front moved through. The air held a cool bite, promising an unseasonably cool evening. He worried whether Katie would be warm enough for an outdoor campout and wondered if he should drive down the hill to the house and fetch her a jacket.

He watched as she and the Amish boy, Cooper, organized the kids into teams for a boys vs. girls night time scavenger hunt. How quickly she had grown. No longer a little girl, she reminded him more of her mother with each passing day.

Dwelling on Kay's death still remained painful, even after 13 years. Several weeks ago when Katie voiced that it would be okay if he dated, that she would understand, he no longer felt guilty about considering that possibility. Katie had clued him in on another fact that he already knew but hadn't acted on. Sheila Cunningham had been sending signals that she was interested.

Stu and Sheila sat around the campfire on lawn chairs along with Declan and Chelsey. All of the other adults had gone home. Now that the kids were engaged in their game, it gave the adults an opportunity to relax.

Declan popped the top of a beer. "I hope everyone enjoyed themselves."

Chelsey laid a hand on her husband's forearm. "I'm sure they did. All of our neighbors were very gracious."

Stu inspected the marshmallows and decided they were done. He pulled one from the stick and offered Sheila the other one.

She took the stick from him. "Thanks."

"You know, Sheila, I had a chance to look around inside the Orr's house," Stu said. "Your finish work is top notch. I didn't see a single nail pop. You do good work."

"She certainly does have an eye for detail," Declan agreed.

Chelsey added, "I love our new home."

Sheila had just popped the marshmallow in her mouth. After swallowing, she said, "Don't take this as a complaint, but by being a female builder, my work is always more critically scrutinized. I have to hold myself to a higher standard, always proving myself. That's why I have to mind all of the details."

Declan crumpled his empty beer can. "Minding the details is always the way it should be. That goes for men as well as women. If everyone minded the details, maybe this country wouldn't be in such a mess…"

Chelsey interrupted. "Please, Declan, you've done enough politicking for one day."

Declan sat back in his chair. "Sorry, I have some strong opinions."

"Really? I would never have guessed." Chelsey stood. "I'm going inside. It won't be long 'til I'm sleeping. It's been a long day."

"Honey, where's Jamal?"

"Inside watching TV."

"By himself?"

"Last time I noticed, yeah, he was alone."

Declan got out of the lawn chair. "I'm going to have a talk with that boy. I didn't appreciate the way he was acting today." He turned to Stu and Sheila. "Stay as long as you like, but I'm going inside with Chelsey."

"I'll take off after saying goodbye to my daughter," Stu said. "That's nice of you to let the kids have the run of your yard tonight. I hope they don't keep you awake."

Declan stretched and walked toward the house. "Ah, let the kids have their fun."

"I guess I should be going, too," Sheila said.

Stu decided to take advantage of the opportunity. "Walk you to your car?"

"Sure," Sheila said.

While they walked, Stu asked, "How are your girls doing? I haven't seen them around lately." Sheila's two grown daughters had both moved from the area.

"Melanie's working this summer in Pittsburgh, she's in grad school, and Crystal and her husband are expecting."

"Congratulations. That'll make you a Grandma."

"Thank you. I'm happy for them, but I'm not sure I like the idea of being called a Grandma. It makes me sound old."

"For what it's worth, you look much too young to be a Grandma." This was no hollow compliment. Stu always admired her looks. Her physical labor as a builder left Sheila fit and trim.

"That means a lot to me coming from you," Sheila said.

They had reached her car. Stu cleared his throat. "You ever hear from Hank?"

She leaned against the car door and sighed. "My ex and I don't talk, but he stays in contact with the girls."

Stu decided to press on. Maybe it was none of his business, but if some sort of infidelity led to their breakup, he wanted to know about it. In a soft tone, he asked, "Tell me if I'm out of line, but what happened between you two? You were such an ideal family. It bothered both Katie and me to see you and the girls go through that. And it happened so fast."

Although it was dark, the Orr's porch light cast enough light for Stu to see that her expression hadn't hardened toward him. "It's not so complicated," she said. "You knew about Hank losing his job when the bank he worked for got bought out?"

"That was bad luck."

"Hank couldn't find another banking job around here with the economy being so bad. It was a real blow to his ego and a fatal blow to our marriage. My business had been thriving, and we were getting by comfortably with just my income. He told me it made him feel inadequate and unwanted which, of course, was ridiculous. I'd have stuck by Hank even if he never found another job.

"One morning I woke up and he was gone. He called a few weeks later and told me he had moved to Baltimore and wanted a divorce. That about sums it up."

Stu glanced at the ground. "I'm sorry for what you and your family had to go through."

"Yeah, it hurt, still does when I dwell on it," Sheila said, "but it's beyond my control now. Life goes on. I have my girls, my business, and plenty of work to do."

Stu admired Sheila's attitude. Here was a woman who could roll with the punches and could be counted on to make the best of it. She was just a little lonely, like him. "Remember the afternoon you first showed Declan this place? I offered the two of you a drink, but he had to leave and you asked for a rain check. Would you like to cash in that rain check now? Since Katie is camping out with the kids, I have the rest of the night free."

Sheila didn't say anything right away. Then she finally responded. "Yes. I'd really like that."

* * *

"Knock, knock," Katie spoke softly before sticking her head between the tent flaps.

Coop had just gotten the boys settled down and had taken off his shoes. He threw a pillow at her and whispered, "This is the boy's tent. No girls allowed."

She giggled and quickly covered her mouth with her hand. She whispered, "I'll bet if those boys weren't in there with you, you wouldn't say that."

She flirted with him. How did she expect him to respond to a comment like that? "What do you want?"

"I need your help with something."

"Just a minute." He grabbed his shoes but then decided to leave them be. Whatever Katie wanted, it wouldn't involve walking very far. He ducked out of the tent and found her sitting by the fire ring fussing with a sleeping bag. The fire had burned out, but the remaining hot coals glowed orange.

"Can you look at this for me?" she asked. "It's Keisha's sleeping bag and the zipper's caught half way up."

"Can't she just climb in and go to sleep?"

"She's obsessing about it. I can't get her to settle down, and she's threatening to go in the house to her bed. I don't want her to wake her parents."

Coop took the sleeping bag from Katie and sat beside her. Holding the bag closer to the embers for better light, Coop saw where the material got caught up in the zipper. It wasn't going to zip up, but he might be able to free it if he could pull the zipper in the opposite direction.

After several tugs, Coop was able to yank the zipper free from the material. "Got it, but the teeth made a hole in the fabric."

"No problem," Katie said. Her voice trembled. "I can get a needle and thread tomorrow from Mrs. Orr and mend it."

Coop looked at her. Katie had her arms around herself and shivered. He took the sleeping bag and wrapped it around her shoulders. "Better?"

"Thanks," she said. "What time is it?"

"I don't know. A little after midnight, I suppose."

"June 21," Katie said. "The first day of summer. I didn't bring a jacket figuring I wouldn't need one."

"Mine's in the tent. You can borrow it."

"Thanks anyway. Once I climb into my sleeping bag I won't need it." She tilted her head back and looked into the sky. "Stars. I didn't think we'd see any tonight with all those low hanging clouds earlier."

"Clear skies. That's why it's on the chilly side."

Katie pointed to a gap between the trees. "From here you can see all the porch lights burning all along the length of Wineberry Hollow. Kind of pretty isn't it?"

"You're kind of pretty, Katie."

She groaned. "I walked right into that one, didn't I?"

"Yep, you threw me a softball, and I smacked it over the fence."

"Have you ever been to a major league ball park, Coop?"

"Actually, no." Coop figured that Katie probably had been, a stark reminder of the differences between the two of them. "Katie, I need to ask you something, and I want you to answer me honestly."

"What is it?" she asked, her voice suspicious.

"If I were English and if I were still in school and if I was going to college, would you have given me another chance?"

"That's a lot of ifs."

He remained silent.

Her tone changed, became more serious. "Coop, don't do this to yourself."

"It's important to me, Katie. I really need to know."

Katie reached over and took Coop's hand, a move so unexpected and startling that he almost pulled his hand from hers. "Listen to me, Coop. We can only be friends. How many times do I have to tell you that? Yeah, I don't agree with your Amish values. We've already been over this. We could never fit into each other's worlds. You're a good looking guy, tall and strong, and I enjoy your company, but the fact that you won't even try to stick up for me when I'm in trouble, I find that to be unattractive. All things considered, that's the real deal breaker."

That again. He would never be able to live it down.

"We had our born to be wild moment, remember? It didn't work. The thing is, being raised Amish is what has defined you, given you a gentle soul, your loyalty to family, your willingness to help others. I'm not sure you'd still have those qualities if you were English."

"But what if I were English and still had those qualities? What if I had plans to go to college…"

"College?" she asked interrupting him. "Why do you keep bringing that up? Do you think that by being educated I'm somehow better than you?"

Coop looked at the ground, unable to maintain eye contact. She had hit the nail on the head. His eighth grade education did make him feel inferior.

Katie let go of his hand and stood. "I will never consider myself better than anyone. I will never be better than you."

With an empty pit where his stomach used to be, Coop watched as Katie walked toward the tent. Halfway there, she stopped but didn't turn around. "If some alternate reality existed where you were English, then there might be a chance, but Coop, I want a man, not a cowering boy."

The same feeling of dread he felt during the night of their date washed over him again.

Without commenting further, Katie disappeared into the girl's tent.

Coop leaned back in the lawn chair and stared into the starry sky. A profound sense of loss overcame him. Contemplating the heaven's infinite vastness made him feel small, further illustrating his powerlessness. Nowhere in God's great universe could he discern how to bring about such an alternate realty where he would have a chance with Katie. Yet, he wished for it. Wished for it with all of his heart.

The old saying popped into his head, *be careful what you wish for*, but he dismissed that notion. Nothing evil could come from a world where he and Katie could be together.

No evil at all.

Chapter 18

Senator Winston Halbert took his seat in the Raven Rock Command Center, a large theater style auditorium that reminded him of the U.S. Senate chamber. Ringing the room stood a large contingent of heavily armed guards. On the stage, a countdown clock displayed on a massive display screen:

0 Days, 0 Hours, 30 Minutes, 42 Seconds

He glanced at the others as they filed in and recognized leaders in their particular areas of expertise, a cross section of the intellectual elite. How had President Kall gotten to so many of these people? Had he blackmailed them the same way he had blackmailed him?

During the past few months, Halbert had engineered a massive bulk food and essential supplies consolidation scheme assuring that each of the enclaves would be self sufficient for up to two years. Under ordinary circumstances, he would be proud of himself, but the heartburn in his gut after looking at the countdown clock left him feeling anything but proud.

What exactly would happen when that clock reached zero?

Halbert's wife, Sally, resisted coming to Raven Rock wanting instead to go to Enclave 2 located near Burlington, Vermont. She didn't understand why he had been so insistent about separating her from her family during the new holiday. He finally convinced her that for political reasons, she needed to be at his side for Armed Forces Homecoming Day. He promised that she could go to Vermont after the holiday, a promise he knew, he might not be able to keep.

Things would have been different if Lenore had agreed to join him at Raven Rock, but she flatly refused. Halbert tried his best to talk her into it using the guise of visiting an exciting new high-tech facility, but she remained obstinate. She'd rather attend one of her girlfriend's parties. Of course, he couldn't reveal the dire consequences of her rebuff. What a shame.

The countdown clock now stood at less than 26 minutes.

President Kall walked down the center aisle of the auditorium shaking hands. When he climbed the stage and took his position behind the podium, Dr. Nika Cho who had been sitting in the front row stood and applauded. This started the chain reaction. Everyone stood and applauded. Halbert glanced around into the faces of those near him. Nobody smiled. This ovation was not one of respect, but rather fear.

The president actually had the impertinence to clasp his hands above his head and wave them in a sort of victory salute to himself. Was he rubbing their faces in it, the fact that most of this crowd was probably coerced into cooperating with him? Did he actually believe that everyone here adored him? The applause went on long enough for two more minutes to click off the countdown clock before Kall beckoned everyone to take a seat.

He clasped the edges of the podium with both hands and spoke. "My fellow colleagues, we stand at the threshold of a bold new era where we, the princes of intelligentsia, take our rightful places as shepherds of humankind. From our citadel here at Raven Rock, we now enjoy the unprecedented opportunity to oversee the rebuilding of civilization into a worldwide utopian society that reflects *our* values, *our* beliefs, and *our* agenda."

Those words brought light applause. Another minute clicked off the countdown clock. 21 minutes remained.

Kall lowered his head for a moment as if in deep thought. Resuming eye contact with the crowd, he continued to speak. "Our predecessors nobly tried to realize this dream through educating the populace, by creating great institutions like the United Nations and prevailing on man's better nature. Although well intentioned, those techniques have proven ineffective. The common citizen concerned with eking out a living neither has the time nor the intellectual capacity to understand lofty ideals that those of us gathered here so clearly see."

The only thing Halbert could clearly see was President Kall's arrogance and condescension.

Kall went on. "As a result, it falls on us to bring about these needed changes in a forceful manner, not out of malice against those who are blind to the truth, but rather out of a will to survive. America's great experiment with democracy has failed. Now we have the means to bring down all of the world's governments and sweep away the moralists who stand in our way. In the wake of this great destruction, a new beginning rises from the ashes, a new United States of America."

The president raised an arm and pointed to his side. "Ladies and gentlemen behold our new standard." Behind him, a great banner unfurled, yellow flames against a crimson background. At its center, a bird with outstretched wings. In its claws, it held the Earth.

More applause, some cheers, and Senator Halbert watched the countdown clock tick down to 17 minutes.

Kall continued, "I trust that you understand the need for discretion and how only a few key individuals have been aware of all of the project's details. I also realize that this is the first time we have all been assembled together, and I know you all have questions, foremost of which concerns the means of this change. Ladies and gentlemen, the time has come for full disclosure."

Kall pointed to a projection booth somewhere behind the crowd and said, "Please."

The familiar map of the 48 Earthburst satellites superimposed at their relative positions above the Earth showed on the display screen directly beneath the countdown clock.

"Two satellites located in each time zone, one each located approximately 30 degrees north and 30 degrees south," Kall said using a laser pointer to highlight features on the display.

Halbert wondered if anyone other than himself thought it to be surreal that the world was about to end while President Kall gave a Power Point presentation. When this was over, would they still call him president? Maybe *His Majesty* would be more to his liking or *Emperor*. Hell, why not go all the way and just call him God?

"What only a few key people have known from the start of Project Earthburst," Kall continued, "is that each one of these satellites is also equipped with a thermonuclear device."

Halbert glanced around. Nobody gasped. Nobody even seemed surprised.

Kall went on. "The altitude of each satellite is 300 miles, the optimal distance for causing maximum damage during the release of an electromagnetic pulse. Simultaneous detonation of these devices at this altitude will be undetectable by the human eye and will cause no physical harm to life on Earth. But it will effectively destroy all modern technology except at our enclaves which have been hardened against the pulse."

Halbert considered what he had heard and tuned out as Kall droned on in further detail. An electromagnetic pulse? Wasn't that the stuff of science fiction? If the science actually existed, then he could visualize how the plan could work. The United States was the world's leading exporter of food and the world leader in the production of meats, fish, and poultry. Without this country's food resources, most of the world would literally starve. Wipe out technology and you wipe out transportation, communication, and essential services.

How long could the unfortunate souls outside of the enclaves survive without electricity? He shuddered after thinking about what was about to occur in the great cities of the world and for the first time Halbert felt a sense of gratitude toward Kall for inviting him onto the team.

He'd be safe. Two years of supplies for each enclave would be more than enough. With a heavily armed army securing each enclave, all they'd have to do would be to wait out the die off and the world would be theirs. Creating the new Armed Forces Homecoming holiday which mandated the families of the soldiers onto the bases would insure cooperation among the troops. In fact, Kall could feed the troops disinformation about another country attacking with some new super weapon. The entire deception fell into place.

Senator Halbert, soon to become Minister Halbert, felt his tension ease. He took a deep breath, sat back in his chair and relaxed.

President Kall concluded his presentation and fielded questions. While Kall spoke the countdown clock clicked off the final seconds.

:03

:02

:01

:00

Chapter 19

Dr. Stewart Hunt downed what remained of his margarita and regarded the woman sitting across the snack bar from him. He had enjoyed spending the last hour with Sheila and was glad he had invited her into his home for a night cap. For a woman in her mid-forties, Sheila had maintained an athletic physique probably as a result of the years she spent working as a building contractor. Yet she still retained feminine qualities, soft brown eyes, shoulder length hair, and a sweet smile which she showed him right now, her perfect teeth an orthodontist's dream.

"You and your family have lived across the street from Katie and me ever since we moved to Wineberry Hollow. How is it that we've never gotten to know each other better before now?" Stu asked.

"Other obligations, I guess," Sheila answered. "You and I are both professionals keeping long hours."

"Long hours and odd hours. Patient emergencies get me out of bed in the middle of the night more frequently than they should."

Sheila studied her empty glass. "You're a good man, Stu. I don't know how this community could get along without you."

"You want another margarita?"

"No thanks, I've had enough." Her eyes met his. "Knowing that a doctor lives among us who is available in the middle of the night gives all of us a sense of security. We may never need your services, but having you a part of our community means a lot."

Stu chuckled, "You make me sound like an insurance policy. Hope you never need it, but glad you have it when you do."

Sheila's eyes widened. She reached over and touched his hand. "I didn't mean it to sound that way. All I mean is we're fortunate to have you as a neighbor."

"Just kidding, Sheila, I get your drift."

Still touching his hand, Sheila said, "On a more personal note, even though we haven't spent much time together, I'm happy that you live right across the road."

He couldn't help but smile.

"You keep the lawn mowed and don't throw wild parties," she added, but when she squeezed his hand, he knew she was teasing.

Sheila removed her hand and sat back in her chair. "Seriously, now that my girls have grown and moved out, and since Hank left, it's sometimes hard to handle being alone. I'm used to cooking for a whole family and having someone to talk with at night. I speak with Crystal and Melanie at least once a week, and I often consider calling them more often, but they have their lives, too. I hate intruding."

"I don't think your girls would consider it a burden if you called them every single day."

"It's hard to explain, Stu, but you'll find out real soon when Katie goes to college. It's tough to let go."

Katie leaving home was not something Stu wanted to think about. "Where does the time go? I still remember her as a baby, carrying her in my arms." That thought also evoked memories of Kay. Eventually, when Katie left, would he be pained in the same way he was when Kay died?

"Speaking of time." Sheila looked at her watch. "It's almost 1:30. I should go." She stood and slipped into her jacket.

"Hold up." Stu reached for his windbreaker. "I'll walk you home."

"It's been a long time since someone offered to see me safely home. Thank you, Stu. It makes me feel special."

"My pleasure." Stu rifled through his pockets to make sure he had his house key and led her out the front door.

The way to Sheila's house was well lit. She had left her porch light on, and when Stu's motion sensing flood light popped on, the illumination was as bright as the full moon.

Sheila rubbed her arms. "It's chilly."

Neither of them said anything else until they reached Sheila's door. She twisted the key in her lock and faced him before pushing the door open. "I'm glad you asked me over. Thanks for letting me clear the air about Hank."

"I enjoyed your company, Sheila. Let's get together more often."

"I'd like that," she said. "Can I cook dinner for you and Katie sometime soon?"

Stu considered it thoughtful of her to include Katie. "Call us, and we'll be right over."

They looked at each other in awkward silence. Stu felt silly how a man his age should be so nervous. Before he could summon up his courage, Sheila took the initiative and leaned in to kiss him.

When their lips met, Stu thought someone had discharged a shotgun right beside his ear.

He jerked away from Sheila. She yelped.

Stu clasped his hands to his ears and shouted, "What the hell was that?" Sparks sputtered from atop the power pole at the end of Sheila's driveway. They rained down like fireworks and died after hitting the road. His nostrils filled with an acidy stench.

"The transformer must've blown." He took a few deep breaths to regain control of his wits. The unexpected explosion had scared the crap out of him.

"Lightning?" Sheila asked in a shaky voice.

The storms had passed through earlier that day. Stu looked up into clear skies, probably the clearest he had ever seen and adorned with thousands of stars. "It couldn't have been lightning. There's not a cloud in the sky."

"I heard about meteorites that sometimes fall from the sky. Is it possible that one hit the transformer?"

"I doubt it," Stu said. "Maybe some sort of power surge."

"Anyway, that was some kiss!" Sheila exclaimed and started giggling.

He glanced in the direction of Sheila's voice but couldn't see her. Stu looked around and discovered that he couldn't see anything. Except for the stars in the sky, his surroundings lay in utter darkness.

Sheila fumbled for the door knob. Stu heard the squeak of hinges as she eased it open. "You have a flashlight?" he asked.

"Yeah, it's in the drawer of my bedside nightstand. Wait here while I feel my way through the house."

A few minutes later, Sheila returned, the beam from her flashlight lighting the way. She picked up the phone. "I might as well call the electric company." She clicked the receiver. "That's funny. The line's dead. I thought the telephone lines had their own power."

"The substation must be out," Stu said. "Try your cell phone. Maybe there's still power to the cell towers."

She reached into her purse and powered it on. "It's not working."

"If the outage is that widespread, the power company probably already knows about it. When we wake up in the morning, I'm sure the lights will be back on."

"I hope so."

"Do you have generator?"

"Yeah, but it's at a job site. Do you?"

"I have a small generator wired to the house circuit to power the office. I have drugs that need to stay refrigerated. If the power's not restored by morning, come on over. You're welcome to use my shower. The generator runs my water heater and well pump, too."

"Thanks, Stu, I appreciate that."

Not knowing what else to say, he asked, "Are you going to be all right?"

"I'm a grown woman and not afraid of the dark, but thanks for caring."

He turned to leave. "I'll see you tomorrow."

"Wait." She handed him the flashlight. "Take it. That exploding transformer might have knocked down some wires. It could be dangerous, you walking across the area in the dark."

"You have another flashlight? I don't want to take your only one."

"I won't need it. I have a candle for the bathroom, and then I'm going straight to bed."

"I'll give it back to you in the morning."

Stu left Sheila's house and closed the door behind him. He walked down her driveway and shined the flashlight at the transformer hanging from the pole. No wires had fallen. Everything seemed intact, but he could still detect a caustic odor probably from melted insulation or burnt transformer fluid.

He entered his dark house and wondered why he didn't hear the engine from his generator. It should have kicked on automatically after the power went out. Stu walked through his kitchen and living room and through the sliding glass doors onto the cement slab that served as his patio. The generator sat in a weatherproof enclosure. Stu shined his light on the contraption and tried starting it manually.

Nothing.

"Hmm, battery must be dead." No big deal. He would drive to Wynot in the morning to get a new battery. The meds in the refrigerator in his office would stay cool for at least a day as long as nobody opened the door.

Katie would never mess with anything in that cooler unless specifically instructed to do so, but he might be gone for the battery before she got home from chaperoning the kids at their campout. Stu taped a DO NOT OPEN note to the door handle just in case.

Probably unnecessary, he thought. The power will be restored by morning. The repair crew always got the lights back on within a few hours.

Stu brushed his teeth and plopped into bed. He thought about Sheila and how much he had enjoyed spending time with her. He looked forward to seeing her again and before nodding off made a mental note to return her flashlight right away in the morning.

Chapter 20

The call came at half past midnight. Captain Doug Sloat and his platoon patrolled the inside fence line near the northwest corner of Enclave 38 when he felt the vibration from the cell phone in the pocket of his ACU.

Colonel Muncie called from HQ, the man's voice sounding urgent. "Captain Sloat, you and your men are to cease your patrol immediately and redeploy to Gate W3."

They had been called into action a few hours earlier as part of a base wide emergency drill, maneuvers periodically scheduled by the brass to keep the men battle sharp. The timing for the maneuvers had surprised Sloat, this being the eve of Armed Forces Homecoming Day and the many wives, girlfriends, and other family members visiting the enclave. He had inwardly questioned the point of going through the trouble of bringing all of the civilians onto base since the soldiers they visited weren't going to be available to entertain them, and he had expected the phone call to be orders to stand down and return to Sheridan Hall.

Sloat spoke into the mouthpiece. "Sir, is this a continuation of our drill?"

"Negative, captain, you are to proceed directly to gate W3 to provide backup for the personnel stationed at that gate."

During the weeks he had been assigned to Enclave 38, Sloat had never known the gates to be a security risk. "Trouble, sir?"

"That's for you to find out."

Not one to normally question orders, Sloat would usually proceed with haste, but he wanted to make sure he and his men knew what they were getting into. "Colonel Muncie, may I ask what this is about?"

"You may ask," Muncie said, "but I have no further intel on the situation."

Sloat picked up on the unspoken message from his superior. Do as you're told. As he was about to hang up, Colonel Muncie spoke again. "Relax, Doug, as far as I know the enemy is not at the gate. No need to charge in there locked and loaded. Just keep your eyes open and be available if needed."

For what? "Yes, sir, on our way. Please inform the officer in charge that we will be approaching from the north road on foot and should be able to rendezvous there." He glanced at his watch. "Around zero one hundred."

After terminating the call and relaying the orders to his men, Sloat and his platoon proceeded toward their objective. He still thought it odd. They were in rural Pennsylvania, the nearest town being West Milton with a population of a few thousand. What's the worst they could expect? A couple of drunk kids with deer rifles? Surely the contingent at the gate could handle something like that without the backup of an entire platoon.

The one positive aspect of this night was they were soldiering. This was what he and his men were used to, not the other silly social services they had been ordered to regularly perform around the enclave. During the past few weeks, they had pulled janitorial duty at Sheridan Hall, worked at the power plant and motor pool, and had even harvested wheat. If this is what President Kall had in mind for his so called domestic security initiative, Sloat figured he could be performing manual labor much easier as a civilian and probably at a higher pay grade.

Sloat's platoon approached Gate W3 with caution and spread out, observing the area. Seeing nothing amiss, Sloat passed the word down the line to stand by. He hailed the night watch and stepped forward.

A female officer greeted him introducing herself as Lieutenant Napoli. She wore a crisp uniform with short-cropped hair under a boonie. Behind her, in the gatehouse, Sloat saw about a half-dozen soldiers, all eyes fixed on him.

"My orders were to report here," Sloat said. "What's your status?"

"All quiet," she answered in a stern tone. "I have no earthly idea why the brass would want to order babysitters for us at this lonely gate and frankly, I view their lack of confidence in me and my squad as an affront."

Definitely, she could take care of herself. This woman had backbone.

In a gruff voice matching hers, Sloat said, "Lieutenant Napoli, I'm sure you and your team are well prepared and fierce warriors inviting all comers who might be spoiling for a fight. On the other hand, be advised that we reported as commanded, and I am as clueless about this situation as you are. We can stand here and piss about it, or we can share information and maybe figure out what the brass has up their sleeve."

"Very well," she said, "but with all due respect, captain, I'm in charge here. This gate is my turf."

Lieutenant Halfjack leered at her. "Well, don't you have some sauce, addressing a superior officer that way. If I were in his shoes, I'd be inclined to take you to the woodshed for a spanking."

"That'll be enough, lieutenant," Sloat told him with a raised voice. He turned to Napoli and moderated his tone. "Duly noted. I won't get in your way unless I have to. My orders were to provide you with support."

Napoli regarded Halfjack through narrowed eyes. She turned her attention to Captain Sloat and softened. "Good. That means we'll get along just fine." She motioned with her head toward the gate house. "I've got a fresh pot of coffee. Care to join me?"

"Don't mind if I do," Halfjack said.

Lieutenant Napoli snapped at him. "The invitation is for the Captain. Not you."

"Aw, come on. I was just kidding around."

Sloat said to Halfjack, "Get the men squared away. Divide them into teams and assign a watch."

"Yes, sir." Lieutenant Halfjack executed a limp salute before walking away.

Sloat accepted Lieutenant Napoli's offer for coffee. They walked inside. "I've never been to this part of the enclave and being night, I can't picture the lay of the land. What's the purpose of this gate?"

Lieutenant Napoli reached into a file drawer and withdrew a map. She unfolded it on the counter. "Gate W3 controls a minor access road leading directly to the river. It's used by base personnel working in maintenance."

Sloat examined the map. "It appears that your access road leads directly to the river with no intersecting public thoroughfares."

"Correct, with one exception. There is an unimproved road not on the map that can be used during emergencies that connects to the main highway approximately here." She pointed with her finger. "It's accessible only by Humvee or other vehicles with a high ground clearance."

He examined her hand resting on the map. No wedding ring. "If the intersection with the highway is camouflaged, then very few people would even know of this gate's existence."

"It is camouflaged, and your assumption is correct. This is a low profile entrance."

"But not necessarily a low value target."

"How so?" she asked.

"With everyone paying more attention to the main gates, an enemy force might be able to sneak onto base through this back door."

Napoli bristled. "Not on my watch."

"Of that I have no doubt."

"Besides," she said, "unless your imaginary force somehow launches their assault from an armada on the river, this gate is too inaccessible."

"Point taken," he admitted. "So, what do you suppose this is about? I mean, my platoon being sent here and this military exercise?"

She shrugged. "Your guess is as good as mine. Just another mysterious order to tack on to a long list of other illogical and ill-conceived decisions."

"Such as?"

Napoli looked around as if making sure nobody in her squad listened in. They were all busy in the next room. "Permission to speak freely, captain?"

"Proceed."

"How long have you been in the Army?"

"Long enough. Why?"

"Have you noticed the difference in the Army between when you first upped and now?"

"You'd have to be blind not to notice the differences."

"Do you like what we've become?"

Sloat waved his hands in front of his chest, palms out in a back off gesture. He chuckled. "Oh, no you don't. You're not going to get me to publically question the wisdom of our commander-in-chief."

She cocked her head. "Do you really think I'm trying to set you up?"

He considered it. "No. Not really."

"Then I'll say what needs to be said since you gave me permission to speak freely." She sighed. "None of what has gone down during the past few years makes sense. The domestic security initiative, the isolationism, the building of these enclaves, even today's Armed Forces Homecoming Day."

"Copy that," Sloat said.

"You have anyone visiting?"

"No. I have no significant other, if that's what you mean, and my folks didn't want to make the trip from Idaho, even on the government's dime."

Napoli interrupted, "Yeah, and what's that about? Why suddenly would Uncle Sam think it vital to reunite the military with their families. I tell you this new touchy feely stuff makes me nervous."

"I've been giving that a lot of thought lately, too. The only way it makes sense is to turn all of the enclaves into self-sufficient concentration camps made up of military personnel and their support structure. Throw in loved ones to keep up the morale and give the soldiers a reason to stay within the enclaves to defend them."

Napoli refreshed her coffee cup and held out the coffee pot to Sloat. "More?"

He held out his cup and let her fill it.

When done, she said, "You present an interesting scenario, one I've considered myself, but it doesn't take into consideration the overwhelming majority of citizens outside of the fence."

Sloat thought carefully about revealing more of what he had been thinking about. The desire to air his private thoughts overwhelmed his instinct for caution. Something about Lieutenant Napoli made him trust her. Maybe it had been the fact that she had led off the conversation by revealing her thoughts to him. "What if our president doesn't give a damn about the citizens outside the fence?"

They exchanged glances. She said, "The people outside the fence were the ones who elected him. You know how the military is predominantly Republican. Most of our troops no doubt voted for the other guy."

"And you know that it's easy to get elected by pandering. What if Kall pulled out all the stops to get into the White House and doesn't really care about the country's future?"

Lieutenant Napoli laughed. "What politician do you know who would admit such a thing?"

Sloat liked the sound of her laughter, girlish, belying the no nonsense attitude the woman portrayed. He took a sip of coffee and stared at her over the rim of the cup. "Perhaps a pathological one?"

Napoli maintained a neutral expression. "Perhaps." She paused before continuing. "Anyway, if Kall is planning anything evil, he'd better get on with it. After Armed Forces Homecoming Day ends, the civilian families are going to clear out and go home."

Sloat considered how they had just shared some fairly intimate thoughts, two practical strangers. He found himself strangely attracted to her. "What about your family? I told you about mine. Do you have a significant other?"

She eyed him. "No, and I'm not looking for one at the

moment."

The two officers stared at each other. He was about to ask Napoli where she was from when the claxon on the outside of the building blared.

"That's the alarm for general quarters," Napoli said. "Outside."

They rushed from the gate house and found Napoli's men mixing with Sloat's platoon. After a few moments of confusion, Napoli's squad took their positions along the gate, rifles ready. Sloat scattered his platoon as backup. Five minutes later, the claxon ceased blaring.

Captain Sloat ran to Lieutenant Napoli's side, his ears ringing. "What the hell was that all about?"

"You tell me."

Both of their cell phones activated simultaneously. "I guess we're about to find out." Sloat pushed the receive button.

The recorded message they both heard came straight from President Kall. "Ladies and Gentlemen, this is your commander-in-chief. I regret to inform you that a short time ago enemies unknown detonated upper atmospheric thermonuclear devices. The resulting electromagnetic pulse has destroyed the country's power grid and rendered all non-military electronic devices inoperable. As you are no doubt aware, an attack of this nature is considered a precursor to a full blown nuclear strike. As a result, I am ordering all military personnel to enter a posture of full military readiness, and I am ordering a total lockdown of all military enclaves. Until further notice, nobody enters and nobody leaves.

"As I mentioned, we have not yet had time to establish the source of this assault, but rest assured our response will be swift and decisive. Once we know more, I'll pass along information through the command structure. In the meantime, be vigilant, be safe, and God bless the United States of America."

Sloat and Napoli stared at each other. "Wait a minute," Sloat said. "If what he says is true, how is it that our gear hasn't been affected? Why aren't the lights out?"

"Military equipment and this entire enclave is hardened against EMPs," Napoli told him. "Out there," she nodded with her head toward the fence, "they're toast."

Just the scenario he had postulated a few minutes ago. How he wished he were wrong.

Sloat scanned the horizon. Even under normal circumstances he wouldn't be able to see lights. They were in the country far from the nearest farmhouse. How could he verify what the president had just said?

He remembered a cell tower on top of the ridge on the other side of the river. A beacon flashed atop the tower as a warning to low flying aircraft. Sloat searched the blackness and found it. "Look," he shouted, "the strobe light still flashes. The president must be mistaken."

He felt nearly giddy. It had been a gut-wrenching scare. If that beacon still worked, then it couldn't be all that bad. Somewhere, a viable power source powered that beacon.

And then, with no warning, the beacon went dark.

Chapter 21

Being used to waking up with the chickens, Coop thought he would be the first one out of his sleeping bag in the morning. His eyes opened at the sound of whispers. The glow of dawn shone through the door slit of the tent. Nate Orr and one of the other boys were having a discussion.

"Good morning," Coop said in a low voice so as not to wake the others. He yawned.

The two boys stared at him with serious expressions.

"What's the matter?"

Nate fielded his question. "Trace and I went inside the house to play video games."

Coop sat up in his sleeping bag. "Not a good idea. Your parents probably wouldn't like being woken so early. It's best you remain outside."

"Doesn't matter anyway, the power's out," Nate said.

"There's nothing to do," Trace added. "I'm bored."

"No electricity, eh?" Coop said. "Welcome to my world, boys."

"What do we do now?" Trace asked.

Coop stretched. "Let's step outside. See what's stirring." He led the two boys out of the tent and took a deep breath. "It's a beautiful morning, clear, crisp air and yesterday's rain took away all the humidity. This is the kind of day when it's a pleasure to be working outside in the fields."

The corners of Nate's mouth turned down and he muttered, "No TV."

"Hiya," Katie said. She popped out of the girls tent, her charges trailing behind. At the same time, the three boys who remained in the boy's tent made their appearance.

"Morning all," Coop said.

The kids started fussing. Katie winked at Coop. "Gotta keep 'em busy, dude."

"Doing what?" Coop asked. "They're little lost lambs without electricity."

Keisha Orr tugged at Coop's trouser leg, trying to get his attention. When Coop looked at her, she asked, "Does having no electricity mean that things are fubar?"

Katie shrieked. "Keisha, that's a bad word."

"It is not. Daddy says when things are fubar you have to improvise."

Katie knelt to be eye level with Keisha. "Your father was in the Army. You shouldn't always repeat words that he says without asking him first what they mean."

"What does it mean?" Coop asked.

Katie stood and started to say something, but her face turned red. "Never mind, Amish. Your ears might catch fire if I told you."

"I'm hungry," the McMurphy girl said. Coop couldn't remember her first name because it was so unusual.

"Siobhan, you're always hungry," Greg Yost told her. "That's why you're so fat."

"I am *not* fat," the little girl yelled and started chasing her tormentor around the yard.

Declan Orr stepped onto the porch. He wore an army green muscle shirt with matching shorts, white socks and sneakers. He bellowed, "Aha, I see that the natives are restless."

"Sorry if we woke you," Katie said.

Declan waved off her comment. "Gotta couple dozen eggs and some bacon for our breakfast, but the stove won't work. Power's out." He turned and yelled through the screen door. "Jamal, go out to the shed and hunt up the Coleman. We'll be cooking with the camp stove until the power comes back on."

He looked at Coop. "By the way, does this happen often, the power going out?"

"Sorry, but I can't say since we don't use electricity."

Comprehension lit up Declan's face. "My mistake, no need to apologize."

"It doesn't happen very often, maybe once or twice a year, and it never stays out very long," Katie said.

Mrs. Orr joined her husband on the porch. "What's going on?"

Declan filled her in.

"Cooking on the Coleman reminds me of the times we used to camp out," she said. "Fond memories. We should plan to camp out some more before the kids get too old."

Declan stared off in the distance. "My memories of cooking out aren't as fond as yours. Warmed over MREs with enemy fire zinging overhead." He put his arm around his wife. "What kept me going was thinking about you and the kids."

Chelsey kissed Declan on the cheek. "That was another time, another place. You're with us now. Don't let your mind drift back there."

"Affirmative," Declan said. He released his hold on his wife and shouted, "Jamal, I don't want to have to tell you again. Go hunt for the Coleman."

Coop heard an angry shout come from inside the house. "Cool it, man, I'm getting dressed."

Declan's forehead wrinkled. "Don't know what I'm gonna do about that boy."

"Give him a little time to get used to things," Chelsea said.

After holding his hand over the campfire, Coop said, "Mr. Orr, it won't take much to get this fire going again. Plenty of embers remain. You can save your propane for another time."

"Outstanding idea. I like a man who knows how to improvise."

"Thanks, sir."

"How old are you, son?"

"Eighteen."

"You're a man then. One of us. That's old enough for you to call me Declan."

Coop felt his face flush. "Please understand that I can call you Mr. Orr or sir, but it's not in my upbringing to address an elder by using his first name."

Declan put his hands on his hips. "Well, son, I certainly wouldn't want you to feel uncomfortable, but I want you to understand something. I can sense that you're more of an adult than most kids your age. As my lovely wife continues to remind me, I'm no longer in the Army. Since you are an adult, that makes you and I equals. If you feel the need to address me as Mr. Orr, then I'm going to call you Mr. Stover."

"That's not necessary, sir."

"I beg to differ, Mr. Stover, and it would be unwise of you to contradict me." The smile Coop saw on Mr. Orr's face belied the sternness of his tone.

"Okay, Mr. Orr. I'll gather up some kindling to get this fire going again."

Declan relaxed his posture and chuckled. "By all means, Mr. Stover, carry on."

They divided up the chores. The boys gathered wood to rebuild the fire, and the girls carried out the eggs, bacon, and cooking utensils.

Katie spoke softly so that only Cooper could hear. "Seems as if you made a new friend in Mr. Orr."

Coop spoke equally as soft. "Since he's my new friend, maybe Mr. Orr won't be too embarrassed to tell me what fubar means."

After pursing her lips, Katie punched him in the arm, "Cooper Stover, don't you dare ask him about that."

He rubbed the spot on his arm where Katie had punched him and made a face pretending that she had hurt him. "I won't ask him if you tell me."

Katie made a fist and waved it under his nose. "Nooo, dude. I'm not going to tell you, and you're not going to ask Mr. Orr. Got it?"

Although Coop was curious about that word, he kept up the act mainly because he enjoyed the way she continued to tease him. "Sheesh, Katie, you sure can be bossy."

"That's because you need to be bossed."

"I think you're taking advantage of my non-violent Amish nature. You keep punching me in the arm knowing that I won't hit you back."

Katie lowered her gaze and shuffled toward the house.

Now what had he said to upset her?

* * *

Cooper fried bacon in an iron skillet over the campfire and then reused the grease to fry eggs. Mrs. Orr retrieved left over hamburger rolls and paper plates from last night's party. The kids ate first. Coop slid an egg onto each of their rolls. They laid cheese and bacon strips on top. After the kids finished and started playing, Coop repeated the process for the adults.

Katie watched the kids play and periodically interceded when they got to squabbling with one another.

Mr. and Mrs. Orr joined Coop at the campfire. Jamal strutted out of the house and stood on the porch. The scowl on the young man's face looked more than unfriendly to Coop. It was downright hostile. He wondered if Jamal was just angry with the world in general.

Mr. Orr spoke up. "Jamal, go fetch us some folding chairs."

Jamal flashed a narrow eyed glance at his father and gathered up the chairs. He leaned them against a tree near the campfire where Coop worked. Coop tried making eye contact, but Jamal ignored him.

"Don't leave the job half done," Mr. Orr said. "Set up those chairs so we have a place to sit, and wipe them down while you're at it."

Jamal glared at his father. He bowed at the waist and said, "Yes, Massa."

Coop cringed. If an Amish kid were to back talk his parents like Jamal just did, especially in public, he could expect a good licking when he got home. He figured Mr. Orr to be a no nonsense parent and worried that he might get physical with his son right now in front of everybody.

Mr. Orr approached and stood eyeball to eyeball with Jamal. "Get out of my sight before I rearrange your face."

"Declan," Mrs. Orr said in a warning tone.

Jamal took a step back. "You always boss me around like I'm your slave."

Mr. Orr stood his ground. "I wouldn't have to boss you if you carried your weight around here." He pointed at Coop. "Look at this young man building a fire and cooking breakfast for everyone. Nobody has to tell him what to do. He sees something needing done, and then he does it. That's the kind of maturity I expect from you."

Great, Coop thought. Now Jamal was going to dislike him even more.

"Yeah, well I'm not him," Jamal said.

"Agreed. You have a long way to go to equal this man," Mr. Orr said. He pointed at the house. "Go inside. I won't have you eating with adults until you start acting like one."

"Fine," Jamal mumbled. He strutted onto the porch and disappeared inside the house.

Mrs. Orr looked at her husband. "You forget that Jamal is only 15. Don't expect too much from him. He acts like an adolescent because he still is one."

"Understood, but Mr. Stover here is only three years older."

"Three years may not be much of an age difference for adults, but there's a world of difference between a 15-year-old and an 18-year-old."

Mr. Orr looked at Cooper. "Those eggs ready yet, Mr. Stover?"

"Yes, sir. Let me slide one onto your hamburger roll." He slipped the spatula under one of the eggs in the skillet and placed it onto the bun.

"Well done, Mr. Stover."

"Thank you."

After serving everyone else, Coop served himself last.

Katie reserved a chair for him beside her and motioned for him to sit. She said, "I wonder exactly when the power went out last night. It seems to be taking a long time to fix it."

"Maybe an automobile accident along Cove Road. Somebody could have struck a power pole." That thought worried Coop. His mother and Hattie had driven the buggy home. Could someone have hit them? It was always a danger to travel the roads in an Amish buggy. He dismissed the idea. Someone would've come to tell him.

Mr. Orr said, "Damn peculiar that none of these kids' parents have come to pick them up yet. It's past zero eight hundred."

Coop looked at Katie. Did she understand what Mr. Orr meant by that?

Katie met his glance. "After eight o'clock."

How had Katie known his question? Did she know him so well that she could read his thoughts?

"I'll do dishes," Katie volunteered.

"That's not necessary," Mrs. Orr said. "There aren't that many. I'll use the dishwasher."

"Negative," Mr. Orr spoke out. "It takes electricity to heat the water and run the well pump. I don't want the pressure to drop to zero. No telling how much longer this power will be out, and we might need that water for emergencies. Furthermore, there will be no showers, either."

Mrs. Orr looked at her husband and said, "Really, Declan, aren't you being a bit too cautious?"

He looked into the sky and said, "Maybe so, but I'm feeling ill at ease. From being in the Army, I've learned to pay attention to that ill at ease feeling. It's usually a foreboding."

"Ease up, soldier. This is Pennsylvania, not the Middle East. Everything is going to be fine." She looked at Cooper. "How do you folks get by with no electricity. Maybe we can copy what you do."

"Hand dug wells and muscle powered hand pumps provide our water. We boil the water on top of the wood stove and use it to do dishes and to fill up the washtub."

"That's a lot of work."

"It's not so bad once you get used to it. It becomes part of the daily routine."

Continuing to glance at the sky, Mr. Orr said, "Fat chance of us being able to hand dig a well on top of this hill."

"We won't have to," Mrs. Orr told him. "Why do you keep looking up?"

"Busiest time of day for air traffic is in the morning. I don't see a single jet trail."

Coop spoke softly to Katie. "Can you give me a ride home?"

"Sure. What's the hurry?"

"Chores."

She glanced at the Orrs. "I can take a couple of kids with me in my car and drop them off."

"Good idea," Mr. Orr said. "I don't know what's up with these kids' parents. I should be able to fit the rest in my Suburban. I'll follow you."

Coop helped Katie to gather the kids and divvy them up. Sammy Wetzel, Sadie Doaks, and Lila Kent would ride in the backseat of Katie's car since they lived closest to Coop. The rest of the kids would squeeze into Mr. Orr's car.

After Katie got everyone buckled up, she fired up her old Buick.

They waited for Mr. Orr to back out of the garage. After a few minutes, he walked over to them. Coop rolled down his window.

"The Suburban won't start," Mr. Orr said, "neither will Chelsey's Honda. Both are dead as doornails."

"What a coincidence," Katie said. "Can I give you a jump?"

"I don't believe in coincidences," Mr. Orr said. "I'm going to try the Mustang."

"Mustang?" Coop asked while Mr. Orr walked toward the garage.

"Some old car he has that makes all you guys drool."

A minute later, Coop watched the old car pull out of the garage. The kids in the Suburban had already gotten out and trailed behind the Mustang. Mr. Orr pulled even with Katie's Buick and shut off the motor. He got out of the car, eyes wide, scanning the area. Something about the man's demeanor, his erect posture and wide eyed stare gave Coop goose bumps.

Mr. Orr motioned for Katie to roll down her window. "Get these kids home. This is important. Don't leave Wineberry Hollow. Tell everyone you see to stay home. Their lives depend on it."

"What's wrong, Mr. Orr?" Katie asked. Coop could tell from the sound of her voice that Mr. Orr's words had frightened her as much as they had frightened him.

"We're under attack." He said it as calmly as if he had told them that the sky was blue.

Coop wondered if he was about to find out what fubar meant.

Chapter 22

The urge to pee woke Stanley Cox. He got out of bed, shuffled to the bathroom and took care of business. On his return trip to the bed, Stan noticed a halo of daylight peeking around the drawn curtain of his hotel room. The idiots at the front desk must've forgot his wake up call. He checked the clock on the bedside table. Damn, the thing had quit working.

He checked his watch. It had stopped. Stan was supposed to meet Toss for breakfast. The big man wouldn't like it if he showed up late.

Toss had introduced him the night before to an overlord who went by the name of Forsythe. The meeting had turned out to be a total bust. Toss had promised Stan big things, but after the meet and greet, Forsythe had told Stan that he would, "be in touch." What did that mean? He had expected an immediate promotion or some other reward for ridding the world of an undercover DEA agent.

Stan stepped into the shower. In the middle of rinsing off his shampoo, the hot water ran out and the water pressure slowed to a gonorrhea trickle. The cold water shocked him fully awake, and he raced to finish. His teeth chattering, Stan got out of the shower and slipped into a plush white robe provided by the Corning Palace. A palace with no hot water? This hotel was a joke.

A placard on the bathroom counter advertised the robes for sale in the gift shop for $175.00 each. Screw that. He was going to steal this one rationalizing that it was due him for the cold shower and busted alarm clock. Besides, the room was registered in Toss's name. Let him pay for it.

Still feeling cold, he unlocked and slid open the door to the balcony and stepped outside. Damn, it was chilly. Yeah, this was Corning, New York and not the tropics, but it was also the first day of summer. The air should be warmer than this. From his suite on the top floor, the view of the Chemung River, colorful downtown shops, and nearby museum appeared tranquil.

He inhaled and found the air surprisingly fresh. Last night he nearly choked on exhaust fumes. What changed?

Stan scanned the streets below. Pedestrians milled around Market Street, but nothing else moved. What, no traffic? Stan leaned over the railing and found vehicles frozen in place as if they all ran out of gas at the same time and drifted to a stop.

Could he still be sleeping? Hallucinating? Nah, he hadn't done any drugs last night.

"Spooky, ain't it?" Toss called from the neighboring balcony.

Startled, Stan nearly lost his balance and fell over the rail. He recovered and turned to greet his benefactor. "I'm surprised you're up. My alarm didn't work."

"Wasn't the alarm that woke me," Toss said. "Was the quiet."

Early Sunday morning on a nice day like this, Stan figured the city should be bustling. Instead, they were greeted with near complete silence.

"Something ain't right," Toss said.

Obviously. "What do you make of it?"

Toss grabbed the balcony's hand rail and looked straight down. "Don't know."

They spent a few minutes observing. Stan heard nothing. No car engines, no tooting horns, no construction noises, not even a church bell. Then, in the distance, he heard the tinkle of breaking glass followed by a gun shot.

Toss stepped back from the rail. "I think we best get out of Dodge as soon as possible."

"What, and skip breakfast?" Stan joked.

Grim faced, Toss said, "Get dressed. We're leaving."

Stan walked back into his suite and changed. He stuffed the pilfered robe into his gym bag along with yesterday's clothes and met Toss in the hall. They made their way to the elevator which, of course, didn't work.

Toss led the way down the stairs to the underground parking garage. People huddled together in small groups, speaking to each other in murmurs. They gawked at Stan and Toss with quizzical expressions. Some of them had raised the hoods of their vehicles and tinkered with their engines.

On the balcony, Toss had used the word spooky. The word fit. As the realization of their predicament took hold in Stan's mind, chills raced down his spine.

Toss pushed the button on his key fob, but the doors to his sedan wouldn't unlock. "Damn it." He slid the key into the slot and unlocked the doors manually. After the big man took his place behind the wheel, he reached across and opened the door for Stan.

Stan climbed in and buckled his seatbelt. He fixed his eyes on Toss's big paw of a hand as the man twisted the key in the ignition switch.

Nothing. Not even a click.

Toss exhaled and sat back in his seat.

"What do we do now?"

Toss reached beneath his blazer and pulled out a handgun. He worked the lever and extracted the magazine.

"What are you doing?"

"Making sure I have a full clip. You still carrying your revolver?"

Stan reached inside his gym bag, pulled out his father's .22, and held it out for Toss to see.

"How many rounds?" Toss asked.

"Cylinder holds 8."

"You bring any extras?"

"No. Didn't think I'd need to."

Toss inhaled. "Use them sparingly. Make every shot count."

Stan's heart raced. "What are you talking about now? Who are we going to shoot?"

"Anyone who tries to mess with us."

"Why would anyone want to mess with us? Where are we going? In case you haven't noticed, nobody's going much of anywhere."

Toss met Stan's gaze, his green eyes narrowing. "Instincts, kid. All those abandoned cars. None of 'em working. Whatever we're experiencing is much more than a simple power failure. I don't think it's going to end anytime soon, and it ain't gonna end well."

Stan sensed this too. "I hear you."

"At best, we might have a few hours to get out of this town before all hell breaks loose. By the time the sun goes down tonight, there will be mass panic. This place'll become a war zone."

Stan shuddered. "If you can't drive, how are we going to leave?"

Toss stowed his handgun inside his blazer, unbuckled his seat belt, and opened the car door. "We walk."

Walk? Stan grabbed his gym bag and exited the vehicle. "Sure, you can walk. It'll only take an hour or two to get to your place in the suburbs, but how am I supposed to get back to Wynot? It'll take me days to walk that far."

"S'pose so," Toss said. He walked briskly toward the daylight at the top of the underground garage's ramp. "You're in good shape and it's early morning. Should be able to do 20 miles before nightfall. Quickest way for you is west to route 15, then due south. I'd advise finding someplace to hole up overnight out in the sticks away from people."

Stan hurried to catch up with him. He shielded his eyes after they emerged into the bright daylight. "What about water? Food?"

"There'll be stores along the way. You can buy what you need."

The people they passed on the street acted lost, bug eyed, not knowing what to do. Toss moved purposefully, his jaw set, eyes straight ahead, arms swinging by his side.

At a corner market, they walked past a uniformed police officer harried by a crowd of people. Stan heard him explain, "Look folks, I don't know anything more than you do. Everyone needs to remain calm."

"My baby needs formula," a lady shrieked. She held her infant in front of the officer as if it would make a difference. "I got to get into that store."

The cop held his hands out in front of him. "Be patient. I'm sure the owner will be here soon."

"But he needs his formula right now," the young mother said, her voice cracking.

Stan felt a hand on his shoulder. Toss's.

"Keep moving," he uttered. "We can't be concerned with what goes on around us or we'll never make it out of here."

Stan felt kind of sorry for the mom and her kid. He even felt sympathetic toward the cop. That guy was going to have a lousy day for sure.

They walked on.

After a mile or so, Stan got thirsty. He spied a gas station, but it looked abandoned. Two young boys on bicycles stopped. One of them rattled the door. The kid then cupped his hands to the window and peered inside. He looked at his buddy and shrugged, nobody apparently there. The kids pedaled away.

"Hold up," Stan said.

"Now what?"

Stan pointed at the gas station. "I really need water for my walk home and might have trouble getting it later when the shit hits the fan. You saw what went down back at that market. If it weren't for that cop, they'd already have smashed their way in. Don't know about you, but I'd rather keep a step ahead of any angry mobs."

"Good point." Toss looked around. He moved his hand to the inside of his blazer and stepped toward the gas station. "All right. We'll buy what we can. If that won't work, then we'll take what we need."

Chapter 23

The odor from mucking out Tony and Bonnie's stall wasn't nearly as pleasant as the fresh air Coop enjoyed while camping out on the Orr's lawn. The overnight showers ushered in a crisp morning and unseasonably low humidity. Coop took advantage of the nice weather to catch up on chores around the barn. While forking the soiled straw from the stall into an old wooden wheelbarrow, he considered the behavior of his English neighbors. It had been three days since the power went out.

The morning after the Orr's party, he had hitched a ride home with Katie. They dropped off Lila Kent first. They found Lila's father working beneath the hood of his truck. At first, he thanked Katie for delivering his daughter and apologized, saying that he couldn't get any of their vehicles started and that the phones were out. When Katie explained that nobody's vehicles worked except for her old Buick and Mr. Orr's antique Mustang and that Mr. Orr advised that everyone should stay close to home, Mr. Kent raised an eyebrow and grew silent.

Katie went on to tell him that in Mr. Orr's words they were, "under attack."

Mr. Kent checked the sky. Then he gave Katie a suspicious look before taking Lila by the hand and disappearing inside his house.

Next, they had pulled into Sammy Wetzel's driveway. The lad had just grabbed his bow from Katie's trunk when his father burst from the butcher shop and in a raised voice complained about the coolers being off line, how nothing worked, and how he needed to deliver a side of beef to one of his customers before it spoiled.

He had wanted to borrow Katie's car.

When she had turned him down, for a moment, he saw desperation in Mr. Wetzel's eyes and worried that he might pull Katie out of her seat and just take her car. She had sensed something, too and had driven away quickly.

Their last passenger was Sadie Doaks, daughter of the blacksmith. When Katie had driven up their lane, Mr. Doaks walked onto his front porch resting a shotgun across his arm. Even after they explained the situation, said goodbye to Sadie, and drove away, Coop had looked in the side mirror and saw Mr. Doaks staring after them, shotgun still resting on his arm.

Coop set down his pitch fork and pushed the loaded wheelbarrow behind the barn to the manure spreader. After dumping the contents into the hopper he pulled a handkerchief from the waist band of his trousers and wiped his brow. He shielded his eyes and stared into the sky. No airplanes. No vapor trails from high flying jets.

Could Mr. Orr be right? Were they under some sort of attack? The very idea seemed silly to him except that all his neighbors were acting as if they were in shock. It didn't feel real to him. Nothing had changed in his life. He would still finish mucking out the stalls, Hattie would still gather eggs from the chickens, his mother would still do laundry in their ringer washer, and after lunch he would walk the fields to check on the summer wheat and sweet corn.

His simple Amish way of life would go on as usual.

Coop thought about his English neighbors and their dependence on electricity and automobiles. They took for granted the conveniences that modern life afforded them. Generations had grown up away from the land, and now the possibility of doing without technology turned their lives to chaos and filled them with fear.

He recalled a sermon he had once heard from his deacon about how those who worshipped the god of Science would suffer distress when that god proved to be false. At the time he had questioned that message. How could science be considered an enemy? The miracles of modern medicine had saved countless lives, even many of those among his Amish neighbors. Coop had worked it out that it was not science itself, but man's *attitude* toward science that led to bad things. Just as everything else in life, there had to be a balance.

What had the English done to themselves? A better question, what were they going to do now? Coop pushed the wheelbarrow back inside the barn. He had work to do. The English would have to solve their own problems.

After finishing the barn work, Coop figured he had about an hour before lunch. He would be able to tolerate that amount of time in the direct sun. Always conscious of his fair complexion, he donned his straw hat and went to fetch Bonnie. He planned to hitch her to the manure spreader and distribute the waste in their fallow field.

As he walked out of the barn, Katie turned into the driveway. He had made a conscious effort all morning to drive her from his thoughts, but here she was. The sight of her brought a smile to his face. She wore cut off shorts and a tee shirt with a logo that read "Hollister." What was Hollister? Her hair hung in wet strands.

Coop considered how he must smell after cleaning the stable and stood a few paces downwind. "Good to see you, Katie."

"I feel like crap," she said. "I just had to use water from our hot tub to wash my hair and we have to carry buckets of water inside to flush the toilets."

"Poor baby," Coop said.

"Shut up."

He chuckled. "Would you like to have lunch with us?"

"That's not why I stopped by. Dad wanted to know if you could meet with him and Mr. Orr."

"Me? Why?"

"I'm not sure, exactly. They plan to go on some sort of road trip and want to ask you a few questions."

What could they possibly want to know from him? "When?"

"Now. I'm your chauffer."

Coop looked at his clothing and work boots. "I suppose I can spare a little time, but I'll need to change clothes and freshen up. Come on inside."

He led Katie into the house. His mother was in the process of pulling pies from the oven.

Hattie stood on a chair and washed dishes. "Katie!" she exclaimed, got down off the chair, and gave her visitor a hug.

"Are you still here, little one?"

"Mama and Papa said that I can stay the rest of the summer with Auntie Ruth and Cousin Cooper."

Mother wiped her brow and said, "The child is a big help to me. A real blessing. And she helps me keep my mind from dwelling on Amos. I love having her." Mother then raised an eyebrow at Katie no doubt wondering what she was doing here. Coop pondered it too. The harder he tried to distance himself from Katie, the more she seemed to show up in his life.

"Back to your dishes," Coop's mother said to Hattie.

"I'm here to fetch Coop if you can spare him for a little while.

My father wants to ask him for advice." Changing the subject, Katie asked, "How are you able to bake pies with no electricity?"

"Propane," Mother answered.

Coop had a thought. If the English vehicles didn't work, how could the propane truck make deliveries? How much fuel did they have left?

"It smells delicious," Katie said. "What kind are they?"

"Blackberry. Fresh picked."

"I'm going to clean up, so I'll leave you alone for a few minutes," Coop said. He figured that Katie and his mother would get along well.

Coop pumped water from the well and filled a wash basin. He washed in cold water and pulled on a clean shirt and trousers. He wished he could wear shorts. They would be so much more comfortable, but of course, the ordnung governing his congregation forbade them. How could wearing short trousers damage anyone spiritually?

Returning to the kitchen, Coop found Katie finishing a slice of blackberry pie. "I'm ready when you are," he said.

"Thank you, Mrs. Stover." Katie carried her plate and fork to the sink where Hattie waited, standing on a stool so that she could reach the counter. His little cousin took the dishes from Katie and plopped them in the dish water.

Coop turned to his mother. "I shouldn't be gone long." Ordinarily he would give her a goodbye kiss on the cheek. Since Katie was there, this would be considered a public display of affection, another action his faith frowned upon.

Silly rules.

Coop climbed into Katie's car. "This is very mysterious. Don't you have an idea why your father wants to see me?"

Katie turned onto Cove Road heading in the direction of her house. "Not really. He and Mr. Orr got to talking about food and mentioned your name. I think they want some advice about farming."

So many other farmers, older and more experienced could provide that kind of information. Why had they asked for him? During the short trip, Coop observed many of his neighbors hanging around out of doors. Of course, with no air conditioning their homes would be ovens. Even on a relatively mild day like today, English weren't used to the heat. They all stared, bewildered looks on their faces. Scared.

"This is surreal," Katie said.

Coop thought that to be a good word to describe the situation.

Katie pulled into the driveway behind Mr. Orr's old Mustang. She led the way into her house where they found Dr. Hunt and Mr. Orr sitting at the dining room table studying maps.

Dr. Hunt stood and shook Coop's hand. "Thank you for coming."

Mr. Orr said nothing. He stared at the maps lost in thought.

"How can I be of help?" Coop asked.

Dr. Hunt pointed to empty chairs. "Sit, Coop. You too, Katie."

They sat across the table from the two older adults.

After Dr. Hunt took his seat, he cleared his throat and said, "Declan and I have reason to believe that something terrible has happened. As you know, everything electronic is broken. Nothing works."

It couldn't be as bad as Dr. Hunt was letting on. "Katie's car works. Mr. Orr's car works."

Orr glanced up from his maps. "They have simple carburetors and distributors. Those old cars were manufactured before computer chips were built-in. Just about every vehicle built during the past thirty years is going to be fried."

"What would cause such a thing?"

"EMP," Orr said.

What was that? He wasn't going to get further explanation from Mr. Orr because the man had lowered his gaze back onto the maps.

"Electro-magnetic pulse," Dr. Hunt clarified. "The detonation of a nuclear device in the upper atmosphere creates a ground induced current of enormous intensity."

Coop exchanged a glance with Katie and saw from her expression that she was just as puzzled as he was. "Do you want to put that in plain English, Dad."

Dr. Hunt sat back in his chair. "Think of the damage a million simultaneous lightning strikes within Wineberry Hollow would cause."

"That would kill everyone," Coop said.

"That's just an illustration of the impact of an electro-magnetic pulse, but an EMP produced by an upper atmosphere thermonuclear device would be harmless to humans. It's the after effects that would wreak havoc. The electrical grid has gone dark."

"For how long?" Katie asked.

Orr looked up from his maps. "I've studied EMP attack scenarios as part of my military training. Power plant transformers are so expensive that no company can afford to keep spares. They're replaced as part of a regular schedule. Delivery time for a transformer takes a year or longer. What makes matters worse is large transformers are no longer manufactured in this country."

"If our electric company can't produce electricity, can't we borrow some from electric companies in other states?" Katie asked.

"Sure we can," Orr said. "That's the purpose behind regional electrical grids. If a natural disaster such as a hurricane takes out an individual plant, the rest of the producers on the grid can compensate and support the affected area. But here's the big picture. There are over 2,000 large transformers in use throughout the United States. The annual worldwide production capacity for these large transformers is less than 100. An enemy military strategy would include taking out our country's entire electrical grid."

Katie frowned. "If that were to happen, it would mean…"

"Teotwawki," Orr interrupted.

It sounded like a Native American word to Coop.

"Teotwawki," Orr repeated. "Military jargon for: The end of the world as we know it."

Dr. Hunt's face turned ashen. "In other words, game over."

Chapter 24

"Dad, you're scaring me," Katie said.

"I'm sorry, sweetheart, but you need to know what Declan and I suspect."

If this were true, Coop felt sorry for his English friends. They would suffer. "I still don't understand. What do you want from me?"

Dr. Hunt and Mr. Orr looked at him. Orr fielded his question. "My years of experience as an Army trainer has honed my ability to quickly judge a man's character. You have leadership abilities,

Mr. Stover."

Coop smiled, "Thank you for the compliment, but I've never led anyone. My faith encourages humility and submission."

"The most important attribute of a leader is humility," Orr said. "You may be young, but you set a fine example the way you handle yourself, your maturity in the face of your father's passing. Your work ethic. Folks look up to you, respect you, precisely because of your adherence to your faith."

Mr. Orr had a point. The Lord was mankind's greatest spiritual leader but also a humble individual. Coop didn't see himself the way Mr. Orr saw him. "I still don't know what you want from me."

Dr. Hunt leaned across the table. "Let me ask you a question, Cooper. In your opinion, do you think that the combined Amish farms in Wineberry Hollow could produce enough food every year to feed all of the rest of the people in the valley?"

Why such a question? "I suppose so. We could probably feed many times more than the total population of Wineberry Hollow."

Dr Hunt and Mr. Orr glanced at each other. Some silent form of communication.

Coop added, "But almost everything we produce that we don't keep for ourselves goes to market. It's how we make our living."

Orr looked at Coop, his face wearing a sad expression. "Son, I hope to god I'm wrong about what I suspect, but if I'm not, there won't be a market. Transportation is down. Very few vehicles are operational. With no electricity, there will be no gasoline produced or shipped. Gas station pumps won't work."

Dr. Hunt picked up the conversation. "No electricity means no refrigeration. With modern just-in-time inventory systems, supermarket shelves will be bare within a few days, sooner if people panic."

Scary words ran through Coop's head. Chaos, anarchy, mayhem, mass starvation.

"If this is indeed the worst case scenario, the people living in Wineberry Hollow are going to need to organize and help each other," Dr. Hunt said.

That seemed sensible to Coop.

Dr. Hunt went on. "We were hoping that you could speak to the Amish families. Explain to them what we think has happened. Be a liaison between your people and your English neighbors. We need your help and experience on how to live a simple life. I don't know what we can offer the Amish in return except our pledge to protect you from harm, if it comes to trouble."

Coop had trouble grasping the fact that these capable, confident men were actually asking him, an 18-year-old, to be an ambassador of sorts. "Do you seriously believe that loss of electrical power is widespread, beyond the valley?"

"I sure hope not, Coop," Mr. Orr said.

"Since there's no television or radio, how will you know for sure?"

"Dr. Hunt and I aim to find out. He and I are going to take my Mustang for a ride. We have enough gas to get as far as Williamsport and back. If the lights are out as far as Williamsport, then we can assume the worst case scenario."

Katie stood. Her voice trembled. "I don't get it. If we're under attack, why haven't we been nuked? Where is the fighting? Where is our Army? Can't they help us?"

"Those are all very good questions," Mr. Orr said. "You father and I hope to find some of those answers on our trip."

Dr. Hunt got out of his seat and hugged his daughter, tried to calm her. "I'm not going to insult you and say that everything is going to be all right, but we have each other and our friends and neighbors. That counts for a lot."

He let go of her. "Besides, this power problem might just be something fluky that happened. It might affect only Wineberry Hollow. Mr. Orr and I will find out."

Katie straightened and placed her hands on her hips. "Yeah, well I'm coming with you."

"Out of the question," Dr. Hunt said. "It might be dangerous."

"That's why I'm coming. I'll be out of my mind with worry if you leave me. My worst nightmare is that you'll go away someday and not come back." She paused and bit her lower lip. "Like Mom. She didn't come back."

"This has to be a decision between the two of you," Orr said, "but allow me to suggest that it might not be a bad idea to have Katie travel with us. People are going to be scared which'll make them dangerous. They see two old soldiers out and about, especially me being black, they might shoot first and ask questions later. A young lady like Katie being with us will make us appear less of a threat."

"You'll appear an even lesser threat with me in my Amish hat sitting in the back seat," Coop said. "I'm coming, too."

Orr scratched the whiskers on his chin. "Cultural diversity at its finest. Sure would make the libs proud."

"No can do, Coop," Dr. Hunt said. "Your mother would never forgive me if something happened to you, and I'd also never be able to forgive myself."

Coop felt something akin to anger or was it pride? Dr. Hunt couldn't have it both ways. Either he was a kid who couldn't make his own decisions or the leader they had made him out to be. He said a silent prayer and then spoke. "If you want me to convince my congregation to follow your lead, then I need to see for myself the state of affairs outside of the hollow. I want to give those I speak with an accurate witness of the facts from my own eyes. It will carry more weight with them. They may not fully trust your conjecture. You want my help? Then I must come along."

Mr. Orr chuckled. "See what I mean, Stu, I was right about this young man. He's confident and capable."

"And a man who refuses to defend himself if we get into trouble out there," Dr. Hunt added. "Amish will not fight."

Katie sneered. "You got that right."

Coop considered these words a low blow. A few moments ago, the doctor spoke of protecting the Amish. Now the man wasn't even willing to protect him during this simple journey. Coop hung his head, turned, and left the house. The Orrs and the Hunts were good people, but they'd have to manage their affairs without him. He hoped that whatever happened, it wouldn't be too difficult for Katie. He'd ride Tony up to see her in a few days, make sure Katie had enough food and other necessities.

He started walking Cove Road toward home. It would take him an hour to cover the few miles, give him plenty of time to think. Could these English be correct in their assumption that the country had collapsed? That would definitely impact both the English and the Amish.

He turned after hearing the sound of an automobile engine. The old Mustang pulled even with him and stopped. Mr. Orr had lowered the convertible top. He drove and Dr. Hunt rode shotgun. Literally. He carried one across his lap. Katie sat in the back, two rifles laying at her feet.

Dr. Hunt got out. "I didn't mean to offend you, Coop. You're right. I can understand your position. You have a big stake in this, so you should come with us. I just want you to know that you may not like what you see once we leave the hollow. It's possible things could get rough. Are you prepared for that?"

"I will not resort to violence, if that is what you mean."

"Even if someone attacks you?"

"I trust in God. If I am to die today, that would be Gottes Wille."

"Chicken Coop," Katie said, her voice dripping with disgust.

Dr. Hunt sighed and pushed the seat back forward. "Get in the back with Katie."

She turned away from him as he took his seat. Mr. Orr gunned the engine and they were off.

He wasn't going to hurt anyone, even if they meant to do him harm, but as Coop studied the forlorn expression on Katie's face, he knew that she still hadn't forgiven him for his failure the night of their date.

They made two stops along Cove Road. First, a short visit at Coop's house so that he could tell his mother that he'd be later than expected, although he didn't fill her in on the details of what they were up to. In a silent prayer, he asked God to forgive him. A lie of omission was still a lie.

Their second stop, at Dr. Hunt's request, was at the Foose household. After they pulled into the driveway, Dr. Hunt got out of the car and carried a small insulated cooler to the Foose's front door, like the kind a person would carry a six-pack of soda in.

Since the Fooses were Amish and Coop knew them well, he decided to hop out of the Mustang and join the doctor as he knocked on the door. Maybe this visit had something to do with the Foose's new baby.

Dr. Hunt gave him a hard look. "Ordinarily your coming to the door with me would be a violation of HIPAA privacy laws, but under the circumstances, I don't think anybody will be in a position to enforce it."

Timothy Foose answered the door. He and Grace were just a few years older than Coop. Timothy invited them in after waving a greeting to Mr. Orr and Katie.

Grace joined them carrying the baby. Little Lucas trailed behind pulling a toy horse on wheels at the end of a string.

Timothy addressed the doctor. "We didn't send for you. Everyone is healthy. The medicine has worked wonders for Lucas. He doesn't get as tired anymore, and we watch what he eats." He faced Coop. "Wie geht's?"

"Things are well with my family," Coop said.

Dr. Hunt cleared his throat. "I'm here regarding Lucas." He handed off the cooler to Timothy.

Timothy opened the lid and wore a puzzled expression. "Another bottle of insulin?"

"For Lucas. I kept this in my office for emergencies. How much do you have on hand?"

After thinking for a moment, Timothy said, "Part of a bottle and a full one just like you gave me."

"How many syringes?"

"I don't know. Enough for the two bottles, I suppose."

Dr. Hunt sighed. "I know this goes against what I've taught you, but it might be a good idea for you to hold on to the used syringes for a while. They're supposed to be disposable, but in a pinch they can be sterilized and reused."

Timothy exchanged glances with his wife. "You expect the power to be out for a long time, don't you? What happens if we run out of insulin before we run out of syringes?"

"As far as I know Lucas is the only person in Wineberry Hollow with type 1 diabetes. I'm going for a drive with Declan Orr. We'll see about finding more supplies."

Cooper saw little hope of that from Dr. Hunt's expression. He rested a hand on Timothy's shoulder but couldn't think of anything consoling to say to his friend. He wanted to tell him not to worry but didn't want to lie.

Timothy removed the bottle from the cooler and handed the cooler back to Dr. Hunt.

"Keep it," Dr. Hunt said. "It's insulated. Refrigeration is done for, so add ice to the cooler as long as your supplies last, but not so cold that it freezes. Insulin will degrade if you can't maintain it at a cool temperature. Do you understand?"

"We keep pond ice in a root cellar," Grace said.

"Thank God for the old ways," Dr. Hunt said. "You'll be better off than most."

After climbing back into the Mustang and driving away, Coop asked Dr. Hunt, "Don't you think we can find more medicine for little Lucas at the pharmacy in Wynot?"

Dr. Hunt rested his forehead in his hand and said, "I hope so. I wasn't completely truthful with the Fooses. Lucas may be my only Type 1 diabetes patient in Wineberry Hollow, but there are several of our neighbors living with Type 2 diabetes. They also need insulin. And that's just the tip of the iceberg. What am I going to do about my patients with severe asthma when their rescue inhalers run out? What about those with heart problems or patients requiring blood thinner or those on meds for mental health reasons?"

Katie spoke from the back seat. "Daddy, a lot of people are going to die, aren't they?"

Dr. Hunt said nothing and stared straight ahead through the windshield.

Chapter 25

After Mr. Orr turned the car onto Route 6, Coop smelled something burning. Not the sweet smell of a campfire or the comforting aroma of a wood stove, but an acrid stench that reminded him of an earlier time during his youth.

When he was 10-years-old, Coop had overheard some of the elders at a picnic discuss how to evacuate a groundhog from its hole by igniting a smoke bomb made up of sugar and saltpeter. The idea of making a smoke bomb proved irresistible. The family kept plenty of sugar in the cupboard, and his mother always stored saltpeter for curing meat. Figuring that more would be better, he grabbed an entire unopened five pound bag of sugar and mixed it with an equal amount of saltpeter in a metal bucket.

He waited until his father hitched the horse and drove off with the family buggy. Coop pretended to be busy pulling weeds from the backyard garden while his mother hung a load of laundry. After she had finished and retreated to the house, Coop retrieved the bucket from its hiding place beneath the porch and carried it to the stone driveway.

He tried lighting the material in the bucket with a match but nothing happened. Coop realized that the small flame from a match wasn't enough to ignite the mixture. He eyed the clothes neatly clipped to the wash line. Among them hung five pillowcases. Surely one of them wouldn't be missed.

Coop heard his mother's voice coming from the laundry room. She sang, *What a friend we have in Jesus*. Guessing that she would be preoccupied, Coop snatched one of the pillowcases, poured the mixture from the bucket into the pillowcase, and set the bundle on the driveway. For good measure, he doused the bundle with kerosene.

His fingers had trembled as he scraped the match against the striker. He stared at the flame dancing at the end of the matchstick, his emotions a jumble of excitement and fear. He touched the flame to the edge of the pillowcase, let go of the match, and ran. The smoke bomb had detonated with a *whomp* and he had felt the heat from the blast on the back of his neck. As it turned out, more was not always better. He learned later that he should've used only a palm full of each ingredient. The pillowcase and mixture of chemicals blazed with a brilliant orange fireball. Thick, black smoke belched into the air, the slight breeze carrying the obnoxious fumes directly onto the freshly hung laundry. He was sure the clothes would catch fire and spread to the house and then to the barn. Coop remembered how he had screamed for his mother.

Katie's voice pulled Coop back from his daydream. "Something in town must be burning."

Mr. Orr pulled over and let his car drift to a stop. Since the convertible top was down, he grabbed the top edge of the windshield and pulled himself up so that his head cleared the glass. He sniffed the air.

"You suspect trouble?" Dr. Hunt asked. "Looting maybe?"

"Wouldn't think something like that could happen so soon in a small town like Wynot or even Wellsboro." Orr lowered himself back into his seat. "Although the larger cities could be burning."

"Like Williamsport?" Katie asked. "It's only an hour or so away by car and we're heading in that direction."

"The source of that stink is a lot closer than Williamsport," Orr said.

Coop noticed how they had yet to see another working vehicle.

Ever since they left Wineberry Hollow, he had seen nobody outside of their houses. On a temperate summer day like this one, why weren't the farmers in their fields? Why weren't children playing?

"Keep driving, I know a way around the town," Dr. Hunt said.

Orr stepped on the accelerator, and they resumed their journey. After a mile, Dr. Hunt directed Orr onto a back road where they finally noticed signs of life. Cows grazed on alfalfa. A middle aged man dressed in overalls stretched a strand of barbed wire between two poles.

Orr pulled over.

A younger man looking to be in his teens, presumably the man's son, took a few steps backwards toward a shotgun resting against a fence post.

"You won't be needing that," Orr said to the youngster. "We're just passing through with the intention of avoiding the town."

Dr. Hunt smiled at the older man. "Do you know if Wynot is safe? Is the drugstore open? I'm a doctor, and we're in need of medical supplies."

The man turned his face to the side and spat a wad of chew. "Haven't been to town for some time."

The smile on Dr. Hunt's face faded. "That's too bad. I was hoping you'd know."

"Say, mister, how come you're able to drive this car when nothing else with an engine works?"

"It's a long story," Orr said.

"I could use a good running motor. You wanna sell it?"

"The car? No."

The man exchanged glances with his son who resumed his backpedaling toward the shotgun.

"No you don't," Orr said. He tromped the accelerator, the rear wheels throwing stones in their wake as they sped away. The expected boom from the shotgun never came.

Coop gasped for air after realizing he had been holding his breath.

Dr. Hunt's face had lost all of its color. "Think he would've tried it?"

"Don't know," Orr said, "but the kid wouldn't have stood a chance. I'd a dropped him with my Glock. Figured the wisest course of action was to get the hell away and avoid any confrontation."

Dr. Hunt glanced into the backseat at Katie and Coop. "Damn it. I knew we shouldn't have brought these kids."

"You're probably right," Orr said, "but it's too late to turn back. People are getting panicky. Things will deteriorate quickly. Better see to our business right now."

Coop's heart pounded. That young man might have shot them.

From the front seat, Dr. Hunt coughed. "That reek is getting worse. Couldn't be from the town, we've already skirted it."

Orr pointed after they rounded a curve. "There." Smoke streamed from the other side of a hill. He downshifted and ascended the grade.

The air grew thick and tasted like metal. The caustic stench irritated Coop's lungs just like the smoke bomb had. Back then, a tarry goo had puddled on the driveway where the pillowcase had once been. In one hand, his mother held a bed sheet. "Ruined," she shouted while waving the sheet in front of his face. "I'll never be able to wash the horrible smell from this laundry. All of our clothes are ruined." In her other hand, she held a long handled wooden spoon. Coop had never seen such anger in his mother's eyes. In Amish households, fathers meted out punishment, but on that day, his mother happily assumed the mantle of disciplinarian.

An audible click got Coop's attention. Dr. Hunt had raised his shotgun, cocked it, and rested the barrel on the ledge of the door. They approached the summit of the hill.

"You two kids take cover in case there's trouble," Dr. Hunt said.

He and Katie ducked behind the seat backs.

Coop still recalled the painful welts on his backside from that wooden spoon, but he also remembered the relief that had washed over him after realizing the house and barn wouldn't burn. On that day, he didn't die. What were they going to find when they crested the hill? He worried how this time he might not be as lucky.

Coop felt the vibration from the tires as the car rolled onto the gravel making up the berm of the road. The car slowed to a stop. He and Katie remained crouched behind the seat waiting for some sort of signal from the two men in the front seat.

After a long silence, Dr. Hunt muttered, "My god."

Katie cautiously sat up. She gazed into the distance and clamped a hand over her mouth.

Coop rose from his position behind the seatback and whispered to Katie. "What is it?"

She raised her other hand and pointed.

In the distance, Coop saw a ribbon of highway, U.S. 15. Between the top of the hill and the intersection with Route 15 lay a verdant forest except for an ugly gash where the trees had been torn up, their trunks snapped like broken toothpicks. The scar trailed off to a fallow field and ended in a smoldering crater. Unrecognizable debris lay everywhere. Sunlight glinted from a large mirrored piece of metal sticking into the ground.

Coop squinted, trying to make it out. Painted on the metal was some sort of triangular shaped logo and the word: DELTA.

"I hadn't given it much thought," Mr. Orr said, "but an EMP strong enough to compromise the nation's electrical grid would be strong enough to fry avionics. All non-hardened aircraft in the sky during the pulse would've dropped like a plumb bob."

"We have to do something. There could be survivors. People might be hurt," Katie said.

In the rear view mirror, Coop caught a view of Mr. Orr's face. The man squeezed his eyes closed and shook his head. "There are no survivors. Not from that."

"You don't know that for sure," Katie said, her voice sounding petulant. "We have to check. Dad, you're a doctor."

Dr. Hunt turned to face his daughter. "Mr. Orr has already stated the obvious, Katie. We won't find any survivors."

Coop felt relieved that Dr. Hunt and Mr. Orr didn't side with Katie. He didn't want to face the horror of what they might encounter at the wreckage.

"What we really need to do is get upwind from these noxious fumes. God only knows what poisons we're breathing in from that toxic brew. Let's move on and check out the highway," Orr said. He shifted the transmission into gear and pulled out.

Katie grew reticent and slouched in her seat. Coop suspected she knew there was no hope for those poor victims of the crash and probably experienced frustration over their inability to do anything for them. He said a silent prayer for the lost souls.

They descended the other side of the hill, the view of the

wreckage disappearing off to their left. The air cleared as they approached the route 15 intersection. Up and down the highway, stranded cars rested in place. When their engines stopped, it looked like some drivers had allowed their vehicles to drift to the side of the road. Others just let them die right in the middle of the traffic lane.

As they drew near to the intersection, a small band of people walked onto the roadway. Orr abruptly stopped the car about a quarter mile away and studied them. More people streamed from the underpass shouting and waving.

"They must've taken shelter there after the pulse," Dr. Hunt said.

Orr sat in the driver seat, his expression cold. "End of the line. We aren't going to Williamsport. I think we know now the true nature of the situation, that it's widespread. Maybe it impacts the whole country."

Coop counted ten people, but he couldn't be sure if more remained under cover.

Mr. Orr turned the car around.

"What are you doing?" Katie asked.

"We're going home," Orr answered.

"What about those people?"

Dr. Hunt spoke up. "Declan, wait. Don't drive off. Let's consider this for a minute."

Some of the people from the crowd behind them began to yell. Two men began to sprint in their direction.

Orr looked him in the eye. "Listen to me. I've lived through situations like this in the Middle East wars. Villages destroyed. People starving and desperate. The natural inclination is to give in to your humanity and try to help. But hopelessness turns people savage. They will do unspeakable things to survive. They'll tear you to pieces for the few drops of water in your canteen." He pointed a thumb over his shoulder. "You want to take a chance with these people? You want to risk your daughter's safety and the safety of young Cooper?"

"This isn't the Middle East. It's the United States of America," Katie said.

Coop glanced back. The men sprinting in their direction would be on them in less than a minute.

"Not your call, we're leaving," Orr said.

"You have guns, so I don't think they will try anything," Coop interjected.

"We should at least hear what these men have to say," Dr. Hunt said. "What they have seen and heard might be helpful to us."

One of the approaching men shouted. "Don't you even think about driving off, asshole."

Orr took a deep breath and exhaled. In one fluid motion, he leapt from the driver's seat onto the road, pulled the Glock from his waistband, raised the weapon in a two handed grasp, sighted along the barrel, and pulled the trigger.

Chapter 26

The round in Mr. Orr's handgun detonated with a sharp crack.

Coop covered his ears.

"That's close enough," Orr said, his voice deep and authoritative. "The next shot won't be over your heads."

The two men stopped. One of them, a stocky man with an unkempt beard and wearing a red bandana, stumbled to the side of the road, placed his hands on his knees and vomited. Probably from the exertion, Coop thought. The other, a wiry young guy wearing jeans and pointed cowboy boots raised his hands over his head.

"Don't shoot, mister, we're unarmed," Boots said, but his cold eyes stared at them unblinking. Coop didn't trust him.

"Who are you people? How'd you get this car to work? Are any more of you coming?" Boots fired off questions and Coop noticed that while he spoke he inched closer to them.

"I'll ask the questions," Orr said. "Turn around and start walking back to the bridge. We will be right behind you."

Boots didn't move.

Bandana straightened and strained to speak up, still winded. "Better do as he says."

Boots relaxed. "All right. We'll do it your way." He turned and walked. Bandana joined him still breathing heavily.

"Coop, you and Katie stay here," Dr. Hunt said.

"Screw that," she said. "I'm coming."

Dr. Hunt wore a hurt expression. "What's gotten into you,

Katie? Why the back talk? This isn't like you."

"I'm tired of being treated like a kid."

Coop also had no desire to be left behind. He turned to Dr. Hunt and mumbled. "I'll keep an eye on her."

Katie smirked. "You? Get real, dude. I'm better off by myself." Before anyone could say anything, she marched forward, following the two strangers.

"Let 'em come," Orr said to Dr. Hunt. "Bring the shotgun. Keep it at the ready. Don't hesitate to use it if things go bad."

Coop and his party walked in a straight line about ten paces behind Boots and Bandana. When they got to the bridge, Orr said, "Hold up," and they all stopped.

For a while, nobody spoke while the crowd from the bridge sized them up.

Coop studied them, too. A mixed group of men, women, families huddled together with their children, all of them wide eyed, frightened. One man, a bandage wrapped around his head, lay against the side of the bridge. A woman at the very back of the crowd squeezed her teenage daughter in an embrace. The girl appeared to be the same age as he and Katie. Possibly a year or so younger. She wore a vacant expression.

Boots took a step forward, hitched his thumbs in his belt, and stared at Mr. Orr. Coop's ill feeling toward this man increased. He hoped Mr. Orr also regarded him with suspicion.

"Your call," Boots said. "You said you had questions?"

"First things first," Dr. Hunt said. "Anybody here need medical attention?"

Boots laughed. "Look around. None of us are in such good shape. Other than a few scraps of food that we shared amongst ourselves, we haven't eaten since the world went to shit. You have any food to spare? How about clean water? We've been taking water from the creek and boiling it, but it tastes awful."

Dr. Hunt started toward the man wearing the bandage on his head. "What happened to him?"

"He fell," Boots said.

Bandana raised his hand. "Sir, I'm not feeling so well, diarrhea I think. I'm heading for those bushes. Just wanted to let you know so you won't shoot me."

"You have a gun stashed down there?" Orr asked.

"No, sir."

"Just remember. I'll be watching. When you come back out, keep your hands up where I can see them."

Coop didn't like it. His throat went dry. How could Mr. Orr keep Bandana covered while Dr. Hunt tended to the wounded man?

"What's wrong with her?" Orr asked. His question was directed to the girl in her mother's embrace.

"Don't mind those two," Boots said. "That girl is...well she's...special, if you get my drift."

"Anyone else hurt?" Mr. Orr spoke up.

Everyone remained silent. The hairs stood on the back of Coop's neck. He sensed something to be terribly wrong here.

Boots relaxed his posture. "Mister, as you can see, we're harmless. I'm sorry for the way we greeted you, but you can imagine how relieved we were to see help finally arrive and then how pissed off we got when it looked like you were going to leave us. You can understand that, can't you? Why don't you lower your gun and tell us what's going on in the world? What do you say?"

Orr kept his gun pointed in Boot's direction at a 45 degree angle. "What do I say? I'll tell you what I say. I say that you and your buddy are thugs. I say that you two have been terrorizing these folks. I say that you ordered everyone here to keep their mouths shut while you did all the talking."

Boots grimaced. "C'mon, man, it's not like that at all. What could the two of us with no weapons do to them? Look at all of these other able bodied men. They wouldn't let me harm them or their families."

"You have weapons," Orr said. "Where are they?"

"Weapons? I have no weapons." He waved his arm in a grand sweeping motion. "Ask any of these people. Do I have weapons?"

A few people uttered a half-hearted, "No."

Others remained silent and shook their heads.

"See," Boots said, "I've been honest with you."

"Then I don't suppose you'd mind if we have a little private conversation with that girl and her mother." Orr paused and motioned for the two to approach.

The mother and daughter gave Boots a wide berth and walked toward Katie.

Coop felt a sense of dread well up inside him. He looked in the bushes but could no longer see Bandana. Why did the women approach Katie? Why didn't Dr. Hunt or Mr. Orr hear them out. Maybe he should stand by Katie in case anything happened.

Orr continued speaking. "If they tell us that something else has been going on..."

Coop saw a flash of fear cross Boot's face.

Boot's voice turned gruff. "Nobody has harmed anybody here."

"Tribal bullies, petty warlords, little men suddenly drunk with power. I've dealt with your kind before and you all have a certain stench about you," Orr said.

Boots pointed a finger at Orr. "There's no cause for you to cast aspersions at me."

Orr and Boots continued their heated exchange, but Coop stopped listening to them. He watched Katie. The woman and her daughter huddled up with her. Katie's lips formed a straight line and she narrowed her eyes.

"Oh, no," Coop mumbled. Orr's suspicions had been accurate.

From the corner of his eye, Coop saw a flash. Bandana ran from a hiding place behind one of the bridge abutments toward an older man standing under the bridge. Bandana must have snuck to the other side of the bridge after disappearing in the bushes.

Distracted by his exchange with Boots, Orr didn't see it. Dr. Hunt remained busy tending to the wounded man.

"Behind you," Coop yelled.

Too late. Bandana grabbed the man, stood behind him and held a gun to his head.

Katie screamed.

The assembled crowd erupted into chaos. They all began talking at once.

"What's going on?" Dr. Hunt asked.

Coop made a motion with his hand for Dr. Hunt to stay where he was.

Orr now pointed his handgun at Bandana.

"Well done," Boots shouted at Bandana. Then he yelled, "Shut the hell up. All of you."

The crowd quieted.

Coop's fear turned to anger. As Mr. Orr said, these two men were indeed thugs.

Boots tromped toward Orr. "Okay, asshole, give me the gun."

Orr pointed the gun at Boot's forehead. "Stop."

Boots obeyed, but laughed. "Kill me and my partner pulls the trigger. That innocent old man will die."

"But you'll be dead, too," Orr said. "Tell your friend to stand down."

Boots smirked. "It appears we have a stalemate."

"Not quite." Dr. Hunt had left the wounded man, cocked his shotgun, and pointed it at Boots. "Have you forgotten about me? Let that gentleman go."

Now that Dr. Hunt had Boots covered, Orr switched his attention and gun back to Bandana.

"You can have 100 guns pointed at me, but the fact remains, if you shoot me, that man dies. Now, both of you drop your guns," Boots said.

"I have a better idea," Orr said. He aimed his gun at Bandana and fired.

Chapter 27

Bandana's head exploded in a red mist. He dropped straight to the ground.

Dr. Hunt turned his attention away from Boots and turned to Orr. "Are you insane?"

Orr pointed his handgun at Boots. "Don't you move." Then to Dr. Hunt. "Quite the contrary, I'm a crack shot with this .45. It was the only logical course of action."

Katie ran to the side of the bridge, leaned against the bridge abutment and gagged but didn't vomit.

Coop walked over to her. "You okay?"

"Leave me alone."

The seriousness of what had just happened finally caught up with Coop. He began to tremble. Mr. Orr had just killed a man. He fell to his knees and then placed his hands on the pavement. Breathing hard, he thought he might faint. Black spots danced in front his eyes, but then his vision cleared. Slowly, he got to his feet.

Coop glanced at Katie. She sat against the side of the bridge, eyes closed, knees drawn to her chest.

Orr kept his handgun pointed at Boots while Dr. Hunt yelled at him for his recklessness. In time, he calmed down.

The other people grew animated. One of them, a middle aged woman with greasy hair and a dirty yellow blouse yelled at Orr to shoot Boots. They seemed less tense now and began to speak among themselves. The wounded man who had been tended by Dr. Hunt walked over to Orr and Dr. Hunt.

Without taking his eyes from Boots, Orr shouted Coop's name.

"Yes, sir?"

"Pick up that dead man's gun and bring it here."

Coop glanced at the ground where Bandana lay dead, the small gun at his side. He didn't want to touch it, but he also didn't want any of the others to pick it up either. With a trembling hand, he picked up the gun and delivered it to Orr.

"Give it to Corporal Clark," Orr said referring to the wounded man. Did that mean the wounded man was a soldier?

The man held out his hand. Coop handed over the gun.

Clark inspected the firearm, checked the chamber, and said, "Seems to be intact." He pointed it at Boots. "Want a piece of me now, scum?"

Boots took a step back, the color draining from his face.

Clark told them what had happened. "All of our vehicles died at the same time the night the lights went out. Man, it was pitch dark except for the glimmer from the stars. I immediately suspected an EMP pulse and thought I was going to die from a nuclear blast. Then when that aircraft drilled into the ground, holy Christ, I damn near had a heart attack. That's something I never want to see again. After awhile, when nothing else happened and I had a chance to collect my wits, I got out of the car and met up with other stranded motorists. Many of them who lived close enough to their homes decided to abandon their cars and walk. The rest of us gathered together and walked down the exit ramp. Took shelter beneath this underpass."

Orr gestured toward Boots and the dead man. "Who are these two and what was their game?"

A slender man with neatly cut black hair and matching mustache gently pushed his way to the front and stood by Coop.

Clark nodded to the man, a signal that he should pick up telling the story.

"My name is Tomas Ortiz," he said with a Hispanic accent. "I was hauling a load of Campbell canned food, a truckload of soup and beans and the like bound for a distribution center in Carlisle, PA when my rig stopped rolling. You'll find it parked about a quarter mile north. After the first day, we all grew very hungry. I offered to open the trailer and break into one of the pallets."

He pointed at Boots and then at Bandana's corpse. "These two bastardos camped out here with us and volunteered to walk with me and carry back the cans. As soon as I unlocked the back of the trailer, they grabbed my key and shoved a gun against my head. They hijacked the food intending to keep it for themselves. They doled out just a little to the rest of us in return for all of our money."

"Money," Orr said with disgust. He glared at Boots. "Don't you know that money is no good anymore."

Boots sneered. "The lights have to come back on sometime."

Clark picked up the conversation. "I thought I had an opening and tried to grab the gun from the dead guy over there. He was the only one with a gun, but his partner here yelled out a warning." He touched the bandage wrapped around his head. "Got pistol whipped for my trouble."

The rest of them began to speak and wanted to introduce themselves and tell their stories.

Orr ignored them, held up a hand, and asked the crowd for silence.

"Why aren't you in one of the enclaves?" Orr asked the corporal.

"Bereavement leave." Clark's lips turned down and he lowered his voice. "Just buried my sister a few days ago. Died in childbirth."

"Sorry to hear that, corporal," Orr said. He stepped away. "Listen up, people. Me and my neighbors are not the cavalry. We are not here to rescue you. We've come from a good distance away on a scouting trip and can do nothing more for you. We're going to leave."

"I don't understand," the woman with the retarded girl spoke up, her voice breaking. The girl clung to her mother. "You have a working automobile. Things must be better where you come from."

"It's an old car with primitive electronics. No computer modules, no fuel injection, nothing that the pulse could fry," Orr said. "I swear that we're no better off where we come from."

"But you're in your home with your families, you have shelter," the woman shrieked.

Coop couldn't believe that they were going to leave these people to fend for themselves. They'd be alright in the short term. It was summer and they had a truckload of canned food. But what would happen when the food ran out and when winter came?

Katie motioned to the retarded girl and her mother. "We can't just leave them behind. Sarah can't take care of herself and her mom can't take much more stress."

"No can do," Orr said.

"Some of us have skills," said a tall thin man wearing a Phillies baseball cap. He stood clustered around a woman his age and two pre-teen boys which Coop surmised must be his family. "I'm Blair St. John, a dentist. This is my wife Heather and my two boys, Stan and Bruce. Take us with you and we can contribute to your community in a meaningful way."

"The man has a point," Dr. Hunt said.

St. John spoke again. "You could take us in just for the short term. We'll be anxious to leave, to return to our homes once this crisis is over."

Orr took a breath and looked glum. "The crisis is only beginning."

"Orr is right," Clark said. "Life as we know it is over. We've just been set back 100 years, maybe more."

"Whose side are you on, anyway? They intend to leave you, too," a prune faced old woman said. She introduced herself as Daisy Crane. She and her middle aged son, Harold, lived in Harrisburg and had been on their way to visit relatives somewhere in New York.

Orr shook his head. "There are too many of you. We have one car and only enough gas to get us home."

"There might be a way," a soft spoken man said. He walked over to Orr. Coop observed that the man walked with a slight limp. He was old with white hair, but his brown eyes twinkled. "My name is Pete Damroth. I'm a mechanic, a damn good one if I might say. You have any old pre-computer tractors sitting around where you come from? I could get one of 'em working and we could find a wagon to hitch it up to. If my fellow pilgrims can hold out a few more days, we can return and fetch 'em."

Damroth pointed to the highway. "As for gasoline, there's an overabundance. There's plenty of abandoned vehicles with tanks full of gas just waiting for the taking."

Coop took an instant liking to the man. He was practical and his demeanor reminded him of how an Amish man would react. A thought popped into his head. "One of our neighbors, Carl Miller, has an old school bus sitting in his back yard. It's old, at least it looks old. He's had it ever since I was a boy intending to convert it into a recreational vehicle of sorts. Far as I know, he never got around to it."

"There you go," said Damroth.

Coop looked at Mr. Orr whose expression appeared less tense. Might his resolve be softening?

Dr. Hunt must have noticed it too. He turned to Orr and spoke. "Declan, the thin veneer of civilization is quickly crumbling. It's only been a few days and these people have already suffered at the hand of thugs. Anarchy reigns."

"Don't you think I know that," Orr snapped. "My soldering days are behind me, yet I've just had to kill a man."

"Not a man," Katie said in a deep, cold tone. She shot a quick glance in the direction of the body. "You put down a dog."

Coop didn't understand the reason for debate. Mr. Damroth, the mechanic already provided the solution. These people were human beings, God's children. He took the straw hat off his head and gripped it. "Excuse me."

To Coop's surprise, everyone stopped talking and looked at him.

"I'm not well traveled or educated and don't know much about the world and how it works or about politics." He grew nervous speaking to so many people and stopped to take a breath. "But I do know that the people living in Wineberry Hollow are kind and peaceable."

He turned to look at Dr. Hunt. "The lawlessness that you speak of may someday come to our community, but I pray it does not. The people of my faith have been brought up to love our neighbors as we love ourselves. Our very lives revolve around working together, helping one another. We have the means to help these folks."

Coop straightened his back attempting to portray confidence, although he certainly didn't feel confident. He squeezed the straw hat in his hand and announced, "I, for one, will not leave these people."

Coop stepped away from his group and stood with Mr. Damroth. He looked each of his companions in the eye. Dr. Hunt wouldn't hold his gaze and glanced at the ground. Katie wore a hint of a smile.

The expressionless Mr. Orr said, "Son, I was right about you, and you make me proud, but I'm afraid you haven't thought it all through well enough. Suppose we agree to integrate these folks into our community. We would have to go home, make arrangements, and return by running a gauntlet of other people. People with guns who are out of their minds with desperation, ready to kill to possess a motor vehicle. They might mistakenly associate us possessing a working car with the fact that we might also have food. We would have to fight them off. There will certainly be more bloodshed.

"Then, there is also the possibility that we might run across more wanderers. How many can Wineberry Hollow absorb, Cooper? We can't save the whole world."

"We may not be able to save the world, but we can save these people. Speaking for myself, if I lose my life in the attempt, then I consider that Gottes Wille."

Orr wrinkled his brow. "God's will or tempting fate? It's a foolhardy plan, son."

"Nevertheless, I am staying. I will lead them to Wineberry Hollow even if we all have to walk."

Corporal Clark interjected, "Sir, perhaps you could return for us with an organized force of men. Volunteers."

"That would be risky for all the reasons I just mentioned," Orr said.

The corporal smiled. "I respectfully disagree, sir. Undisciplined, roving mobs would be unlikely to bother you were you to enter the field with an army visibly displaying superior firepower."

"Spoken like a true soldier," Orr said.

"We can put it to our neighbors," Dr. Hunt said. "See if they might be willing."

Orr paused as if considering everyone's position. He spoke to the stranded ones. "My companions seem determined to lend you a hand. Since nobody elected me the final authority in these matters, and since I'm new to their community, I'm in no position to stand in their way."

Cheers rose from the crowd and words of thanks.

"Listen up," Orr spoke again in his normal authoritative tone. "Nothing is certain in a situation like this. I can guarantee you nothing. My companions and I will return home with your mechanic, Mr. Damroth, and hope that he is as good as he says he is. We will make an effort to come back for you, but only if the people in our community agree it's worth the risk. Anything can happen. You still need to assume that you will be living beneath this underpass for a long time. You have to become organized. Prevent from happening what has already happened to you. You'll need to become hard people, suspicious of others who may want to join you, ruthless, and cunning so that you don't end up as victims."

Orr turned to Corporal Clark. "You have some protection now, a firearm. Can you lead these people, soldier?"

The corporal stood erect. "I'll do my best, sir."

Orr glanced at Boots. "You'll have to deal with him, you know, and you do understand that you have only one option."

The corporal's face slackened. "I know that."

Placing a hand on the young corporal's shoulder, Orr said, "A soldier's lot in life is not an easy one. We do what most others cannot do." He turned and walked in the direction of the Mustang.

Coop wondered if he should stay behind anyway, but then he realized that he would be needed to convince his neighbors to rescue these poor souls. Relieved that everyone had agreed with him, he rejoined his companions.

The mechanic, Pete Damroth, squeezed into the backseat. Katie sat in the middle on the hump.

"Let's get the hell out of here," Dr. Hunt said.

"Aye," Orr muttered and started the engine.

As they drove off, Coop looked behind at the disappearing faces, some of them waving goodbye. He felt a tap on his shoulder and found Katie smiling at him. "Congratulations, Chicken Coop," she said. "You finally showed some backbone back there."

Instead of feeling insulted, Katie's words warmed him. His face flushed. With the convertible top down the wind roared past his ears. He spoke softly so nobody but Katie could hear. "Maybe you'll think differently of me now?"

She tilted her head as if regarding him. Then she turned away.

Chapter 28

Mr. Orr drove his old Mustang toward Wynot. They all gawked again at the debris field from the crashed jet but said nothing. Coop sensed that speaking would somehow disrespect the lives that had been lost. Maybe the others felt the same way. A few miles after they passed the crash site, Pete Damroth opened up.

"I live in Bradford with my son and his wife. My Martha died a few years ago. As a matter of fact, I was on a return trip from visiting her brother in Towanda when my car quit."

"How far is Bradford? Is it close enough for us to take you home?" Coop asked.

"Two hours by car. Less than a hundred miles, I suppose. If I were a younger man, I might try to walk it. Figure it would take five days at 20 miles a day." Pete patted his side. "Arthritis is my hips put that notion out of my head."

"I noticed you walked with a limp," Katie said.

He glanced between Katie and Coop. "You two are too young to understand about aches and pains that come with age."

"You sure you're healthy enough to work?" Orr asked. His voice sounded skeptical.

"My hips may be shot but there's nothing wrong with my hands," Pete said, his voice taking on an indignant tone. "I wasn't lying to you. I'm a retired master mechanic. I may not move too fast anymore, but if a motor is fixable, I can do the job. Take this car for example, four-barrel carburetor and 289 cubic inch engine. I worked on plenty of old Mustangs. Surprised to see this one in such good shape, especially for a '66."

"I meant no disrespect, and the way you talk, well, maybe you do know something about cars," Orr admitted.

"Turn me loose with one and you'll see."

"You missed the Wynot bypass," Coop said after Orr drove past the turn off.

"We're taking the main road into town. Dr. Hunt wants to stop at the pharmacy."

The small town was only about half the size of Wellsboro but lay on a direct path between Route 15 and Wineberry Hollow. Coop visited Wynot several times each year because it was the location of the Amish market. The townsfolk were normally friendly, but after the trouble they had just experienced, Coop asked, "You think it's safe?"

"Don't know," Orr said. "Everybody be on your toes."

As they approached the town limits, a yellow Ryder truck sat cross ways blocking both lanes of traffic. Between the front end of the truck and a street light, a gap just wide enough existed for a car to squeeze through.

Orr slowed to about ten miles per hour and headed for the gap.

A man stepped into the gap holding a shotgun across his chest. He wore dark trousers, a white shirt with epaulets, and a necktie. He looked like a law enforcement officer half out of uniform. The man raised a hand, palm forward.

Orr stopped the car.

"State your business," the man said.

Dr. Hunt spoke, "Rawland, it's me, Stu Hunt."

The man squinted. "Didn't recognize you, Doc. Who's that with you?"

"My neighbor, Declan Orr, is our driver. My daughter, Katie, a friend, Pete Damroth, and another neighbor, Cooper Stover." To the passengers in the car, Dr. Hunt said, "This is Rawland Toomey, Deputy Sheriff."

Deputy Toomey's gaze lit on each of their faces. He settled on Orr with a hard stare. "What are you people doing here?"

"Passing through," Dr. Hunt said. "We've been scouting and are on our way home. Need to stop at the pharmacy."

"Pharmacy's closed," Toomey said.

"I was hoping to get Dan to open up for me. Need to buy some meds."

"Like I said, pharmacy's closed."

Orr spoke. "Unless you own the pharmacy, that's not for you to say."

Toomey's eyes widened. He repositioned his shotgun to point

toward the car. "I don't need to explain myself to the likes of you." After a pause, he added, "Boy."

The two men stared each other down.

Dr. Hunt said, "C'mon Rawland, you know me. We're not looking for trouble. There's a little boy with diabetes back in the hollow. That's the only reason we're here."

Toomey sneered, "We have people in town with diabetes, too."

"I don't want to buy out the entire inventory. Just enough to get us through until things return to normal."

"Things might not return to normal for a long time. Maybe never."

"All the more reason for us to work together," Dr. Hunt said. "If we're in this for the long haul, we'll need to help each other out."

"We have a doctor in town. Don't need your help."

"That's short sighted, Rawland. I'm not talking about just my services. What happens when the grocery store runs out of milk, eggs, fresh fruit, and vegetables. You have cows in town? Chickens? These are things we have in the country that your town will need. Right now, meds are what I need."

Nobody spoke for a few moments. Toomey broke the silence. "So you're offering to trade?"

Dr Hunt said, "The system is broke. I suspect we'll all be trading with each other for the time being."

Toomey wiped the back of his neck with his hand and let his gaze roam over the Mustang. "I don't know how you got this automobile to work, but since you mentioned how you want to trade, I'm willing to make you an offer. Give me this car, and I'll let you walk into town. You can deal with Dan at the pharmacy and then walk home."

Katie spoke out. "That's fifteen miles."

Toomey shrugged. "That's the deal. Actually, I'm allowing you the better of it. I was thinking of just confiscating this car for emergency purposes."

Pete Damroth sat up in his seat. "You have no right to do that or to keep us from driving through this town."

"I'm the highest ranking law enforcement official around here, old man," Toomey said, "and with the world gone to hell the way it has, I can do what I want. I've declared martial law."

Orr grunted. "You dumb ass. This is still America. Only the

President of the United States has the authority to declare martial law, and it's the military's job to enforce it. Not some home grown zealot like you who has no sense of decency."

"Wrong, boy. This gun is my authority." Toomey whistled. From behind the Ryder truck stepped three more men, all of them armed with rifles. They spread out in front of the Mustang.

Coop wondered how this could be happening. Why were these men acting so unreasonably?

Toomey eyed Orr. "Where'd you get this working automobile, boy? Did you steal it?"

"No." Orr's voice remained level. Coop's mouth went dry. How could Mr. Orr remain so cool, so normal? Wasn't he scared?

"Prove it," Toomey said. "Let me see your registration card."

"I'm not showing you squat," Orr said using the same normal tone.

"Your refusal makes you automatically guilty," Toomey said. He pointed his shotgun at Orr's face. "I'm taking this vehicle one way or another. If you resist, I'll blow you away…boy."

Katie flinched, "Don't shoot. We'll give you the car."

When Deputy Toomey glanced at Katie, the distraction was long enough for Orr to pull his handgun. He aimed it at Toomey's head and said, "I won't be able to drop all four of you, but if this ends in a firefight, you're going to be the first to die for sure."

Dr. Hunt raised his shotgun and pointed it at the nearest of Toomey's posse. "He won't be the only one to die."

The man at the business end of Dr. Hunt's shotgun began to quiver. "Hey, I didn't sign up for this. What do we do now, Rawland?"

"I'll answer that," Orr said. "I'm going to put the car in reverse and back away. You men relax. Nobody needs to get hurt."

Pete Damroth leaned forward. "Mr. Orr, you won't be able to keep that gun pointed and shift gears at the same time. Let me have that pea shooter of yours. I'll keep you covered."

"No, I'll manage," Orr said. Using his free hand, he shifted the car into reverse and then gripped the steering wheel. "In case you get the idea to open up with those rifles after you're beyond the range of my Glock, just remember that there's innocent people in this car."

The doctor added, "Including my daughter. I won't hesitate to shoot."

Orr backed the car slowly, keeping his handgun pointed at Toomey.

The men in the posse looked at each other. One of them lowered his rifle. The others followed suit. Deputy Rawland relaxed his posture and pointed his shotgun at the ground. He shook a finger at them.

His meaning was clear. They had better not return.

Chapter 29

Being just a week past the summer solstice, the long hours of sunlight made the adjustment to a world without electricity easier on the English. Coop was used to living without electric lights and had grown up mastering how to function by lamplight. His neighbors, though, seemed to regard the night as something unnatural, something to be feared. Good thing it was summer. If it were winter, with its 7 AM dawn and 5 PM dusk, Coop wondered how the English would ever get anything done.

Sam Wetzel, the butcher, had visited yesterday to borrow a hand plane to shave a sticking door. He kept eyeing the sky and commenting about how he needed to keep moving so as to be home long before dark.

Pete Damroth, refugee from the Route 15 underpass, moved into a spare bedroom at the Miller farm. That suited everyone as he worked on the old school bus owned by Carl Miller and had it tuned up and purring like a kitten within a day after they had returned home. Now, he busied himself working on other old vehicles within the valley, trying to make them functional. Most of the classic autos were beyond repair, but Pete did manage to bring a few old tractors back to life. Yet, the blackness of night unsettled even this old man. Home long before twilight, he admitted being easily spooked by night noises.

Strange people, the English.

Coop regarded the night as a thing of beauty, a gift, and a reminder of man's puniness as compared with the vastness of God's great universe. In the absence of artificial light, the myriad of stars Coop observed on a clear moonless night humbled him, filled him with a sense of well being. How could anyone stare at that infinite glory and not realize how powerless they were as compared to God?

Then again, maybe that was why so many of his neighbors feared the night for its undeniable manifestation of humankind's lowliness.

Today, gray clouds blanketed the sky. It would probably rain this afternoon. Since mid-morning, guests began to arrive at his farm conveyed by all manner of transportation for a mid-day meeting. Some arrived on horseback, some in buggies. Many of them walked. Declan Orr arrived in his Mustang, Dr. Hunt and Sheila Cunningham in Katie's old Buick. Two neighbors drove their tractors and Fred Doaks, the farrier, arrived in a mule drawn cart.

This seemed a waste of daylight to Coop. He could be working. Meetings like this should be held in the evening after farms chores had been completed.

But that meant the English would have to travel home in the dark.

A steady stream of Wineberry Hollow residents had made their way to Coop's farm, but now as he stood at the end of the driveway looking up and down Cove Road, he saw nothing moving. Everybody who was going to come had already arrived.

Coop walked into his barn and nodded to Dr. Hunt who stood in the back of a hay wagon, a signal that it was clear to begin. The crowd sat on straw bales laid out in long rows forming benches. They engaged each other in low conversation.

Dr. Hunt cleared his throat and asked for attention.

The crowd hushed and turned their faces toward the doctor.

"Let me begin by thanking Cooper Stover for the use of his barn," Dr. Hunt said. By acknowledgement, he tilted his head in Coop's direction. "Being almost exactly in the middle of Wineberry Hollow makes this a convenient location."

Coop stared at his shoes uncomfortable at the verbal recognition, considering his act as nothing special. Of course he would allow them to use his barn. Neighbors helped each other. It should have gone without saying.

Dr. Hunt went on. "I hope nobody resents my leading this meeting, it's just that everyone here knows me, and I know all of you by name. That makes things a little easier on us all. On the other hand, if anybody objects, I'll be glad to turn things over to any one of you."

Sheila Cunningham spoke up. "You'll do just fine, Stu, get on with it." She winked at him.

Coop noticed how friendly Sheila and Dr. Hunt had become ever since the world went dark. Could they be courting?

Looking around the barn and seeing nobody objecting, Dr Hunt said, "The reason we're meeting today is to discuss the situation we find ourselves in and to make some plans. There's been a lot of conjecture over what happened a week ago. None of us knows for sure, but the evidence suggests that we've been crippled by an EMP or electromagnetic pulse. We've seen no activity by our armed forces, no aircraft in the sky, no attempts to reconnoiter, which leads me to believe that the effects are widespread, probably affecting the entire country, maybe even the whole planet."

From behind Coop, someone spoke out, "You can bet your ass the Islamic Fundamentalists are behind this. They live in the stone age and want all of us to be like them."

Dr. Hunt allowed the ensuing murmur to die down before continuing. "What you said might be correct, but it's just as likely something else has happened. Anyway, that doesn't matter now. The reality of the situation is that we need to assume we're going to be without the conveniences we take for granted for a long time, years maybe. That's why I passed the word to all families in the hollow to send at least one representative to this meeting. We're going to need to form a tight knit community and help each other in order to survive."

He paused and looked around. "If you notice that any of your neighbors aren't here, I'm asking that you share with them what we discuss and about the decisions we make here today."

Carl Miller squeezed a baseball cap in his fist and rocked in his seat. "You don't really believe this situation is going to last much longer, do you?"

"I hope not," Dr. Hunt said, "but just the same we need to prepare for the worst."

"What do you have in mind, Doc?" Joe Hutmaker asked.

"There are two things we need to address," he answered. "First, we need to decide how to manage our collective resources. Second, we need to plan how to defend what we have."

"Defend from who?" Sam Wetzel asked. "You expect roving gangs of marauders from the big cities to swoop down on us? How are they going to get here if they have no transportation?"

"That's probably not how it will happen," Declan Orr spoke up from the front row. His baritone voice commanded everyone's attention. "The threat will come from neighboring communities."

A man sitting three straw bales down from Coop uttered, "Who the hell is that guy?" Coop knew the man from seeing him around, but he didn't know his name.

"Come on up here," Dr. Hunt said to Orr. "Might as well let you speak."

Orr stood and stepped up onto the wagon beside Dr. Hunt.

"For those of you who don't know, this is Declan Orr. He and his family moved into the house that Sheila built at the back end of the hollow. Declan recently retired from the military and is an accomplished strategist. He knows what he's talking about. I suggest we take seriously what he has to say."

The two men exchanged glances and Orr began to speak. "I need to get something out in the open from the git go. I'm a black man. If that means that any of you have a problem listening to what I have to say, understand that you ignore me at your own peril. As Stu just pointed out, I've been through some real shit storms during the past few years and have a keen understanding of how panic stricken people react in life and death situations. I also know the minds of thuggish warlords and how to deal with them."

He took a breath. "Are there any questions before I continue? Any objections?"

Coop wondered why Orr thought it necessary to say such things. The people in Wineberry Hollow were not bigoted. He guessed that Mr. Orr had lived through some bad experiences which resulted in his defensive posture. Everyone stared at Orr in complete silence.

"I've seen things," Orr said, his voice lowered but sounding serious. He stared at some distant point just above their heads. "Entire villages begging for scraps, paralyzed by fear of marauders who confiscate their grain, poultry, and cattle to feed their armies. Thugs with guns who lord it over those who have no guns, uncaring if their countrymen starve."

"Things like that might happen elsewhere," Carl Miller

interrupted, "but that's not going to happen here."

"Yeah, we have guns," Sam Wetzel added.

Orr looked Sam in the eye. "Could you defend yourself with your guns against an organized gang? Are you physically and mentally prepared for that eventuality?"

Sam smirked. "You're new here, Orr, so I'll give you the benefit of the doubt. This is Wineberry Hollow, not some big city neighborhood. Ain't no gangs in these parts."

"Not now, but they will come."

Joe Hutmaker raised a hand and stood. "Mr. Orr, we Amish do not fight."

"I understand," Orr said, "so the rest of us will have to fight for you. The price for that protection is your feeding the families in the hollow."

"But we sell our farm goods at market."

"There is no more market," Orr said with a raised voice. Then he softened. "For everyone gathered in this barn, the world has suddenly contracted, its borders, the confines of Wineberry Hollow. Beyond the end of Cove Road lies hostile territory."

"I pray you are wrong," Joe said.

"What do you have in mind, Declan?" Sheila piped in.

"I've studied our situation and with our mailman, Gary Daw's help have developed countermeasures against attack."

Attack? Coop couldn't fathom such a thing, but as he looked around, he read unease on the faces of his neighbors.

Orr continued. "As you are all aware, Wineberry Hollow is a dead end valley, Cove Road being the only way in or out. With a mountain to our north and south, and a mountainous wilderness area at the back end of the valley extending all the way to Pine Creek Gorge. There's only one practical way for marauders to launch an assault and that's through our front door, where Cove Road intersects the township road."

"I suppose a determined gang on foot or horseback could hit us by coming over the mountains," Dr. Hunt speculated.

"That's possible," Orr acknowledged, "but unlikely, at least until they test the path of least resistance first."

"We need to keep outsiders from entering the hollow," a frightened voice from the crowd shouted.

"Exactly," Orr said. "Mr. Daw has informed me that there are

52 families on his mail route made up of 36 residences and 16 large farms, most of the farms run by Amish. Estimating an average of four per household means that there are probably 200 men, women, and children living in the hollow. I'm looking for a minimum of 36 able bodied volunteers to form a militia, 12 per shift, each serving 8 hours a day guarding the entrance to our valley."

"This is insane!" Carl Miller exclaimed. "This power outage will end soon. The Army will protect us. They'll fix it. They'll have to." The crowd erupted in conversation. Coop listened and observed. Many of them agreed with Orr. Just as many scoffed at his notion. All of them, though, Coop could see were frightened.

When the conversations began to die down, Dr. Hunt spoke, "Listen, everyone, I'm as flabbergasted about this as the rest of you. I don't know why we haven't seen or heard anything from the National Guard or anyone else in authority. Since we haven't, I've resigned myself to the fact that for the time being, we're on our own. Now, we're damn fortunate. Due to geography, Wineberry Hollow is defensible. Because of the variety of skills possessed by the 52 families, we're also self-sufficient. We can get through this if we all work together."

Orr took over from Dr. Hunt. "Folks, I'm a newly retired Army Ranger, and I'm stepping forward as leader of the hollow's makeshift militia, if you'll have me. I'm not imposing myself on anyone, but I don't believe anyone here is more qualified."

When Orr paused, Coop looked around. Nobody else seemed eager to take the job.

He went on. "You folks are civilians, so I wouldn't expect the same kind of discipline typical of regular Army troops, but be advised that if you agree to let me lead, I'll expect those who volunteer to obey my orders. This is no joke. It's serious business and our lives may depend on a vigilant, sober, militia."

After Orr stopped talking, Dr. Hunt leaned on the rails of the wagon. "Does anybody have anything to say?"

Hearing nothing, Dr. Hunt said, "Declan, the job's yours."

Gary Daw stood. "Now that there's no mail service, I'm out of work. I'll be the first to volunteer for the Wineberry Hollow militia."

"Glad to have you," Orr said. He stepped down from the wagon and shook Gary's hand.

Others approached Orr and volunteered, shaking hands and patting each other on the back.

Coop looked at the ground. Would the English understand why he and his Amish friends would not join them, *could* not join them due to their faith? Would they resent it? Would they deride the Amish as cowards? Katie hadn't understood. Why should these people?

The situation remained peaceful for now, and his neighbors seemed willing to trade protection for food, finding the tradeoff a tolerable solution. If fighting were to occur and the Amish didn't participate, would the English remain tolerant? Thinking back on his date with Katie, the incident at the skating rink and her reaction, Coop wondered if they would continue to understand.

Almost all Amish made their living from farming and the building trades, the truth being that the English didn't really need the Amish. They could just take the land and farm it for themselves. If the situation grew more desperate, would it come to that?

Chapter 30

The meeting in Cooper Stover's barn had gone on for well over an hour. After the forming of a militia, other matters were discussed, details agreed upon, responsibilities delegated. Everyone would have something to do, some way to contribute to the community. Coop read relief on his neighbors faces after they realized how with careful management of resources, they could indeed be self-sufficient. They had plenty of food and the mountain stream flowing the length of the valley provided a steady flow of water, even during the heat of summer. Besides that, all of the farms had hand dug wells.

Coop considered how all of them having meaningful work assignments assuaged their fears. He thought the meeting would soon end, but Dr. Hunt climbed back onto the hay wagon and asked for everyone's attention.

When they quieted, he spoke. "I have a couple more issues before we leave." He sighed and glanced at the ground before continuing. "You may not have thought about this but we're all going to have to be especially careful about accidents. I have a limited supply of antibiotics and pain medicine. When it's gone, it's gone. Please…just be careful."

Fred Doaks raised his hand and asked, "My wife and I both are on blood pressure medicine. What happens when we run out?"

Dr. Hunt looked the man in the eye. "I know how fond you are of your wife's desserts, Fred. We'll soon be running out of sugar, so Caroline isn't going to be able to bake you those pecan pies you like so much. You won't be eating as much and you'll probably be eating better. Plus all of us'll be doing a lot more physical labor. We'll be losing weight and gaining muscle mass. I suspect your blood pressure problem will take care of itself. Maybe that's one good thing to come from what we're going through. Most of us should get healthier."

Coop heard a few snickers in reaction to Dr. Hunt's comments. He glanced at Tim Foose remembering the cooler of insulin they had dropped off for his son, Lucas. What was going to happen to the boy after his insulin ran out? Tim had his gaze fixed to the ground as if thinking about the same thing.

"Just one more thing," Dr. Hunt said. He nodded in the direction of Pete Damroth and introduced the man to the crowd. "You may have heard rumors about this stranger working on Carl Miller's old school bus. As it turns out, Pete's somewhat of a wizard with old engines. Got that bus running anyway."

Dr. Hunt paused, then said, "Any of you have old pre-fuel injected engines that need fixing, let Pete know. He's staying here with the Miller family. Fixing internal combustion engines is how Pete will be earning his keep."

"What good is that old bus?" someone asked.

"I'm getting to that," Dr. Hunt answered.

Coop sensed the doctor straining to maintain his patience.

"The third day after things went dark, Declan and I along with Cooper and my daughter went on a road trip, to check on things."

"How bad was it out there?" the same man asked who had spoke earlier.

Dr. Hunt lowered his voice. "Bad." He went on to explain about the panicked farmer and his son, the crashed airplane, the battle under the bridge, and the standoff with Deputy Sheriff Toomey. "That was five days ago. It's probably much worse by now."

The doctor paused and pulled a handkerchief from his pocket, wiped perspiration from his brow. "We left eleven people under that bridge, promised to go back for them. That's why Pete's been fixing the bus."

Sam Wetzel stood. "What do you plan on doing with those strangers?"

"We're bringing them back to the hollow," Declan Orr said, his voice authoritative.

Wetzel grew agitated. "Look, we've just been talking about our limited resources and how we need to keep strangers out of our community. Now you want to invite eleven more people in? Eleven more mouths to feed? Where do you suppose they're going to live once they get here? I'm certainly not taking in any refugees."

Orr and Dr. Hunt exchanged glances. Dr. Hunt spoke. "We promised to rescue those pilgrims. We won't be bringing more. Katie and I are going to open our home to one of the families, Sheila Hunt has agreed to do the same. We just need a few more of you to volunteer."

"I'll help," Vicki Clark said, "I have some extra bedrooms."

"The missus and I should be able to share a room," Gary Daw said.

"Some of these pilgrims have skills we can use," Dr. Hunt said. "One man is a dentist who will be a great help to us all. One is an active duty Marine who can help Declan with the militia. Declan and I are going to take that bus to fetch them."

"This will likely be the last trip we make for a long time," Orr said. "That bus is big enough to haul those folks plus a few other things we might scavenge along the way."

Cooper thought about the truckload of canned food. They could stuff a lot in the bus if any remained, if by now it wasn't all looted.

"Might be dangerous," Sheila Cunningham said.

"No might about it," Orr said. "I'll be asking some of you new militia men to ride posse. The more firepower we display, the more likely opportunists will let us be."

As the meeting ended, Coop's neighbors slowly dispersed and headed toward home. Sheila Cunningham got into the passenger seat of Katie's old Buick and waited for Dr. Hunt who remained in the barn with Declan Orr and the men who volunteered to be posse. Coop joined the men.

"Thanks again for letting us use your barn," Dr. Hunt said.

"You're welcome to it anytime," Coop said, but the meeting had bothered him. He needed to tell the doctor what was on his mind. "Can I speak with you outside?"

Dr. Hunt agreed and followed Coop to the driveway. The gray skies had grown darker and a drizzle had started sometime during their meeting. He waved to Sheila still waiting in the car. Coop led Dr. Hunt to the front porch under the overhanging roof.

"When does Mr. Orr intend on rescuing those people from the bridge?"

"Tomorrow or the day after. Why?"

"I won't feel comfortable going along this time," Coop said. "I'm not afraid for my sake, but now that we know the world is violent, if anything happened to me, who would take care of Mother and Hattie?" He cast his gaze to the floor of the porch. "I hope you understand."

Coop looked up after feeling a hand on his shoulder. Dr. Hunt met his gaze, his face wearing a sad smile. "Son, Declan and I understand your position and nobody expects you to leave Wineberry Hollow. It was a mistake to take you and Katie along the first time. Besides, we pledged to protect you. You and your Amish friends are too important to the community. We need you and your knowledge of the old ways."

Coop felt guilty. "I'm no more important than anyone else."

"And you're no less important either. Each one of us'll contribute in his or her own way."

"People will think of me as a coward for not fighting."

"Trust me, Cooper, when I tell you that most of us admire your courage for living the way you do, sticking to your beliefs and principals."

"I don't feel very brave. I feel," Coop tried to put words to it, the weight of responsibility for caring for his mother and cousin and now his English neighbors. The loss of his father, the worry, the fear, the now uncertain future. He swallowed a lump which had formed in his throat. "I feel alone."

Dr. Hunt thought for awhile before speaking. He looked into the gray sky, the drizzle that had now changed to a more steady rain. "I read somewhere that to be a leader is to be alone."

Why did this man continue to think such things about him. "My faith forbids leadership aspirations. I strive to be humble."

"Throughout history some of mankind's greatest leaders have been humble, Jesus Christ, Mahatma Gandhi…"

"…Don't compare me to the Lord. It is blasphemy."

"I'm not being contemptuous of Christianity, Cooper. I'm just trying to correct your skewed viewpoint. You seem to think that leadership comes primarily from wielding power, using physical force. You probably think that Declan Orr is a great leader because of the way he demonstrated courage facing down danger."

"Of course, look how easily Mr. Orr convinced those men to join him in the militia."

"You're wrong, Cooper. Those men agreed to let Declan lead them because of their trust in him, their respect for him. Trust and respect. Those qualities I also see in you. They just manifest themselves differently, in your confident faith, your work ethic, and determination."

Not everyone agreed with Dr. Hunt. Coop was sure his daughter didn't. "I'm just a young man, barely an adult. I'm not the confident person you think I am."

The corners of Dr. Hunt's mouth turned up. "Time will tell."

Declan Orr and the men he had been speaking with came out of the barn into the rain. Orr got into his Mustang. The other men scattered for home.

Sheila rolled down the window of the Buick. "Coming, Stu?"

"I worry about my mother and Hattie, but what would Katie do if something happened to you on this trip to rescue the strangers?" Coop asked. He nodded toward the Buick. "What would Mrs. Cunningham do?"

Dr. Hunt raised an eyebrow. "Nothing is going to happen to me, at least not on this rescue trip. I'm not going."

Coop frowned. Wouldn't these militia men want the doctor? He was no stranger to violence and seemed at ease using a firearm.

"The militia won't let me come. I guess they consider me too important to the community," Dr. Hunt said. "Just like you."

Chapter 31

Winston Halbert, Minister of Logistics, entered the briefing room and took a seat at the conference table along with Dr. Kirk Carano, Minister of Genetics; Lisa Roykirk, the former Secretary of Agriculture and now Minister of Health; General H. James Munjak, Minister of Defense; Patrick Stroehman, formerly a Senator from Massachusetts and now Minister of Communications; and Kall's wife, Dr. Nika Cho, Minister of Culture.

Kall took his seat at the head of the table.

Conflicted, Halbert thanked God for his position of power among this elite group and the safety it afforded him from the chaos outside the enclaves. On the other hand, he feared God's condemnation over his complicity in the extermination of most of the human race. Unlike Kall, Halbert didn't delude himself into thinking that God was using him as His instrument.

The rumor mill buzzed that President Kall had been pleased with the progress of Project Earthburst, but when Halbert exchanged glances with the man, Kall's steely eyed glare projected dissatisfaction. Or was it madness?

The first lady adjusted her posture to lean toward her husband.

One of the overhead fluorescent light fixtures flickered and buzzed. Halbert smirked at the irony. Here they were in the inner sanctum, Kall's holiest of holies where he expected excellence from his staff and the damn lights weren't even working properly.

"People," Kall said. He paused and took a deep breath as if to restrain himself. "I've called you all together to assess our progress at the end of Earthburst's first week. From the reports getting back to me from the field, we're meeting with success."

Reports back from the field? Halbert considered those words and took their meaning to be that Kall had well placed spies in each of their ministries.

"During these briefings I want you all to discuss the project's deficiencies in the frankest possible terms, and I want the unvarnished truth from each of you." He pointed a finger down the length of the table. "If anyone tries to cover their own ass, or if I even suspect a falsehood, there will be the devil to pay. Does everyone understand me?"

Halbert along with everyone else grunted their assent. A scene from the film, *The Untouchables*, flashed through his mind, the one where Robert DeNiro as Al Capone graphically dispatched one of his lieutenants using a baseball bat. In the film his men had been assembled around a similar conference table.

Kall turned his attention to his wife. "Dr. Cho, what's life like beyond the confines of the enclaves? How far along is the devastation?"

Before speaking, she shot her husband a smile. "I'm not aware of deficiencies. All is going according to plan, spectacular even."

Kall sat back in his chair and seemed to relax. "That's good news."

"Military reconnaissance reports widespread panic and paranoia. Every major city is burning," she announced as casually as if reporting a sporting event. "Civil service is nonexistent everywhere. No police, fire, or medical services. Everyone has hunkered down into an every-man-for-himself mentality. Organized gangs occupy grocery stores and food distribution warehouses. As you might expect, the most ruthless among these gang members have set themselves up as despots, controlling the flow of all essential goods and services."

"What about medical supplies?" Kall asked.

"Decimated," Cho answered. "A street junkie's holiday. There isn't a hospital, pharmacy, or doctor's office anywhere that hasn't been looted."

"What's your estimated rate of die off?"

"Our best guess is that we've already lost 25% of the population of the former United States of America. The rest of the world fares much worse. India and Asia are starving. The southern hemisphere is in the height of winter. They're finished."

"Excellent," Kall said and smiled briefly for the first time since the meeting started.

Halbert had signed on to this project with his eyes wide open, Realistically, he had no choice. Now that it was actually happening, discussing the death of humanity in terms of statistics seemed surreal. He still had trouble wrapping his mind around the coldness of it and fully understood that he sat in a room full of monsters.

Dr. Cho continued. "The death rate will accelerate as the

available resources dwindle. The non-essentials will become more desperate, shooting each other over scraps. Another month to six weeks and the die off will be 80% or more in this country. Near 100% in the rest of the world. Non-essentials living in rural areas who work together, the self-reliant types, will survive. If they are far enough out, the gangs won't be able to reach them."

Kall cut her off. "How long can they endure if current conditions continue indefinitely?"

She shrugged. "For the duration. Farmers and their supporters have the knowledge, resources, and wherewithal to persevere."

"How many people are we talking about?"

"In this country? Roughly 2% of the population."

Kall's eyes went to the ceiling, his mind calculating, or did he just now notice the flickering fluorescent tube? "Two percent of 320 million is about 6 and half million. That's too many. How can we get that number down to less than a million non-essentials?"

Non-essentials, the new euphemism for human beings dying outside the walls of enclaves. Halbert was sure that everyone in the room, himself included, would burn in hell.

"I wouldn't know how to force the issue," Dr. Cho said.

"C'mon, Nika, you're the Minister of Culture. What can we use against them?"

"Crop failure should improve our odds," she suggested.

Dr. Carano's hand went up. "If we could identify those isolated pockets of survivability, it's possible to dust their crops with an invasive agent. For instance, we could introduce Ug99 fungal spores into their wheat fields."

Lisa Roykirk pushed back from the table and stood. "No, no, no," she shouted. "You'll kill us all with a stunt like that. If just a single spore were to find its way into our food reserves or onto the fields within the enclaves, it would devastate us."

"I agree, we must find solutions that do not endanger the enclavists," Kall said. He asked Roykirk to return to her seat and glared at Carano. "You're supposed to be among the best and brightest. What the hell kind of a suggestion was that?"

The man squirmed in his seat. "Just thinking out loud. Brainstorming."

"We could wait until harvest time and send our armies to burn their fields," Dr. Cho said.

General Munjak leaned forward and rested his arms on the table. "Or wait until the crops are harvested and confiscate them. Use them to supplement the enclave food stocks. If the non-essentials resist, that'll give us a reason to cull more of the remaining herd, if you get my meaning, sir."

"I get your meaning and commend you on your creative thinking," Kall said. "Use your troops and make it so."

Halbert reconsidered that burning in hell would not be an adequate enough punishment.

"Uh, not so fast," Dr. Cho interjected. "Your troops may be reluctant to follow those orders."

All eyes fell on her.

Kall said, "My wife and I already discussed this phenomenon, so I know what she is going to say, but go ahead, Nika, and enlighten the rest of this council."

Dr. Cho spoke. "Simply put, we may have overestimated the impact of Armed Forces Homecoming Day. Having the families of our troops confined with them after the world went dark should have instilled a sense of good fortune within everyone. Think about it. What luck. Their loved ones would be safely locked away, wanting for nothing, leaving the troops placated about defending against our unknown enemies."

She drummed her fingers on the tabletop before continuing. "Our psychologists realized that the enclavists would feel some concern and compassion toward the unfortunates beyond the fences, but it appears now that their model has been flawed. Apparently, our soldiers and their families exhibit a great deal of sympathy toward the outsiders."

"How has this sympathetic behavior manifested itself?" asked Minister Stroehman.

"Enclaves are under complete lockdown. Standing orders are for our patrolling troops to keep non-essentials away from enclave perimeters using force if necessary. Currently, that isn't working. Enclavists communicate through the fences, exchanging news. When they hear about how bad things are on the outside, their resolve weakens. There have even been incidents where our troops have been distributing food and medicine at the compound gates."

"Unacceptable," Stroehman said, his voice raised. He banged a fist on the tabletop. "That risks compromising the success of the project. Our food and supplies have been carefully determined in advance. Halbert, you're in charge of logistics, how long can we remain self sufficient?"

Feeling numb, it took a few moments for Halbert to realize that he had been asked a question. He responded, "Each enclave has enough food for two years taking into account ongoing dairy operations and farming."

"More than enough time for the die off to run its course," Kall said.

"But not if we give away our supplies," Stroehman added.

Despite his fear, Halbert felt compelled to speak. He leaned over the table. "Do you really believe the good people of the United States of America are going to sit idly by while their fellow countrymen suffer?"

Everyone stared at him. Kall stiffened his posture and spoke. "Let me remind you that allowing the world to continue along its self destructive path when we had the power to stop it would've been insane. All of us would've eventually died. Better for the cream of humanity to survive, don't you think? Also, the United States of America no longer exists. Let's not speak of it in terms of the present tense and relegate it to its proper place, the ash heap of history. Win, if you have regrets I can easily arrange for you and your wife to be deposited outside the gates. Is that what you're asking of me?"

Halbert considered how if he had an ounce of courage, he would take Kall up on his offer, maybe start a revolution from the outside to overthrow the madness he had taken part in. But fomenting revolution was for young people, strong leadership, and Halbert felt old and weary. He had made his bed. Too late for him now. Instead, he needed to undo the damage his words caused. The anger he saw in everyone's eyes made his heart pound. He moved his hands to his lap so the rest of them couldn't see them trembling. "You misunderstand my meaning. If the enclavists were to learn the truth of what we have done, they would consider us insane. We may have killed the country of America, but it won't be as easy to extinguish the American spirit of decency and generosity. That's what our psychologists failed to understand. That's the flaw in the plan."

Halbert breathed easier as the ministers softened their demeanor toward him. He had successfully weaseled his way out of the tough spot his big mouth had put him into. He needed to be more cautious. Next time, he might not be so lucky.

Kall relaxed his posture. "That's perceptive of you, Win. Does anybody have a suggestion as to how we can fix this? How do we extinguish what Win calls the American spirit?"

"Out of sight, out of mind," General Munjak said. "We need to do a better job of isolating the enclaves. Keep the non-essentials far away from the fences. Among the troops there are always a hard core element. Men who follow orders without question. The select few who, if ordered, would stomp puppy dogs or throw newborn babies onto bonfires."

Dr. Cho gasped, "That offends even my jaded sensibilities."

Killing babies or puppies? Halbert wondered.

The general chuckled. "Excuse my colorful military hyperbole, but it illustrates a point. I have men who wouldn't think twice about planting a thick blanket of land mines around the perimeter of each of our enclaves. I guarantee that after a few of their numbers become dismembered, the rest of the non-essentials won't venture near the fences."

Kall leaned back in his seat and locked his hands behind his head. "Sounds good, but I believe that would be too much of a challenge. There's no way to complete a task like that discreetly. Too many people would know, and our involvement would be transparent."

Repositioning himself, Kall leaned forward and rested his hands on the table. "What we need is a way to demonize the non-essentials. Distract the enclavists so they think less of the outsiders and more of themselves."

"Make the non-essentials into enemies?" Roykirk asked. "How do we do that?"

"What would scare the enclavists so badly that they would avoid non-essentials as if they were lepers?" Dr. Cho asked.

Dr. Carano beamed. "You just answered your own question, Nika. It's quite simple, really. We give them a contagion."

"There you go again," Lisa Roykirk said. "Just like your harebrained scheme about infecting crops with Ug99, unleashing something biological could spread to the enclavists. By god, it could even infect us."

"Relax, Lisa, I'm not suggesting we introduce a plague into the world. We can accomplish the same thing by making the enclavists *think* that a contagion exists," Dr. Carano said. He faced Kall. "And I know how exactly how we can accomplish that."

* * *

Win Halbert entered his apartment and headed straight for the liquor cabinet. He called out. "Sally, where are you?"

No answer, but Halbert heard his wife's scuffling from the bedroom. He plinked three cubes of ice into a glass and unstoppered a decanter of gin. Halbert poured the clear liquid and watched as the ice floated to the top.

He tilted the glass and drank as fast as the burning in his throat would allow. Quite a few cases remained in the stash he had amassed, but eventually it would run out. Then what would happen? Had anyone on Kall's team planned for that eventuality? After the die off and dispersal back into the countryside, would the distilleries reopen?

How could all of the great minds who planned Earthburst fail to understand that people would care about their fellow Americans? If they were so self-absorbed to miss that obvious fact, then planning for the reopening of distilleries had to be fantasy.

In his heart, Halbert knew Kall's new utopia was doomed. All of the technology, all of the scheming, and all of the lies would prove impotent, because in the end the intelligentsia weren't able to grasp the fundamentals of basic human nature.

"Sally?" he called.

Still no answer. He took a step toward the bedroom and stopped. Reconsidered. Poured another glass full of gin. Halbert shuffled toward the bedroom door and eased it open. An open suitcase lay on the bed full of clothing.

"What's going on?" Halbert asked.

"What's it look like? I'm leaving."

Halbert grinned, a reaction to the absurdity of the situation. "Where are you going?"

"Home."

"This is our home now."

"Vermont is our home." She latched the suitcase, her face hard set and determined. Halbert knew the look. When Sally got this way she was difficult to reason with.

"How do you propose to get to Vermont? Nothing outside the enclave is operational."

She stopped what she was doing and looked at him. "Win, you're a U.S. Senator, can't you use your influence and get the Army to fly us home?"

He sighed. Halbert couldn't recall when he had fallen out of love with his wife. There wasn't a single incident, just a slow distancing. He continued to go through the motions acting like a husband, doting on her even, but it was all pretend. The spark had gone out a long time ago. Frankly, it surprised him how she didn't sense the change. Maybe she did and was also pretending. Although he no longer loved Sally, she had stuck with him, and because of that he still had affection for her. Enough affection to want to protect her.

Halbert set his drink on the dresser. "Be reasonable, Sally, we're at war. The armed forces can't taxi people around for personal reasons. Besides, we're safe here. There is no life outside of the enclaves."

Sally sat at the edge of the bed. "I hate it here. I don't know anybody. There's nothing for me to do. I'm worried about my brother and his family. Who's going to keep them safe?"

Her brother lived in the city of Burlington and was probably dead by now. Or soon would be. "I don't know, Sally. We have no communications to the outside, just between enclaves." He sat on the bed beside her. "All we can do is hope for the best."

"How long until power gets restored?"

"I really don't know. The damage is widespread. It could take years, maybe a decade."

She took his hand. "Can't you come up with an official reason for us to relocate to an enclave closer to Vermont? Maybe that would be close enough for us to find out more about my brother and the rest of our friends."

Halbert looked into his wife's eyes. They were the same blue color as Lenore's. That thought saddened him. Sally wasn't the only one who felt a frustrated sense of loss. What he had with his young paramour in no way approached love, yet he never truly realized the depth of his emotional attachment to Lenore until she was gone. Washington D.C. had been a den of vipers. At her end, he hoped Lenore hadn't suffered.

Relocating Sally might not be a bad idea. With her gone he could find a replacement for Lenore and move her into his quarters. Maybe a girl from the outside, what the rest of the ministers coldly referred to as a non-essential. He bet plenty of attractive young ladies would trade their dignity for a secure life.

"Sure, Sally, I promise that I'll speak with President Kall. I'll gladly do that for you." Running a hand through her hair, he said, "I didn't realize that you were so miserable. You should've said something sooner. You know that I'd do anything for you. You're the love of my life."

She smiled.

Halbert had played this game for so long that he no longer felt an ounce of shame at the lies he uttered. They came to him automatically, robotically. "Unpack your things," he whispered in her ear. "Please? I need you."

Chapter 32

Deputy Sheriff Rawland Toomey briefed Stan Cox and an older guy from Wynot named Glenn. "Nobody gets into this building unless I say so. Don't let anybody give you any crap about private property. We're in a state-of-emergency, and I've confiscated this facility for the greater good of the community. The food in this warehouse is the town's lifeline. Remember that I'm the law around here. You boys have shotguns. If you need to use them to defend from looters there won't be any repercussions. You'll be doing your duty."

The deputy drove off bobbing up and down on the steel seat of his old Oliver tractor. He parked a quarter mile away at a dairy.

"Who died and put him in charge?" Stan asked.

"He put himself in charge," Glenn answered.

"And the people of Wynot let him take over?"

"Nobody else wanted the job. State troopers are out of commission and the county sheriff got caught out of state somewhere. As Toomey continues to remind everyone, he's now the highest ranking law enforcement officer around these parts. Why? You have a problem with him?"

Toomey stood in Stan's way. He wanted to be the person calling the shots. "No problem. Just seems sort of an asshole."

Glenn pulled a pack of cigarettes from his shirt pocket and offered Stan a smoke. "Yeah, he's an asshole, but I'd rather be working with him than against him."

Stan took one the offered cigs. He set his 12 gauge aside and lit up. "Don't mind if I do. Might as well enjoy these while we can. When they're gone, they're gone."

Glenn shot a glance at the door behind them. "Warehouse is full of smokes. It'll be years till they're all used up. Things'll be back to normal long before then."

Wishful thinking, Stan thought. This was the new normal.

"Anyway," Glenn continued. "We guard the door. If you need smokes just go on inside and help yourself. Hell, help yourself to anything in there. I won't say anything. Of course, I expect you to return the favor. When I go in there, I expect that you wouldn't rat me out, right?"

Stan contemplated how if he were in control of this town, he'd personally shoot Glenn in the face if he caught the guy stealing from him. "Makes no difference to me. Besides this job has got to have some perks."

Glenn stared at Stan and narrowed his eyes. "You don't look like the type who would approve of stealing."

That made Stan laugh. "Yeah, I'm a little angel." When Stan and Toss broke into the gas station back in Corning, he had stuffed a six-pack of Aquafina bottles into a plastic grocery bag and crammed as many candy bars as he could into the gaps between the bottles. He and Toss parted ways after they left the gas station. Stan figured he'd probably never see the big man again.

His career as a drug dealer had come to an abrupt end, but the world going dark opened up a universe of new opportunities. Being an almost wiseguy gave Stan the confidence that he could control his own destiny. He no longer feared being average. He was young, the world would become his, and it would start by him taking over his hometown.

"Your first day on the job?" Glenn asked.

"Yep."

"How'd you get hooked up with Toomey?"

"Long story. Don't feel like talking about it." The forty mile hike from Corning to his house had taken Stan three days. Although armed with his father's .22, Stan had tried to avoid people, but a number of refugees walking home had crossed his path. Mutual suspicion led them to pass in a wide berth. The daylight hours hadn't been too bad, but at night...

Stan shivered after recalling the far off screams, the shots, the fires, and the stench of flesh decaying in the heat. He had seen what normally civilized men and women had done to each other in their desperation.

When he finally arrived home, his parents were overcome with joy after having thought that he had died somewhere. After cleaning himself up and taking a few days to figure out what to do with himself, Stan announced that he wanted to help the town. His proud parents gave their blessing, and Stan walked into Wynot and volunteered his services to Toomey.

Finished with his cigarette, Glenn flicked the butt onto the pavement. "Suit yourself. I was just trying to make conversation." A few seconds later, Glenn tilted his head. "You hear something?"

Stan listened and picked up on the sound of an engine approaching from the west. An old faded yellow school bus rounded the bend.

"Get a load of that," Glenn said. "I haven't seen a vehicle other than a few old tractors since the lights went out."

The bus sped by. Stan saw 10, maybe 12 faces sitting in the bus, but they were too far away for him to identify who they were. Certainly not school kids. Recognizing an opportunity, Stan extinguished what remained of his butt under his boot and grabbed his shotgun. "Toomey's going to want to know about this. I'll go get him."

Glenn's eye twitched. "Hold on. We've been assigned to guard this building. You can't just leave your post."

Ignoring him, Stan sprinted the quarter mile to the dairy, crashed through the door, and found Toomey in conversation with a man wearing a white butcher's apron.

"What the hell is this?" Toomey asked.

Stan took a moment to catch his breath and told the men about the bus.

Toomey's eyes widened. "A fully operational school bus?"

"Yes. Old, but it sped down the road just fine."

"We need that vehicle," the man in the apron said.

"They're heading straight for town and the roadblocks. The

boys will stop them," Toomey said. "Grab your horse, Terry."

Terry yanked off his apron and exited through a side door. Stan followed Toomey to his tractor. The deputy jumped into his seat and fired it up. He motioned with his arm. "You come with me. Stand on the toolbox and grab hold of the fender."

Stan slung the shotgun over his shoulder and climbed on. Terry appeared from behind the building on the back of a brown horse. He shouted to the horse and the animal took off in a gallop. Stan almost lost his balance when the Oliver lurched forward after Toomey popped the clutch.

When they drove past the warehouse. Glenn stared at them, slack jawed.

That retard was worthless.

It took them a few minutes to get to the edge of town. Two guys milled around behind a hay wagon, red faced, waving their rifles.

Toomey let loose with a long string of curses and slowed his tractor to a stop. He pointed to a bearded man wearing a Phillies baseball cap. "Don't even tell me that you let them through."

The man shrugged. "They took us by surprise and got past before we even had a chance to pull the wagon across their path. That bus must've been going 50 or 60. We never expected anything to fly through at that speed."

"Goddamn it, Hoss, you're supposed to be in charge of this roadblock." Toomey got down from the tractor and yelled in Hoss's face. "Do you have any idea how valuable an operational school bus would be to this town?"

"Sorry, boss. That thing was loaded with men pointing guns at us. Billy and I probably wouldn't have been able to do anything about it anyway."

"Which way did they go?"

Hoss pointed straight ahead. "Down the street. Headed for Route 15."

"God help you, Hoss, if we don't catch up to them. Round up as many men as you can find and be quick about it." He turned his attention to Stan. "Kid, you help me hitch up the wagon."

A few minutes later, Stan rode in the wagon along with Hoss, Billy, Terry, and a dozen more guys. Stan figured the old Oliver pulled the wagon along at about thirty miles per hour. Toomey was kidding himself if he thought they'd catch up to that bus.

What seemed like an hour had gone by and Stan gasped after catching sight of a huge passenger jet that had crashed. On the long walk home from Corning, Stan had followed Route 15 but left that highway at the Tioga cutoff, so he hadn't seen the wreckage.

Terry pointed toward the underpass. "There it is."

Sure as hell, Stan saw the bus with a bunch of people gathered round it.

Toomey drove to within a hundred yards, stopped, and cut the engine. He got down from the tractor and looked at the men in the wagon. "Make sure you get it through your pea brains to *not* shoot at that school bus. The main reason we're here is to capture it. Got that. Do *not* shoot the bus."

Stan jumped off the wagon along with the other guys. Toomey didn't know what he was doing. A poor spot for a firefight, the area offered little cover. Most of the guys stood around in a loose formation, rifles across their chests. About ten yards to his right, Stan spotted a groundhog mound. He got down on his belly behind the mound and pointed the business end of his shotgun toward the bus.

The people who had gathered round the bus scattered for the safety of the underpass.

The first person to approach was a big black guy carrying what looked to be an assault rifle. Behind him, Stan counted eight men who fanned out in military precision. They moved quickly, took their positions, kneeled, and pointed their rifles.

Impressive.

Stan shot a glance at Toomey's men. They gawked at the bus wide-eyed as if in shock, Hoss's face paled, and he looked like he would puke. Billy stood frozen in place, hands in his pockets.

Bozos.

Toomey straightened and shouted to the black guy. "You were warned the last time we met, boy."

These guys knew each other?

The black guy took a step forward. "Deputy Sheriff, I don't give a damn about you or your town. We're here to pick up these pilgrims and then we'll be on our way."

Toomey worked the action of his pump shotgun and chambered a round. He pointed the barrel at the black guy. To the black guy's credit, he didn't move, didn't even wince.

"Last time we met there were five of you in an old Mustang," Toomey said. "This time you ignore our roadblock and bring a dozen armed men, testing our defenses. Next time you'll make a move on the citizens of our town. I can't allow that."

The black guy glared at Toomey. Man, he had guts to look down the barrel of Toomey's shotgun. "Let me tell you how this will go down. Your men will lower your weapons. We're going to load up our passengers. Then we're going to return the way we came."

A couple of Toomey's guys snickered.

"Don't be a fool," Toomey said. "You're outnumbered and outgunned. By my authority as a Deputy Sheriff of Tioga County, I'm commandeering your vehicle for the greater good of the citizens of Wynot."

Sneaking a glance at Toomey's men, Stan noticed that the bozos finally were starting to spread out. They might get lucky after all.

"Let me tell you about the facts of life, Deputy Sheriff. We may be outgunned, but every single one of my men has your chest in their crosshairs. If you're determined to see this through, you'll be the first man to drop."

Stan visualized Toomey being perforated by a dozen rifle rounds and decided that nothing would please him more. They had given up their advantage by allowing the black guy's men to take their positions. Toomey was a pathetic leader who should've been shooting instead of talking. Stan entertained the idea of shooting Toomey himself.

"And my men will likewise take you out," Toomey countered.

"Okay then," the black guy said. He aimed his assault rifle from the hip at Toomey. "Let's party."

Stan admired the black guy for his fearlessness.

He didn't know who took the first shot, but suddenly gunfire erupted all around him.

The black guy rolled to his side and disappeared in the weeds. Stan bet he was unhurt.

The spot where Toomey had been standing a split second earlier now lay shrouded in red mist. The blustering moron got what he deserved.

Stan aimed at one of the bushes where he saw a man duck behind and squeezed the trigger. Twigs flew as the shotgun pellets disintegrated the bush, but his target rolled away. Damn number 6 shot was all he had. Shells loaded for rabbits. He needed double aught to be effective at this range.

The black guy's men seemed to concentrate their fire to his left so Stan crawled through the weeds to his right. If he could flank the shooters, he should be able to take out a few of them before they realized he was there.

While he crawled, Stan heard a woman scream and remembered the passengers attempting to board the school bus who had then retreated beneath the underpass. Who were these people and what did they have to do with the black guy and his men?

After an eternity of crawling, Stan realized that he'd never be able to safely close the gap. There simply wasn't adequate cover. He flattened himself best as he could against the ground and started firing in the direction of the muzzle flashes.

He'd be lucky to score a fatal shot from where he was, but the pellets ripped up brush enough to keep the enemy moving. Once those guys moved, they were easier targets for the bozos on his side who had rifles.

Despite his efforts at scattering the enemy, Stan didn't see a single one of them go down. The guys on his side had to be lousy shots.

An elderly woman ran from the underpass waving her arms and screaming. "Stop this. Stop this." Some unarmed guy chased after her, a horrified look on his face. Stan swore he yelled, "Mother," before both of them were cut down by a hail of bullets.

Weird.

Having scored some hits seemed to encourage the guys on his side. They whooped and began to advance while firing. Two of them sprinted off to the side in a flanking maneuver.

This fight might well go their way.

Stan took a few more shots before catching a glimpse of movement in his peripheral vision. An Army troop carrier had stopped in the middle of the highway and soldiers streamed out the back. He decided not to wait to find out which side the Army would choose in this fight.

"Fall back," he yelled. "Fall back."

He might die here, but Stan decided he wasn't going to make it easy. He jumped and sprinted in a straight line back to the tractor.

Bullets whizzed by tearing up the weeds, but the guys on his side returned fire, providing cover.

Stan dove under the wagon and caught his breath. Miraculously, he hadn't been hit.

The Oliver rested on its rims, both rear tires shredded by gunfire. Damn it. He'd be walking home once again. Stan looked around and spotted a patch of woods in the direction of the downed jetliner. He cupped his hands around his mouth and yelled, "Make for the trees. Pass the word. Make for the trees."

He no longer heard shots coming from the enemy, so they must have ceased fire. Stan took advantage of the lull and bolted. He heard the huffing of others behind him. After hitting the woods, he kept running until heavy enough cover lay between him and the soldiers. Stan fell to the ground and gulped air. Sometime later, Toomey's remaining men gathered around.

Terry helped Stan to his feet. "Kid, that took guts putting yourself out there like that, making those guys jump around like jack-in-the-boxes."

"You guys hit any of them?" Stan asked.

Nobody made any claims.

Hoss laughed. "No, but we sure took out that old lady and that guy running behind her."

"That's nothing to brag about."

Hoss stiffened. "Who the hell are you, anyway?"

Stan approached the guy, pulled his father's .22 from his belt and stuck the barrel under Hoss's chin. "My name is Stan Cox. I suggest you remember that."

Hoss stood statue still. "Easy, Stan, I meant no disrespect."

Billy yelled, "This is bullshit, man. I'm all for protecting our town, but chasing people all over the place and getting into firefights over a stupid school bus is bullshit. And now look at us. We're fighting each other."

"Relax." Stan holstered the .22. "You're right, Billy. Toomey is dead. The bullshit stops here. No more aimless fighting."

"Yeah, but what do we do now?"

"How many men did we lose back there?"

"Four," Terry said, "besides Toomey."

"A damn waste," Stan uttered. "I'll take the responsibility to inform their families. Dress it up to make it sound like they died defending the town."

Everyone looked at Stan, and he seized the moment. "We have a long walk home in front of us, fellas. Along the way, I want to talk with each and every one of you, get to know you. We need to reorganize. Nobody is going to protect our town, so we'll have to protect it ourselves. I promise there will be no pettiness like what we just went through. No more wasting time on ridiculous roadblocks. We'll call ourselves the Citizen's Committee of Wynot, and we will have only one purpose. Feed and clothe the people of Wynot and defend them from intruders."

Stan paused. Nobody challenged him, but he wanted to make sure. "Anybody have a problem with that?"

All eyes looked at the ground and Stan knew for sure from that moment on, he would never be average again.

Chapter 33

Declan Orr knelt beside Corporal Jack Clark inspecting the dead bodies of Harold Crane and his mother, Daisy. The corporal wiped the back of his hand across his eyes. Orr gave the young man time to compose himself and asked, "You were supposed to keep these people inside the underpass. What happened?"

Clark stood and sighed. "Sarah, the young retarded girl, started screaming after the shooting started. She became uncontrollable and her mother, Wendy, couldn't handle her. I went over to help. I suppose Mrs. Crane," he glanced at the dead woman, "thought she could make everyone stop shooting. Her son, Harold, tried to pull her back, but too late."

He looked Orr in the eye. "I feel responsible. Should've stopped them."

Orr returned his stare. "No, corporal, you're not responsible. You did what you had to and couldn't have prevented this lady or her son from acting foolishly. It's a damn shame, but don't beat yourself up over it."

"But sir, over the past week I got to know them well. Mrs. Crane was a retired school teacher, Harold was a stone mason. They were good people. Never meant anyone no harm. All they wanted to do was to get back to their family in Harrisburg."

Orr laid a hand on Clark's shoulder. "I've been where you are, and I know that it ain't easy. That's why war sucks. Too many good people die. We all lose."

"Drop your weapons," a voice sounded from the grassy bank behind them. A group of soldiers in uniform held their guns at the ready.

Orr lowered his rifle to the ground. "Easy there men, we're the good guys."

"So say you," one of the soldiers said. Orr saw that he wore a lieutenant's insignia. "I need all you civilians to disarm until I can sort this out. Do it now. I won't ask again."

"Understood," Orr said. He passed the word to his men to cooperate fully with the lieutenant. "I'm Declan Orr, recently retired Sergeant Major, U.S. Army Rangers."

The lieutenant snorted, "Retired or not, ranger or not, you have some explaining to do, mister."

"That'll be all, Halfjack," another soldier said. He approached Orr and extended a hand. "I'm Captain Douglas Sloat."

Orr shook hands with Sloat and saluted. "Is this your outfit, captain?"

"Affirmative. Out of Enclave 38."

"Glad you came along when you did. Our attackers had us pinned down and making a decent fight of it."

Sloat looked at the corpses. "Other than these unfortunate souls, it appears that your men suffered no casualties. All the dead combatants are laying out there in the field. Seems to me you were taking it to your attackers pretty well."

"We've trained a bit, sir."

Sloat cocked his head. "You told me you were retired, Mr. Orr?"

"Yes, sir."

Sloat put his hands on his hips and looked around. "Care to enlighten me on this situation?"

Orr explained their business and how the residents of Wineberry Hollow committed to take in the refugees. He detailed to the captain how the community formed a militia to protect their neighbors and property. Orr also told him about Deputy Sheriff Toomey and how he fancied himself as dictator of Wynot, hoarding food and medicine, wanting to confiscate their bus.

"I suppose I'll need to have a conversation with this Toomey,"

Captain Sloat said.

"No need. That pulpy mess you see over there by the tractor is him. Correction, *was* him."

Sloat glanced in that direction. "Do tell."

"I'd say that's very convenient for you," spouted Halfjack. "We'll never get Mr. Toomey's side of the story now, will we?"

Orr couldn't figure why he was the object of the man's hostility. "The way I told it is the way it was."

"We're supposed to take your word over that of a civilian law enforcement officer?" Halfjack asked in a condescending tone.

Sloat stepped between the two men. "Stand down, lieutenant. Take a handful of men and get busy burying the dead."

Halfjack grunted, managed a limp salute, and ambled off.

Orr shook his head. "Used to have to bite my tongue around self-righteous pricks like him. Glad I don't have to anymore. That man is a blight against good officers."

Sloat's expression remained neutral. "Seeing as how I'm still active military I don't have the luxury of being loose with my tongue, so I will neither agree nor disagree with you. I ask only for you to consider that not long ago we were still seeing action over in the sandbox. Given the new stresses we all face, many of my men haven't yet had a chance to decompress."

Despite Captain Sloat's attempt at diplomacy, Orr could smell degenerates like Halfjack a mile away. "Speaking of our current situation, are you at liberty to discuss what's happening in the world? Now that the military is out and about, can I assume that things will soon return to normal?"

Sloat's lips curled down, and he looked around, observing who might be listening. "Negative, Mr. Orr. Conditions are far from normal. Walk with me."

"Excuse me a second," Orr said.

The refugees shaken by the firefight and distressed over the deaths of the Cranes milled about with blank expressions or sobbing. Orr yelled for Gary Daw. "Get the men together and gather up our guests and their possessions. Help them board the bus. The sooner we get these folks out of here, the sooner they will return to their senses."

Daw nodded toward the bodies already becoming thick with flies. "What about their friends?"

"Unfortunately, we have no time to grieve. We need to get home before dark. The Army will see to it that they get buried." He hated to be brutal like that, but under the current reality, it's just the way things had to be. Orr turned his attention back to the captain. "Okay, captain, let's take that walk."

After strolling out of earshot, Orr asked, "What can you tell me?"

The captain answered, "Those of us in the rank and file military know little more than you do. I can only tell you that an EMP event has made the entire planet dark."

"Who is the enemy? Who are we fighting? I mean, do we know yet who is responsible?"

"The brass is as tight lipped about that as the Pope would be about a mistress."

Orr stroked the stubble on his chin. "It's easy to draw conclusions, isn't it?"

Sloat stopped walking and looked at him. "How so?"

"The recall of the military, the new isolationist policy, the enclaves, and the lights going out during Armed Forces Homecoming Day. Then the communications blackout and obvious absence of any military presence until now. The timing of it all strikes me as dubious."

"What are you saying, Mr. Orr?"

"I'm saying that I don't believe in coincidences."

Sloat resumed walking. "Neither should anybody with half a brain."

"Kall's behind this. That brother ain't right." He studied Sloat's face for a reaction and saw nothing. "You're a good man, captain, and I understand how it would be unbecoming of an officer to criticize his commander-in-chief. I'll interpret your silence as tacit agreement with what I just said."

"You may interpret my silence as fear to speak freely, Mr. Orr."

Orr feared they were running behind schedule, and he wanted to be safely home before night fall. "Can you tell me what you and your men are doing here?"

"Salvage. We're to run the roads and retrieve anything useful for the enclavists. We were in the process of unhitching a trailer load of canned food about half a click from here when your gunfire drew us to your location."

"Campbell soups and beans?"

"Affirmative. You know about it?"

"One of our refugees, Mr. Ortiz, was driving that truck when the world went dark. We were hoping to load up the back of our bus with those cans to take home with us."

"If we hadn't already discovered the load, I'd let you have it," Sloat said. He glanced over his shoulder to where they left Lieutenant Halfjack. "That's no longer an option. *He* knows about it."

Orr appreciated the captain's dilemma but still resented the fact that their food was being confiscated. "So it's to hell with those of us on the outside?"

The captain's lips formed a tight straight line as if trying to keep the words from spilling from his mouth. "If you're asking me if my mission has anything to do with recon and rescue, I'd have to answer in the negative." He stopped walking and faced Orr. "Don't expect help from the military. As a matter of fact, our orders are to avoid outsiders. We wouldn't be having this conversation if it weren't for us stumbling onto your skirmish."

Orr held back feelings of rage. The captain risked much by speaking candidly with him and he didn't want to direct his anger at the man. Those responsible were above the captain's pay grade. "How is it that someone has miscalculated the amount of stores to lay up in the enclaves? If the military is already scouring the countryside for food, what has gone awry with Kall's master plan?"

Sloat lowered his voice. "This is a very dangerous conversation, Mr. Orr."

Orr pointed to the pilgrims boarding the bus. "Dangerous for you? Those are the people who are in danger. My wife and kids back in Wineberry Hollow are in danger. Everybody not deemed worthy enough to occupy space inside the fences of the enclaves are in danger."

Sloat paused before speaking. "There are obviously those in command who don't give a damn about you and your neighbors. I'm not one of those people, and neither are the majority of those serving with me. My mother and father did not join me on Armed Forces Homecoming Day. My home is in Idaho, and my parents didn't want to make the trip. I haven't spoken with them since the world went all to hell. Like with you folks, they are in danger, too. And like with you folks, I'm helpless to do anything about it.

"You're a smart man, Mr Orr, so listen up. If I had an opportunity to speak with my parents, I'd advise them to do exactly what you are doing. Organize. Watch out for one another. Share resources. Above all else, I would advise them to keep a low profile. Literally stay under the radar. Do you hear me, Mr. Orr?"

Orr considered the captain's words and felt chills race up his spine. "My god, is the military coming after those of us who remain?"

"I can't say so with a certainty, but if true, you and your neighbors do not want to be low hanging fruit."

"I get it. We should avoid attracting attention."

Sloat rubbed the back of his neck. "The textbook definition of a sociopath is a person who lacks a sense of moral responsibility or social conscience, someone who feels no remorse. A person like that is also generally fearless, but the one thing a sociopath worries about is people who *do* feel. They tend to underestimate human compassion because they don't understand it. Those of us who can help are doing so, at great risk of discovery."

Orr was beginning to understand. Men like Sloat, men with a moral conscience were probably smuggling enclave food and supplies to the outsiders. Why else would enclave stores be drawn down quicker than anticipated? "You said earlier that anybody with half a brain could put two and two together and figure out that Kall is behind what has happened."

"You may have inferred that, Mr. Orr, but I did not specifically use those words. This points to the commander-in-chief or someone else in a very powerful position. To be honest, I don't know anything for sure. It's all conjecture at this point."

Orr believed the captain was in a good position to draw that conclusion. "Kall must've figured that he could buy troop loyalty by including their families in the enclaves. His error was that decent people don't think like him. Those decent people want to help those of us on the outside. For some reason that jeopardizes Kall's new utopia, so he needs to compensate by accelerating the destruction before good hearted people like you can organize and rise up against him."

The two men started walking back the way they came. Orr

continued, "How am I doing so far?"

Sloat looked straight ahead. "Like I already said, you're a smart man, Mr. Orr."

"The question is, how long will it take for good hearted people to attempt a coup? After all, you did take an oath to protect the constitution of the United States."

Captain Sloat slowed his pace. They were almost back to the underpass. In a hushed voice he said, "In a situation such as you describe, I would imagine good hearted people would proceed slowly and with extreme caution until they know who they can trust. Rumor has it, and this is all rumor, a man code named Mandible, a high ranking military officer is leading a resistance of sorts against Kall. Until Mandible and his organization achieves critical mass, those on the outside need to lay low."

Orr pondered the captain's words.

Sloat continued, "Take your people home, Mr. Orr. God speed and learn from your mistakes."

"Mistakes?"

"Two big ones," Sloat said. "You left your circle of safety. I trust you will not make that mistake again."

"I can assure you that henceforth the door to our community will be barred. What was my second mistake?"

They stopped walking and watched as Lieutenant Halfjack and a group of enlisted men dug graves for the seven dead bodies. The men labored with their shirts off and huffing in the hot afternoon sun.

Sloat moved close to Orr's ear and spoke barely above a whisper. "Earlier you revealed to me that you hail from a place around here called Wineberry Hollow. That's a fact that I'm confident I'll easily forget."

He motioned with his head toward Halfjack. "But it's also a fact that I'm confident *he* will easily remember."

Chapter 34

On most Sundays, Cooper Stover couldn't wait for the long three hour church service to end. This morning he experienced butterflies in his stomach and fretted about what he had to say to the congregation. Dr. Hunt and Declan Orr should not have burdened him with the request that he be their spokesperson. He was not an experienced speaker and not even a baptized parishioner. Would the congregation even listen to him?

Services were held at Elam and Ruth Kroh's home, it being their turn to host the gathering. Earlier that morning, Coop helped their son and his classmate Stephen unload the bench wagon and distribute the *Ausbund* hymnals, four to a bench. Stephen managed to keep his stuttering under control only while talking about Rebekah Hagen, the maidel he was courting. She seemed to be a calming influence in his life. Since the maidels and women would be sitting in a separate room from the men during the service, Stephen wouldn't be able to introduce Rebekah until after the service ended.

Mr. Kroh, a church Deacon, granted permission for Coop to address the men at the conclusion of the service and before they all broke for lunch. Now as they sang the final stanza of *Das Loblied*, he felt a trickle of perspiration trail from his armpit to his waist. After the benediction, Mr. Kroh motioned to Coop.

He stood, fingering his hymnal. In the next room, the women began the process of converting their benches into tables for lunch. The distraction made it more difficult for Coop. Many of the men looked over their shoulders most likely anticipating their meal and socializing, especially after sitting for the past three hours.

"Brothers, I have something important to tell you." Coop spoke too low and most of them didn't hear him. Those toward the back began having side conversations among themselves.

Mr. Kroh cleared his throat. "Brothers."

The room grew silent and everyone turned their attention to the front of the room.

Mr. Kroh gestured with his arm in Coop's direction. "Young Mr. Cooper has requested that we remain a few moments so that he can make an announcement. The sooner we allow him to have his say, the sooner we can partake of that fine coffee I smell and my wife's famous snitz."

More than a few men nodded and murmured their assent at Mr. Kroh's words.

"Go ahead, son."

Coop had rehearsed his opening remarks, but now that all eyes were on him, his recollection evaporated. In fact, he felt a complete fool. After an uncomfortable pause, Coop just decided to tell things as they were with no fancy words and no embellishments. He swallowed and began to speak.

"The day after our English neighbors lost their electricity, I rode in an automobile with Dr. Hunt and his neighbor, Mr. Orr. We drove as far as Route 15 to determine how widespread the problem with the electricity might be. The terrible things I witnessed during that trip, I'm sure will remain a part of me for the rest of my life."

Coop paused a moment and decided he should elaborate so that his audience would take his words seriously. "On three different occasions during that one trip, men tried to kill us for no reason other than to steal our vehicle. I personally witnessed a man die at the hands of another. I smelled the burnt, decaying flesh of those who perished as a result of a plane having fallen from the sky."

One of the elders stood and shouted, "This is outrageous." He pointed a finger at Mr. Kroh. "Elam, what are you doing by having this boy tell us such sensational stories."

Joe Hutmaker stood and in a calm voice said, "I've known Cooper Stover all of his life. He is not prone to fantasy or the telling of tall tales. I say we let him speak about these important matters. These things matter to the well being of our families."

"He's not even baptized," the elder said. "Why should we listen to one who has not committed to the faith."

Coop felt an overwhelming urge to defend himself and blurted, "It is true that I have not taken the step of baptism, nevertheless I feel affection for everyone in this room and beg you to hear my message. I swear that I'm speaking the truth."

The elder narrowed his eyes at Coop. He spoke low, almost in a growl. "You swear, boy? Be warned that oath from your lips to God's ear."

"I accept your counsel," Coop said, "and your warning."

Both the elder and Joe Hutmaker sat.

Coop went on. "These things I spoke of I personally witnessed. Now that more time has passed, I fear the situation to be ever more desperate. Dr. Hunt, whom you all know and respect, and Mr. Orr, the other man I spoke of, both believe the problem to be widespread. They speculate the entire country may be affected. Maybe even the whole world."

One of the men interrupted. "Speculate? It hardly seems

possible such a thing. What are the facts as stated by the law enforcement authorities or government officials?"

Coop grew frustrated. "Communications has ceased to exist. There is no radio. No television. There are no newspapers. Every piece of modern machinery has stopped working. I just got done telling you how airplanes have fallen from the sky. Mr. Orr tells me it has been caused by something called an electromagnetic pulse, a great weapon someone has used. Our English neighbors are in great distress."

Another man interrupted. "We live without electricity. The English will also learn. Perhaps this is for the best. Without all of the distractions caused by electricity such as computers, their devices that play the devil's music, and children who become fat and lazy while playing video games instead of working the fields, it will strengthen their faith."

Many of the brothers nodded and murmured approval.

"I must respectfully disagree," Cooper said. "This is not about trivial distractions. For several generations the English have known no life without electricity. They have become too far removed from the Earth and have lost all knowledge of the simple life. Most live all of their lives in great cities having never turned a single spade of dirt. I fear for those unfortunate souls, for they may already have perished.

"All of us know of and respect Dr. Hunt, and I have also come to respect Mr. Orr. They have asked me to present a proposal. The English living in Wineberry Hollow no longer have the means to travel to their places of work. They are now rooted here. Some wish to work with us on our farms and dairies. Some have formed a militia to prevent outsiders from raiding our community. They want to learn from us and to protect our lives and our property. They ask no payment other than for us to feed them and their families."

"Protect us from what?" another man asked.

"Do you not understand?" Coop answered with a raised voice. "Not only are these English outsiders far removed from the Earth, but they are also far removed from God. They will grow hungry. They will grow desperate. And then they will come. And those who do come possess a brutality that knows no mercy. I have seen such brutality first hand."

The brothers began another round of murmuring among themselves. The elder who had spoken out earlier turned to Cooper and said, "We must accept what has happened as Gottes Wille. It is also His will who among our Amish brethren should live or die."

"Perhaps it is Gottes Wille for us to cooperate with our English neighbors," Coop said. "Demonstrate to them the happiness of a humble life. Allow them to draw closer to God."

The elder furrowed his brow. "Are they willing to respect us and our ways? The scriptures counsel us to separate ourselves from the world, an admonishment we have lived with for centuries. The danger is that we will become influenced by their wickedness rather than they being influenced by our faith. I especially fear for our impressionable young people. We lose too many as it is during rumspringa."

Elam Kroh stood and planted a hand on Coop's shoulder. "The scriptures also tell us to love our neighbors. From what young Cooper here has told us, the only remaining distinction between us and the English is our faith. They have nothing left which they can use to turn any of us away from the church. I believe Cooper's words. I also believe that with the extra help being offered by our English neighbors, we can comfortably produce enough food for everyone in Wineberry Hollow. This is an opportunity provided to us from God, so what have we to fear?"

Nobody else spoke.

Elam let go of Coop's shoulder and said, "As you have taken on the responsibility of being a messenger, so shall you deliver our message back to our English friends. We accept their offer to work on our farms in return for their protection, however those who choose to labor alongside our people must be prepared to submit to our authority. We will dismiss anyone who holds in contempt our way of life. No drunkards, no smokers, no loafers, no blasphemers, and we will certainly allow no disrespect of our daughters."

Coop felt a sense of relief well up inside of himself. "I understand and will convey your reply."

Coop filed out of the room along with the other men. He had already asked permission of his mother to take the buggy to see Dr. Hunt. Mr. Orr and a group of his militia were to rescue the refugees living beneath the underpass today, and he was anxious about their safe return. He hoped that Dr. Hunt had news.

And he also hoped to see Katie again.

While Coop hitched Tony to the buggy, Stephen found him. He towed a girl behind him by the hand. "I...I...I wanted you to meet Rebekah. Rebekah, this is my friend Ka...Ka...Cooper."

Rebekah curtseyed and said, "Pleasure to meet a friend of Stephen's."

Pretty girl with bright green eyes and charming smile, but she looked to be around 15 or 16, a bit young for Stephen. "Where are you from?"

"My papa's farm and orchard lies along the township road."

Coop knew the place and it worried him. "You and your family are isolated. Don't be afraid to seek shelter here in the hollow at the first sign of trouble."

Stephen stood up straight. "Don't worry, Becky, we'll take you in if it comes to that."

"Please don't think of me as rude, but I need to go." Coop climbed into the seat of the buggy and prodded Tony forward. He turned once in his seat and waved goodbye to his friends.

Chapter 35

When Coop arrived at Dr. Hunt's house, he unhitched Tony and tied her under the shady canopy of a maple tree. He grabbed the water bucket attached to the back of the buggy, filled it from the stream that drained the surrounding mountains, and set it beside the tree.

Coop knocked on the front screen door. It disappointed him when Dr. Hunt answered. He hoped it would be Katie instead.

"Cooper?" Dr. Hunt seemed surprised.

"I met with the congregation this morning. Wanted to tell you what they had to say."

Dr. Hunt held open the door. "Come in."

Coop removed his hat and entered. Sheila Cunningham sat on the living room sofa, her eyes puffy, a handkerchief balled in her fist. "Have I come at a bad time?"

Dr. Hunt motioned to a lounger. "Have a seat,"

Sheila ignored Coop. She sniffled and stared out the living room window.

"Have Mr. Orr and his men returned yet?" Coop asked.

"No."

"Until they do, I feel like I'm sitting on needles and pins."

"I'm concerned about them, too. What happened at your meeting today?"

Coop related to Dr. Hunt what he had told the congregation and of their response.

Dr. Hunt exhaled through puffed out cheeks. "That's the first good news we've had in a long time. I'm relieved the elders agreed to our offer. Nice job, Coop. Thank you."

Mrs. Cunningham remained silent and distant. Coop wondered why she seemed so dispirited and wondered if he should risk asking. Most likely she had been visiting Dr. Hunt about some illness.

For a while nobody spoke and Coop grew nervous. He began to fidget.

"Say, Coop, Sheila and I have been engaged in a private conversation. Would you mind visiting with Katie until we're done?"

Coop grasped the arm of the chair. "Is she here?"

Dr. Hunt pointed over his shoulder with his thumb. "She's out back working in the garden."

"May I?"

"Yeah, go on."

Coop's heart raced in anticipation, and he had to make a conscious effort not to sprint through the kitchen to get to the back door. He found her sitting on the grass along the edge of the garden holding a garden fork and pulling weeds.

When Katie saw him, she stood and raised an eyebrow. "Where'd you come from?"

"Just finished speaking with your father about the meeting today." He filled her in on the details.

Looking at the garden, she sighed. "Dad and I used to grow stuff for fun. Now I guess our lives depend on it."

"You won't go hungry, Katie. That was the point of today's meeting."

In the 20-foot square plot grew tomatoes, peppers, cucumbers, beans, and squash at the far end. Not enough to sustain Katie and her father, but it would supplement what his neighbors could share with them. Although it was a sin to work on a Sunday, Coop couldn't help but offer. "If you have another fork, we can make quick work of it."

She rolled her eyes. "Oh, yeah, then what do I have to look forward to. There's nothing to do anymore."

"What's wrong with friendly conversation?"

Katie looked at him dubiously.

"I'll start at the other end. We'll meet in the middle."

"Uh, Coop," she said. "You're not exactly dressed for the occasion."

That's when he realized that he still wore his Sunday for-gut clothes and shoes.

"Don't worry about it. I didn't intend to weed the entire garden at one time and I need a break." She squinted. "This sun is brutal."

Her remark reminded Coop of his fair complexion and that he still held his hat in hand. He planted the straw hat firmly on his head.

Katie peeled off her garden gloves. "Wait for me on the back porch where it's shaded. I'll get out of these grungy clothes." She wore a purple tee shirt, cut off shorts, and flip flops. A red rubber band held her hair in a pony tail.

"You don't need to change," Cooper said. "You're perfect just the way you are."

She paused, considering what he said. "All right, have a seat at the picnic table. I'll be right back with some water from the spring. Seeing as how we have no more refrigeration, it won't be cold, but at least it'll be wet."

When she turned her back to walk into the house, Coop stared at her bare legs and the way her hips moved. "Perfect," he mumbled.

She soon returned and sat on the bench across the table from him. Handed him a glass of water.

"Thanks." Coop drained the glass not realizing how thirsty he had been. He watched the way Katie's throat moved as she drank. She set her glass on the picnic table and the two of them looked at each other.

Katie broke the silence. "God, it's hot out here, but with no AC it's even hotter in the house. How do you Amish stand it?"

"You get used to it."

Katie focused on the tabletop.

"What's wrong with Mrs. Cunningham?" Coop asked. "She

seems out of sorts."

"That poor woman is a wreck. She has two daughters, you know, both in their twenties. Both live in cities. It's driving her crazy not being able to communicate with them. She fears the worst…and she's probably right."

That turned Coop's thought to his friends in Philadelphia, Liam and Andrew. He wondered if he'd ever see them again. "I know how she feels."

Katie leaned over the table and rested her hand on Coop's forearm. She lowered her voice. "Wanna know a secret?"

"How can I say no to that?"

"With Sheila being lonely and alone and Dad being alone, he asked her to move in."

"Are they getting married?"

"I don't know, Coop, don't you think that's rushing it?"

"If they share the same bed, they should get married."

Where Katie rested her hand on his arm, she now squeezed him hard. Then she removed her hand. "Cooper Stover, did I say they were sharing the same bed?"

He felt his face flush. "I just naturally assumed…"

She giggled. "Although that would be good medicine for the both of them."

"Katie!"

"Yeah, as if you wouldn't jump at the chance."

Coop let her words hang. He didn't know what to say or what she wanted him to say.

Katie refocused on the tabletop and tugged at a stray lock of hair that had worked itself loose from her ponytail. She inspected the strands as if looking for split ends. "What's going to happen to us, Coop? When I don't keep occupied and allow my mind to drift, I get so scared."

He started to reach across the table wanting to take her hand. He stopped himself. It would only end up raising his hopes, and he'd get hurt again. "We're better off than just about anyone else I can imagine, especially considering the plans that your father and Mr. Orr have made."

He paused. "By the way, I have just the thing to keep your mind from entertaining sad thoughts."

Katie tilted her head.

"Dominoes."

Her face brightened. "You brought them?"

"Under the buggy seat."

Katie applauded. "I'm gonna show you how the game is played."

"That'll be the day." Coop walked to buggy and checked on Tony. He picked up the box, returned, and emptied the dominoes onto the picnic table.

After an hour, Dr. Hunt and Mrs. Cunningham joined in. She appeared in better spirits than when Coop first arrived but didn't have much to add to their conversations.

As the sun dipped toward the western horizon, everyone's mood became more somber.

Katie turned to her father. "Shouldn't they be back by now?"

Dr. Hunt pressed his lips into a straight line and nodded.

Coop fidgeted knowing that he soon needed to go.

Finally, they heard the rumbling of a motor and blast from a horn. The four of them ran to the road and saw Mr. Orr at the wheel of Carl Miller's old school bus. They waved and shouted as he drifted to a stop in front of them.

He opened the door and flashed a white toothed smile.

"'Bout time, Declan," Dr. Hunt said. "Trouble?"

Orr glanced at the passengers behind him and motioned them forward. "I can debrief you later. In the meantime, I have some worn out pilgrims who haven't slept in a bed for a long time."

First off the bus stepped Wendy and her teen daughter, Sarah. Coop remembered this girl as being a little off, possibly retarded. She clutched a dirty teddy bear to her chest.

Dr. Hunt shook Wendy's hand. "Welcome to Wineberry Hollow. You and your daughter can stay in my house for now. Katie, please show them inside."

Coop watched Katie as she led them into the house.

Next off stepped the dentist. He reintroduced himself as Dr. Blair St. John and his wife, Heather, and his sons Bruce, 13, and Stan, 11.

Sheila pointed to her house across the street. "You're welcome to live in my home. I'll be staying with Dr. Hunt for the time being, so the whole place is yours. Feel free to spread out."

Dr. St. John looked at the ground and wiped his eyes. "We

thought we were all going to die. I'm overwhelmed by your kindness. I don't know what to say."

Sheila rocked on her feet and crossed her arms. "I have adult children out there." She motioned with her eyes toward the front of the hollow. "I pray that someone shows them the same kindness that I show you."

Dr. Hunt cleared his throat and spoke to Dr. St. John. "Actually, there's a method to our madness. Being at the back end of the hollow, we are geographically the most isolated and safest. Since you and I are both physicians, between the two of us we'll be dealing with patients at their most vulnerable."

St. John looked at Dr. Hunt. "You do know that I'm only a dentist."

"I remember," Dr. Hunt said. "Dental health will become increasingly important over the long haul. Besides, you've had some medical training so I expect your assistance to be invaluable to me."

St. John bowed slightly. "Of course. I'll do anything I can to repay your hospitality."

Sheila took Heather's hand. "Come on. I'll show you around."

The family followed her across the street.

Last off the bus stepped Corporal Clark.

"The corporal will be bunking with me and my family for the time being," Orr said. "He and I will be training our militiamen, so it seemed logical that we be together."

"Makes sense to me," Dr. Hunt said. "Where are the others?"

"On the way through the hollow, I dropped Tom Ortiz with Gary Daw who agreed to take him in. We dropped Pete Damroth back at the Millers. By the way, Coop, your mother wants me to tell you that she's expecting you for supper."

"I should go," Coop said. He shot a glance at Dr. Hunt's front door.

Dr. Hunt stroked his chin. "What about that guy and his elderly mother, the Cranes, I believe was their name?"

Orr said nothing. He eyeballed Coop, then looked at Dr. Hunt and just shook his head.

Taking that as a signal that he had overstayed his welcome, Coop said, "Thank you for allowing me to spend the day." He glanced at the door. "Please say goodbye to Katie for me."

Dr. Hunt studied him. "Get your horse hitched. If you're still here by the time Declan and I are done talking, I'll go get her. You can tell her goodbye yourself."

Coop resolved that it would take longer than usual for him to get the job done.

"Hold up," Orr said. "We're already done. I miss my family and I know they're worried sick. How about we catch up on things tomorrow."

"I understand," Dr. Hunt said.

"Come on, corporal," Orr said. The two of them boarded the bus and headed up the dirt lane to Orr's house on the mountain leaving Coop standing alone with Dr. Hunt.

Dr. Hunt regarded Coop and then glanced at the house. "Coop, you're a fine young man. I have a great deal of respect for you, and you're good company for Katie. I sense in her a fondness for you."

Coop grunted. "She thinks I'm from Mars."

"What?"

"Katie sees me as only a friend."

"And do you wish for more than friendship?"

Coop blushed.

"My daughter can sometimes be secretive, and apparently there exists a history between the two of you that I'm not aware of."

Coop stared at the ground and said nothing.

"Look, Coop, our world has just turned upside down. Instead of limitless possibilities, Katie has seen her universe shrink to the size of Wineberry Hollow. Her dreams are destroyed. She's more devastated than she puts on."

Dr. Hunt looked to the sky and sighed. "It hurts me terribly that Katie now faces such an uncertain future. My heart aches for her. Anyway, I'm trying to tell you as her father that right now Katie is vulnerable. I'll not take kindly to anyone who tries to take advantage of her."

Horrified at what Dr. Hunt was thinking and somewhat offended, Coop looked him in the eye and said with conviction, "I would never do anything to hurt Katie."

Dr. Hunt held up a hand toward Coop. "I believe you, son. I know you would never hurt her intentionally. I ask only that you consider something. A few weeks ago, Sheila and I were just friends. You're not blind. You see what's happened. I suppose that may make me appear to be a hypocrite, but there's a big difference between our situation and yours. Sheila and I are older and have a great deal more life experience than you and Katie. Our judgment isn't clouded by the passion of youth."

Coop removed his hat and wiped his brow. "Dr. Hunt, I do not presume to judge the relationship you have with Mrs. Cunningham. I also will not lie to you. My feelings for Katie are more than they should be, but Katie has made it clear that she doesn't feel the same way about me. I just want her to be safe and happy."

"It's apparent to anyone who sees the two of you together that you make each other happy, and don't misunderstand me, I approve of your friendship. All I ask is if she ever experiences a moment of weakness, do the right thing and be strong for her."

Coop considered Dr. Hunt's request. "That's an easy promise for me to make. I will always be strong for Katie's sake, and I'll always be there for her, too." He extended his hand and the two men shook.

"I'll go tear her away from Wendy and Sarah so you can say goodbye."

"Wait," Coop said. "That would be selfish of me. Wendy and Sarah need Katie's attention more than I do at the moment. Let them be. Tell Katie that I look forward to our next dominoes contest."

"Okay, Cooper," Dr. Hunt said as he walked toward the house. "I'll be sure to do that. You say hello to your mother for me."

Chapter 36

Captain Sloat halted his truck in the middle of the lane, killed the motor, and turned off the headlights. He opened the door and cursed at the squeaking hinges. He got out and looked around, opened the buttons of his shirt, and inhaled a deep breath of air. God, it was hot. Summer in Pennsylvania reminded him of the Middle East, the difference being the oppressive humidity in the air here and utter lack of an evening breeze.

Summers in Idaho seemed just right. Hot during the day, but pleasant after the sun went down. Good sleeping weather. He wondered how his parents were doing. Would his father be okay after his cholesterol medicine ran out? Was someone helping them, maybe taking the same risks he now took to help the locals on the wrong side of the fence?

Overcast skies filtered out the stars completing the darkness. Sloat walked a circle in the road and looked around. He saw nothing, not a single point of light. He listened. The only sign of life, the sounds of crickets and a distant tree frog.

He used the beam of a flashlight to find the gate blocking the entrance to the access road and worked the lock with the key entrusted to him by Lieutenant Napoli. She also risked much. What the two of them attempted violated direct orders and could be construed as treason. The lock released and Sloat eased the gate open. He returned to the truck, a cab with an attached 18 foot box, similar to a do-it-yourself moving van. He started the engine and carefully navigated through the gate and onto the rough, unpaved road.

He let the motor run while closing and locking the gate behind him.

Back in the cab, Sloat kept the transmission in first gear and crept along the single lane dirt road leading to Gate W3. To his right loomed a high bank. On his left, a precipitous drop into the Susquehanna River. He hugged the bank. The terrain provided good cover and difficult access to the gate. The access road had been designed for nothing larger than a jeep. In this wide truck, Sloat knew that he pushed his luck. Desperate folks counted on him. Here in Pennsylvania he wouldn't be able to help his family in Idaho, but he would do his best to help other local families.

Sloat knew that he wasn't alone in his insurrection. More than just a few good men disagreed with the manner in which President Kall treated their fellow Americans. They should be opening the enclave gates, sharing resources, not treating the outsiders as pariahs. The military had formed its own underground led by a high ranking officer who went by the moniker of Mandible, his identity a closely guarded secret. Through a covert chain of command using cutouts and dead drops, an organization had been established where participating officers were setup in teams whose members did not know the identities of other teams. That meant if any one team were compromised, the entire organization could not be rolled up to Mandible.

The landmark loomed ahead, an uprooted poplar tree hanging over the road. Captain Sloat drove under the tree and switched off his headlamps. A few seconds passed. In the distance he saw three flashes from a flashlight. A pause. Then three more flashes.

All clear.

Sloat eased the truck forward. Lieutenant Napoli stepped from behind a tree trunk and raised her palm. A cadre of soldiers holding rifles at the ready surrounded the truck. He waited until Napoli approached before rolling down his window.

They exchanged greetings and Napoli ordered her men at ease.

She pointed to a clearing and spoke softly. "That's a boat launch, a gentle slope to the river's edge. You'll need to pull forward and carefully back down the slope. These men will guide you."

Sloat did as Napoli instructed and managed to park the rig with the rear storage compartment door a few feet from the water. He cut the engine and climbed out.

"Give the signal," Lieutenant Napoli ordered a soldier near the river's edge.

Sloat saw the soldier raise a flashlight and point it at the opposite shore. Two flashes followed by two more flashes. From the other side of the river, flashes of acknowledgement.

It took fifteen minutes for the visitors to row across the river, their fleet a mishmash of canoes, bass boats, and one kayak, about two dozen total watercraft.

Lieutenant Napoli greeted the man in the kayak. She introduced the man to Captain Sloat simply as Danny. "Danny and his volunteers collect what they can and distribute to those in need."

"Someday I hope we can meet under more relaxed circumstances," Danny said. "For now, it's safer for the both of us if I just call you captain." He looked at the back of the truck. "What do you have for us?"

Sloat removed the cargo lock and pulled open the doors. A riot of flashlights lit up the interior reflecting off Campbell canned soups and pork and beans.

"The truck is stuffed with eight pallets," Sloat said.

Danny stepped back. "So much. We're grateful, but I don't know how we can handle all of this."

"We'll have to break down the pallets and load individual cases into your boats," Sloat said.

"My volunteers and I might not be able to do this all in one night."

"I need to get this truck back to the motor pool by midnight. We need to get these cases unloaded."

Lieutenant Napoli cut the bands of a pallet with a box cutter. "Let's unload and hide the cases along the shoreline. The captain can return his truck, and you men can make as many trips as needed to ferry these cases across the river. If you don't finish by dawn, we'll camouflage the rest until tomorrow night. Understand that the longer these boxes remain on this side of the river, the greater the risk to me and my team."

"We'll do what we can to finish tonight. Thank you for everything," Danny said. He turned to Sloat. "And thank you, Captain. I know the danger you face and appreciate what you have done. A lot of people are in a bad way. I can't imagine what's going to happen if the situation continues."

"Keep your faith," Sloat told him unable to think of anything else to say. To Napoli, he said, "A word lieutenant?"

He walked out of earshot. Lieutenant Napoli followed.

Sloat spoke in a hushed tone. "How do you know you can trust this man? I mean, how do you know he won't horde this food for himself?"

"My hometown is Lewisburg, just north of here. I don't know Danny personally, but I know people who know Danny. They tell me he's the real deal."

"You're fortunate to be assigned to E38. So close to your home. You get to see your parents, your family?"

"My parents are both dead," Napoli said. She didn't elaborate, but nodded with her head toward the river. "Two sisters live over there. I don't get to see them since I'm restricted to the enclave, but Danny shuttles letters back and forth for me. And yeah, I'm fortunate to have at least that much contact."

"Your men," Sloat said. "You trust them all?"

"Nobody under my command believes the bullshit being fed to us. This is a manufactured crisis. All of us have someone on the outside. We can relate to what must be happening out there, the death, the suffering. Besides, nobody has turned me in yet. I'm not looking to get caught, but if it happens I'll hold my head high for choosing the right side."

"What side is that, lieutenant?"

"The moral one."

They watched the activity of the soldiers and outsiders working together to unload the truck and repackage the food onto the boats. Napoli broke the silence. "What about you? Do you trust all your men?"

"No."

"Let me guess, your second in command, that jerk of a lieutenant. What's his name? Half ass or something like that?"

"Halfjack. Yeah, he's a problem. The man buys into all of this, thrives on it. He's in his element. Flourishes in the chaos that results from a crisis."

"What about the rest of your men?"

"There are a handful of men I can trust. Don't know about the rest yet. After we returned from our recon mission today, I chose a trusted few to retrieve that trailer load of canned food. I drove this extra truck and we loaded up the eight diverted pallets. While we were gone I assigned Halfjack and the rest to help in the dairy to keep them out of the loop."

"I'll bet they hated you for that."

"Actually, the prospects of working in that air conditioned dairy enticed the men better than another jaunt into the field in this heat. Since nobody was able to count all of the pallets on the broken truck, none of Halfjack's ilk should suspect anything missing. Once I return this truck, we'll be in the clear."

The two of them stopped talking and watched the first small row boat push off with as many cases as the pilot dared to load on it. The small boat sat dangerously low in the water.

"I envy you that you can leave the enclave," Napoli said. "What's it like out there, from your point of view? How bad?"

Sloat would've like to share his feelings with the lieutenant, but didn't want to burden her with gory detail. Still, he felt the need to tell someone. "I've witnessed some terrible things," he started. As he recalled the images, Captain Sloat fought to contain his emotions. How they had to drive past masses of humanity, mothers begging for food for their children. They couldn't stop for fear of being swamped by the hordes lining the highway. "Remember in the times before, the story of what happened in New York City during a blackout?"

"I recall stories of riots and burning," Napoli said.

"The mayor of New York at the time labeled it a night of terror. The looting, pillaging, and fires overwhelmed law enforcement. The rioters had their way. The city burned. All that happened in just one night of darkness. What do you think it's like out there after weeks of darkness?"

"Survival of the fittest," Napoli murmured.

"Exactly. You should see Williamsport, or what used to be Williamsport. It's gone now. Uninhabited and uninhabitable."

"Where have all the people gone?"

"Dead," Sloat said, "or they soon will be. Grocery Stores are cleaned out. There's no food within a three day walk from Williamsport. Soon there will be no food anywhere. Smaller towns can last longer, but only if the people don't panic and work together. I fear that eventually they too will succumb.

"Lieutenant Napoli, would you know what to do? I sure as hell wouldn't. Nobody grows their own food anymore except maybe for small gardens. We've forgotten how to survive on our own."

Despite the heat, Captain Sloat saw the lieutenant shiver. "No, sir, I wouldn't have a clue. Will anyone out there make it?"

Sloat recalled the one bright spot of his day. "Isolated pockets of Amish farmers and their friends stand a chance. I met a man today. If he and his neighbors don't get careless, they should do okay."

"The Amish," Lieutenant Napoli said. "What irony. The majority of humanity who consider themselves enlightened, who scorn the simple life, now find themselves at the mercy of people like the Amish. I guess the meek really will inherit the Earth."

"Affirmative," Sloat said. "Blessed be the meek."

Chapter 37

Cooper Stover sat on a straw bale just inside the entrance to his barn and listened to the rain drumming against the roof. The storm had started at dawn as a downpour, but by lunch it had tapered off to a steady gentle rain, the kind that would last the rest of the day. The *Purina Dog Chow* thermometer hanging from Coop's porch post read 70 degrees, and he welcomed the break from the summer heat which for the past several weeks had been relentless.

The murmuring voices behind Coop belonged to men of the Wineberry Hollow militia who had assembled in his barn. While they waited for the meeting to begin these men spoke of sore muscles and lost weight and changing habits since the world went dark. How they went to bed early, because there was nothing to do at night. How bored their kids were without computers, TV, or playing video games. They also spoke about the appreciation they had gained over how hard the Amish worked on their farms.

Coop listened and tried comparing himself to them. He did the same things now as always, working the farm, tending his animals, caring for his mother and little cousin Hattie, and helping his neighbors. The world going dark didn't change his daily life in the same way it had changed for the English, yet he shared with them a sense of anxiety, the fear of an uncertain future. Everyone in Wineberry Hollow enjoyed plenty to eat for now and would continue to do so if everyone carried on with their share of the work. In retrospect, Coop needed the extra hands provided by his neighbors. Since his father's passing, these friends had greatly eased his workload. If God saw fit to continue blessing them with rain at regular intervals, everyone would reap a bountiful harvest.

Coop often thought about the world beyond their valley. He recalled the hostility of men during their road trip, how ready they had been to steal Mr. Orr's vehicle and do them harm. If something such as this could happen in a small rural community, how much worse must it be in the cities? How many had died during the past month? Maybe the real question was how many had lived?

Declan Orr called for the meeting to begin. After everyone settled down, he glanced at Coop and said, "First off, I'd like to thank Cooper for allowing us to use his barn again. It suits us well to meet here when it rains."

These men normally assembled everyday at the Kroh farm located at the entrance of the hollow. Coop understood that they trained and drilled there, but Elam Kroh, being somewhat of a pack rat, stuffed his barn full of old farm equipment leaving no room for an assembly as large as this one, the thirty or so men Coop had counted.

"For the past month, I've tried to pass on to you men specialized knowledge concerning guerilla warfare, military tactics, and establishing lines of defense," Orr said. "We've studied our situation and the geography of the hollow, considered protective tactics, and planned for unexpected contingencies. I can tell you from firsthand experience that during battle nothing ever goes exactly according to design.

"Despite our planning, there are a few other items we need to consider. Being a member of this militia means that every man supplies and maintains his own rifle. Most of you are familiar enough with your own firearms, but the disadvantage this presents is a possible shortage of ammunition. In the army, we all carry the same caliber. Here, if my neighbor carries a .30-.30 deer rifle and he runs low on ammo, I can't help him because I carry a .223 autoloader. Some of you have equipment at home to do your own reloading which is a big help, but over the long haul we will eventually exhaust our supplies."

Orr stopped and looked out over the assembly. "When that happens, we'll be faced with the possibility of defending ourselves with homemade bows, rocks, and hand-to-hand combat."

"I sure hope it doesn't come to that," one of the men mumbled.

Orr flashed the man a sympathetic smile. "I share your sentiments, my point being that we need to preserve our ammo, meaning that we need to limit target practice to just a few shots per week for each of you. That's not optimal, but it's our wisest course of action."

Coop had a deer rifle and shotgun. He wondered if he should share his ammunition with the militia. What if he did so, and it enabled one of these men to kill someone? Would God consider him just as guilty as the man who pulled the trigger? The thought of attackers ransacking his farm saddened Coop and disgusted him. He hoped that day would never come and decided that he had heard enough. He stood and brushed straw from the back of his trousers. On rainy days like this one he usually helped out Sam Wetzel with butchering. They took occasional breaks during which he and Sam's son, Sammy, would practice their archery skills. Unlike bullets, arrows could be re-used and through trial and error, young Sammy had become an accomplished bowyer. He turned to leave.

Mr. Orr called out to him. "Mr. Stover, can I prevail on you to wait a moment? I need to ask you something."

Coop nodded but remained standing by the door. What more did Mr. Orr want of him?

"You may have heard me discuss before how the militia has split into three units, men who work together guarding the entrance to the hollow. Any attack will most likely come from that front since it represents the topographical path of least resistance." Coop remembered Orr speaking these words before. He had heard them on several occasions. It struck him that the men already knew what Orr was saying. The review probably served as a reinforcing reminder, part of their drilling.

"My team will stand guard from dawn until early afternoon. Corporal Clark and his contingent will take over until the sun goes down. Gary Daw and his men have volunteered to stand watch over night.

"The plan we've put in place is this. During the first sign of trouble, one of the men will jump on a horse and ride the length of the valley Paul Revere style alerting the rest of the militia to immediately muster. In theory, that's a solid plan, but we need a backup." Orr glanced in Coop's direction.

What backup? Why did Orr look to him. Coop spoke, "You know my position. I cannot fight. I will not betray my faith."

"I'm not asking you to fight, Cooper, but you and your Amish neighbors could provide a valuable service."

What did the English want from the Amish if not to fight? He waited for Orr to explain.

Orr fixed his gaze on the rain falling beyond the door. "I noticed that just about every Amish farm has a good sized dinner bell. I've heard the one at the Kroh farm. Sure is loud."

The bells had to be loud so workers in distant fields would hear the call to dinner. "That is true. As you know we carry no personal telephones."

"Can you hear the Kroh's farm bell from here?" Orr asked.

"Only when the wind blows the right way."

"How about Mr. Wetzel's bell. Can you hear that one?"

"Yes, clearly."

"And the Wetzels ought to be able to hear Kroh's bell."

Coop supposed that would be the case.

"Our backup plan is to alert everyone in Wineberry Hollow through the ringing of the farm bells. At any time of the day or night if you hear the constant ringing of Mr. Wetzel's bell, I'd like for you to jump on your bell and ring it with everything you got as an alarm to the next farm down the line. By my reckoning, if everyone remains vigilant about listening for the bells, the alarm can be sounded the entire five mile length of the hollow within minutes."

He stopped and looked Coop in the eye. "The question remains if performing this service violates your faith. Could you do this for us? Could you and your Amish neighbors ring their bells if we were being raided?"

What could be morally wrong about sounding an alarm? It would cause nobody direct harm and may possibly save lives. If his people learned to hide upon hearing the bells, would the bell ringers be culpable if upon hearing those same bells, the English chose to fight and possibly kill? "I cannot see how sounding an alarm would violate the tenants of our faith, but I should seek the opinions of the older men of my congregation in this matter."

"If those elders agree with your assessment, can I count on you to approach the farmers and explain what we need? Maybe arrange a test run sometime next week?"

"Yes. I will do this for you."

Mr. Orr thanked Cooper and started a discussion with his men about building a barricade across Cove Road.

Coop bowed out and walked through the rain to the neighboring Wetzel farm. When he arrived, he recognized Katie's old car sitting in the driveway and his heart raced. Was she here? He hadn't seen her for a month, since the day they played dominoes and the refugees arrived.

He knocked on the door to the butcher shop and eased it open. "Mr. Wetzel?" he called. "Sammy?" Nobody answered and after looking around Coop didn't see anyone. He tried the back door of the house.

"Hello, Coop," Sammy said. The young man opened the door and invited him in.

Coop removed his hat and stepped into the kitchen. Dr. Hunt sat at the table sewing a cut to Mr. Wetzel's thumb. Mrs. Wetzel worked over a basin washing dishes and Sammy watched Dr. Hunt with a keen interest.

"I apologize if I am intruding," Coop said.

"Glad you're here," Mr. Wetzel said. "Damned if I sliced open my thumb while cutting up a hog. It's going to slow me up for awhile. You think you and Sammy can finish the butchering for me? Now that it's started, it needs finishing before the meat spoils from the heat."

Since refrigeration no longer existed, Mr. Wetzel butchered at least once a week and an allotment of fresh meat was divvied up among all the families. Each family who owned animals contributed as they could. Occasionally, someone brought in a deer to supplement. "Of course, I will gladly help."

"You need to be more careful. Antibiotics are running low and an infection in a wound like yours could mean big trouble," Dr. Hunt told Mr. Wetzel in a scolding voice.

"I hear you," Mr. Wetzel mumbled.

"That goes for you, too, Coop," Dr. Hunt said. Then he turned to Sammy. "How old are you, son?"

Sammy straightened and said proudly, "Just turned 13. I'm a teenager now."

"You be careful around your father's knives," Dr. Hunt said. "Accidents can happen real quick."

"I worry about his schooling," Mrs. Wetzel said. She had finished the dishes and dried her hands on a terry cloth towel. "What are the children going to do come September?"

Dr. Hunt closed his medical kit. "Funny you should mention that. My daughter and I discussed the possibility of starting up a school for children in the hollow. Nothing advanced, maybe just basic education following the Amish model of sending kids through the 8th grade. Maybe we could integrate our kids with the Amish students, or if that wouldn't suit our Amish neighbors, we could use someone's barn and hold our own school."

Coop considered the possibility of offering his barn for the school. If Katie was going to be a teacher, that meant he would get to see her every day. He almost cheered aloud considering that possibility.

"As it turns out, one of the refugees who lives with us, her name is Wendy, is a teacher. Her daughter, Sarah, is special and Wendy doesn't like leaving her for any length of time. She'd be able to be with Sarah if she agreed to take the teaching job."

This dashed Coop's hopes.

"That would be a wonderful idea," Mrs. Wetzel said. "Our Sammy would attend. He's going to be an 8th grader."

Sammy groaned. "Aw, Mom, do I have to?"

"Yes," Mr. Wetzel said, and from the man's sharp eyed look, Coop knew that settled the matter.

Coop walked outside with Dr. Hunt. They stood on the porch while Dr. Hunt fumbled with an umbrella. "How are things with you and your family?"

Dr. Hunt set his medical kit on the porch and regarded Coop. "We're all fine, Wendy, Sarah, Sheila, and me." He smiled. "But I suppose what you really want to know about is how Katie is doing?"

Coop felt himself turning red and lowered his gaze to the ground.

"Katie's been keeping herself busy. She helps me when folks come to the house needing medical assistance. She also serves as a helper for Dr. St. John, the dentist who moved into Sheila's house with his family. In between, she helps Wendy tend to her daughter. Sarah is 14 and can sometimes be difficult to handle."

Coop swallowed. "Does Katie ever mention me?"

"Not to me," Dr. Hunt said. He must have read disappointment in Coop's face because he followed up that statement with, "but Katie doesn't tell me everything anymore like she did when she was younger. I think it's because with maturity comes sensitivity. She mistakenly believes that it would burden me somehow, sharing her troubled thoughts with me."

How awful, Coop thought. Keeping ones emotions bottled up like that. But wasn't that exactly what he did? Coop wanted to see Katie again, but what new reason could he come up with to stop by?

Dr. Hunt picked up his kit. "Gotta go." He set his kit in the back seat and climbed into the passenger seat. He rolled down the window. "Coop, get in the car with me for a minute."

He raced around in the rain to the passenger door and climbed in. After shutting the door Coop saw Katie's iPod hanging from the dashboard and his thoughts flashed back to the night of their date.

Dr. Hunt cleared his throat. "What I wanted to tell you is a couple of evenings ago, I sat with Katie on our front porch. A beautiful evening, not like with all this rain. We didn't talk much. I sat there watching her while she watched the sunset.

"Having raised Katie, I can sometimes read her thoughts. She mourns the passing of her old life in the times before, as do all of us who are English. I wish I could get you to understand the emotional devastation, especially for someone like Katie who held such lofty goals.

"Son, I honestly don't know if she thinks about you. She's terribly lonely, though. That much I can sense."

Coop pondered that. He knew all about loneliness.

Dr. Hunt went on. "Living back the hollow with all of us old farts and now with an emotionally challenged teen, Katie has nobody her age to pal around with."

Was this an invitation by Dr. Hunt to call on Katie?

"You know, maybe another girl her age."

So much for the invitation.

"Anyway, since you wanted to know, that's how I read Katie." He stared at Cooper, expectantly.

What did Dr. Hunt want him to say? "Would you tell Katie that I asked about her?"

"Of course."

Coop got out of the car his mind swirling with confusion. He waved as Dr. Hunt drove away. Had there been some hidden meaning in Dr. Hunt's words? He wished these English would plainly speak their mind.

Chapter 38

Stan Cox sat atop his old farm tractor creeping in low gear toward the warehouse porch. The crowd parted as he drove through, some of them waving a greeting, some cheering. His heroic actions during last month's ill fated raid by Sheriff Toomey and how in the aftermath Stan organized the Citizen's Committee of Wynot elevated him to hero status among the town's residents.

Heroic actions? Sure, he had taken a risk by sneaking close to the people who had driven in on the bus. He had peppered them with his shotgun and had warned his side when the Army showed up. In reality, Stan understood that Sheriff Toomey had intended on stealing that bus and doing god knows what to the people in it.

During the long walk back to town, Stan had persuaded his men to spin the story to gain support from the people for their new citizen's committee. He appointed himself the committee president and new sheriff and promised to make all his men deputies. By the time they returned, the story quickly spread how the Citizens Committee of Wynot or CCW had bravely defended the town from wanton attackers, pillagers, rapists, and murderers. Four good men had lost their lives, but they had fought bravely and eventually repelled their attackers. A lie, but who would be the wiser?

Stan dismounted from the tractor and walked up the ramp to the warehouse loading dock. From this platform, everyone had a clear view of their leader, and he of them. A good spot for a public address, or in Stan's mind, to hold court. To his left stood Hoss, his bodyguard, big and brutish but dumb as nails, holding a shotgun across his chest. Terry the Dairyman, Toomey's former lieutenant, took a position to Stan's right. Unlike Hoss, Terry demonstrated keen intelligence and had become Stan's chief advisor.

"We love you, son," Stan's mother shouted from the crowd. She waved. Standing beside her, his father beamed with pride. Their son, the leader. Their son, the hero. Such praise for an 18-year-old kid who six weeks ago had been a drug dealer and cop killer. If they only knew. If only the world had not gone to shit, what would they have thought of him then?

"I love you too, Mom. You too, Dad," Stan shouted, knowing the boyish display of affection would earn points with the crowd. Sure enough, everyone he made eye contact with wore a big smile.

Time to begin, to lead his flock. "Hello folks, thank you for taking the time to come to our first general town meeting since the world went dark."

His greeting drew sighs and murmurs from the assembly.

Stan motioned with his hand for calm. "Those words, *The World Went Dark*, are hard for me to say, and I know they're hard for you to hear, but after six weeks we need to face up to the fact that this is our new reality. America as we've known her is no more. Our government is gone. Our cities are dead. Law and order is what we, the people, make of it."

He pointed to a spot just over their heads. "If any organized help existed out there, they would have already come. I'm here to tell you that there is no help. We're on our own now."

Stan paused. He wanted that thought to sink in. He also

discovered how much he was digging this. If his high school speech teacher could see him now. Maybe he hadn't possessed book smarts, but he had plenty of street smarts. He had observed how President Kall operated, learned from him, and gained an understanding of power politics: Scare the people. Give them an enemy to rally against. Then propose a solution and lead the way. After six weeks, his flock despaired. They were hopeless, frightened, and would be open to any suggestion that would restore normalcy to their lives.

"We're on our own," Stan said again for emphasis, "and that's why I organized the CCW. There is no need to be despondent." Such a good word, *despondent*, a big word, made him sound more intelligent. "We will stand together as a community and help each other. Isn't that what decent human beings do?"

He motioned with his head toward a woman standing in the front row holding an infant in her arms. "Mrs. Olson, we all know that your husband was one of the victims of the attackers. He gave his life defending this town. Since that time, the men of the CCW have seen to your every need, right? We've come every time you called for us and kept up with the work around your house, brought you food and medicine when your baby got the colic."

Her husband had been one of the fools who took a shot at the old lady when she had appeared from the underpass. Not much of a hero.

Mrs. Olson said nothing and nodded dumbly. Not the outpouring of gratitude that Stan hoped for. She wasn't much help.

He tried again. Searching the crowd, Stan let his gaze fall on an elderly man. "Mr. Symington, I personally used my tractor to haul in a load of firewood and helped you rank it, didn't I?"

The old man shouted, "That's right and God bless you, son."

That was more like it. A perfect moment, Stan knew, to woo the crowd with some self deprecation. "You know, in the before times, I probably would've complained if you'd asked me to help you, maybe even would've said something like, 'do it yourself, old man.' I was just a kid then. Still am, really, but this tragedy has forced me to grow up too soon. I had big ambitions. I wanted to make a difference in the world, but this calamity has stolen my youth, my joy." He faked a choke, rubbed his eyes, and took a moment as if composing himself. Peering out over the crowd, Stan continued. "Well, that's life. I can't change the world, but I can commit myself to serving the good people of my town."

The line about "serving the good people of the town" was a cue for Terry Dairyman. Just as the two of them had rehearsed, Terry laid a hand on Stan's shoulder and said loud enough for the crowd to hear, "It's okay, Stan. You're not alone in this."

"Thanks, Terry." Stan turned his attention back to the crowd. "All of us who are members of the CCW pledge our lives to this town. We will protect you, because nobody else will. We're young and strong and will come when you call, because it's the decent thing to do. We will make sure that nobody hoards or withholds food and basic necessities from you or tries to take advantage of you."

"What about the food?" Billy called out from the crowd. Stan expected the question because he had planted the man there for that purpose. "I'm down to my last sack of rice, my last can of beans."

Stan pointed behind him to the doors of the warehouse. "Help yourself. The CCW has seized this warehouse and the town supermarket so that all of you can freely take what you need. Some of you may think we are bullies for doing this, but somebody needs to monitor these stores of food to make sure that nobody panics and empties out these places. While people go hungry, we won't abide selfish hording."

Billy shouted out. "Last time I was in that warehouse I found slim pickings. Food isn't going to magically replenish itself. When it runs out, then what happens?"

The people in the crowd began to murmur.

"Settle down folks," Stan said and then he mustered a confident, reassuring tone. "Nobody in our community will go hungry. The CCW promises you that."

"How?" Billy asked. "You gonna call down manna from heaven like Moses did?"

Several people in the crowd snickered. Billy obviously enjoyed his role a bit too much.

Stan pointed down the road. He found it curious how the crowd always looked in the direction he pointed. It made him feel like a magician. "Last week, one of our Amish neighbors a few miles outside of town came to us because his little girl got tangled up in some rusty barbed wire. Many of you probably know who I'm talking about. It was Sam Entrinken. I fetched Dan, the pharmacist, and we went to Sam's farm. Gave his daughter a tetanus shot. Sam may not be a townie, but he is our neighbor. We couldn't withhold life saving medicine from Sam's little girl. That wouldn't have been Christian.

"While I was at his place, something caught my attention. Mrs. Entrinken was canning tomatoes from their garden, a rather large garden I might add. I couldn't help noticing that her pantry was well stocked. Rows and rows of put up vegetables, far more than she needed to feed her family this coming winter. The fields looked healthy and with all of the rain we've been getting it's likely to be an abundant harvest. Also, I counted forty milk cows. What's one family doing with all that milk? There are no more milk pickups."

Billy raised a hand interrupting Stan exactly as planned. "Did they pay you for your kindness in tending their girl? Maybe slip you some food?"

Stan sighed. "They didn't offer and we didn't ask for any." Technically not a lie. Although Stan and Dan the pharmacist didn't carry away any food, the Entrinkens had fed them a grand dinner.

"That's gratitude for ya," a woman from the crowd shouted.

"Listen, folks," Stan said, getting the crowd to refocus on him. "Now we're getting to the real reason why the CCW has called this meeting. Billy is correct when he says that we'll soon be out of food. As a community, we need to make a tough decision. Our Amish and non-Amish farm neighbors who live beyond the limits of our town produce more than enough food to meet both their needs and ours. Obviously, we're going to need them to donate a fair share. Those of us in the CCW are asking for your support and blessing on a mission to meet with these neighbors."

"You mean beg for handouts?" Leroy asked. Leroy was another of Stan's men planted in the crowd.

"I'm sure they'll help us after we explain our situation."

"Son, you're young and naïve," Leroy said. "Those people will gladly sell us what we need until they own everything we've worked our entire lives for, including the shirts off our backs. Especially that Sam Entrinken. He's so tight his ass squeaks."

Stan allowed the crowd to murmur over Leroy's comment.

Many were becoming visibly upset. Stan fought hard not to smile. His plan was working. His Social Studies teacher once referred to this political strategy as triangulation. Pit two groups against each other, but stay above the fray. Agitate while appearing righteous.

"Frigin' Amish," one of the older women in the crowd shouted.

Now that the crowd was suitably stirred up, Stan knew exactly how to ply them further. "Let's not get carried away. We're asking you for authorization to meet and talk, appeal to their better nature. We can't just demand that they give us their food, can we?"

"You think they give a damn about us?" Billy asked. "Like you said, Sam Entrinken has more milk than he needs. He probably dumps the excess on the ground when he could be donating it for the benefit of our kids."

"That's sinful," one of the town ladies shouted.

Stan held his hands out in front of him, palms up, as if surrendering. "Certainly you're not suggesting that those of us in the CCW raid the farms and just take what we need?" He glanced at Terry Dairyman who had remained at his side.

Terry picked up on Stan's cue and stepped forward. "Folks, there's no call for the outlying farmers to be selfish. As you know I own the dairy down the street. You can see my cows from here. You might also know that for the past few weeks I've been donating every drop of the milk that my cows produce, because I don't have anybody to sell it to anymore. In return, many of you have been kind enough to provide me with feed, supplies, and other necessities in exchange for milk. That's the way things should work in this new reality. Neighbor helping neighbor. The CCW is also protecting me and my family and property from marauders. That's an adequate arrangement as far as I'm concerned. Now, I do what I can, but my cows can't produce enough for this entire town. We need other like-minded individuals. In return we should offer them protection by annexing their farms into our community."

"But we don't have enough manpower to protect outlying areas," Stan said. It wasn't an objection, but rather a statement to prime the crowd into agreeing with what he knew Terry was going to say next.

"We will if the CCW can enlist more volunteers," Terry responded. "I'm sure that civic minded, healthy men will step forward to join our ranks."

A calculated move. Stan wanted more men for his army, but he needed to find a way to make the people think it was *their* idea. He didn't want it to appear that he was power hungry. Besides, with little to do and having idle time on their hands, joining the CCW would provide restless men with a release. Raiding farms also held out the possibility for personal gain. Stan addressed the crowd. "Is this true? Are any of you men interested in volunteering?"

He felt a trickle of perspiration run down the side of his face when nobody stepped forward right away. People in the crowd glanced at one another until a wiry guy wearing a dirty white tee shirt elbowed his way to the front. He spit on the ground, looked up at Stan, and said in a low quiet voice, "Count me in."

Now that this first person had agreed, a flood of men stepped forward, all of them pledging their support.

"You men do understand that what we propose may be met with resistance," Terry said.

"What'ya mean?" the wiry guy asked. "Amish don't fight. It'll be easy pickings."

"What's your name?" Stan asked.

"Rog."

"Well, Rog, not all of the farms are run by Amish, and they may have already formed alliances with non-Amish neighbors."

Rog looked around. "There's a lot of us. We can take 'em."

It's what Stan wanted to hear. This man, at least, was willing to fight. He suspected that the others would also harden once hunger tugged their gut.

From his spot in the middle of the crowd, Leroy raised his hand. Stan glanced his way. "You have a question, Leroy?"

"Yeah, how do we know how much to take from those farmers?"

Could he sell this next part of the plan to the townsfolk? Would they back him? In the before times, they would've been repulsed by his suggestion. Funny how people changed when distressed. Stan decided to give it his best shot and go all in. "Confiscation is an ugly business, something that I'm struggling with right now with my conscience. On the other hand, I can't stand by and watch the people of this town starve. Through no fault of our own we find ourselves in desperate times which call for extreme measures."

He nodded at Leroy. "Sir, you have a valid question. When we call on our neighbors, what if an unscrupulous few of them hold back and horde more than they need while we suffer. How will we know?"

The din from the crowd grew loud enough that Stan became concerned that they could no longer hear him. He shouted, "There is only one solution."

They quieted and turned their attention back to him. Stan waved his index finger in the air. "One solution." After a brief pause while he wrinkled his brow to give the appearance that he pondered the subject with great difficulty, Stan went on. "The only way this is going to work, the only way to insure that every farmer donates his fair share is to confiscate absolutely everything they produce."

Stan saw several jaws drop, but before anyone could protest, he raised his voice, "Please hear my reasoning." He lowered his tone and continued. "In order to insure that farmers get the same allotment of food and milk as the rest of us, we need to gather it *all* together in one centrally managed and guarded facility." He pointed a thumb over his shoulder at the warehouse. "This facility should serve that purpose very well.

"Every day, all of the families living in our community including the annexed farms can travel here to receive their appropriate ration. Now, some of you may object that this sounds a lot like Communism. I, too, find the situation repugnant, but as I said before, we live in desperate times. We didn't cause the world to go dark, but we need to adjust to a new reality. That reality includes our neighbors who own farms. We're all in this together. The producers have no right to hold out on us or lord over us what they possess."

He took a breath. "Does anybody object?"

During the next few minutes, the crowd debated, but the momentum swung his way. The people were terrified, and he had offered them an easy way out. When the timing felt right, Stan spoke up, "Folks, do we have your support? Will you authorize the CCW to act on your behalf? Let me see a show of hands."

An overwhelming majority approved.

"All right then," Stan said and sighed. "This is going to be unpleasant and something that I don't want to do, but I've already committed to serving you. As your sheriff, I promise that I'll do my best to honor your decision."

"Use any means necessary," Larry shouted from the crowd. "You and your men have our backing."

The meeting adjourned and the people dispersed. To Stan, it seemed as if they held their heads higher now than when they first arrived, as if they had found new confidence. As long as he provided for them, Stan knew, he would maintain his power.

"You have your army, sheriff," Terry Dairyman said, "and a mandate."

Sheriff? Stan considered a different, more fitting title:

Warlord.

Chapter 39

Declan Orr knew that respect could either be forced through tyranny or earned through competent, consistent leadership. While fighting the Islamofascists in the Middle East, he had witnessed the impact of both ways. Using a heavy hand on villagers who aided the enemy gained their outward compliance, but it also reinforced what they had been taught about American brutality, made them believe in America as being the Great Satan, strengthened their resolve and ultimately made them more eager to resist. At best, tyranny represented only a short term solution.

The military eventually changed strategy and adopted a longer view. They facilitated local leaders in the rebuilding of schools and hospitals, assisted them to reconstitute their own police forces, encouraged merchants to reopen their businesses. In essence, this strategy involved helping the beleaguered people rediscover their lost self-esteem. During that process, those newly empowered citizens began to cooperate. They still resented American troop presence, but their general attitude shifted from open hostility to a reluctant tolerance.

Orr adopted this latter view when dealing with the men under his command. He always led by example, never asked anyone to do anything they hadn't seen him do first. He often put himself on the line for his men, and they responded by unquestionably following his orders.

He also used the "respect earned" approach with his neighbors in the Wineberry Hollow militia, training them how to defend their families, instilling confidence. He made it a point to rotate among the three shifts of watchmen, serve alongside them, give them the benefit of his experience. Orr understood that these citizen warriors weren't ever going to be as disciplined as professional soldiers, but to their credit, they grasped the potential threat and took his leadership seriously as well as their duties.

Orr stood at the edge of Elam Kroh's pasture, turned his face toward the sky, and closed his eyes, let the setting sun warm his face until beads of perspiration surfaced on his brow. He lowered his face and regarded Jamal, shirtless and sprawled out on the grass in the shadow of the Ford Mustang.

What was happening with his son? He had tried damned hard to become a father to the boy, even gave up his military career to spend more time with the family, moved them to the relative safety of the rural countryside. Leadership by example wasn't earning Jamal's respect. If anything, it made him haughtier. Should he change tactics and treat the boy more harshly? Instill a little fear? Orr knew how to be a soldier, but he wasn't nearly as effective as a parent. Nothing seemed to work. Grasping at straws, he decided to bring Jamal along during today's exercise, make a helper out of him, observing how his son would take to the job.

It had been a disaster. During today's training exercises, he had asked Jamal to fetch water for the men, carry their gear, interact with them, hoping he would learn by observation how decent people behaved and got along with one another. Jamal resisted every request Orr made of him, whined, complained, refused to even take an interest in the military maneuvers going on around him. By mid-afternoon, Orr had given up. Let his lazy slug of a son doze in the shade.

This situation needed to be dealt with.

Orr walked over to Jamal and tapped the boy's foot with the point of his boot.

Jamal opened one eye. "What?"

Orr said nothing. He just glared down at his son.

Jamal closed his eye and rolled over on his side, facing away.

"You slept enough for one day." Orr slipped a key into the latch and opened the trunk, pulled out a cooler they used to carry water and set it on the ground beside Jamal. "Get up and gather the empty canteens from the picnic tables. Use Mr. Kroh's well pump and fill them. Stash the full canteens into this cooler."

Jamal mumbled something that Orr couldn't hear.

"What you say?"

He remained on the grass, but twisted his head to face his father. "I said do it yourself."

The militia had drilled hard that day on their mock exercises. Orr was hot and tired and fed up. Reaching down, he grabbed Jamal under his arms. In one smooth motion he hauled his son to his feet, pressed the boy against the side of the car, and stood nose to nose with him. In his fiercest, no nonsense drill instructor voice, he said, "I told you to do something, and by god, one way or another you're going to do it."

Jamal stared back in wide eyed shock and fear, but that moment was short lived. He stuck out his chin in defiance. "Yeah, whatever."

Orr released him and took a step back. Jamal moseyed to the cooler and gripped it by one handle, dragging it in the grass as he walked to the picnic area.

The cranking of the bus engine drew Orr's attention. One of his men had started it up. He walked a few steps toward the bus to get a better view of what was going on and saw a horse drawn buggy coming down the township road toward the intersection with Cove Road. The men guarding the intersection waved to the buggy and the driver backed up the bus enough for the buggy to pass.

Since the rescue of the refugees, the militia had repurposed the bus as a barricade to the entrance of the hollow. As a rule, the militia didn't approve of anyone coming or going. The residents of Wineberry Hollow had voted and adopted a policy of isolation for the sake of security. Every resource available from the outside world could be found within the hollow and most people remained content to stay put. Whether it be food, fuel, clothing, or medicine, if it didn't exist in the hollow, it likely wouldn't exist out there.

Although Orr didn't like it and considered it foolhardy, some allowances had to be made for friends and family living on the outside. He recognized the buggy and roan colored horse. Young Stephen Kroh courted a girl, Rebekah Hagen, from an outlying farm. Almost every evening after his chores were done, he'd either visit her family, or like this afternoon, fetch her back to have supper with his family. Not a good situation as he would have to leave the hollow again to take the girl home.

Orr heard a loud thump and turned. Jamal had dropped the cooler into the Mustang's rear compartment and slammed shut the trunk lid. The boy stood, staring, arms crossed. Orr tried to relax and calm himself. "Son, work with me here. What's it going to take to make you happy? You need to open up, because I'm out of ideas."

Jamal slouched against the car. Stephen and Rebekah passed by in their buggy and waved, horse hooves clopping against the macadam. A few moments passed and the horse left the road and headed for the barn.

"Huh," Jamal uttered. He pointed to his chest. "What I want? I'll tell you what I want. I want my life back. I want to go back to our house at Fort Benning, to my friends. And I had girlfriends there, too." He waved an arm around. "This place sucks."

"Oh, so that's it. You're looking for a girlfriend."

Jamal stomped a foot. "I am not looking for a girlfriend, at least not from the stable of booty they keep around here."

Orr shot a glance at Stephen helping Rebekah down from the buggy. "Plenty of girls around here. Look at that Rebekah. She's pretty. Dr. Hunt's daughter is pretty, too, except she's older…"

"…Yo, have you got your head up your ass? Has the fact that they're white escaped your notice?"

Resisting the urge to backhand his son across the face, Orr said, "It's not the color of your skin that'll make girls around here turn up their noses at you. It's your attitude."

"You don't know nothing about it," Jamal shouted.

"Let me tell you what I *do* know. Let me give you a wakeup call. All of your old friends from Fort Benning are likely dead. Our old house is likely burned to the ground. That old way of life is over. Welcome to your new life, Jamal, your new reality. Get used to it, because it's all you're going to have for a long, long time. These decent people have accepted us as their own. I haven't found any racist bullshit here, and I suggest you harness any lingering resentment. Just put it behind you. There's no room for that crap anymore."

His words deflated Jamal. The boy hung his head.

"Get in the car," Orr said. He slid into the driver's seat and

Jamal joined him after a few seconds. He drove onto Cove Road and pointed the car toward home.

Jamal gripped the dashboard. "If this is all there is, then I want to fight."

Confused, Orr said, "You've been fighting me ever since we moved here. What are you talking about?"

"I want to fight," Jamal repeated. "I want to join your militia. Give me a gun so I can kill something."

"If it comes to fighting, son, I need you to hole up with your mother and Nate and Keisha. You can protect them."

"Why can't I fight alongside you?"

Orr shot a glance at his son. The boy looked serious. "You're only 15."

"So what's the difference? If I'm old enough to pull the trigger while protecting Mom at home, then I'm old enough to join the militia."

"There *is* a difference," Orr said.

Jamal leaned against the passenger door. "Why did you ask me what would make me happy if you're not going to listen to what I have to say?"

"I listened, son. Just can't make it happen for you."

"Why not?"

"I already answered that question. My decision stands. End of discussion."

They drove past Wetzel's butcher shop. Cooper Stover and Sammy Wetzel stood in the driveway, talking. Orr waved.

Jamal pounded the dashboard and shouted, "Goddamn it."

Orr decided he'd tolerate the outburst. He had opened a dialog with Jamal, opened the door just a crack, and that was a start. "You're alive, son. Life may be hard and it may be unfair, but it's better than the alternative."

* * *

Coop felt the whoosh of air against his face as Mr. Orr drove by.

"Did he just curse at us?" Sammy asked.

"I heard what Jamal said, but I doubt it was directed at us. We didn't do anything."

"That kid is whacked. I don't think we'd have to do anything for him to curse at us."

Coop walked toward the house. "Forget about it. Let's see what you got."

Sammy beamed. "Good enough to outshoot you, I'll bet."

"We Amish don't bet." Coop reached into his pocket, and pulled out a piece of hard candy. "But if you score higher than me, I'll give you this root beer barrel. We only have a few pieces left at the house and they probably won't make 'em anymore. Ever." Coop planned on giving it to him anyway, win or lose.

Sammy cheered. "All right."

They walked into the backyard. Sammy pointed to a paper bag about 15 paces away with a crude target drawn on it and resting against a dirt pile backstop. He retrieved his bow from the back porch and a quiver of arrows. Handed the bow to Coop. "You go first."

Coop inspected the workmanship. "Nice job, Sammy. Your tillering skills certainly have improved. This is your best one yet."

"My shooting's improved, too. You'll see."

Coop tugged at the bow string. "I don't doubt it."

"Sixty pound draw more or less," Sammy said. "I'm getting stronger."

"Do tell."

"Check out these arrows," Sammy handed Coop the quiver. "Poplar, just like you suggested. Used chicken feathers for the fletching. Of course, I have no points but I sharpened the ends good with a knife seein' as how the electric pencil sharpener don't work anymore."

"Doesn't work."

"Huh?"

"You said the pencil sharpener *don't* work. Proper grammar is *doesn't* work. Dr. Hunt tells me they may start up a Wineberry Hollow school in the fall. Make sure you attend."

The ends of Sammy's lips turned down. "I guess school isn't important anymore."

"School will always be important." Coop nocked an arrow and tentatively pulled back on the bow string. Sammy had become an accomplished craftsman, but the first time Coop tried any bow, he always had it in the back of his mind that it might snap.

This one didn't. Coop sighted along the shaft and let the string slip from his fingers. The arrow punched a hole through the paper bag about six inches to the left of the bull's eye.

"You're gonna have to do a lot better than that," Sammy told him.

Coop feigned annoyance and nocked another arrow. This shaft was slightly thicker than the first one. It was hard to maintain consistency when making your own arrows. His second shot punched through about an inch left of the first shot.

"You're getting worse instead of better," Sammy said.

Coop ran a hand through his hair. "I'll just have to make this last shot count." He pulled back on the string and thought how the first shots went left. He would compensate this time and shoot to the right. He aimed along the shaft, made a slight adjustment and let go. The shot penetrated wide right.

"I give up," Coop said and handed the bow to Sammy. "Your turn."

The youngster stuck a finger in his mouth and held it up to the wind.

"Quit stalling and show me what you have."

"I'm not stalling. Just practicing my showmanship."

Coop groaned.

Sammy's face suddenly turned serious. He nocked his arrow, stood perfectly erect and sideways to the target.

Good form, Coop thought.

Sammy released the bow string. The arrow whooshed through the air into the paper. Bull's eye. Sammy held out a hand, palm flat.

"Okay, okay," Coop fished the root beer barrel from his pocket and handed it over.

"Told you I was getting good."

"I'm impressed," Coop said. "Can you do that consistently?"

"Watch me." Sammy nocked another arrow. This one stuck less than an inch below the first. His third arrow a little to the left of the first two. A tight group considering the primitive equipment.

"Bravo," Coop said and applauded.

Sammy bowed. "Want to go another round?"

"Nope. Hattie will be cross with me if I give away all the root beer barrels." He glanced at the setting sun. "Besides, break time is over. Got to get back and put the chickens to roost."

Sammy walked with Coop around front to the end of the

driveway. Coop stopped. "You're good enough to shoot deer with that bow. That's a useful skill. Someday we'll run out of bullets."

"Yeah," Sammy said. He looked down the road. "The militia should learn how to use bows."

"They'll probably have to someday."

"I'm going to join up as soon as I'm old enough," Sammy said.

Coop chuckled. "You're only 13. Don't be in such a hurry to grow up."

Sammy's brow wrinkled, his face turning serious. "Coop, does it ever bother you knowing that you aren't supposed to fight?"

He thought back to that night at the skating rink. "Sometimes."

"I'd shoot an arrow through someone in a heartbeat if I had to. I mean if they were hurting my mom or something like that."

Coop ruffled the boy's hair. "That would be terrible, Sammy."

He expected Sammy to say something like, "I hope it never comes to that." Instead, the youngster stared down the road in the direction of Kroh's farm where the militia men trained and guarded the entrance to the hollow.

"I could do it," Sammy uttered. "If I ever had to."

Chapter 40

Dark clouds gathered on the western horizon. Rain would come this evening. Win Halbert studied the sky. A perfect afternoon for an outdoor staff meeting. The breeze ahead of the approaching storm cut through the August heat and humidity leaving the air shirt sleeve comfortable and smelling of cedar. The promise of rain guaranteed a short meeting. Halbert didn't relish being around Kall and his minions, so a short meeting suited him just fine.

He left the Raven Rock underground command center a half hour before the start of the meeting and strolled around the recreation area just outside the entrance to the Northwest Portal. A crowd of soldiers played a game of touch football, their wives and kids sitting on blankets, enjoying a picnic dinner, cheering. Two teens jogged by commenting on an upcoming dance at the enclave's rec hall. As Halbert walked on, he watched a group of young girls enjoying a game of hop scotch. Two older men, probably fathers of soldiers, lamented that the Raven Rock facility had no golf course.

Surely these people could not be oblivious to the fact that a few miles away, beyond the confines of the enclave, people were starving. To them, life went on as if they were in ignorant bliss. What defect in the human psyche allowed people to ignore the suffering of others? Did this explain why Nero fiddled while Rome burned? Why Germans turned a blind eye while their Jewish countrymen vanished in the middle of the night? Why Bosnian Serbs so violently turned on their Muslim neighbors in the late 20th century?

Of course, the people he walked among had to be fully aware of Kall's atrocities, just like he was. And just like him, they were too frightened to do anything about it. Or maybe they were just biding their time.

After the first few weeks, Kall had taken Halbert to task for improper planning. As Minister of Logistics, he was accused of not laying up enough stores. In time, he had been vindicated by Kall's spies. Personnel from every enclave had been caught passing food to non-essentials. The practice had been condemned and those responsible punished. Despite the crackdown, enclaves continued to hemorrhage food and medicine. Everyone had friends or family on the outside. Thus the reason for today's staff meeting. They would brainstorm on how to stop the illegal redistribution of goods. Halbert clearly saw what Kall and his team of monsters feared to admit. They wouldn't be able to stop it. Real Americans wouldn't stop. Earthburst would fail, was already in the process of failing.

Yet he played along with them having already cast his lot. As the prophet Isaiah admonished, he would eat and drink. Tomorrow he would die.

Halbert strolled to the meeting tent, an olive colored canvas big top with open sides. The contingent of armed guards searched him and let him pass. Once inside, he helped himself to a bottle of water. Why didn't Kall serve anything stronger at these meetings? An oversized picnic table served as their conference table. Halbert took his seat on a webbed folding chair and waited.

His colleagues soon joined him. Kall and Nika arrived precisely at 5. "Afternoon," Kall said and held a chair for his wife. He took a seat beside her and lit a cigarette. "One of the reasons I wanted this meeting outside was so I could enjoy my one true vice. Nika doesn't like me smoking underground."

"I don't like you smoking at all," she said.

He puffed and held the cig at his side. "I've called you together to discuss the fraternization of enclavists with the non-essentials. Incidental contact by our military is to be expected during reconnaissance, but other personnel confined within the compounds have no business comingling with the outsiders. Too many become sympathetic and corrupt, stealing and then redistributing our supplies."

Kall took another drag. "Today it stops."

General Munjak spoke. "I still say we need to mine a buffer zone around the fences."

Minister Stroehman butted in. "The contraband flows right through the gates. This isn't a scenario where fences are being breached."

"I agree," Halbert said. He might as well offer an opinion, show the others he was a part of their team. "Planting land mines around the perimeter would be ineffective. This activity is facilitated by our enclavists. Not the non-essentials."

"Until now, we haven't been serious enough about solving the problem," Munjak said. "The problem can easily be solved by shooting people. Make it a capital offense. Any enclavists caught in the act should be summarily executed. Any non-essentials seen within range of our facilities should be dispatched by snipers."

Kall sat back and blew a smoke ring. "You think we have enough hard core element at each facility to carry out those orders?"

Health Minister Lisa Roykirk shook her head. "It would be a gamble. Shooting at our own people would cause a great deal of psychological stress to our soldiers, not to mention the morale problem it would cause when the enclavists found out. Something like that we wouldn't be able to keep under wraps."

"During a previous meeting, Dr. Carano introduced a workable solution," Nika Cho said.

Roykirk rolled her eyes. "Yeah, he wanted to introduce a plague."

"He had another idea, a brilliant one. My husband and I discussed it with him in great detail and agree with its viability." Cho looked at the Genetics Minister. "Tell them about it, Dr.

Carano."

In what Halbert figured to be a conciliatory gesture, Carano laid a hand on the table and leaned in toward Roykirk. "Lisa, I hope you know all that talk about Ug99 and unleashing a plague was just brainstorming on my part. Of course, I understand the risks of doing something rash as that. I'm no fool."

Roykirk raised an eyebrow but said nothing.

Carano began, "What I concluded at the end of that meeting was that we could accomplish the same results by making the enclavists *think* that a contagion exists. What I have in mind is doable."

He took a breath and looked around the table. "Have any of you heard of Creutzfeldt–Jakob Disease?"

Halbert searched his brain. "Isn't that related somehow to mad cow?"

"Quite right. CJD is the human variant of bovine spongiform encephalopathy more commonly referred to in the vernacular as mad cow disease." Carano stared into the space behind Halbert. "Do you remember news footage of cattle in Great Britain that were afflicted in the latter part of the 20th century?"

"Those poor animals," Lisa Roykirk muttered. "I remember them convulsing, falling to the ground, bleating."

Carano raised his index finger. "It manifests similarly in humans, the ataxia and myoclonus."

"Want to put that in English, Dr. Carano?" Kall asked.

"Loss of coordination, twitching, and trembling are typical of early stages," Carano explained. "The prion proteins responsible for the symptoms kill off healthy brain cells and eat holes in brain tissue. Under a microscope, diseased tissue resembles a sponge, thus the term spongiform. As the disease progresses the victim suffers memory loss, personality changes, seizures, psychosis, and inevitably death. There is no known cure."

"A hell of a way to die," General Munjak observed.

"Indeed." Carano stopped and looked at them as if they all knew how that mattered.

Minister Stroehman asked, "Are you suggesting that we somehow scare the enclavists by circulating rumors about the existence of CJD among the non-essentials?"

"No, not rumors. We make it real. We showcase this disease in all its brutal glory for all the enclavists to see. A few months from now, our people will have nothing to do with the outsiders. More than likely they will shoot non-essentials on sight."

That seemed a stretch to Halbert. "I suppose you already have a plan?"

Dr. Carano's eyes twinkled. Halbert nearly gagged with the realization that the sick SOB would enjoy unleashing such misery into the world.

Carano said, "If you'll remember from the mad cow scare, nearly the entire bovine population in the British Isles was slaughtered for fear of the disease jumping the trans species barrier. Popular thought held that humans drinking milk, eating cheese, or ingesting meat from tainted cattle could be susceptible to the disease. Although this has never been conclusively proven, it has never been disproven either. Due to the nature of the affliction, the authorities agreed to err on the side of caution."

"Wisely so," Roykirk agreed.

Carano continued. "Spongiform encephalopathy also exists in other species. As we already know, in cattle it's mad cow disease. In sheep and goats, it's known as scrapie. In deer and elk, it's known as chronic wasting disease or CWD."

He shifted in his seat and leaned on the table. "Consider a scenario where starving non-essentials kill and consume a deer infected with CWD. If those people later developed Creutzfeldt–Jakob, one would assume that the disease was transmitted from that deer."

Having been uncharacteristically quiet, Kall now chimed in. "Would all of you agree that such a conclusion would appear logical?"

Like the rest of the people assembled around the table, Halbert answered with a nervous nod.

Carano licked his lips and continued. "What if the condition appeared to become pandemic?"

"Wait a minute," Roykirk interrupted. "I'm no expert on this subject, but I seem to recall that CJD is not contagious."

Carano shrugged. "You know how fickle diseases can be, always mutating and evolving. It should be easy enough to advance the concept of a new strain."

General Munjak raised a hand. "All I'm hearing are a lot of

theories and what ifs. As a military man I'm only interested in the execution. How are you going to conjure a diseased deer? Then how are you going to feed that deer to your target and cause them to contract CJD? Then how do you make the disease jump from person to person while keeping it under control? From arresting its spread within the enclaves?"

Dr. Carano frowned. "Let me finish and I'll answer that for you."

"Go ahead," Kall said, "tell us."

Carano cleared his throat. "Minister Roykirk is correct. The disease is not communicable. However, we do know that it can be transmitted by contaminated human growth hormone harvested from the pituitary glands of cadavers who died of CJD. You may recall that injectable HGH had been widely advertised as a panacea for aging. Because of the risks of contracting CJD, the FDA banned that therapy.

"In the before times, I had the privilege of working at the CDC. They had numerous CJD infected cadavers used for study. President Kall assures me that the CDC remains intact..."

"...The facility relocated to Enclave 9 in the Carolina foothills," Kall interrupted.

"So we have access to contaminated HGH," Carano said. "Enough to infect thousands."

"Won't work," General Munjak grumbled. "If we round up non-essentials and stick them with needles, they're going to remember that. They'll know how they got sick."

Not only did Dr. Carano's eyes gleam, but the grin he wore caused Halbert to wince. He guessed that what came next would lead to something monstrous.

Carano tapped the tabletop with his finger. "The plan is to fan out and visit all of the enclaves. Spread propaganda about the new highly virulent contagion and then inoculate all enclavists. Everyone will be required to submit to an injection with something harmless like Ringer's solution. Randomly mixed in among the vials, however, we will place a few contaminated doses. When those random enclavists become symptomatic, we'll blame it on contact with the outsiders, the poor enclavists apparently already having contracted the disease prior to the inoculation."

Monstrous didn't begin to describe their scheme. Halbert

squeezed the bridge of his nose in an attempt to quell a waxing headache.

"A regrettable, but necessary sacrifice," Kall said.

"I concur that it should eliminate the comingling," General Munjak said.

"Excellent," Kall said. "Let's make it happen."

While the rest of them fine tuned the plan, Halbert daydreamed. If humankind were to survive these times, what would they write in their history books? How would history describe one man's rise to such power that he was able to perpetrate such an atrocity?

The meeting concluded. Rain drops started tapping against the tent. All of them stood ready to leave, to retreat back into the tunnel complex.

"Could you wait a second?" Kall asked Halbert. "I need you for something."

"Sure," Halbert answered knowing he had no choice. He hoped he wouldn't have to endure a dressing down over some perceived infraction. Being subject to mood swings, one never knew what to expect with Kall.

After everyone departed, Kall said, "I've been thinking about your request for a transfer away from Raven Rock."

"As you know, my wife wants to relocate to Vermont. I'd like to join her." A lie. Halbert had little desire to spend more time with his wife, but putting up with her would be a damn site better than staying at Raven Rock under Kall's thumb.

"All right," Kall said. "Do me a favor and I'll do you a favor."

He had already sold his soul. What more could Kall want from him?

"Although I never met Lenore, I understand she was a beautiful lady. Too bad she didn't come with you. I'm sure you miss her terribly."

Why would Kall bring this up now? "I'm afraid I don't follow…"

Kall chuckled and patted Halbert on the back. "I like you, Win, and am glad you joined my team, glad you were willing to put our political differences behind us. That way of life is long gone. Water under the bridge." He sat on a corner of the picnic table. "I can't give Lenore back to you, but there will be other opportunities. I've made you a powerful man. And I also realize that you feel a certain obligation toward your wife. You want to take care of her."

He pulled a pack of cigarettes from his shirt pocket and lit up. "But you don't really want to move to Vermont, do you?"

Was he that readable? Halbert sighed. "No."

Kall took a drag from his cigarette. "What I have in mind is to send you someplace else. Someplace with more…opportunity."

Halbert waited for the details. The devil, as he knew, was always in the details.

"I want to send you to Enclave 38 in Central Pennsylvania. By taking up residence there you will become my ambassador. More importantly, my eyes and ears."

"I don't understand, sir, does a problem exist with the current administrator at E38?"

"No, no," Kall said after taking a drag. He blew smoke. "I just need to correct a miscalculation on my part."

What? The great Lord Kall was admitting to a mistake?

"I placed top ranking military men in charge of the enclaves but realize now that they require civilian oversight. For instance, in these meetings you hear the things that General Munjak says. He tends to be rash. I've observed that all brilliant military minds tend to be reactionary in situations where discretion is required. Win, I know you have it in you. You're one of the most discreet men I've ever known."

"Me? What makes you think that?"

Kall stared at him with unflinching eyes. "Lenore."

Unable to hold Kall's gaze, Halbert looked away.

"Here's the deal, Win. Comingling with non-essentials didn't originate with the enclavist civilians. It had to originate with the military. After all, they're the ones with the means and they control the assets. I have intel that an officer located at E38 who goes by the code name, Mandible, is responsible for the distribution of our resources there. What I don't know is whether the command structure at all others enclaves encourages the activity. As a result, I'm placing a trusted civilian advisor in each of the enclaves. You're part of my inner circle, so I'll need to keep you geographically close. E38 is less than an hour away by chopper. I'll expect you to return from time-to-time and continue to attend strategy meetings and implement my agenda.

"I'm granting you complete autonomy over E38, Win, full control. Do you want the job?"

Hell yes, he wanted the job. Lord Kall was offering him a fiefdom. He'd be out from under Kall's direct watchful eye. And with Sally in Vermont, he'd be far removed from her watchful eye, too. "Just to be clear. Assuming that illegal activity exists and that it's being perpetrated by our military, you want me to ferret it out?"

Kall stubbed what remained of his cigarette against the edge of the picnic table. "Ferret it out and report it to me."

The two men shook hands and walked into the rain. Kall's goons escorted them, holding umbrellas over their heads. Halbert's mood swung from joy to fear. Joy over what he had been offered. Fear in the knowledge that Kall could no longer trust his military.

How much time did they have until the Earthburst project completely crumbled?

Chapter 41

Coop pulled a plain white handkerchief from his waistband and wiped his brow. The worst of the summer heat and humidity had finally departed. The late September air carried the earthy odor of forest duff and chilly nights had already painted foliage near the top ridges of Clymer Mountain yellow. In a few weeks, the entire valley would explode into a riot of color.

The screen door to the house banged. Coop's mother approached carrying a glass of water and handed it to him.

"Thank you." He downed the drink and handed the glass back to her. "I always feel better after the harvest is in."

She glanced at the ground, her expression somber. "Your father used to tell me the same thing."

Coop hugged her. "I miss him, too." He wasn't sure he meant it, but the words comforted his mother. Since the world went dark, his English neighbors provided abundant help and Coop was grateful for their assistance. But he had been the person in charge, telling the English what needed to be done. By contrast, last year, he had done most of the work himself and his father had been a stern taskmaster.

"The corn is in," Coop said, "the grain's in the bin, hay's in the barn, and straw, too. Only thing left to do is planting the winter wheat."

The sound of children's voices drifted from the barn. "It must be cramped in there now that the barn's full. You sure there's enough room for the English school?" Mother asked.

"They do not complain," Coop said, "and since we live in the center of Wineberry Hollow, this is a good location."

"I find no fault with your decision, Cooper. I'm proud of you for offering to host them."

"You know, Mother, it would be more convenient allowing Hattie to attend this English school instead of sending her the two miles down the road to our Amish school." Coop understood that an Amish education included Bible study, but Hattie was just a child and had plenty of time to absorb their faith.

Mrs. Stover glanced into the distance. "It's hard on me having her gone, but it's the English world that has changed, not ours. We must still adhere to the ordnung of our congregation which forbids our children from attending the English run schools."

The barn door opened and children streamed out led by Sammy Wetzel. "Done for the day, woo hoo," he shouted. "Stop by after supper for some target practice."

"Can't today," Cooper said. "Maybe tomorrow."

"See ya, then," Sammy said. He took off running for home.

Little ones queued in a line to board a horse drawn wagon. Mr. Damroth waved to Coop and his mother. He had modified the wagon by adding a roof which kept him and the kids dry when it rained. He also served as their driver. Coop marveled over the man's ingenuity.

Coop waved back and then walked into the barn to see Mrs. Godfrey or Wendy as she preferred him to call her. He saw Sarah first, Wendy's daughter. "Hello, Sarah."

The teen refused to acknowledge him and stacked a set of books onto a shelf he had recently built into the wall. When Coop first met Sarah, she had been frightened of him. He later learned that she was scared of everyone and rarely spoke. Wendy had explained that Sarah was a special needs child, and it took a great deal of time for her to open up to strangers. Some days she spoke with Coop. Most days, like this one, she ignored him, lost somewhere in her own world.

"Hello, Cooper," Wendy said.

She sat on a metal folding chair behind her desk which consisted of a sheet of plywood spanning a set of sawhorses. Now that harvest was in and he had more time, Coop would build her something better.

He removed his hat and stood facing her. "Did they all behave for you today?"

"Goodness no," she said. "It's in kids' nature to *not* behave. Being a teacher requires channeling bad behavior into constructive learning."

Coop wasn't sure what she meant so he changed the subject. "I'll bet you were a good teacher in the times before."

"That's what I was told. Of course, I was only a third grade teacher then. I must say it's quite a challenge teaching first through eighth grades all in one room." Wendy always smiled. She might have been a good looking lady at one time. Lines on her face and thinning hair made her look older than she probably was. Raising a special child like Sarah probably took a lot out of her, too.

"It's only the first week of school," Coop said. "Give the kids time to adjust. I'm sure they'll do well."

"We should've started a month ago," Wendy said. "The traditional year starts the week before Labor Day, you know."

"The children were needed for the harvest." Thinking about tradition and how things had been done in her world meant that Wendy still longed for the past. This new life remained difficult on the English.

Wendy stood. "I'm ready."

They walked outside.

Since Wendy and Sarah lived with Dr. Hunt and Katie, the arrangement was made for Wendy to drive Katie's old car to school every day. Until all of the gas in Wineberry Hollow was exhausted or went bad. Then Coop didn't know what they would do. Horse and buggy probably. Coop opened the passenger side door for Sarah and held it for her.

She studied him for a few moments before climbing in.

Coop got in on the driver's side and slid into the backseat.

Wendy took her seat behind the wheel and started the car. After turning onto Cove Road she glanced at her daughter and said, "Sarah, tell Cooper what you learned today."

The girl leaned against the door and said something that Coop couldn't hear.

"Don't mumble," Wendy scolded.

Sarah straightened. "Two plus two is four. Four plus four is eight. Eight plus eight are sixteen. Sixteen and sixteen are thirty two. Inchworms measure marigolds. The cow jumped over the moon."

Suddenly, Sarah jerked. She turned and pressed her face between the seats and peered at Coop. "What are you doing back there, Cooper? This isn't your car."

"No, it isn't my car. It's Katie's car," Coop said.

Sarah's face lit up. "How did you know that?"

"Because I know Katie."

"Mom, he knows Katie."

"And I know Dr. Hunt. I'm visiting this afternoon to chop firewood so that all of you will stay warm this winter."

Sarah turned and sat back in her seat. "He knows Katie."

"Nice of you to help out," Wendy said. "Dr. Hunt has been so busy helping patients and Katie and I aren't strong enough to wield that maul. It takes us forever just to split logs."

"I'm glad you asked me to help. Where'd you get the firewood?"

"Chain saws still work. The men at our end of the valley have been cutting firewood all summer. It's how some of them pay for Doc's services. Most of what they deliver, though, is too thick to fit into the woodstove."

Coop had a chainsaw, too, one of the seemingly ironic allowances of his particular Amish sect. Owning a chainsaw wasn't prideful, but owning an automobile was akin to having one foot in hell.

"Do you like lasagna?" Wendy asked. "It's what I'm serving for supper tonight. It could be our last lasagna ever. We've reached the end of our store bought pasta."

He wondered if Wendy had assumed the role of cook as part of the arrangement for the Hunts taking her in. "Sure, lasagna is fine, but you don't need to feed me."

"Nonsense. One good turn deserves another."

Coop had wondered all day if Katie would be around. He knew how she split her time working for both her father and Dr. St. John.

Would she even be home or would she be across the street at the dentist office? Two months had passed since he had any contact with her. The harvest had filled Coop's time and kept him from thinking about her. Now that harvest season had ended and the long winter approached, how disappointed he would be to work all evening at Katie's home and not be able to see her. He longed to ask Wendy if she would be there but didn't want to be so direct.

Coop had made his feelings about Katie clear to Dr. Hunt. Would he have let anything slip to Wendy? In the Amish community, such talk would be considered unseemly, but these English probably made light of such things.

An idea flashed into Coop's brain and he tried an indirect approach. "You sure there will be enough to go around? There's you and Sarah and Dr. Hunt and Sheila and Katie. If all of you are dining together, I would hate to think that my extra mouth might deprive any of you of the last of your pasta."

"Don't worry, we'll have plenty for everyone," Wendy said.

Could he assume then that everyone including Katie would be there for their evening meal? A few minutes later, Wendy turned the car into the Hunt's driveway. He'd soon find out for himself.

"Woodpile's in the back." Wendy turned to Sarah. "Go tell Katie to set an extra plate this evening."

Now that Coop knew for sure that Katie would be home, his anxiety eased.

"I'll show you around," Wendy said.

"No need, I've visited here before," Coop reminded her. "Don't you remember that I was here the day you and Sarah arrived in Wineberry Hollow?"

"Were you?" she asked. "That day was a blur. So much happened. Anyway, since you know your way around, I'll let you get to work. If you need anything just knock on the back door."

The two of them parted and Coop walked around back. The fire wood lay in an unorganized pile. He estimated two wagon loads. Spying the chopping maul resting against a wheelbarrow, Coop grabbed the tool and balanced it in his hands. Satisfied that the iron head remained secure at the end of the handle and wouldn't fly off, he began chopping.

A half-hour later, Sarah brought him a glass of water. "Here you go, mister."

He took the drink and once started couldn't stop. Thirstier than he thought, Coop downed it all. He handed the glass back to Sarah. "Thank you. That was dee-licious."

Sarah giggled and imitated him. "Dee-licious."

He resumed chopping and Sarah stayed there watching him. She sat on the picnic bench and silently studied him.

Absorbed in his work, it surprised Coop when Katie spoke, "Better watch yourself, Coop. I believe you have an admirer."

She sat beside Sarah, a hand around the younger girl's shoulder.

Coop set the maul on the ground. "Hello, Katie." She looked different. It took a moment for him to process that she had cut her hair. It no longer hung down her back and stopped instead at the top of her shoulders. She had let it grow back to its natural golden brown color. "I almost didn't recognize you without your pony tail."

She grimaced. "No more hair dye, you know. My roots started showing. Decided to cut it until it evens out. Besides, hauling water from the stream is a hassle, so I don't wash my hair every day like I used to. It's easier to take care of this way."

The cut framed Katie's face, the way her hair curled under her chin. "It's cute. I like it."

She squinted at him, her skin creasing near the corners of her eyes. Had she lost weight?

"I didn't do it for your approval," she said.

Coop looked her over. Katie *had* lost weight. Her knees looked knobbier than before, her cheeks hollower. She slouched as if defeated, not the erect, self confident posture that he had grown to admire.

"Why are you staring at me? It's giving me the creeps."

Coop's face flushed. His cursed complexion again. "C'mon, Katie, it's been such a long time. I'm happy to see you."

"Happy? God, Coop, you might be the only person on Earth who's happy."

Sarah drew back, probably sensing Katie's tension. She slinked into the house. Katie remained rooted to the picnic bench.

Her attitude frustrated him. Unable to think of anything kind to say, he turned his back, picked up the maul, and got back to work. He hoped her hostility would evaporate in time for supper, otherwise the meal was going to be unpleasant.

Out of the corner of his eye, he spotted Katie. She had pulled on a pair of work gloves and started stacking the split wood against a tool shed.

"I'll do that after I finish," Coop said. "You don't have to."

"Don't tell me what I can or cannot do," she snarled.

Her tone hurt his feelings. He hadn't done anything to deserve her anger.

Coop continued to chop and Katie continued to stack. A few minutes later, he couldn't stand it anymore. He let the maul drop to the ground and faced her. "Katie."

She shot a glance his way and picked up another piece of wood, added it to the stack, and stopped, her back turned. She spoke so softly that Coop barely heard her words. "How do you do it? How do you stay so centered?"

He pulled his straw hat from his head and dragged a forearm across his brow. Perspiring from the hard labor, he hoped he didn't smell. Fingering the hat in his hands, Coop said, "I need to take a break. Sit with me...please."

They returned to the picnic bench and sat side-by-side, Katie angled away from him.

Coop took a deep breath before speaking. "Don't resent me for the fact that the Amish never had electricity, or automobiles, or tap water, so we don't miss those things. This terrible time in the world is not our fault."

"I know that," Katie mumbled.

"Still, it causes us distress. Both the English and the Amish suffer."

She looked at him, lines furrowing her brow, a look of incredulity, disbelief.

"Yes. It distresses us that it is unsafe to venture beyond Wineberry Hollow to visit friends and relatives, that we can no longer take our produce to market, that we bear the responsibility of feeding not only our families, but your families, too."

"I'm sorry to be such a burden," she said.

"I didn't mean it that way, and you know it." He regretted the anger that had crept into his tone.

She shot him another look but said nothing.

Coop went on. "We Amish are not insensitive. It hurts us to witness your suffering. The only thing setting us apart is our religious beliefs. Otherwise we are just men and women, the same as you. We're happy and thankful for what we have. Running hot water, washing machines, flush toilets, and the television do not define us. They never have. You can live without those things, too. Eventually you might even become happier, although I'm sure you still miss those things now."

Katie glared at him. "How dare you think of me as being so shallow and selfish. I've told you all about myself, what motivates me, about my dreams and aspirations, about my wanting to become a doctor. Apparently you weren't paying attention. Apparently you're just like every other guy who thinks they're humoring me by letting me talk, when in reality they don't give a damn about what I have to say and just want to score. Is that what I am to you, Coop? Just some girl to be conquered?"

"Where does this ugly talk come from?"

She shouted. "This isn't about my missing the stupid television."

Coop raised his voice to match hers. "Help me out here, Katie. It's like we're speaking two different foreign languages. Just tell me what I've done to make you so angry."

Her mood softened and she relaxed. "Martha Goode is expecting a baby any day now. Things are...well things are complicated. Her baby might not live. Terry Maxwell had an abscessed molar today. Dr. St. John had to extract that tooth with no nerve block. I can still hear Terry's screams in my head. Billy Taggard and his friend were horsing around with a pitchfork. His friend accidently ran a tine through Billy's arm. The stupid kid and his parents were too prideful to come see Dad about it right away. Now Billy has a bad infection. He might lose his arm."

Katie faced Coop, looked him in the eye. "He's 12. We have no anesthesia. I can't sleep worrying about how that poor kid is going to handle it if we have to saw off his arm."

"I...I don't believe I know any of those people," Coop said.

"Yeah? We'll try this on for size. You know Tim and Grace Foose, don't you?"

"Of course."

"Then you know about their little boy, Lucas, who has diabetes. They have maybe one more week's supply of insulin. There is no more. Anywhere. After their supply runs out...little Lucas is going to die. He's going to die, Coop, and there is nothing my father can do to stop it."

Coop felt the kick to his gut. The Fooses lived for their children. It would tear them to pieces.

"That's not the half of it," Katie said. "Do you want me to keep going. Want me to tell you more horror stories?"

Coop squeezed shut his eyes and shook his head.

"Don't be so quick to judge me next time."

They remained silent for a while. Coop considered how Katie's empathy for others caused her such pain. How could older men like Dr. Hunt and Dr. St. John function? Did age and experience allow men to better separate their feelings from their patients? In the distance Coop heard a dinner bell, probably coming from the Miller farm, a reminder that Wendy would soon be serving her promised lasagna. Except Coop had lost his appetite.

He glanced at Katie. What could he do to make things better for her? To see her smile again? Maybe he should invite her to spend a few days at his farm. Do a different kind of work. Get her away from the sight of daily human suffering. It would sting if she rejected his offer but it was worth the risk. If he could talk her into it, he knew it would do her a world of good. Forcing a smile. Coop said, "For the record, I *did* pay attention to those things you told me about yourself."

She met his glance with her own. "Yeah, I'm sure you have no impure thoughts in your Amish head."

Something nagged at the back of Coop's mind. Something that didn't have to do with Katie. What was it?

"I didn't mean to take it all out on you. I shouldn't be such a bitch," Katie said and moved her hand to eye level. She held her index finger and thumb together with about a half inch of air between them. "And maybe I do miss the TV about this much."

Coop finally grasped the meaning behind his nagging feeling. He gasped and sprang to his feet.

Katie got up after him and studied his face. "Coop, what's wrong?"

"The dinner bell. It hasn't stopped ringing."

Chapter 42

Declan Orr raced down his stone driveway in his Ford Mustang, dust flying in its wake. After pulling onto Cove Road, Katie Hunt and Cooper Stover flagged him down. "No time to delay," he muttered after rolling to a stop.

"Is there trouble?" Katie asked, her eyes wide.

"Somebody set off the chain of bells. My wife and kids have already made their way to the hidey cave. You and the ladies in your household need to drop everything and take cover in the shelter, too. Just like we practiced during the drills. Do it now."

Katie tugged at Cooper's shirt sleeve. "C'mon, Coop, there's plenty of room for you, too."

Coop shook free from her grip. "I need to get home to mother. Can you drop me off, Mr. Orr?"

He didn't want a passenger, but felt obligated to give Cooper a ride. "Get in."

"Stay safe, Katie," Coop said and climbed into the passenger seat. Orr observed Dr. Hunt on the front porch, waving and motioning for Katie, Sheila, and Wendy and Sarah Godfrey to gather together. He'd get them moving.

"Hold on," Orr tromped the gas pedal.

"Where have you sent the Hunts?" Cooper asked.

"Jamal and I expanded an existing hidey cave in the side of the mountain near the house. We planned for this eventuality. Our families know to hide there."

"How did you do such a thing as building a cave?"

"Picks and shovels." Orr thought back on it and mused how Jamal seemed to enjoy working with him on the project. The one time since moving to the hollow that the two of them actually got along together.

"They're safe then?" Coop asked wearing an intense stare.

Evidently he cared a great deal about the Hunts, most likely Katie in particular. He noticed how this young man had taken a shine to her.

"Safe as can be under the circumstances."

"We have a root cellar," Coop said. "Do you think I should hide there with my family?"

"That would be a good choice." Orr pulled over at the edge of

Coop's driveway. "Son, this could be nothing, but you should consider it as potentially serious. Do you understand?"

"I pray it is nothing, as you say." Coop exited the vehicle and ran into the farmhouse.

Orr sped away. He spotted Gary Daw and Tom Ortiz hurrying down the road, rifles in hand. They jumped in.

"Any word?" Orr asked as he drove away.

After recovering his breath, Daw said, "Not a scheduled drill. I assume this is for real?"

"Not someone who screwed up and rang the dinner bell one too many times, accidently setting off the chain?" Ortiz asked. "It is dinner time, you know."

Orr hoped that's all it was. "We'll soon find out."

He saw the old school bus parked across Cove Road, serving as their physical barrier. A score of men gathered around the bus, rifles at the ready peering down the township road. Some of the men huddled around a horse and buggy talking to an Amish couple. When Orr got closer he recognized them as young Stephen Kroh and his girl friend, Rebekah Hagen.

Orr parked the Mustang near the buggy and sprang from the car. "What's the situation?"

Corporal Jack Clark hustled over to Orr. This was his watch, his squad of men. "Three wagons headed this way pulled by old tractors. A dozen to twenty men or so riding in each wagon. They're armed."

"How far out?"

"Don't know for sure."

"I don't understand, corporal. Where did you get this intel?"

Clark pointed to Stephen Kroh.

Stephen embraced Rebekah who acted inconsolable. She uttered, "They must have stopped at our farm. What will they do to my family, my mother, father, and brothers? I shouldn't have come."

"Then you, you, you wouldn't be safe, either," Stephen stuttered.

Orr exchanged glances with Clark and then turned his attention to Stephen. "Tell me what you know, son. Make it quick."

Stephen licked his lips and took a breath as if trying to calm himself. "Rebekah's family farm has an orchard." He pointed down the township road. "That way."

"Get to the point," Orr scolded. "We may not have much time."

The young man's eyes rounded. "We pick, pick, picked apples and from the side of the hill saw them ka, ka, coming."

"Who?" Orr pressed. "How many?"

Stephen corroborated what Clark had already told him. Three tractor drawn wagons carrying a large contingent of armed men. "I ran for the buggy. Becky's father told me to ta, ta, take her with me."

"I shouldn't have left them," Rebekah whined. She turned her attention to Stephen. "What will they do to my family?"

"They should be safe in the roo, roo, root cellar."

"How long ago did this take place?" Orr asked.

"The horse and buggy pulled in close to half an hour ago," Clark said.

"Doesn't wash. Tractor drawn wagons should easily have gotten here by now. Why would they have stopped?"

"I don't know," Clark said.

Orr motioned with his head for Clark to join him out of earshot. In a low voice, he asked, "You believe their story?"

"Affirmative. Based on the way the two kids are acting, they're genuinely frightened. Also, it's my experience that Amish people don't take to lying. Not in their nature."

"You have any suspicions?"

"Affirmative," Clark said, "and none of my suspicions have a happy outcome. Either they stopped at and are currently raiding that poor girl's family farm, or they're gathering intel before a planned assault."

Orr took his field glasses and scanned the road and terrain between them and the Hagen's orchard. No movement.

"Did those strange men see you when you drove the buggy away from the farm?" Orr asked Stephen.

"I suppose they did." Stephen spoke slowly and concentrated, probably to keep from stuttering. "We could see them, so they could see us."

"We witnessed no apparent pursuit," Clark added.

"They were too far off to stop, stop, stop us. I whipped my horse into a run to get here," Stephen said.

Orr scanned again with the field glasses, a feeling of unease taking hold of him. He had expected a frontal assault to take advantage of the easiest terrain. Could he have underestimated these attackers?

"What do you make of it?" Clark asked.

"Hard to say." Orr scanned the field directly across the road from their position. "You have men in the spider holes."

"Yes."

"Not a pleasant assignment, but it sure will surprise any attackers."

The sun hung low in the west. Maybe one more hour of daylight. They needed information, especially if their defenses needed realigning. Orr glanced at the Mustang. The car will have the advantage of speed. I'm going to ease down the road to see what I can see. If there's trouble, I can outrun them."

"With all due respect, Declan, you can't outrun a bullet," Clark said.

"Noted. That's why I want you to ride shotgun with me and pick two men for the backseat. If I have to do some fancy driving, I'll be needing cover."

"Got it." Clark walked off to choose his men.

Orr heard the sound of a vehicle on Cove Road behind their position. Some of the men around him tensed and pointed their weapons in the general direction of the approaching vehicle. He recognized Katie's old car. "It's Dr. Hunt. Lower your weapons." What was he doing coming here? He was supposed to be back at the hidey cave.

The doctor pulled in beside Orr's Mustang and got out. From the passenger seat, Jamal emerged, grim faced, toting a shotgun.

"We're here," Dr. Hunt said.

Orr looked between the two of them. Dr. Hunt wore a blank expression as if expecting Orr to say something. Jamal rested the shotgun across his arms and walked toward the bus barricade.

"Unless you men need anything else, I'll get out of your way," Dr. Hunt said.

"Wait a minute. What the hell is this? Jamal get back here."

Dr. Hunt wrinkled his brow. "You mean you didn't want me to deliver Jamal to you? That's what he told me after I got to the cave."

"Jamal," Orr yelled.

Jamal stopped walking and turned but he didn't approach his father. "I'm not waiting around in no hidey hole with a bunch of women. I come to fight."

Orr gritted his teeth. He had no time for this. "Get your ass over here."

"No."

"What did you say?"

"I can shoot as well as anyone here."

Orr had always reminded himself that the men in the militia were civilians. These were not professional soldiers, and he didn't want to treat them as such. He worked hard avoiding slipping into a drill sergeant persona, but Jamal had worn out his patience. He hated for these men to see what they were about to see. But what could he do? He wasn't able to reach Jamal as a father. The time had come to get rough.

He strode over to Jamal and yanked the shotgun from his grasp. Orr wanted to throw it on the ground, but a weapon in these times was too valuable to risk damaging. He banged his forehead against Jamal's. The boy drew back, his haughty expression morphing into one of fear.

Keeping his hands at his side, Orr stood erect no more than an inch from Jamal's face. "This is not a goddamned game," Orr yelled. "Any time now we may have to shoot and kill people and be shot at and killed."

"Yeah, well I can handle it."

"Shut your mouth, boy, before I ram a fist down your throat." He had never threatened his son like this before, so his words carried weight.

Jamal winced.

"You cannot handle it," Orr yelled. "When you wipe the sweat from your eyes and find out it isn't sweat but blood spraying from a wound from the man beside you, you won't be able to handle it. When your nostrils fill with the smell of shit from the dead men laying around you whose bowels have released, you won't be able to handle it. When you blast someone in the torso with this shotgun and watch as his guts spill out all over the ground, you won't be able to handle it."

He took a breath. "You're no soldier, hell you're not even a man, you're just a 15-year-old, undisciplined, ungrateful, boy. I don't want a boy getting in my way when the shooting starts, and these men don't want that either."

Orr pointed to the road. "Get the hell out of my sight. Go back to the cave with your Mama or I'll plant my foot so far up your ass my toe will be sticking out your mouth."

Jamal's jaw trembled and he slowly backed away.

Dr. Hunt cleared his throat. "Sorry about this, Declan. I had no reason to believe your son would lie to me. I'll drive him home."

"Not your fault, Stewart," Orr said. "And the boy is going to walk home. Don't you dare drive him."

After a pause, Dr. Hunt said, "You sure, Declan? It's five miles and the sun's going down."

"Boy wants to be a man. Men aren't afraid of the dark."

Dr. Hunt grunted, got back into his car, and drove away.

Orr turned his back on Jamal. "Corporal Clark," he said. "You picked your two men?"

"Hey, old man," Jamal yelled.

Orr turned and saw his son give him the finger. The boy ran off across the Kroh's field.

He'd deal with Jamal later. No time now.

"We're ready," Clark said, acting as if he ignored the exchange between Orr and his son.

"Good. Let's go."

Orr, Clark, and two men named Quinn and Tungstall climbed into the Mustang. Orr cranked down the convertible top. "The farm is no more than a mile away. The road's narrow, and it'll be hard to turn around so I'm going to back down the road. If we need to make a quick exit, I'll drop it in gear and smoke tires. I want Quinn and Tungstall in the back to rest your rifles on the rear deck lid. Clark, you watch our flanks. Keep your eye on the mountain."

Orr motioned for the militia to roll the bus out of their way. A minute later, they were on the township road and proceeding rear end first toward the Hagen's orchard.

In reverse the transmission wound tight at 20 miles per hour and made a whining noise that could be heard for a long distance. Orr kept it between 10 and 15 to cut down on the noise, but the slow progress frustrated him.

Minutes later, from the backseat, Tungstall called out, "Contact."

Orr hit the brakes and the car halted. The men in the back peered through their rifle scopes at the farm. Orr used his field glasses and scanned the farm and barnyard. "I count three wagons and an undetermined amount of men." He lowered his field glasses. "Jesus, there are a lot of them."

"They see us yet?" Clark asked.

"Negative," Quinn said. "They appear to be loading supplies into one of the wagons. Bushel baskets of apples."

"Any sign of the Amish folk that live there?" Orr asked.

"Negative."

Safely hidden away somewhere, Orr hoped.

"Uh oh," Tungstall blurted. "We've been spotted."

Orr brought the field glasses to his eyes in time to see one of the men grab a rifle and point it in their direction. Then a muzzle flash.

"Incoming," Clark shouted.

Tungstall and Quinn ducked behind the seat backs. The front windshield exploded into shards of flying glass.

"Go, go, go," Clark yelled.

Orr dropped the Mustang into gear and peeled out. After they rounded a bend in the road and were safely out of rifle range, Orr shouted. "Anybody hit?"

He heard three nos. Then Orr unleashed a string of curse words that he hadn't used since he left the Army. After getting the anger out of his system, he said, "I'll never be able to find a replacement for that windshield. Somebody's going to pay."

Chapter 43

Stan Cox had been rooting through the kitchen cupboards when he heard the rifle shot. Cursing under his breath, he walked outside to find out which of the fools had shot off his gun. He'd warned his men before about wasting ammo.

"Trouble, boss," Leroy said. "Visitors in a car. Didn't know who they were. Never saw 'em before. I shot at them and run them off."

It would change everything if he could find an operational automobile, something faster than the tractors. "A car? Which way did they come from? Which direction were they heading?"

"They didn't pass by. I looked up and saw the ass end of a

convertible. It was as if they backed the car down the road."

Hoss joined them. "Transmission's probably shot. Probably has no forward gears."

"Hell it don't," Leroy said. "Driver laid a patch of rubber after I shot at them. Think I took out their windshield but don't know if I hit anyone."

Stan figured the old car belonged to someone living in Wineberry Hollow. "When we finish up here, we're going to make an appearance on Cove Road. Ask some questions. We'll find out who has a working vehicle."

Terry Dairyman approached.

"All them apples loaded up?" Stan asked.

"Yes."

During the raids, Leroy and Hoss bore the responsibility of watching the road while the rest of the men plundered and loaded wagons. Stan never worried about anyone coming to the rescue of the farmers, but he felt more secure having someone watch their six. Today, this move had paid off in spades. In hindsight, he wished the two guards would've had the presence of mind to lure the vehicle closer instead of shooting at it. "I want the two of you to march up the road about a hundred yards and hide. If they come back, let them by you. Then we'll have them in a cross fire."

"Good idea, boss," Leroy smacked Hoss on the arm. "Let's go."

After the two men walked out of earshot, Terry said, "It's almost dark. We should be heading back."

"But they spotted a working car. That's worth checking out."

"Can't it wait for another time?"

"Why are you so reluctant?"

"We don't normally stray this far from home."

True. The CCW had annexed all of the farms within a manageable area. The citizens of Wynot no longer needed to fear starvation. As a matter of fact they had more than they needed. The only reason Stan had brought his men to this farm is he remembered the apple orchard, fresh fruit still being a scarcity. "We'll have enough daylight to take a quick look," Stan said. "One pass down Cove Road and then right back out. If we see that car sitting out in the open, we'll take it. If not, we'll call it a day."

Terry said nothing, but Stan caught a look of disapproval on the man's face.

"Round up the men," Stan said.

A few minutes later Stan mounted the lead tractor and pressed the starter pedal. The engine coughed and black smoke belched from the upright exhaust. He thought again how great it would be to lead the CCW with a car instead of this smelly farm tractor. Waving his arm, he beckoned for the other two tractors to follow and headed toward Wineberry Hollow. Along the way, he stopped long enough for Hoss and Leroy to jump aboard the wagon with the rest of the men. "Anything?"

"Nothing," Hoss said.

"Stay sharp. Let me know if you see that car sitting around."

Stan proceeded up the township road. Was that a school bus parked across the entrance to Cove Road? He drove up to the road block and stopped.

"Unhitch the wagon," Stan ordered. "I'll hook the tractor to the bumper and pull that bus out of the way." Did the yokels living in the hollow actually believe that a mere school bus would stop them?

A big black man stepped from behind the bus with a gun leveled at Stan. "I wouldn't do that."

A dozen or so men streamed out on either side of the bus. The setting sun cast them with long, intimidating shadows. These men had taken his crew by surprise.

"You men in the wagons keep your hands where we can see them," the black guy ordered.

Nobody had seriously threatened the CCW until now. Most of the farmers rolled over when they came to call. This man had these people organized. And they appeared to be serious.

"Easy does it, men," Stan shouted. "Do as he says." The men grumbled but did as they were told. Fifty pair of hands shot into the air including his own.

"State your business," the black guy said.

Stan looked the man over and recognized him as the leader of the group he had skirmished with at the Route 15 underpass. He glanced at the bus. Could it be the same one he had seen at that battle? Forget about the car. An operational bus would be more than excellent. The CCW would be able to travel in comfort during rainy days and they could stay warm during the upcoming winter.

"My name is Stan Cox. Who might you be?"

"Call me Mr. Orr."

"You in charge here?"

"I'm the one pointing a rifle at your face. That good enough?"

Stan grinned. "Mr. Orr, I'm president of the Concerned Citizens of Wynot and the fine folks of that community also appointed me Sheriff of Tioga County."

Orr glared at him. "I doubt that you're the sheriff."

"I am now," Stan said. "Ever since your men shot the deputy."

That revelation appeared to take Orr aback. He relaxed the grip on his rifle and lowered it so that it pointed at Stan's feet instead of at his head. "You were there that day?"

"Yeah. A bad scene for sure. Don't hold it against me, though. I was just following Deputy Toomey's orders."

"Orders to shoot unarmed, innocent pilgrims?" Orr asked.

Stan hung his head doing his best to act naïve. "I didn't know what Toomey was leading us into. That man was a fool. He got what he deserved."

"Looks to me like you're picking up right where he left off, raiding defenseless farmers. What did you do to the folks living at yonder farm?"

"Nobody was at that farm. We had come to purchase or trade for apples, that's all. We figured the farm was abandoned so we helped ourselves." Stan had seen the root cellar and guessed the occupants had hid there. Most farm families headed straight for the root cellar at the first sign of trouble. Stupid yokels. Didn't they know that would be the first place he would look if he really intended to find them? Actually, it always worked out for the best. He and his men pretended that they didn't know and took what they wanted. It was less bother that way, and he didn't want to hurt any of the farmers anyway. Otherwise there would be nobody to work the fields for the next harvest.

"We aren't interested in trading with you," Orr said.

"Not a problem," Stan said. "We're on our way back to Wynot. It's just that one of my men reported seeing a working car headed this direction. Since I'm the sheriff, I decided to check and see if the people in that car might be bothering you folks."

"Car belongs to me," Orr said, "and one of your men owes me a new windshield."

Stan lowered one of his hands and held it over his heart. "A regrettable misunderstanding."

"Unlike your band of thugs, my men don't shoot first and ask questions later. That would also have been a regrettable misunderstanding."

Stan wondered about that. He decided to press their resolve. Were these men actually willing to shoot at his men? Orr wouldn't have a problem doing so, but what about the rest of them? "See here, Mr. Orr. You have no cause to call us names. These men are my deputies. By the way, since your car has a shot up windshield, I'm sure it has little value to you now. Want to trade for it?"

"No."

"Want to trade for that bus?"

"No."

Stan smiled. "As Sheriff, I have the authority to confiscate it, you know? For the greater good."

"You could try." Orr raised the rifle again to point at Stan's chest.

"Come now," Stan said in his most reasonable tone. "We have you outnumbered 4 to 1. You don't want to tangle, do you?"

"Don't be so sure that you outnumber us," Orr said.

That comment made Stan queasy. He looked around to assess where others might be hiding and then decided it was a bluff.

"Enough with the games," Orr said. "Get your wagons turned around and head back the way you came. We don't need your kind around here."

Stan flushed with anger. He resented how Orr questioned his authority and wasn't used to back talk. "We will leave when I'm good and ready."

"No. You'll leave now." Orr pulled a whistle from his shirt pocket and blew into it.

From the field opposite his position, Stan heard a grating noise and turned his attention that way. A dozen trap doors sprang open, revealing hidden men, each one pointing a weapon their way. The CCW still outnumbered these defenders, but strategically they were outmatched. In a firefight, he and his men would be cut to pieces.

He was beaten.

"Mr. Orr, I'd like permission to lower my hands to start up my tractor. We will be on our way as you requested."

"You can leave after we collect your weapons."

Stan stiffened. He would sacrifice himself and every last man with him before enduring such an outrageous insult. "No way in hell are we going to do that. You try it, and this meeting will end in a senseless bloodbath, and a lot of that blood will come from your men. You want that? Allow us to leave with our weapons and nobody needs to get hurt."

"Do it then," Orr barked. "If you ever return we'll consider it an act of aggression and open fire. This is your only warning. That includes the farm you just plundered. Don't bother those people again."

Boiling with rage, Stan's hand shook when he gripped the steering wheel. Nobody taunted him and got away with it. This incident could lose him the respect of his men. He resolved that somehow he would return and kill Orr. Burn whatever house he lived in to the ground.

He opened the throttle and the tractor bucked. The jerking threw his men in the attached wagon from their seats. They yelled in protest. Stan turned a tight circle on the township road and proceeded to drive away. He thought about stopping at the farm with the apple orchard, pulling each of the Amish out of their root cellar and shooting them all in the head. Of course, the CCW wouldn't allow him to do that, but he was angry enough to go through with it just to spite Orr.

As they approached close enough to see the orchard, Stan caught movement from the corner of his eye. He turned and was greeted by a screaming man wielding a tree branch like a club. "What the …" He couldn't get the rest of his words out before the man leaped onto the tractor and knocked him out of his seat.

Stan fell to the ground. The huge rear tractor wheel barely missed rolling over his leg. His head banged against the pavement. He saw stars. The screaming man stood over him, tree branch raised like a golf club, Stan's head the golf ball. He instinctively raised his hand to ward off the blow, but Hoss and Leroy tackled the attacker.

Stan didn't remember passing out, but when he came to, he found himself sitting on the road against the tractor wheel. What had happened? From the side of the road he heard Terry Dairyman yelling at someone. As his head cleared, Stan remembered being angry. Remembered that someone had jumped him.

He tried standing. Suddenly Hoss appeared and helped him to his feet. "You all right, boss?"

"My head aches, but otherwise I believe I'm okay."

The fading twilight made it difficult for Stan to see who Terry was screaming at. He walked their way holding one hand over the knot forming at the back of his head. Terry had a man pinned against a tree with his forearm to the man's throat. A black guy, like Orr. After doing a double take, Stan saw that it wasn't a man, but a teen. Hell, he had been attacked by a kid.

"Let him speak," Stan said.

Terry Dairyman lowered his arm from the kid's throat and the kid started coughing.

"What's your name?" Stan asked.

After the kid was able to breathe again, he bellowed, "You ain't so bad."

"I asked you for your name."

The kid spit on the ground. "Come over here and make me tell you."

Stan shook his head. What made the people around here so damn defiant? "All right, I'll go first. My name is Stan Cox. Seeing as how you're obviously out to do me harm, I figure the least you owe me is to tell me your name."

The kid stood erect and raised his chin. "Jamal Orr."

"Orr? You kin to that big guy who gave us all that trouble back there?"

"My dad."

Stan raised his arms to the heavens and thanked the Lord. Was he living right, or what? He'd see if Orr would be willing to trade with him now.

"What do you want us to do with him?" Terry asked.

Stan grinned. "Oh man, my imagination is running wild."

"Coward, you won't fight me," Jamal uttered.

"What's wrong with you? You have a death wish?" Stan asked.

"I can show my old man that I can fight. If I have to I can kill."

With that statement, Stan started to understand what might be going on. "I take it your father doesn't want you to fight along side of him?"

"Thinks I'm too young. I wasn't too young to knock you on

your ass."

An idea formed in Stan's head. If he could pull this off it would be so, so, sweet. He touched the back of his head and twisted his face from the pain. "Yeah, Jamal, you certainly did knock me on my ass. In front of fifty bodyguards, you were able to surprise us and do this to me. I must say that I'm impressed. Your father underestimates your abilities and your guts."

Jamal stood taller at Stan's words.

"You're a hell of a warrior, Jamal. Tell you what. Since your father doesn't appreciate you, how would you like to join up with me?"

Jamal's eyes shifted from side to side. "You're just a bunch of outlaws."

"That's what your father wants you to believe. It's what he wants all of the people living in Wineberry Hollow to believe so that he can hold on to his power. He's wrong, Jamal. I am the legally appointed sheriff of Tioga County. All of these men you see are my deputies. We are the good guys."

Jamal waved an arm. "Yeah, tell me another one."

"It's true." Stan reached inside his jacket pocket and produced a badge and ID. The badge he had stolen from Toomey's office, the ID was an old luggage tag. He tossed it to Jamal. Jamal looked it over.

"You think all of these men would back me up if I wasn't legal?"

A flicker of doubt flashed across Jamal's face. "If you're the law then why you stealing apples from the Hagen's orchard?"

"Not stealing, Jamal. The Citizens Committee of Wynot appointed me and my men to go out into the country and ask the farmers for aid. They have a lot more food than they need, but the people in the towns are going hungry. It's a redistribution of resources. We didn't hurt anybody. In fact we allowed some folks in a horse and buggy to drive away just as we got to that farm. If you want I can prove it to you. We can stop by the farm. You can talk to them."

"So you're a modern day Robin Hood?"

Stan smiled. "Something like that."

"Uh, huh," Jamal said.

"I could use a man like you. Come with us. We have a

bunkhouse setup in our warehouse. Prove to your old man that you're better than he thinks you are."

Jamal remained silent for a minute before he spoke. "What if I say no?"

Stan shrugged. "You can go home to your father with your tail tucked between your legs."

"You'd let me go, just like that?"

"If I wanted to harm you, Jamal, the deed would already be done. As Sheriff, I could charge you with assault and haul you to jail, but I see now that this has all been a misunderstanding. I'm willing to let it go." If the kid said no, he'd send him back to his father one body part at a time.

After another long moment, Jamal glared at him. "So what do I have to do to join up?"

Chapter 44

Stan walked into the woods away from his men, an arm around Jamal's shoulder. The sun had set and they couldn't see each other. "I wanted to speak with you alone, man-to-man." He found it easy to stroke the kid's ego, something Jamal's father should've done from time to time. When they were out of earshot, Stan acted as if he wanted to confide in his new recruit.

"Here's the deal, Jamal. I know that you're sincere, but some of my men have doubts. They suspect that you may be a spy?"

In the dark, with his hand still on Jamal's shoulder, Stan felt the young man bristle. He quickly added, "Not me. I trust you, but put yourself in their shoes. You are the son of the man who opposes us. Wouldn't that make you somewhat suspicious?"

Jamal remained silent.

"The fact remains that your father and his men are guilty of obstruction. That makes them criminals, Jamal. It doesn't matter that they think they're doing the right thing. They are standing in the way of something we desperately need."

"What's that?" Jamal asked.

"A working vehicle."

"You want to take my dad's Mustang?"

"No, not that."

"Katie Hunt's car then? She's my neighbor."

Stan froze. Katie? Since the people of Wynot had appointed him sheriff, Stan was regarded as the most eligible bachelor in the county. Stan had enjoyed the comfort of plenty of ladies. He didn't think about Katie anymore and her rejection of him, but now that Jamal had brought up her name, Stan decided that she represented unfinished business. He would pay Katie a visit. But why would Jamal bring up her car? Oh, yeah, he remembered her ugly old rust bucket. Did that thing still work? "No, Jamal, it would be wrong of me to take Katie's car or even your father's car. That's personal property. I wouldn't do a thing like that. What we need is the bus. The bus is community property."

He explained to Jamal how vital the bus would be to ferry around supplies and how it could also serve as an ambulance for sick and wounded people. "Using that bus as a glorified road block instead of putting it in service is wrong. You can see that, can't you?"

"S'pose so. How you going to get it from my father."

"Here's the plan. This is going to take some guts on your part. Are you up to it?"

Jamal grunted.

"I'll take that as a yes. It's a simple plan. I want you to pretend to be my hostage. I trade you for the bus."

"He's going to shoot you if you go back there," Jamal blurted. "You won't get the chance to talk with him."

"Quite right. Your father and his crew are probably on high alert and expecting us to return. All of their attention is focused on the township road. We need to surprise them with something they aren't going to suspect."

"What would that be?"

"I know a little about Wineberry Hollow. I know that Cove Road is the only way in and out. The hollow is easily defended because it's surrounded by mountains. If we knew an easy way to get over the mountain, we could surprise them by approaching from behind on Cove Road instead of the township road. What can you tell me about the mountain? Do you know a way in?"

"Not really," Jamal said. "We only moved here just before the world went dark."

"Think, Jamal, you must've done some exploring. Mountains like these are usually honeycombed with old logging roads."

"Yeah. There's another black family living in the hollow. They have a long driveway off of Cove Road that comes up to this side of the mountain. I remember Mr. Doaks telling us it was an old logging road that keeps going past his property to the top. The end of his driveway, I think, is less than a mile from the township road. We could go over the top from this side and catch his driveway."

Jamal paused. "Thing is you won't be able to take your tractors over. Those mountain roads are rough."

In the dark, Jamal wasn't able to see the ear-to-ear grin on Stan's face and Stan didn't have to worry about hiding it. "Perfect."

"Uh…"

"What is it, Jamal?"

"My father. I'm pissed at him, but you aren't going to hurt him."

"I don't want to hurt anybody, Jamal, but I'll lay it out for you straight. If your father shoots first, my hands'll be tied. My men will defend themselves." Stan paused. "But I'm sure it won't come to that."

The two of them emerged from the woods and joined up with the waiting men. Stan explained the plan.

"This is crazy," one of them said. "This kind of activity is not what I signed up for."

Many others grumbled in agreement.

Stan needed to regain control quickly. "Listen up. I realize that we're pretty far beyond our boundaries. When we started out today, the purpose was to bring back fresh fruit to the community from the apple orchard, right?"

Nobody disagreed.

"That's why we're in this neighborhood. While we were here minding our own business securing those apples, an old automobile bearing men with weapons came up on us with unknown intent. Our purpose for investigating Wineberry Hollow was to secure that vehicle. That's when we discovered the bus. Now we are presented with an opportunity. You're all correct. This is beyond our area of control, and I don't want to come back to this place for a long time."

Leroy spoke up. "Boss, I suspect that the objection here isn't about relieving the good citizens of Wineberry Hollow of their bus.

It's about hiking over the mountain at night."

"You afraid of the dark, Leroy?" Stan asked in a mocking tone.

Some of the men laughed and made comments.

"No, boss."

"Leroy, I didn't say we'd be doing it tonight. Use your head, we wouldn't be able to see. I don't think we have a single flashlight among us."

"When then?" Leroy asked.

"Tomorrow at first light, and not all of us. This is going to be a stealth operation. All fifty of us maneuvering through the woods will sound like a herd of elephants. I'm asking for only a handful of volunteers."

"You know I'm with you," Terry Dairyman said.

"Hoss and I don't have nothin' to do tomorrow," Leroy said. "We'll come."

"Shoot, if you two are going, I'm coming, too," Billy said.

"Been spoiling for some action," Rog said. "These passive Amish are no fun."

"Counting Jamal, that's seven. Should be enough," Stan said.

"Wait," Glenn said. "I want in on this, too."

Stan didn't care much for Glenn, thought he was lazy and never forgot how on his first day on the job, Glenn had suggested that they steal cigarettes from the warehouse. He didn't trust the man. Still, he might have a use for him in this venture. "All right, you're in. Let's head home and get some rest. It's been a long day."

Stan arranged for the men participating in the morning raid to ride alone together in one of the wagons on the return trip home. Everyone except for Jamal and Glenn. Once underway, he huddled up with them. These men were his enforcers, ruffians, over the edge types, and Stan knew they looked forward to a good scrap.

"We ran into a hornet's nest today, didn't we fellows," Stan said.

"I didn't like it much taking orders from that Orr guy," Rog said.

"Neither did I. This incident made me look bad. Made us all look bad. Tomorrow, we're going to take that bus, but that's not all we're going to do."

"You thinking about payback, boss?" Leroy asked.

"Serious payback. We've done a lot for the CCW and precious

little for ourselves. We've never skimmed anything off the top. I ain't complaining about that, but tomorrow, when we hit Wineberry Hollow, I'm not going there as a member of the CCW, and I'm not going there as sheriff. I'm going there with you men, my band of brothers, and we're going to exact our own brand of justice. If any of you have second thoughts, I'm not going to object if you back out."

"Back out?" Rog said. "I'd say it's about goddamned time we did something for ourselves. The CCW is a decent gig and gets us respect in Wynot, but it sure isn't personally profitable."

"Wait a minute. What about the kid and Glenn?" Leroy asked.

"Jamal doesn't know that we're planning extracurricular activities and Glenn's going to be his baby sitter while we're out having fun."

"That works for me," Leroy said.

"What do you have in mind?" Hoss asked.

"Jamal tells me that his family lives at the very back end of the hollow in a new house. He also tells me that the community's medical facilities are located nearby, a doctor's office and a dentist. I can vouch for that. I know the doctor." And his daughter, Stan thought, but he didn't want to get into that with the men. He would dream about Katie tonight, the payback he had planned for her.

Billy spoke up. "You mean they have their own doctor and dentist?"

"Their own butcher, their own blacksmith, and their own new school at an Amish farm. Wineberry Hollow is a self contained community. If we take out their resources, they won't be so independent anymore. Then we can revisit anytime we want and take what we need."

"You got all this information out of the kid?" Terry Dairyman asked. "Is it reliable?"

"I believe him," Stan said. "I already told you about how I know the doctor, and in the before times Sam Wetzel was our family butcher. The kid was exact about those two and their locations, so I have no reason to believe he's lying about the rest. In the morning when we crest the mountain, we'll hit the blacksmith first. That one's going to be a bit dicey because we'll have Jamal with us. We'll have to make sure we don't become too exuberant there. The plan is to leave the kid and Glenn behind while we bust up the school. We'll commandeer an Amish horse and buggy and take care of the doctor and dentist and take out Jamal's father. On the way back from that raid, we may or may not take out the butcher shop depending on the time. We grab Jamal and Glenn and finish our business at the barricade. Drive the bus home."

"How are you going to get Glenn and the kid to cool their heels while we take care of all that other business?" Leroy asked.

"I got it all worked out," Stan said. "Every last detail."

Chapter 45

The two hour tractor ride from Wineberry Hollow to Wynot left little time to sleep for Stan and his handpicked band. The next morning they left Wynot at 4 AM for the return trip. He wanted to be in position and ready at the first glow of dawn for their raid. Anger over losing face during the encounter with Orr coupled with the lack of sleep left Stan in a foul mood. He embraced the feeling knowing he'd be primed to take out his irritation on the good citizens of Wineberry Hollow.

Stan drove the tractor while his men in the wagon dozed. The open air stung his face and he wore a wool hunting coat as a shield from the cold. Now that autumn was upon them, the weather presented a challenge. During the summer, a light jacket sufficed during their dawn patrols. No longer adequate against the late September chill, he and his CCW brethren had to bother with heavier coats and foul weather gear. He didn't enjoy carrying around the extra weight.

By now they had enough stores laid up to see the community of Wynot through the winter. The patrols would soon end.

Instead of driving to the exact spot they had parked during the previous evening, Stan pulled into a turnoff some distance from the Hagen's orchard. Although still dark, this time he and his men had each brought a battery powered flashlight.

They disembarked from the wagon. Stan tossed his wool hunting coat in the back, happy that his arms could move freely. The crew walked up the road moving quietly past the Hagen's farmhouse until reaching a low spot where they would be able to follow a gradual incline up the mountain.

Stan and Jamal led the way. His men crashed through the woods like bears on a rampage. If Orr had set up a watch, they'd be detected for sure. Jamal assured him that a fortified entrance was the hollow's only concentrated defense. There were no watches in the mountains. According to Jamal, they didn't have enough manpower which sounded reasonable to Stan.

It took an hour, and they finally reached the top of the mountain as the sun's yellow face peeked above Wineberry Hollow's eastern ridge.

No longer cold, perspiration ran from all of their red faces. Clear skies allowed the Earth's built-up heat to escape overnight. Now those clear skies would allow the sun to quickly heat the atmosphere. Stan figured it could hit 50 by noon. Maybe even 60.

"We'll pause here," Stan announced. "Check your weapons."

All of them carried handguns in various calibers. Each man also brought a long barreled weapon, either a rifle or shotgun. Stan carried a modified AR-15, his father's .22 revolver in a holster on his right hip, and a hunting knife.

Jamal grumbled. "Don't see why you won't let me have one of those pop guns."

Stan handed Jamal a set of binoculars. "You're supposed to be our hostage. Try these instead. Where's the blacksmith's place?"

After glassing the slope, Jamal lowered the binoculars and pointed. "See that smoke through the trees? That's gotta be coming from the Doaks's woodstove. Nothing else is around there.

They followed the ridge until stumbling onto the logging road that Jamal had described the previous night. Quietly as they could, they made their way down the road until, through the trees, Stan could make out the silhouette of a house. They approached to the edge of the tree line before he raised an arm and motioned for his team to huddle up.

In a voice barely above a whisper, Stan said, "Hoss, you and Leroy circle around the west side of the house. Rog, you and Billy circle east. Glenn, stay put right here with Jamal until one of us comes to fetch you. Terry Dairyman and I will bust through the back door."

Looking at Jamal, Stan asked. "Who all lives here?"

"Fred Doaks and his wife, Caroline, I believe is her name. They have two kids. Sadie is around 8 and they also have a boy a little younger than Sadie. Can't remember his name."

"Any mean dogs or anything else we should know about?"

Jamal shook his head.

Stan took a deep breath to calm his nerves. Prior excursions had involved an overwhelming number of CCW members, forty to fifty at a time, calling on mostly passive Amish families and farmers frightened out of their minds at such a force of men. This guerrilla style mission was different, dangerous, but also exciting.

He raised his hand over his head and drew an imaginary circle in the air. Hoss, Leroy, Rog, and Billy moved out. He gave them until the count of thirty and turned to Terry. "Let's go."

The two of them charged across the back yard and stopped, one on each side of the threshold to the back door. Stan slowly opened the screen door, held it, and nodded to Terry.

Terry tried the door knob. It didn't surprise Stan that the door was unlocked. Country folk rarely locked their doors. They rushed in, rifles at the ready and found themselves in a family room. Hurrying along, they turned a corner and entered the kitchen.

A black lady held a frying pan over a wood stove. She looked up and saw them. Her eyes went wide. She shot her hands to her face resting a palm against each cheek and screamed.

Stan's ears hurt so bad that he almost dropped his rifle. Jesus, how could women scream so loud? "Shut up," he shouted.

Terry raced across the kitchen floor and wrapped a hand around her throat.

"Listen to me," Stan said. "Caroline, right? Do as I ask and we will not harm anybody."

At that instant, Hoss and Leroy burst through the front door.

"Bedroom. Kids and husband," Stan directed. The two men understood immediately and disappeared down a hallway.

"Do anything you want to me, just please don't harm my children," Caroline said.

Hoss and Leroy returned, each towing a screaming child in pajamas.

Stan pointed to the dining room table. "Sit them down." Then to Caroline, "Go to them and get them to keep quiet."

Caroline Doaks ran to the table and hugged both kids close to her chest. They continued to sob but stopped their wailing.

"Where's your husband?" Stan asked.

She said nothing but her eyes flashed to the east wall.

"Go see what's out there and check on Rog and Billy. They were supposed to come around from that side," Stan ordered Leroy.

"Sure thing, Boss."

"What do you want?" Caroline asked, her voice cracking and eyes still saucer wide.

"Right now I need for your husband to join us."

"What's he ever done to you?" she screeched. "I don't even know you."

"Relax, Caroline, we don't want to hurt him. That's not why we're here."

Leroy walked back through the front door wearing a grin. A heavy black man followed, hands tied behind his back, his nose bloodied. Rog and Billy followed, their rifles pointed at the center of the man's back.

"Fred Doaks, I presume?" Stan asked.

The man shot him a menacing glare while Leroy led him to the dining room table. Leroy made him sit beside his wife. Caroline took a napkin from the table and dabbed at the blood running down Leroy's nose. The kids resumed their wailing.

It took several minutes until everyone calmed down.

"It's all clear out there," Hoss said.

"Who are you?" Fred asked. "What do you want?"

"Breakfast," Stan said. "We've already had a long morning and are about to have an exciting day. The bacon in the fry pan smells delicious." He glanced at Caroline. "Please, make us something to eat."

She exchanged glances with her husband. Fred nodded and she started working.

"Hoss, go get Glenn and the kid."

Moments later, Hoss led Glenn and Jamal into the house.

"What are you doing here?" Fred Doaks asked when he saw Jamal.

"Mind your own business," Jamal muttered.

"What? You with them?"

Jamal ignored him.

Stan began to explain. "You citizens of Wineberry Hollow are too independent. Think you have your own little self contained world. Think you don't need outsiders. My men and I are here to change that."

"What are you talking about?"

"Your ironworks keeps the hollow's horses shod, makes useful tools and implements, fixes damaged wagons. We're not going to harm you or your family, but we are definitely going to put you out of business."

He motioned to Hoss and Leroy. "Go take care of it."

Stan followed Hoss and Leroy a few minutes later and found them pounding away at the coal forge with sledge hammers. Pulverized fire bricks lay in a heap, the furnace broken to pieces. "All the king's horses and all the king's men."

"Huh?" Leroy asked.

"Never mind. You're done here. Come inside and get something to eat."

After they returned to the house, Stan asked, "What time are the kids expected at school?"

"Eight," Caroline said as she handed a plate of scrambled eggs to Glenn. "Mr. Damroth will soon be coming to fetch Sadie and Carl in the school wagon. Please, don't hurt him."

Stan clucked his tongue and said, "I already told you that nobody needs to get hurt if they do as we say." Looking into the kids faces, he said, "Good news. You get to play hooky today, but I'm going to need you to get dressed."

"I'll need to pick out their clothes," Caroline said.

Stan regarded her. "All right. Billy, you go with her."

While the kids got ready, Stan addressed Fred Doaks. "Jamal and my man Glenn are going to hang out here while the rest of us take care of our remaining business. We'll be leaving you and Caroline tied to these dining room chairs until we return about noon. We'll lock your kids in the bathroom. Then we'll be out of your hair…if you remain cooperative.

"My men and I will be riding on that school wagon. Before you think about attempting anything heroic or stupid while we're gone, always remember that if anything goes wrong, I'm ordering Glenn to take care of your kids first. Understand?"

Fred gave a curt nod.

A few minutes later, Rog shouted, "Tractor's coming up the

driveway."

Caroline brought her little ones, Sadie and Carl, into the kitchen. She begged, "Please don't do this."

"The kids are my leverage," Stan said.

They wouldn't let go of their mother and started sobbing. So did Caroline. She made no move to prod them forward.

Rog pulled his knife and held it to Caroline's throat. "Come on now, or I'll hurt your mommy."

The kids wailed and Fred struggled up from his dining room chair. Hoss pushed him back into his seat.

"Put the knife away," Stan said. "Terrorizing these kids is not what we need right now." He smiled and took them by the hand. "I won't let anyone hurt your mother, but you have to come with me to the bathroom."

"Be good, babies. We'll be right here in the dining room," Caroline called after them. She sobbed.

After locking the kids in the bathroom, Stan stepped onto the front porch.

The man on the tractor stared at him. "What's going on here?"

"I understand that you're Mr. Damroth?"

"That's right."

"Take the day off. I'll be driving these kids to school today."

"Like hell you will."

The old man had guts. "Tut, tut," Stan said and held his rifle in the direction of the wagon full of kids. "Rifle, kids, armed men, do I need to spell it out for you?"

"I guess not."

"That's better. What's your next stop?"

"These Doaks children live the furthest out. This is my last stop before heading for the school house."

"Excellent." Stan turned to his men. "All aboard." Then to Damroth, "Nice and easy, step down from the tractor."

Damroth did as instructed.

"What do we do with him?" Rog asked.

"Have Glenn tie him to a chair in the dining room along with Fred and Caroline."

Stan looked at the school children in the wagon, all of them staring at him. "No need to be alarmed, kids. Which one of you wants to be my navigator to the school?"

Chapter 46

Coop checked the calendar. September 28. Knowing that winter wheat needed to be in the ground about two weeks prior to the first frost, he decided today would be perfect. A little warm for working the fields, but the weather could easily turn nasty this time of year. He needed to take advantage of the time God gave him. Coop walked into his tool shed and pulled the lid from the white plastic bucket containing his seed. He ran his hand through the grain, brought out a fistful, and let the seeds trickle through his fingers back into the bucket.

He heard the old tractor pull into the driveway and figured it to be Mr. Damroth and the school kids. Coop glanced out the door and took in the sight. Men with guns sitting with the children. At first the thought unsettled him, but then he figured that Mr. Orr probably arranged for men in the militia to provide an escort because of yesterday's trouble. Were they afraid that the strangers would return? He had been told that the militia had driven them away.

Coop didn't want to second guess Mr. Orr's intentions, and it really wasn't his affair. He was glad he hadn't been there at the head end of the hollow to witness the violence. He put the thought out of his mind and loaded the bucket of grain onto a wheelbarrow. Next, he set about gathering tools. Just as he was about ready to push the load out of the tool shed, Mother burst through the threshold out of breath and trembling.

Tears streamed down her cheek. "They're going to burn our barn."

"Mother, what is this you are saying?"

She pointed a finger out the door. "The men. They're set to burn."

Obviously Mother had misunderstood something, but what was up with these men? Coop left the tool shed and walked their way with his mother several paces behind him. The scene was indeed strange. All of the school children stood gathered near the house, quiet as church mice as if shocked into silence. A man held a rifle on them. Why?

In a sign of deep distress, Sarah Godfrey sat on the ground swaying back and forth while fanning a hand in front of her face.

Wendy appeared to be arguing with one the men. Coop didn't remember seeing this one before. He appeared unkempt with a dirty white shirt. She waved a finger under his nose.

The man she argued with slapped Wendy. Hard. She fell to the ground.

Coop stopped dead in his tracks. Mother came up from behind and laid a hand on his arm.

The corners of Wendy's eyes leaked tears, and the man who had slapped Wendy hoisted her to her feet.

Coop approached, his heart pounding in his chest. "What are you doing?"

The man ignored him and said to Wendy. "I asked you if everyone was out?"

Wendy held a hand to her face where the brute had hit her. Coop saw that whatever fight she may have had had gone from her. "Yes, all the children are out."

"Light 'er up," he called to someone standing in the barn.

Coop's breath caught. "Do you really mean to burn our barn?"

The man who had been in the barn stepped out. "Sure do."

When Coop laid his eyes on the man, every hair on the back of his neck stood up.

Stan. Katie's Stan.

These men were not a part of Mr. Orr's militia. How did they get past the entrance to Cove Road. Had there been some sort of fight? Had the militia been defeated?

Coop removed his hat and stepped forward. "Please, do not burn my barn. The lower level is loaded with straw. Such a hot fire could spread and take the house."

"You own this place?" Stan asked.

He acted as if he didn't recognize Coop. Was it possible? Coop had been dressed in English clothes during their ugly encounter. "My mother and I own this farm."

Stan displayed a rueful smile. "Too bad, but you allowed your barn to be used as a school. I'm going to send a message to anyone who entertains such notions. Your barn will burn."

"Remain here," Coop said to his mother. He approached Stan to within ten feet. His body began to tremble uncontrollably. One date he had enjoyed with Katie. One date where he dared pretend to be English just to fit in. He had paid for his sins that night, but obviously it hadn't been enough. God had seen fit to punish him again. Would the humiliation, the degradation, follow him the rest of his life? For just that one sin? How could God be so cruel?

Coop got to his knees. "I beg you. I will do whatever you ask. Please show mercy."

"You freaking Amish make me sick," Stan said. "Get up."

Coop hesitated.

"I said stand up."

With quivering knees, Coop rose.

Stan looked him in the eye and frowned. "Do I know you?"

Coop turned away. He felt as if he would vomit.

"You're pathetic," Stan said. "It's so much easier when you Amish hide in your root cellars. Why don't you all go there now. Get out of my sight."

Another man appeared at the entrance to the barn. He displayed a lighter with an open flame.

"Put that out, Hoss," Stan said. "You might accidently drop it and start the whole thing burning."

Hoss tilted his head. "I thought that was the idea, boss."

"On our way back," Stan said. "Do it now and you'll have everyone in the hollow come running. We have something else to do first."

"Like what?"

"Destruction of their medical facilities, and a visit with an old girlfriend."

The humiliation Coop felt vanished. In its place, a rage burned hot as the flame from Hoss's lighter. He balled his fists and yelled, "No."

The world went quiet like a winter snow falling on the fields. Every eye looked on him, those from the savage men, the children, and Mother.

He and Stan stared at each other.

"Wonders never cease," Stan said. "Uncharacteristic backtalk from an Amish man. What did I say that struck such a nerve? I don't get it. You grovel at the thought of my burning your barn, but display righteous indignation about the community medical facilities?"

Coop squeezed shut his eyes and unclenched his fists. He had to keep a cool head. He had to think of some way to prevent Stan from harming Katie.

"What's the matter," Stan said. "Cat got your tongue? Explain yourself."

If he could only think of something. He prayed for insight. He silently begged God to keep this monster from Katie. He would take the punishment, the further humiliation upon himself if only Katie would be spared.

"Hey, I'm talking to you mutie," Stan said.

Their eyes locked and Coop saw a grin form on Stan's face. "No," Stan said. "It can't be. I can't be that lucky." He marched right up to Coop and stared at him. When Coop cast his gaze to the ground, Stan said, "It *is* you. It's really you."

"Cooper, what is this man talking about?" Mother asked.

"Cooper?" Stan asked. "So that's your name?" He laughed, set his gun down and clapped his hands. Then he started dancing. He actually danced.

This time, Coop couldn't hold it back. He shrank away a few paces and retched, his breakfast spewing from his stomach onto the ground.

Stan laughed even harder and pointed. Now in front of Mother and all the school children he had been made an object of mockery and derision. One small consolation. At least Hattie wasn't there to witness it. At least she was safe at the Amish school.

"Help him to his feet," Stan said after regaining his composure. "Tie his hands and put him in the wagon."

Two of the rough men took hold of him and dragged him along. They made him get onto the school wagon. Then they shoved him. He fell to the ground.

"Please, don't harm my son," he heard his mother say. More humiliation. Having to endure the entreaties of his mother.

Stan spoke. "School teacher, take your kids back into the barn. If anyone moseys by we want everything to look nice and normal till we return. Hoss, you and Leroy will stay here to make sure everyone behaves while the rest of us complete our other business."

He pointed to Coop's mother. "You join them."

"Gottes Wille," she mumbled and followed Wendy.

Really? Coop wondered. Is this what God wanted?

Coop pushed himself up and sat on the wagon bench. As the

children re-entered the barn, he saw Sammy Wetzel dart behind the shrubbery alongside the house. Coop feared for the boy. If those men saw him they might beat him. What was he doing? He should comply with their wishes. He sat there, his head down. What would Stan do to him now? The greatest mercy he could show would be to execute him. In fact, Coop would embrace that considering it a victory.

Minutes later, Stan climbed onto the wagon and took a seat beside Coop.

Coop didn't care. Whatever Stan had planned, it didn't matter anymore.

"Cooper, is it?" Stan asked. "Are you two still together?"

Coop understood Stan's meaning. "We never were. Together."

Stan sneered. "You and me both, pal." He looked down the road and sighed. "She sure is a tough nut to crack." He smiled. "Or should I say a tough cherry to pop."

"Katie is a human being. You talk as if she were an object."

"Hey, I'm a human being, too," Stan said. He slid closer to Coop. Their hips touched. "The thing I can't figure is her and *you*. How could something like that even happen? It boggles the mind."

"Let me join the others in the barn," Coop said. "I'll cause you no trouble."

"Where would the fun be in that?"

"What fun?"

"You and I have some unfinished business," Stan said, his voice cold like ice. "Katie and I also have some unfinished business. Why don't the three of us finish our business together? My business with Katie, well I imagine you know what that is. My business with you?"

Stan grabbed the point of Coop's chin and turned his head so that their eyes met. "My business with you is you get to watch."

Chapter 47

Stan thought it through. Leaving Damroth behind at the Doaks place may have been a miscalculation. The old man could have driven them to the back end of the valley. If anyone saw them along the way things would appear normal with Damroth in the driver's seat. The alternative Stan had decided on was to force

Cooper to drive them. He figured everyone in the hollow knew the young Amish man. It would be very unlikely that anyone would suspect anything afoul if they saw him driving. The mutie was too chicken shit to try anything heroic. Besides, it went against his religion, Gottes Wille and all that.

To Stan's surprise, Cooper refused to drive them at first. Stan threatened that things would not go well for Katie if he didn't cooperate. That's all it took to get the Amish man to do as ordered. The fool. Was the mutie so naïve that he really didn't know how it would end for both him and Katie?

How sweet to be able to finish his business with both of them. Stan still couldn't believe his luck in having discovered the mutie's identity, although it raised other questions. Stan glanced at the back of Cooper's head and the ridiculous straw hat he wore. Why would an otherwise devout Amish man like Cooper don English clothes? And why would a hot chick like Katie go out with this guy when she was so obviously out of his league? Within the next few minutes, he meant to have the answers to those questions.

As they approached the tail end of the hollow, the trees grew closer to the road. The old tractor's engine noise echoed louder in the trees which added to the squeak of wagon boards rubbing against each other. Stan told his men to keep their guns down and out of sight. Terry Dairyman and Billy and Rog looked ill at ease, their gazes darting from house to house, farm to farm. Did anyone living along the road appear alarmed? Other than an old woman hanging laundry on a line, nobody even looked their way.

Stan shouted for Mutie to drive past the Hunt's driveway and park in the field at the foot of Jamal Orr's driveway. That kid willingly provided a lot of intel. Stan hoped it would all prove to be accurate. For Jamal's sake, it had better.

Cooper shut off the motor but kept his eyes forward. Did the mutie think that ignoring Stan would somehow change his fate?

The four men jumped off the back of the wagon and shouldered their weapons. Stan motioned with his head toward the entrance of the Orr's driveway and said, "Billy, Rog, you know what to do." He watched as they disappeared into the woods.

"Wouldn't mind tagging along with them to see justice done to that big black man," Terry uttered.

"We have our own mission just as rewarding," Stan said, "and you're my wingman."

Terry smiled. "Let's get 'er done then."

"Climb on down," Stan ordered Cooper.

The Amish man obeyed and stood beside the tractor, a vapid look on his face.

Stan shoved him. "Lead the way. March right up to your sweetheart's door and knock. Remember to smile."

They walked single file up the driveway, this being their riskiest moment. Stan didn't want to be spotted too early. He needed to get inside the house. To his relief, they stepped onto the porch no one having seen them. Cooper knocked.

A woman answered. Someone Stan had never seen before.

"Cooper?" The woman asked from the other side of the screen. She frowned. "Is something wrong?"

Cooper removed his hat. Fingered it. "Sheila, these men." He stopped.

"What is it?" she asked and opened the door.

Terry grabbed the door and stepped inside.

"Who are you? What is this?"

In a quick motion Terry smacked Sheila in the jaw with the butt of his rifle. Without so much as a whimper, she crumbled to the floor out cold.

Cooper dropped to his knees and cradled Sheila's head. He raised his voice. "There was no need to harm her."

"Shut up or the same will happen to you," Stan said. Where was Katie and her father? Had they heard the commotion? He caught movement coming from the back yard. Stan looked through the kitchen and dining room and out the sliding glass door which led to a patio. Katie and her father worked at the far edge of the yard stacking firewood.

"Check the rest of the house," Stan ordered Terry. "We'll wait here for you."

"Bring a pillow from one of the beds," Cooper ordered, his voice surprisingly uppity.

Terry met Stan's gaze. "Do as he says," Stan said.

A minute later, Terry returned. "Clear." He threw a pillow at Cooper who eased it under Sheila's head.

"Not a bad looking lady," Terry said leering at the prone woman.

"You want to have a go at her? Be my guest," Stan said. "The mutie and I have business outside."

"No, you must not do such a thing," Cooper shouted.

Terry laughed while unlatching his belt buckle. "Who's going to stop me? You?"

"C'mon, Mutie," Stan said. He grabbed Cooper under his arm and hauled him to his feet. Even after his verbal protest, no physical fight could be found in the man. Not much of a man at all.

Stan slid open the door to the patio and pushed Cooper over the threshold.

Katie saw them. She dropped the log she was about to hand to her father. Dr. Hunt didn't see them right away. He straightened from his bent position and rubbed his hip. The shocked look on Katie's face must have clued him in. He followed her gaze.

Stan saw a flash of recognition in Katie's father's eyes. Dr. Hunt asked, "What's this man have to do with you, Cooper?"

Cooper continued to finger his hat but said nothing.

"He doesn't speak much," Stan said with a laugh. He drank Katie in, head to toe. "From past experience we already know that, don't we Katie?" Stan didn't like her new haircut but admired the way perspiration made her face glow and the way her tee shirt clung to the curves of her breasts. She seemed skinnier than before. No doubt from doing more physical labor and eating less. The fear displayed in her eyes turned him on.

"What's he talking about?" Dr. Hunt asked Katie. Then he turned his attention back to Stan. "Where's Sheila?"

"Entertaining the troops," Stan said.

Dr. Hunt glanced at the patio door and stepped forward. Stan raised his rifle and pointed it at him.

Dr. Hunt froze. "What do you want?"

"Me," Katie said in a matter-of-fact tone. "He wants me."

* * *

Sheila Cunningham emerged from a deep fog, her jaw on fire. Probing the hot area with her tongue, she realized that she had lost teeth. She tasted blood. Swallowed blood. Was she dreaming? Was she in bed? If so, the hard mattress hurt her back.

She couldn't breathe. Something heavy lay on top of her. Sheila gasped for air.

She heard a man's voice. "Welcome back, darling." She felt

him groping her body and grunting.

Then Sheila remembered. The Amish man, Cooper Stover, and the strange men who accompanied him. One of them had hit her.

She flailed her arms and tried to scream. "Get off me."

"We just got started." He grabbed her wrists and forced her arms above her head pinning them to the floor. He leaned in and kissed her roughly on the mouth.

She pinched his lower lip between her teeth and bit down hard.

The man yelped and tried pulling away. She clamped down determined to tear flesh from his face. He released her wrists and gouged at her eyes. Hot white sparks flashed beneath her eyelids. Liquid squirted from the corners of her eyes. Excruciating pain distracted Sheila, and she relaxed her bite and let go of his lip.

They both screamed.

Sheila bucked. The man fell off her and landed on the floor. With her eyes watering from the assault and unable to get them open, Sheila spit blood and tried to ignore the pain. Scrambling to her feet, she felt her way along the wall and headed for the kitchen, the block of knives on the counter being her goal.

She felt her way past the refrigerator when suddenly her head jerked back. The man grabbed a fistful of hair and forced her to her knees. "You'll die for ruining my lip, bitch."

She fell forward against the man's legs. With his testicles within reach, she grabbed them and squeezed. The scream escaping from the man was the loudest cry she ever heard. He punched her in the temple. A relatively anemic punch but forceful enough to knock her to the floor.

Knowing that he would kill her, Sheila willed herself to not slip back into unconsciousness. Her eyes had swollen shut making it impossible for her to see. Crawling on the floor, she bumped into the stove. Grabbing the edge of the counter, she pulled herself up.

The man groaned just a few feet away. She heard him vomit. Feeling around on the counter top, she tried locating the knives.

"Oh, no you don't," the man said, his voice weaker now and rasping. Sheila heard him scrambling along the floor in an effort to reach her.

Where were those damn knives? The block should be right in front of her. She waved her arms along the counter in a panic sending pots flying, her hands banging into the coffee maker and the microwave.

Hands closed around her ankles. Knowing that he would try to jerk her off her feet, Sheila tried kicking, but his grip was too strong. He yanked her feet from the floor.

As she went down, Sheila's fingertips brushed the tops of the knives neatly stowed in the wooden block. She fell on top of her attacker. The block fell on top of her and bounced off, the knives falling free of their nest and clattering against the linoleum.

The man pushed her off and rolled on top of her. One of the knives ended up beneath her hip. The man wrapped both hands around her throat. Instinctively, she grabbed hold of the man's wrists trying to break his hold.

He was too strong.

God, it hurt. She couldn't breathe. Despite the pain and swelling, her eyes bugged open.

Through a film of sticky liquid, Sheila saw the man staring down at her, grimacing. This was it, then. In a few moments, she would be dead. The handle of the knife beneath Sheila pressed against her hip bone mocking her as if saying, "So close."

Weakening and her lungs burning from lack of air, Sheila reached for the knife and closed her hand around the blade. The sharp edge sliced into her palm as she unwedged it from between the floor and her hip sending a new bolt of pain through her.

With her hand slick from blood and barely able to grasp, Sheila managed to right the knife in her hand. Gathering her little remaining strength and resolve, she plunged the knife into the man's side.

* * *

Coop listened with horror to the screaming and crashing taking place inside the house. Certain that Stan's partner was killing Sheila, he turned toward the patio door.

"Hold it," Stan yelled and pointed his rifle at his chest.

In that moment, while Stan was distracted, Dr. Hunt grabbed a log of firewood and flung it at Stan. Stan must have seen it coming and ducked just in time. Too bad. That log was right on target and would've brained him.

Dr. Hunt grabbed another log and sent it flying at Stan. For an older man, he was quick.

Stan raised his rifle stock to ward off the blow. Before he could point the barrel at the doctor, another log flew his way. Then another. The last one slammed into his shin bone, and he howled.

The next log Dr. Hunt reached for was a thick one. Its weight slowed him down just enough so that Stan was able to point his rifle and shoot from the hip. He squeezed the trigger. The rifle bucked.

Coop stopped breathing unable to fathom what had happened. A red bloom in the middle of Dr. Hunt's chest indicated that Stan's shot had found its mark.

Dr. Hunt slumped against the wood pile and reached a hand toward Katie. He tried speaking but coughed blood.

Katie shrank back and screamed.

Dr. Hunt melted to the ground, blood gouting from his chest and mouth. His eyes met Stan's. Dr. Hunt's body relaxed and his stare went vacant.

Recovering his senses, Coop shouted, "What have you done?" He ran to Dr. Hunt and knelt at his side. "This man was a healer, a good friend to everyone. You have taken the life of a man who was put on this Earth as a gift from God."

Katie gawked at her father's dead body but didn't approach. She brought both fists to her mouth and chewed on her knuckles. She stopped screaming and rocked on her feet making mewling noises.

"You could've stopped me, Mutie. You stood right beside me while God's gift hurled those logs at me. While I was warding off Doc's missiles, you could've taken me down. You're built like a tank, so you know you could've, farm boy. Instead, you just stood there."

"You are despicable," Cooper shouted. He straightened and gazed at Stan's gun. Could he close the gap in time to tackle the murderer before being shot?

As if reading his thoughts, Stan jerked his rifle, pointing it at Coop. "I'd really like for you to try, Mutie, in fact I'm going to force your hand." He looked at Katie. "What do you think, Katie doll? Am I to blame for pulling the trigger or is your boyfriend to blame for being too slow to knock the gun from my hands. C'mon, it would've been easy for him."

"Bastard," she said, her face beet red. She sat on the ground and rested her father's head in her lap.

Coop's anger matched Katie's. This vile man needed to be

stopped. Humility be damned. If given the chance, he was going to kill Stan Cox. Glaring, he uttered, "I am not afraid of you."

Instead of seeing desperation on Stan's face at Coop's newfound determination, the murderer smiled as if amused. "Why don't you frigging do something about it then?"

"Put down that rifle and I'll tear you to pieces."

"I'm happy to oblige, Mutie, I've got no problem at all with that request." Stan lowered the rifle to the ground and wiggled his fingers at Coop. "Come."

Enraged, Coop bounded toward him. Quick as lightning, Stan drew a handgun from his belt and aimed it square at Coop's chest.

"Nooo," Katie screamed.

Coop stopped short. "Now who's the coward."

"You're the one who stopped. If you think you can stop me, come and try."

"Don't do it, Coop," Katie begged. "He's just looking for a reason to kill you."

Stan walked in her direction keeping the gun pointed at Coop. "I don't need no reason, Katie doll. I'm just seeing how much humiliation Mutie will take."

His entire body trembled from the adrenaline surging through him. "Leave. Her. Alone." Each word, he shouted after taking a ragged breath.

Katie backed away from her father's body until she bumped into the woodpile,

"You going to take off your clothes or are you going to let me do it for you?" Stan asked.

Katie held her fingers in front of her like claws. "I'll scratch out your eyes if you try."

In a quick movement, Stan swatted her hands away and shoved her to the ground.

Coop lunged, but once again Stan was too quick and trained his gun on him.

"Don't do it," Katie shrieked. "No matter what happens to me don't give him the satisfaction of killing you. If you get a chance, run."

"Run," Stan said mocking Katie's girlish voice.

"I'll never run again from the likes of you," Coop said, the coldness of his tone surprising him.

Stan narrowed his eyes and pointed the gun at Katie. "If you run, I'll put a bullet in her face. Her death will be on your hands. I want you here."

Still on the ground, Katie scooted backwards away from Stan until once again hemmed in by the woodpile.

Stan placed a foot on her stomach, forcing her flat against the ground.

Katie grabbed his foot and tried to trip him, but Stan kicked her in the ribs. She yelped and went limp. She glanced at Coop with a resigned expression. "Let him do his worst, Coop. I don't want you to die on my account."

Stan spoke, "Maybe if you had been this easy in the before times, this wouldn't have been necessary. Your father would still be alive. That means you share some of the blame, too."

"Don't listen to him, Katie," Cooper said. It dawned on him that she would let Stan have his way with her in order to save his life. Feeling frustrated and impotent, he remained rooted in place.

"How far must I push you, Mutie?" Stan untied Katie's sneakers and pulled them from her feet. He unbuttoned and unzipped Katie's jeans. He grabbed the waist band and tugged them from her hips, never taking his eyes off Coop. "How far?"

Coop tried another approach. Maybe Stan wanted him to beg. So be it. He would beg. Clasping his hands in front of him as if in prayer, he uttered, "Don't do this to her. Please."

Stan pulled Katie's jeans from around her knees and slipped them completely off. He tossed them to the side. "I don't want you to beg, Mutie. I want you to try and stop me."

"You'll just shoot him," Katie said, her voice sounding detatched.

"Indeed I will," Stan said. "Well, at least I'll try. Who knows? Your boyfriend might get lucky. While I'm in the throes of passion, he might be able to overtake me before I can squeeze off a shot. He might be able to cover the twenty feet or so separating us. Think you can do it, Mutie?"

"Katie had feelings for you once. How could you do this to her?" Coop reasoned.

"You're not even going to try?" Stan tugged Katie's tee shirt over her head and arms, balled it up, and gently slipped it under her head. "Why not make her comfortable? Poor girl just lost her father." He ran a hand down her thigh and leg and positioned himself between her legs.

Desperate for an opening in which he could intervene, Coop balled his fists and waited for Katie to fight him, distract him. But she just lay there.

"Absolutely delicious. Perfect," Stan said. "It strikes me that you're enjoying this, Mutie. I'll bet you've never seen this much of a girl. Thrilling, isn't it? So soft they are. Skin so smooth. Who knows? You might get off watching me do her. The way she is now, all traumatized, she probably won't object if you take a turn after I'm done. Hell, she probably won't even remember. You can rape her, and then blame it all on me."

Katie's head lolled to the side. She met Coop's gaze. What did he read in her expresssion? A pleading? Expectation? Dismay? Disgust?

"Enough," Cooper said.

"Really?" Stan bent, and while keeping an eye on Cooper licked Katie's torso from her navel up to the valley between her breasts.

Katie shuddered.

Stan unzipped his trousers and freed himself. "Katie Hunt, our time has finally come."

"No," Cooper said. He picked a small log from the ground, one of the projectiles Dr. Hunt had thrown at Stan. "I will not allow this to happen."

Stan grasped the elastic of Katie's panties with one hand. His other hand held the gun trained on Coop.

Cooper started toward him and raised the log in both hands like a baseball bat.

Stan pulled back the hammer on the revolver. "Too bad, Mutie. You aren't going to win. You never stood a chance against me."

Stan's body suddenly convulsed and his eyes went wild. A stick protruded from beneath his throat. Not a stick, Coop realized, an arrow. Blood soaked through Stan's shirt and pulsed onto Katie's belly. The revolver dropped from his hand.

Coop turned.

A grim faced Sammy Wetzel stood at the edge of the lawn, bow in hand.

Chapter 48

Declan Orr hadn't slept a wink. His fool of a son running off and not returning home had sent Chelsey into a panic. During the night, she had paced around the house and periodically ventured outside calling Jamal's name, begging him to show himself if he were hiding nearby.

Far as Orr was concerned, Jamal could damn well stay away until he learned some respect. A night alone in the woods might clear the boy's head and make him realize how good of a life he had. Orr remembered sleepless nights on far away battlefields, pondering whether the next day might be his last. Now *that* had been stressful. Although the world had changed, Jamal was surrounded by family and friends. He had no worries. He'd better get over his self absorbed funk, because Orr had run out of patience.

Chelsey had been too out of sorts to see Nate and Keisha off to school. Earlier, he had walked with his two younger children to the bottom of their driveway and watched them board Mr. Damroth's makeshift school bus. At 12 and 10, these two had adapted easier. At 15, Jamal was in that difficult in-between time period, no longer a child, but too young to be a man. Orr remembered his own adolescence and had to admit that growing up as a poor kid in Detroit hadn't been easy. But he had gotten through it, just as other kids get through it. Jamal had no excuse.

Damn him for worrying his mother.

Chelsey stood on the front porch still wearing a housecoat and watching the yard. Her hands gripped the porch rail.

Orr laid a hand on her arm. "He'll be fine."

"You don't know that," Chelsey said in a calm tone, her bloodshot eyes and puffy face a further indication of her anxiety.

"Jamal may be arrogant and rebellious, but he's not stupid. He can take care of himself."

"He's just a boy, and you let him wander off. You didn't even try to stop him," Chelsey said, her voice reflecting exasperation.

Orr recognized the tone. When Chelsey got this way and dug in her heels, there would be no arguing with her. Saying nothing, he stepped off the porch and headed into the trees. He had a hunch that Jamal might have spent the night in the hidey cave. That would make sense, Jamal knew how to get there even in the dark.

He found the entrance to the cave. "Jamal, you in there? Come out, son."

No response. He entered and found the cave empty. Orr wiped his brow with his sleeve. Fool kid. Where could he be?

Orr exited the cave. Could Jamal have returned to the militia encampment. The kid at this moment may be pestering Corporal Clark. He hoped not. Then again part of him wished it were true so that Chelsey could quit worrying. Making a move like that might make sense to Jamal. He was familiar enough with the shift schedule and would know that his father wouldn't be there.

He decided to drive out to the encampment and see. Good idea anyway to check on the mood of the men after last night's incident. They had all been jazzed about turning away the bullies, but having experienced combat, Orr understood that sometimes outward ebullience covered underlying nervousness. Physically they had performed well for non-professionals, maintained discipline, but could these inexperienced peaceable folk handle the psychological impact of having their homes and families threatened?

While walking toward his Mustang, Orr heard small arms fire and halted. His military mind kicked in. Number of shots? Bearing? He had heard two pops in quick succession coming from the vicinity of Dr. Hunt's house.

"Chill," Orr said aloud. Somebody probably just shot a deer. After last night, he was jumpy.

From the corner of his eye, Orr detected movement, a flash of blue jeans among the foliage. He eased behind a tree trunk and watched. Two men approached the house, paralleling the driveway and using the woods for cover. They moved slowly, holding rifles and trying not to rustle the brush.

Orr didn't recognize them, and from their actions, they obviously planned an assault. Were these the only two? He scanned behind them but could detect no other movement. Were those previous shots hostile fire? How did these men get past the encampment?

Before he could get answers to those questions, Orr knew he had to neutralize this situation first. From here, he had a clear view of the front porch. Chelsey had gone inside. He hoped she would stay there.

Two of them, he thought, and they had rifles.

Orr looked at his bare hands. What could he do? A few yards from where he stood, a steep bank about eight feet high dropped off onto the driveway. His best plan of action would be to jump the two men as they passed by. The problem was that he would have to jump onto the road and attack as they walked through the woods on the other side. The plan was precarious at best, but there was no time to consider other alternatives. Would the element of surprise give him enough advantage to take them down? If they were trained soldiers, he wouldn't stand a chance.

The two men pulled even with Orr and stopped. Had they sensed him?

One of them spoke in a low voice but loud enough for Orr to hear. "What are you doing, Billy?"

Billy inspected his rifle. "Making sure I chambered a round. We should split up. Give me about five minutes to circle around. We'll bust in simultaneously, me from the back, you from the front."

"How will I know when you're ready?"

"I'll fire a round through the door before I kick it in. When you hear that come running. Remember, Stan doesn't want us to dick around. Listen, Rog, we need to pop everyone in the house, especially the big black dude, and join back up with Stan right away."

"You don't need to repeat the boss's orders to me," Rog said. "I'm no retard."

"Just making sure. Be ready." Billy snuck away toward the house.

Orr prayed for Chelsey to stay inside, and realized that God had already given him a huge advantage. Now he needed only to take down Rog, overpower him, take his rifle and intercept Billy before he invaded the house. His timing needed to be perfect, otherwise Chelsey would die.

Orr breathed deeply calming his mind and racing heart, like he had done too many times in the past before a big battle. He counted slowly to one hundred, figuring that would give the two men enough separation to allow him to make his move.

Ninety-eight, ninety-nine, one hundred.

Orr moved toward the bank at the edge of the driveway and

jumped. He damn near cleared the driveway but landed hard. His knees buckled under the impact, and he somersaulted into the trees. The forward momentum carried him through the roll and he popped back up onto the balls of his feet, fists at his side.

The wide eyed, slack jawed expression on Rog's face reassured Orr that he had taken the man completely by surprise. Before Rog could react, Orr smashed him in the jaw with his fist. As Rog went down, Orr grabbed the man's rifle and yanked it from his grasp. It took every ounce of Orr's will power to not pull the trigger. He would have, except it would give him away.

Using the toe of his shoe, Orr jabbed Rog in the ribs. The man was out cold.

How much time had passed? He needed to move. Orr abandoned cover and ran right up the middle of the driveway toward the house. He assumed that Billy would circle around the house to the right since they had come from that side of the driveway.

Orr circled left to meet the man head-on. The safest course of action would have been to sneak up from behind, but Orr didn't want to risk that he had fallen too far back. Not with Chelsey's life at stake.

He cleared the side of the house just in time to see Billy point his rifle at the back door.

"Yo," Orr shouted.

Billy jerked around in Orr's direction.

Orr aimed for the middle of Billy's chest and fired.

Billy dropped his rifle and stumbled backwards, his arms wind milling.

Orr shot twice more, one to the chest, and one to the face.

Chelsey burst through the back door and seeing the man down covered her mouth.

"It's over," Orr said not giving her a chance to speak. "Get back in the house. I'll be joining you soon."

She looked between him and the dead man before shuffling backward through the door.

Orr found Rog where he had left him. The man had regained consciousness and sat on the ground with his back leaning against a tree trunk. He held the front tail of his shirt over his face to staunch the bleeding.

"Spill it," Orr said. "Tell me everything."

Rog snickered. "Screw you."

Orr squatted in front of Rog, reached out, and twisted his nose. Rog howled.

"How did you get past the encampment?" Orr asked. "How many are you? What's the objective?"

After spitting a mouthful of blood, Rog said, "We bypassed the road block. Came in over the top of the mountain."

It made sense to Orr. He anticipated that would be how a surprise attack would happen, but he didn't expect that it would occur so soon. "I overheard you talking about your leader, Stan. How does he play into this?"

Rog held the shirt to his nose and pointed with his head toward the valley below. "He has some dealings with a girl down there, but I don't know what that's all about, I swear it."

Could he be referring to Katie? "Anybody else?"

Rog told him about Hoss and Leroy waiting at the school for their return.

"Is that it?"

"Are you going to kill me?"

Orr sensed that the man was holding something back. "Any reason why I shouldn't?"

"How do you suppose we knew how to breech that mountain, how to find the school, how to find your house?"

The sudden realization caused an iron weight to drop into Orr's gut.

The smirk on Rog's face grew wide. "You want to see your boy again, you'd better keep me alive."

Chapter 49

Deep sorrow flooded through Declan Orr's soul after seeing Dr. Hunt dead. Such a terrible loss to the community. Such a good friend. Just as it had been during those countless times on the battlefield when he had lost good friends, they still remained in the thick of danger and there was no time to grieve. Sheila Cunningham had killed her attacker with a steak knife. Battered and barely able to see through swollen eyes, her hand bandaged, she limped from the house helped along by young Sammy Wetzel, one of her arms around his shoulder. The way the story went, the lad had killed the gang's leader by shooting an arrow through his back. Katie Hunt shuffled behind Sheila in zombie like shock, another look Orr had seen countless times among battle fatigued troops. How did she and Cooper Stover figure into this? It would all have to be sorted out later.

He sent Katie and Sheila up to his house with instructions to join Chelsey in the hidey cave. He wanted the women to be safe in case things went bad. Cooper had confirmed that only two men had stayed behind at the school, but Orr wasn't sure whether he was getting the whole truth from Rog about the rest of the plan.

Orr set Rog in the school wagon and tied his hands and feet. Sammy sat beside Rog wearing Stan's baseball cap. Orr looked at Cooper. "The two men at the school house are expecting you to return as the driver. With luck, they'll see Rog here and assume that Sammy and I are Stan and Terry. I hope to surprise them and take them out before they discover the truth."

Cooper's hands trembled. "Take them out? There has already been so much death."

After having witnessed the depravity of the thugs, how was it possible this young man still held on to his Amish sensibilities. He leaned in toward Cooper, got in his face. "Man up. Two of my children are in your barn."

"As are most of the children living in Wineberry Hollow," Cooper said. "As is my mother and Wendy Godfrey and Sarah."

"Then I'm glad you grasp the seriousness of the situation. Drive this rig home and act like nothing unusual has happened. I'll take care of the rest."

Cooper's eyes widened. "You intend on fighting those men yourself? Shouldn't you have help?"

"The only organized help is at the road block. We won't be able to drive past your farm to get to them without being seen. Even if we did, a show of force might get those kids killed. You're going to have to trust my judgment. This rescue falls squarely on my shoulders and yours." Orr stopped talking and stared into Cooper's eyes. "Can I depend on you? If not, my only other choice is to have Sammy drive. He has the brass to do it, but I'd much rather it be you."

They both glanced at Sammy. Orr figured that once the

adrenaline wore off, the weight of having killed a man would come crashing down on Sammy. He didn't want the boy to be driving when that happened. The way Cooper eyed Sammy led Orr to believe that the Amish man also understood this.

"Yes, I will drive," he finally said.

"Get us there at a leisurely pace. Attract as little attention as possible and drive right up to the entrance of the barn. After you park, I want you and Sammy to dismount on the far side keeping the tractor between you and the barn. Got it?"

Cooper nodded.

He turned to Sammy. "Have I made myself clear?"

"Crystal."

As they rode down Cove Road, Orr thought out his plan. The barn had no windows to speak of. Just before they pulled even with the barn, he would roll out the back of the wagon and sneak around the blind side opposite the road. Using this tactic, he hoped to get the drop on the two attackers.

He turned his attention to Rog. The man was restrained and wouldn't be able to do much, but he could yell a warning. Orr fashioned a gag out of an oily rag he found lying in the wagon and tied it around Rog's neck after wedging the material in his mouth. Orr wished he could've killed this vermin earlier, but he believed that a remnant of the gang held Jamal, and Rog knew where they were holding him. He needed to keep the man alive. For now.

Had Jamal willingly betrayed his neighbors? Did his son hate him so much that he would be capable of such treachery? Orr hung his head. Was he that imperceptive of a father to not have seen the depth of Jamal's pain?

Orr snapped out of it. His inadequacies and Jamal's crimes would be dealt with at a later time. His other two children needed him now.

The barn came into view. Orr leaned over to Sammy and said, "Remember what I told you. Put the tractor and wagon between you and the barn. It took a lot of guts to do what you did at Dr. Hunt's house, but I need you to stay out of this battle, son. I don't want to be distracted by worrying about you and Cooper. Do you understand?"

"Yes, sir," Sammy said.

God, this boy was younger than Jamal and today he had killed a man. Whatever happened next, this day would mark a turning part for the residents of Wineberry Hollow. His neighbors who may have adopted the notion that the world had become somehow more idyllic or romantic since the world went dark would finally understand. With the loss of electricity also came the loss of civilization and decency. Until now they had been sheltered, but evil had found them at last, just as Orr knew it eventually would. But today, evil would not prevail. Not on his watch.

Almost at the driveway, Orr jumped off the back of the wagon, ran to the back of the barn, and pressed his back against the wall. He clicked off the safety to his rifle and ran around to the other side of the barn. He peeked around the corner just in time to see a man emerge from the barn.

"Rog, is that you? Who's that with you? Where's Stan and the others?"

Damn it. Where was the second man?

"What the hell?" The man said. He must have seen the gag in Rog's mouth. The man pulled a handgun and yelled, "We got trouble, Hoss."

Orr stepped into view. "Don't move."

The man reacted by pointing his weapon at Orr. Orr took him out with two shots to the chest.

Inside the barn, kids started screaming.

Orr shuffled closer to the door. "You in there. Give it up. You're surrounded."

"Daddy, Daddy," a small voice shouted. It was Keisha.

Aw, shit. He hadn't anticipated that. Moments later the second man showed himself carrying Keisha around her waist, a handgun pressed to her temple. His face was pale, eyes wide with fear. His hand shook. Not a good situation.

A lump formed in Orr's throat. Could he risk putting a round into the man's forehead?

Before either of them had a chance to say anything, Nate raced from the barn. He pummeled the man's back with his fists and cried out, "Don't you hurt my sister."

The man's concentration faltered, and he swatted at Nate with his gun hand.

Orr took advantage of the distraction provided by his son. He pulled the trigger and watched the man's head explode.

Orr ran to Keisha and Nate and gathered them up, one in each arm and squeezed them close to his chest. "I'm sorry you had to see me shoot those men. So sorry you had to live through that." Whatever psychological damage this incident would inflict on his little children, at least they were alive.

The next few minutes Orr spent commiserating with the adults, Wendy Godfrey, Cooper Stover, and Cooper's mother. The consensus was to have Cooper drive all of the children home immediately. Orr argued against that plan since he wasn't sure where the remnant of the gang were holed up. His argument prevailed and the decision was made to keep the children in the barn for the time being until the situation became more clear. Cooper and Sammy would stand watch outside. Wendy Godfrey would remain inside the barn with a shotgun. She told them in no uncertain terms that she had no reservations about using the shotgun if it came to someone threatening the children.

Once the children settled in, Orr drove off with the tractor and wagon, Rog his only remaining passenger. After reaching the roadblock at the entrance to Cove Road, Corporal Clark and his team gathered around.

Orr filled them in.

"All of that went down while we dilly dallied here at the roadblock?" Clark asked.

"Not your fault," Orr said. "You couldn't have known."

"What now?" Clark asked.

Orr turned his attention to his prisoner. He mounted the wagon and removed Rog's gag. "Where are the rest of your gang? Where's my son?"

Rog spat and cursed. "I almost choked to death on that oily rag. I need water."

"It'll go worse for you if you don't talk." He held a canteen to Rog's lips and let the man drink.

Rog smirked. "I'll talk, but first I need some assurances."

"You're in no position to bargain."

"Sure I am. As long as you want to see your kid again."

"What do you want?"

"Turn me loose. Let me drive away in that fancy Mustang of yours. Give me a pen and paper. I'll write it all down and leave it in the mailbox of those people who own the orchard. By the time you get there with this old tractor I'll be out of rifle range."

"Dream on," Orr said. "That's not going to happen."

"Those are my terms. Either agree or take your chances and kill me now. Of course, doing that would be as good as killing your son."

"I have a better idea." Orr turned to Clark. "Find me a bucket and a tarp."

Rog's eye twitched. "What are you going to do?"

Orr pointed over his shoulder. "Let's take a walk, you and I, to yonder stream."

The men untied Rog from the wagon slats but kept his wrists and ankles tied. They carried him to the bank of the stream.

"Lay him on his back. Let his head dangle over the bank's edge."

The militia men did as Orr told them. Gary Daw straddled Rog's chest to keep him from rolling onto his side.

"Get off me," Rog sputtered.

"In due time," Orr said.

Clark returned with a blue tarp, the cheap plastic kind with brass grommets they used to be able to buy at any hardware store. Orr unfolded the tarp, took it in both hands and shook it out. He laid it on the ground like a table cloth beside Rog. "Get his ankles," he said to Clark.

After Clark pinned Rog's ankles and with Gary Daw on his chest, the man had been rendered immobile.

"Now. Tell me what I want to know," Orr said.

Rog's eyes went wider now, the haughtiness having left his expression. "Kill me and your boy is as good as dead."

Orr leaned over Rog until their noses touched. "Who said anything about killing you?" He dipped the bucket into the stream and filled it. With his free hand, Orr laid the tarp over Rog's face and sealed it tight over the man's nose and mouth.

Beneath the tarp, Rog protested, but his protests were muffled.

Orr raised the bucket over Rog's face and slowly poured a steady stream onto the tarp in the area of his nose and mouth.

Rog's protests stopped and he began bucking and writhing. Clark and Daw kept him pinned. After the bucket emptied, Orr pulled the tarp from Rog's face. The water tight tarp prevented any of the water from penetrating, but Rog gasped for air, his face displaying terror.

"You tried to drown me," Rog shrieked.

"The only liquid on your face is your own snot and sweat," Orr said. "The gag reflex is one of man's strongest impulses, and I can trick your mind into thinking you're actually drowning."

"Screw you," Rog yelled.

"I've water boarded tougher SOBs than you can possibly know, battle hardened soldiers, terrorist extremists, so I know that one or two more times is all it'll take. Save yourself the misery and tell me now what I need to know." For emphasis, Orr dipped the bucket into the stream and refilled it.

The smirk reappeared on Rog's face. "It wasn't so bad after all."

"Oh, yeah? Let me remind you then." Orr slid the tarp back onto Rog's face and poured. No sooner had he started than the man thrashed wildly.

This time, when Orr removed the tarp, tears streamed from Rog's eyes. "Enough," he sobbed. "Enough."

Orr nodded to Clark and Daw to let him up.

Rog pulled himself up to a sitting position. "We left your boy at the blacksmith's place. One guy is minding him and the blacksmith's family."

"Only one?" Orr asked.

"Yes, Glenn is his name. We were going to return there after our other business, get them, and present ourselves here. With the boy as our hostage Stan figured we could exchange him for your bus."

"Foolhearty," Gary Daw said. "A suicide mission."

"Could've easily worked if things hadn't gone our way," Orr said. "Of course, it wasn't so lucky for Dr. Hunt or the rest of the innocents who had to suffer through this."

Daw pointed at Rog. "What do we do with him?"

"Keep him bound at the wrists and ankles. Put him on the bus. I'll need a half dozen men to remain here to stand watch. The rest of us need to go and finish this." Orr turned to Rog. "If any of what you told us turns out to be untrue, this'll be the sorriest day of your life."

Chapter 50

Glenn stepped onto the Doaks's back porch and glanced at the sky. The sun hung almost directly overhead playing peek-a-boo with scattered fluffy clouds.

Where was Stan?

Stan had said that they would be back before noon to wrap things up. It worried Glenn that something might have gone wrong. If the rest of his group stumbled into the full force of Wineberry Hollow's militia they wouldn't stand a chance.

He walked back inside not wanting to let Jamal alone too long with Fred, Caroline, and the old man, Damroth. The kid was too young and Glenn didn't trust him. The past hour he had acted bored, like he no longer had the nerve to see the mission through. Stupid kid. There was no turning back now.

"I really need to go to the bathroom," Caroline Doaks said. She had been complaining for the last hour, but Glenn didn't want to risk untying her from the chair.

"Nothing stopping you," Glenn said. She could pee in her pants as far as he was concerned.

"C'mon, man, that would be nasty," Jamal said. "What harm is there in letting her go to the bathroom?"

Glenn tapped his finger against Jamal's chest. "You wanted to be a part of this. You started this, even. Stan left me in charge until he gets back, and I expect you to follow my orders."

"Bullshit," Jamal said. He walked behind Caroline's chair and began untying her hands.

"What the hell do you think you're doing?"

"If I wanted to take orders, I would've stayed with my old man. I'm letting this lady go to the bathroom."

Glenn glanced at the rifle he held across his arm and fought back the urge to punch a bullet hole in the middle of the kid's forehead. Stan wanted Jamal alive to use as a hostage to exchange for the bus. If he killed him, that plan would fall apart, and Stan would be pissed to say the least. Still, he couldn't allow this teen to disobey his orders without consequences. He'd have to figure some way of punishing him without killing him. "You go with her then. Keep the bathroom door open, and mind those kids in there. Make sure they don't follow you out. Don't want them running around the house causing a distraction."

Jamal untied the bindings on Caroline's ankles and helped her to her feet. He shot a defiant look at Glenn as he accompanied Caroline into the hallway leading to the bathroom.

Fred Doaks glared at him.

"What are you looking at?" Glenn raised the butt end of his rifle and jerked as if he would smash it into the man's face. Fred flinched and Glenn laughed.

Pete Damroth grunted and said, "I'd like to see you try that if he wasn't tied up."

"Shut up, old man."

After Jamal returned with Caroline, he faced Fred and Damroth. "How about you guys, you have to go?"

"No way are you going to untie *them*," Glenn said. The old man he could handle, but Fred Doaks's arms were as big around as his legs and all morning he had fixed his gaze on Glenn like a cat sizing up a cornered mouse. That man was crazy enough to try something.

"I'm good for now," Damroth said.

Fred looked at Jamal and shook his head. Glenn wondered if the kid would've actually tried to untie the man. One move in that direction and he would've shot him, Stan be damned.

"Bind her," Glenn ordered Jamal.

"Why?"

"Because I said so."

Jamal put pressure on Caroline's shoulder, a signal for her to sit. She did so, but he made no move to tie her.

Glenn grabbed a length of rope from the kitchen counter and threw it at Jamal. "Get to it."

"No," the kid said.

Glenn had reached the end of his patience. He pointed his rifle at Jamal. "You will tie her to that chair or by god I'll put you out of your misery."

Jamal stood and pointed his chin at Glenn. "You need me. You won't shoot me."

Glenn clicked off the safety. "Like hell I won't."

Caroline jumped up out of the chair. "Don't shoot." She turned to Jamal. "It's okay. Do as he says."

"You shouldn't ought to worry about her. She's just a woman,"

Jamal said.

Glenn laughed. "Just a woman, eh? Boy, you have a lot to learn."

"I am not your boy," Jamal said. Caroline sat in the chair.

"Just a figure of speech, kid. I never did buy into that political correctness crap."

"And I'm not a kid, either."

"I'll concede that point. You're just a 15-year-old dumb ass."

Jamal straightened and narrowed his eyes. "Old enough to kick your skinny ass."

Glenn pictured the long armed, wiry kid wailing away at him. He kept the barrel of his rifle pointed in Jamal's direction. "Maybe someday you'll get a chance to find out. Would be my pleasure to teach you some respect."

"Why not now?" Jamal sneered. "You ain't nothing without that rifle."

Glenn laughed to cover his nervousness and stepped to the front window. He peeked out from the side of the curtain. Nothing unusual outside. Where the hell was Stan?

"They're not coming back. You know that, right?" Damroth muttered.

"I don't want to hear another word out of you, old man," Glenn said.

"It's all gone wrong. They'd have returned by now. If I were you, I'd cut and run."

Damroth's prescience spooked Glenn. He had been considering that exact possibility. He couldn't wait around forever. He could abandon the kid and hike out the way they had come in. Stan had the keys to the tractor in his pocket, so he'd end up having to walk back to Wynot which would probably take the better part of two days. Better walking than dead.

Glenn also worried about leaving too soon. What if Stan and the group were just delayed? What if they arrived just a few minutes after he left? He'd end up being a laughing stock, made into a pariah for being craven.

After thinking it through, Glenn made up his mind. He'd wait another hour. At the end of that time if there was no sign of Stan, he'd assume they'd all been caught and would bug out. He'd let Damroth and the Doakses live, didn't really have anything against them, but he would seriously consider shooting the kid. Jamal was the one who got them involved in this crazy plan. He deserved to pay the price for its failure.

When Glenn turned, he noticed that Jamal still hadn't tied Caroline yet. "I'm not going to tell you again…"

Jamal's eyes went wide. "What is that? I hear someone outside yelling."

Now Glenn heard it, too, the muffled cry of a voice saying, "You in there. Open up."

"Shit." His heart pounded. He motioned for Jamal. "Open the door, but don't step outside."

For once, the kid did as he was told. He eased open the front door and peered out.

"Come out, hands held high," a gruff voice ordered from outside. "You're surrounded and your gang has been neutralized."

"Dad," Jamal yelled.

This had turned into a nightmare. Jamal's father had come for him and the kid was about to bolt. He was alone now, Glenn knew. All alone. Glenn grabbed the back of Jamal's shirt collar and pressed the business end of his rifle against the middle of Jamal's back. "Time to play your role of hostage."

Jamal scoffed. "You crazy fool, can't you see it's over?"

"Not as long as I have this rifle to your back." He tried projecting confidence while fighting back the urge to vomit. "Step out, real slow. Just a couple steps onto the porch. No further."

Glenn pressed Jamal through the door.

"You okay, son?" Orr asked.

"Yeah."

Orr stepped from behind a tree. "Give it up. This whole place is covered. Don't try to be a hero."

Glenn glanced from side to side. He didn't see anyone else but didn't doubt that others were watching. "Here's how it's going to go," Glenn said. He hated it, the high pitch of his voice compared to Orr's, betraying his lack of confidence. "The kid and I are going to step back into the house. You're going to go get me a vehicle. I don't care if it's the bus or that old Mustang. Just bring me something that still runs. When you return, I'll drive out of here."

"That's not going to happen," Orr said.

What was wrong with the man? "In case you haven't noticed, I have a rifle shoved into your son's back."

"I see it."

"Then do as I ask, or I'll waste him."

Orr held a handgun. He raised it to the height of Jamal's knee. "Do that and you'll die, too. I promise you that."

"He means it," Jamal said.

"Shut up, kid."

Orr raised his handgun. The son-of-a-bitch was out of his mind. He was going to try a shot. Glenn scrunched down as small as he could make himself and hid behind Jamal. To do that, he had to remove the point of his rifle barrel from Jamal's back. He repositioned and aimed the rifle toward Orr by resting it against Jamal's rib cage.

Jamal tensed and grabbed the rifle barrel.

Glenn reacted by yanking the trigger. He batted the kid away.

Orr made a gurgling noise, not quite a scream, doubled over, and dropped to the ground.

"Dad," Jamal yelled. He glared at Glenn. "You shot him. You filthy bastard."

Before Glenn could recover his wits, Jamal grabbed the rifle with both hands. The kid yanked it from Glenn's grasp. He held it over his head like a club.

Glenn raised his arm as Jamal brought it down. The blow landed against his forearm and he felt it snap. Jamal pitched the rifle away and jumped on him. They both fell to the ground with Jamal landing on top.

Glenn's broken arm wouldn't move, but it didn't hurt yet. He knew the pain would soon come. Jamal towered above him. The kid raised a fist, murderous rage in his eyes. Glenn remembered the sheathed hunting knife on his belt and grabbed for it with his good hand.

Jamal's fist landed square on Glenn's nose. His field of vision exploded into dancing white spots.

Before the kid could land another punch, Glenn pulled the knife free from its sheath and plunged it into the boy's abdomen. He pulled the knife across the kid's torso opening him from kidney to kidney.

Jamal screamed.

By now a horde of Wineberry Hollow militia men swarmed

him, grabbing, pulling, pinning him to the ground. One of them pointed a gun at this face.

Glenn felt the kick as the bullet punched through his forehead and then nothing.

Chapter 51

As an accomplished politician, Winston Halbert was used to telling people what they wanted to hear. He could wear a straight face and sell lie after lie to his constituents and could make them think it was their idea. The Academy Awards people had it wrong. The most masterful actors in any given year were not world famous professional entertainers, but rather the relatively unknown men and women who in the before times had walked the halls of the U.S. Congress.

Advancing a self-serving agenda was nothing new to Halbert, in fact he used to enjoy the game, the scheming and plotting. Back then, it had been about the accumulation of wealth and power. Sure, some people got hurt, some lost fortunes, but they didn't die. That had changed now. Holding Earthburst together meant saving his life at the cost of other's lives.

Halbert was damned to Hell and he knew it. So, why should he care about the atrocities being carried out under his watch? Maybe he held on to enough of his humanity so that some things still disgusted him, the inoculation program being at the top of the list. A large segment of E38 inhabitants refused to submit to the program. As overlord of the enclave, it had fallen to him to enforce compliance. Everyone was required to receive an injection to maintain the sham.

Everyone also included children. He shuddered after calling to mind the terrible sights he had seen, what he needed to show these others. To convince them.

Halbert had called a series of meetings to drive home the issue. He glanced at his notes and read that today's meeting included the soldiers assigned to Sheridan Hall. He stood behind the podium in the chapel of the enclave's medical center and scanned the sea of faces assembled before him. Most of the young men looked like kids to him, sporting peach fuzz instead of whiskers, some having facial complexions still marred by acne.

Ah, well, just another meeting, another acting job, another performance. Halbert gripped the sides of the podium and cleared his throat. Everyone turned their attention to him.

"For those of you who haven't met me yet, my name is Winston Halbert. I'm not comfortable with formalities, so everyone here is welcome to call me Win." He read in his notes to smile at this point, to put his audience at ease. Scanning the faces in the crowd, he noticed that nobody returned his smile. Another tough room.

"As you know, I've been appointed by your commander-in-chief as civilian oversight to this enclave. That makes it my responsibility, the well being of both military and civilians living here. These are difficult times, to be sure, but we're doing alright and will continue to do so as long as everyone within the fence heeds precautions." He scanned the room while speaking, making it a point to settle on everyone's gaze during the course of his presentation.

"I called you here to discuss that word I just spoke. *Precautions*. We have good reasons for imposing restrictions and for asking you in the military to enforce those restrictions. President Kall doesn't want to see anybody suffer, but sometimes we have to make difficult choices for the greater good. Listen to me carefully, for I'm about to be blunt. Comingling with outsiders risks extermination of the entire human race." Halbert paused to let the words sink in. As expected, they all gawked at him like he was insane. Let them think it. He had a trump card to play.

Down the hall.

In the isolation ward.

"By our very nature as Americans, we are a compassionate people. I understand how it goes against our good nature to stand by while our fellow citizens suffer. I'm not immune to wanting to assist starving people, our neighbors without hope, when it seems that all we need to do to ease that suffering is to open our storehouses and share the bounty of what we have."

Halbert banged his fist against the top of the podium. "But our creator also imbued us with a sense of self-preservation. We need to be in a position to take care of ourselves before we can help others, and I'm here to tell you that we have fallen inept at taking care of ourselves."

One of the officers rolled his eyes after hearing this. Halbert glanced at the man's nametag. Sloat. He made a mental note of the name.

"If we aren't careful, before this winter is over and a new harvest begins, we are going to run out of food. The residents of E38 might well join the masses of the starving. You want to know why?"

He paused and studied the audience before continuing. "Because you are allowing it to happen. The theft and smuggling of stores to outsiders is seriously jeopardizing the lives of the citizens living within this enclave."

"No way. Not on my watch," another officer shouted out. The man's name tag read, Kettering.

Halbert shrugged. "Okay, maybe not you, but it could be one of you others." He pointed to a man in the back. "Maybe you." He pointed to another man sitting to his left. "Maybe you." He pointed to the man named Sloat. "Or you," and allowed his finger to linger. That would teach this upstart officer to roll his eyes in derision.

A sharp look from Kettering to Sloat caught Halbert's attention. Was it possible that he had hit on something? Returning his hands to the podium, Halbert went on. "For those of you who never heard of me and think that I'm just some old man standing up here spouting off, let me tell you a little about myself."

He detailed his history as owner of a food distribution network in the before times and how President Kall had appointed him Minister of Logistics based on his rise from bag boy to magnate. "So you see, I do know what I'm talking about, and I have been closely monitoring the situation."

A low murmur arose. Good, they were taking him more seriously now. He allowed the din to go on for a few moments before continuing. "Starvation is bad enough, but now we face another threat, one even more terrible and insidious. The outsiders have been eating all manner of things. Foul things. Many of you haven't believed the intelligence concerning Creutzfeldt–Jakob Disease, but the outsiders are a real threat to us. Once contracted, there is no cure for this disease, but we can protect ourselves by avoiding contact and through preventative inoculation. Under military orders, every one of you has been inoculated, but some of the civilians living among us have been resistant."

A hand shot in the air. Halbert hated being interrupted. In an irritated voice he asked, "You have a question?"

The man attached to the hand stood. "My name is Ortega, sir. The civvies of E38 have trouble believing what they are unfamiliar with. They don't get it. Nobody likes having a needle stuck in their arm unless they have an incentive."

Soon they would have plenty of incentive. "Understood, Ortega. It's our job to make them understand. You have to make them believe."

Another hand went up, this one belonging to the eye-rolling man named Sloat. What did he want? Halbert pointed at him. "Go ahead."

"I'm Captain Sloat, sir," he said after standing. "I've been inoculated, but that's because I was ordered to. My duties include wide area patrol outside of the enclave. I have moved among throngs of citizens and have seen no evidence of CJD. I understand the civilian point-of-view, because with respect, sir, it's also difficult for me to believe what I haven't seen."

In a few minutes, this man would believe. "Just because you haven't seen it doesn't mean it's not real, captain. Starving people will eat anything. For instance, the whitetail deer population around these parts are infested with chronic wasting disease. Our scientists have proven that through human ingestion of those diseased animals, the affliction has jumped the trans-species barrier and manifested in humans as CJD."

"We should just shoot everybody outside the fence to mitigate the risk," the man with the Kettering name tag spoke.

"That'll be enough, lieutenant," Captain Sloat said. Kettering and Sloat exchanged dirty looks. Definitely something going on between those two.

"I get it," Halbert said. "In order to convince the civilians, you'll need to be convinced yourselves. That's why we're meeting here at the med center. I'm going to prove it to you."

The room fell silent.

"I hope none of you have eaten lunch yet." Before they could respond to his statement, Halbert strode toward the door. "Follow me."

The soldiers filed out of the chapel behind him. Halbert led the way down the corridor and stopped in front of a set of double doors. A sign with bold black letters against a yellow background hung beneath a small wire mesh window embedded in the door. The sign read:

DANGER - QUARRANTINE AREA

Turning to face them, Halbert said, "All of you have been inoculated, right? If not, you'll need to return to the chapel and wait." Many of these men had seen military action. They feared no man, but when confronted with the unknown? Some of them paled.

He pushed the door open. "Be convinced, gentlemen, and then convince your families and neighbors to get inoculated. The threat is indeed real."

As Halbert held the open door, unearthly screeches reached their ears, tortured, shrill, gurgling noises. Soldiers stepped across the threshold, but Halbert refused to enter himself. He had seen it before and wasn't going back into that room. His guilt prevented him.

Closing his eyes, Halbert recalled the scene. An enlisted man quivered on the floor, chained to his bed. A young wife in the throes of a perpetual seizure, her dead eyes fixed on the door, bleated like a dying lamb. The child haunted him most. A boy of about seven, banging his head against the floor, bloodying his face. How could President Kall allow the tainted doses to be administered to children? They could've packaged the smaller syringes separately eliminating the random chance of infection among young ones. Knowing Kall, the man probably ordered those doses himself for the impact it would have on the recalcitrant.

It didn't take long for the officers to beat a hasty retreat. After the last man exited, Halbert closed the door on the chamber of horrors. "Now do you believe?"

A sea of heads bobbed, but not all of them. A few always remained skeptical, Captain Sloat being one of them. Enough of the others had been convinced. His point had been made.

"Poor bastards," one of them said. "How long must they suffer through that?"

"The child isn't expected to live the day," Halbert said. "The two adults may linger another week or two."

Sloat spoke. "Have you interviewed them? Were you able to determine the vector of the disease?"

"Both of the adults commiserated with outsiders," Halbert lied. "We aren't sure how the boy contracted the disease."

"My god," Kettering uttered, "that's fubar."

"Indeed, it is," Halbert agreed.

Someday, in the future the truth would come out about the tainted inoculations. Schemes like these always had a way of being exposed given enough time. When that day eventually came, Halbert prayed that it would be after he was dead.

Chapter 52

Cooper Stover stood among the crowd at graveside hat in hand and looking at the tops of his shoes. Elam Kroh donated a corner of his field for use as a cemetery since no graveyards existed within the hollow. The militia had buried all the dead. Three individual graves for Dr. Hunt, Declan Orr, and his son Jamal and one common grave for the seven marauders. Questions had been asked and answers had been demanded, his Wineberry Hollow neighbors desperate to make sense of such an unthinkable tragedy.

How could this have happened?

They had pieced together that answer quickly enough. Fred and Caroline Doaks explained Jamal Orr's betrayal and how he had led the invaders over the mountain logging road behind their home. Those men had simply bypassed the militia's blockade at the entrance to the hollow.

Why had the attackers come?

Speculation held that the invaders didn't need to raid the hollow. They probably had plenty of stores to get them through the upcoming winter from the farms surrounding Wynot. Why would they undertake such a mission just to steal an old school bus? Was it just out of spite? Jealousy? Why Dr. Hunt's home? What had the doctor ever done to those men?

Cooper didn't remain silent. He didn't want Katie to have to explain and suffer again through the memory of her assault and father's murder. He confessed his one-time date with Katie to his congregational elders and to the militia. All of it. He explained his deception of wearing English clothes, his humiliation over Stan's confrontation, and how that incident had exacerbated the boy turned sheriff's hateful grudge toward Katie, motivating him to exact his terrible vengeance.

Such tragedy over one sin, one night. Ten men dead. Would God finally now be satisfied? Had he paid the full measure for his transgression?

He hadn't cared that his congregation now considered him to be a pariah, but it hurt him, the impact this had on his mother.

Cooper kept his eyes to the ground while mourners took turns eulogizing Dr. Hunt, Declan Orr, and even Jamal. He couldn't meet anyone's gaze. Probably never would be able to again. No matter what his neighbors thought or how they reasoned it out, Cooper clearly understood the truth as he saw it. Had he not asked Katie for a date, none of this would have happened. They wouldn't be burying ten men. He alone was responsible and bore the bloodguilt. It weighed him down, made his life unbearable.

Chelsey Orr took a turn at speaking. Cooper glanced her way. She stood between the graves of her husband and son holding hands with her two remaining children. The kids wore stoic expressions. Chelsea straightened and opened her mouth.

"Throughout history good men have answered the call to protect the innocent from the evil that men do to each other." Her voice held firm, but Coop recognized the suffering displayed on her face. Lowering her gaze to Declan's grave, she continued, "My husband was one of those men. He loved his country, loved his family, loved his life."

She let go of Keisha's hand and wiped the sleeve of her jacket across her eyes before taking her little girl's hand again. "Declan saw a lot of evil during his life. When he could stomach it no more, he brought us here to Wineberry Hollow. 'God-fearing people live here,' he told us, 'a great place to raise a family.' And he was right. You welcomed us into your community with never a hint of the racism we encountered in the so-called enlightened cities. You went out of your way to make us comfortable here."

After stopping to take a breath she went on. "Despite your kindness, evil has found a way to take my husband from me." She turned her attention to Jamal's grave. "And my son, too.

"I don't blame any of you for what has happened. If we wouldn't have relocated among you folks we'd probably all be dead by now. Please forgive Jamal for losing his way and for the part he played in this."

She sniffled and nodded her head toward Katie who sat at graveside on a lawn chair. Coop saw in Katie's eyes a hollow, haunted look. "Katie Hunt, you've lost both your parents to violence now, such a terrible thing, but don't for one second believe that you're alone. You've been such a joy to my children. Nate and Keisha and I will never abandon you. We're here for you, and I suspect all of your neighbors feel the same way."

Katie didn't look up, didn't even acknowledge Chelsey.

Chelsey looked into the crowd. "Your spirit of community is precious. Declan understood that and did everything he could to preserve it. He was a soldier and realized the importance of a protective militia. Its formation is his legacy to Wineberry Hollow. He would want us to move forward and not just survive but thrive."

Tugging her children with her, Chelsey shuffled over to the common grave of the attackers. The mourners watched her movement. Cooper wondered what she was going to do now. She let go of her children's hands and pointed at the grave. "We know very little about these men. Whoever they may be, they too have parents, wives, and children. How awful that their loved ones may never know what happened to them. Do they have children who even now wait at the door for their fathers to return home? Before the world went dark I wonder, were these honorable men? Did the horrors of this new reality forced upon them cause these poor souls to choose a darker path?

"My point, dear friends, is in order to thrive we need to let go of any lingering hate. These men may not deserve our forgiveness, but we must find a way to freely grant them that gift. By doing so, we make our stand, we demonstrate to what's left of the world that human decency still exists, that we refuse to succumb to the darkness, that we will live our lives to the highest standards of civilization."

Chelsey dropped to her knees and hugged her children, one in each arm. Looking at the mound of earth covering the bodies of the men responsible for the death of her husband and son, she said, "I forgive you." Then she wept.

Coop heard nothing but Chelsey's sobs. The entire gathering watched her. Caroline Doaks approached and attempted to help Chelsey to her feet. Chelsey waved her off. She stood on her own and took her children by the hand. She went to Katie and kissed her on the forehead and expressed words of condolence that Cooper couldn't hear.

Katie touched Chelsey's cheek, a comforting gesture. She stood from her chair and walked away with Chelsey and the kids. Sheila Cunningham followed cradling her bandaged hand.

Coop regarded Sheila. That woman had also suffered. Not only at the hands of a ruffian, but also at the loss of Dr. Hunt. He figured that the two of them would soon have married. Coop felt some measure of comfort in the fact that the four women living in Dr. Hunt's house, Katie, Sheila, Wendy Godfrey, and her special daughter, Sarah, would see each other through.

What bothered Cooper about Katie was her lack of tears. It couldn't be healthy, her bottling up her emotions. He wished she wouldn't try to be so strong. Nobody expected it of her. He thought about it and realized that in all the time he spent with Katie she never cried. Not even when Stan had murdered her father. Maybe it just wasn't in her nature.

After Chelsey's eulogy, nobody else had anything to say. It was as if Chelsey had said it all. The crowd dispersed.

"Cooper, come," his mother said. She took his arm.

"Go ahead and take the buggy. I'll walk home."

She gave him a questioning look.

"Don't worry, Mother, I'll be along soon. I just need some private time."

She dipped her head and walked away with Hattie.

When only a handful of people lingered in conversation with each other, Coop approached the graves of Dr. Hunt, Mr. Orr, and Jamal. He squeezed the brim of his hat in his hand and uttered, "Mrs. Orr spoke of forgiveness. Could you forgive me if you knew that I set in motion the plague that brought about your deaths?"

The sun moved low in the sky and a cold breeze tickled Coop's face. Nightfall would soon come.

"Hey, Coop," said Sammy Wetzel.

The young man startled Coop. "I didn't see you."

"I noticed you still standing here. I just got done talking to one of the militia guys down at the school bus. Corporal Clark is in charge now."

"I remember him," Coop said. "He was one of the refugees, and he moved in with the Orrs. I hope Chelsey allows him to stay on. Up on that hill by themselves, they should have a man with them."

"That Mrs. Orr is really brave," Sammy said, his lips turned down. "Her being able to talk like that over her husband's grave."

"Her words were powerful."

"Gary Daw told me that Corporal Clark executed that prisoner, the one named Rog."

Coop had already heard about it. "They shouldn't have done that. That is exactly the point Chelsea was trying to make."

Sammy glared. "We couldn't take the chance of letting him return home and blabbing to everyone about the back door into our valley. Anyway, Corporal Clark figures the rest of the CCW isn't likely to bother us anymore. When those men don't return, the others will be scared. Besides, winter is almost here."

Although Sammy didn't speak of it, Coop knew the 13-year-old had to have suffered grave consequences after taking Stan Cox's life with that arrow. Sure Coop was grateful. Sammy had saved his life and Katie's life, but at what price? A child stood with him, not a man. And even men suffered from the taking of life. Now, this talk of executions and military tactics. Children should be concerned instead with baseball and farm chores. Cooper asked him. "Are you okay?"

From the expression on the lad's face, Coop knew that Sammy understood his meaning. "You don't have to worry about me. Dad and I talked about it."

"Good. You know you can talk to me too, if you ever feel like it."

Sammy grinned. "Carl Miller told me that he saw some trout in the stream on his farm. I haven't eaten fish in a long time. It's evening so they should be biting. Want to come fishing with me."

Ah, the resilience of youth. Despite Coop's misery and guilt, he knew he had at least one friend, this young man who would stick by him. He didn't deserve such a friend, but was nevertheless grateful. He laid a hand on Sammy's shoulder. "Come on. Let's go tell your papa to oil up his fry pan."

Chapter 53

Captain Sloat sat in the waiting room watching a fly dive bomb Colonel Muncie's administrative assistant, Ekaterina, or Cat as they called her. The woman sat at her desk working her keyboard. She waved a hand in front of her face shooing the fly away only to have it land on her forehead a few moments later. Exasperated, Cat stopped working and grabbed a fly swatter from somewhere inside a file drawer. She stood and scanned the room for her harasser, but the fly had disappeared.

"They do that all the time," Sloat said. "Amazing how they can vanish when you have a weapon at hand."

Cat grinned. "Let that fly show itself again and I'll be ready." She sat and resumed tapping her keyboard.

The colonel had ordered him to report to his office at zero nine hundred. Sloat looked at his military issue watch and saw it was nine-oh-five. He had received the order last night by messenger, but no reason had been provided as to the nature of Colonel Muncie's request. Sloat hated not being prepared and tried to anticipate what his commander wanted of him. Would Cat know? "The colonel is running late. Anybody in there with him?"

"I thought you knew," Cat said. "Your Lieutenant Kettering has been in there since eight. Is he in some kind of trouble?"

Halfjack? Why would he be meeting with the colonel? "I'm afraid that I'm in the dark. Anything else I should know?"

"Kettering," Cat spat out his name with disdain. "The man gives me the creeps. Always hitting on me, and he knows I'm happily married. I hope the colonel is chewing his ass."

Since the world went dark, Halfjack had become increasingly harder to control. Was it possible that he had stepped over some line? Could that be what the meeting was all about? If so, the colonel was being uncharacteristically patronizing. If his lieutenant was sexually harassing Cat, the colonel should've asked him to handle it. Then again, Cat was his administrative assistant which made it personal. Sloat said, "I wasn't aware. If Kettering ever bothers you again, be sure to let me know. I'll see to it he backs off."

Before Cat could respond, the door to the colonel's office opened and he waved for Sloat to enter.

Sloat stood and nodded to Cat. "Remember what I said."

"Will do," she said without looking his way, her fingers tapping the keyboard.

Sloat entered the office and stood at attention. Colonel Muncie closed the door and walked to the window. He separated the slats of his Venetian blind and stared outside. Lieutenant Kettering sat in a chair, a smug expression on his face.

Muncie let go of the slats and they slid back into place with a snap. He turned and leaned on the desktop, palms down. The colonel wore a frown. "Captain Sloat, have you been diverting food and supplies to the non-essentials?"

So that's what this was about. Somehow Halfjack had found out and had turned him in. Sloat glared at his subordinate.

"Don't look at him," Muncie said. "You look at me, soldier, and answer the question."

Sloat knew this day would come, it had only been a matter of time. He also knew that it would go worse for him if he tried to deny it. "Sir, those people that you refer to as non-essentials, they are human beings, American citizens."

Muncie slapped the desktop with his hand. "A simple yes or no answer will suffice, captain."

Although Muncie still wore his frown, his eyes remained soft. If the colonel were angry, Sloat would expect to see his eyes narrowed. He couldn't read the man. And he wouldn't lie. "Yes, sir, I have been diverting food and supplies to civilians living beyond the fence of this enclave."

"Convicted by his own words," Halfjack said. "You're a fool, Sloat."

"Captain Sloat is your superior officer," Colonel Muncie shouted. "Until that status changes, you will treat the man with due respect."

"Sorry, sir," Halfjack said with a sneer, "but after our meeting with Win Halbert, after seeing those poor, sick bastards, I find this action repugnant."

Muncie looked Sloat in the eye. "Why are you being so willfully disobedient?"

"I believe I already answered that question, sir. American citizens are starving. I swore an oath to defend my countrymen. I've been doing that the best I can."

Halfjack waved his hand in a mocking flourish, "Captain Sloat, sir, you have disobeyed a direct order from your commander-in-chief, President Kall. The non-essentials are dangerous plague carriers."

"Shut up," Colonel Muncie said. "If you say another word, Lieutenant Kettering, I'll throw you in the brig."

Halfjack stared at the wall behind the Colonel.

"On second thought, you're dismissed, lieutenant. You're no longer needed here."

"As you wish, sir." He stood, saluted Colonel Muncie, executed a perfect about-face, and walked out of the office, shutting the door behind him.

"He's a dangerous man," Muncie said. "Blinded by ambition."

"Sir?"

"Now that he's done with you, he'll be coming after me next."

Sloat didn't know what to make of the colonel's comment so he remained silent.

Colonel Muncie motioned to the chair previously occupied by Halfjack. "Have a seat, Captain Sloat."

After Sloat did as the colonel asked, the colonel sat in his desk chair and leaned back. He laced his hands together behind his head. "Who else is involved in your operation?"

If he were going down, he wouldn't drag anyone else down with him. He wouldn't betray Lieutenant Napoli and her soldiers. "Sir, I will not lie to you, so my only recourse is to say nothing."

Muncie raised an eyebrow. "You're refusing a direct order to answer my question?"

Sloat sighed. His next statement would most likely get him court martialed. After years of serving as an exemplary soldier, he was about to throw it all away. He hoped it was worth it. "With deepest regrets, I must refuse to respond to that question."

Muncie unlaced his fingers and leaned forward across his desk. "You're playing a dangerous game, Captain Sloat. People are in near hysteria over the CJD outbreak."

"You really believe those unfortunate souls we saw contracted the disease from outsiders?"

"What are you implying, captain?"

"I haven't seen a single sick person outside of the fence, but I have seen starvation. Until evidence proves otherwise, it's my intent to help the starving."

Muncie stared at him, regarding him. He said, "Are you a student of literature, Captain Sloat?"

What did this have to do with anything? "Sorry, sir, my experience is limited to killing the enemy and breaking their toys, and my fellow citizens are not the enemy."

Colonel Muncie's lips turned up into a wan smile. "A poet named Yeats once wrote, 'Things fall apart; the center cannot hold.' It appears that is exactly the situation we find ourselves in."

"Sir, the only words of poetry I know were written by John Lennon, 'Happiness is a warm gun.'"

Muncie ignored Sloat's comment and his face turned serious. "Your Lieutenant Kettering has been spying on you, personally tracking your activities." He pointed to a folder on his desk. "The man has photos of you in a compromising situation passing crates to civilians."

"It appears I overestimated my ability to keep him out of the loop."

"This is serious, Captain Sloat. Lieutenant Kettering means to see this through."

"With dogged determination," Sloat said. "I know him better than you, sir."

"I'll need to buy him off," Muncie said.

"Sir?"

"He wants a promotion and command of his own platoon. Your days of reconnaissance and patrolling the country side are over. It's his job now."

Having nothing further to lose, Sloat said, "Do with me what you will, but that man has a sadistic streak. He's not suited for the job. Without me to keep him in check, he'll bully survivors unmercifully. While wandering the countryside, any non-essentials he sees with the shakes, even if it's Parkinson Disease, he's liable to shoot on sight confusing the symptoms with CJD. Besides, many of the men under my command have no respect for him. They aren't going to like this."

"The damage is done. I either give him what he wants or lock you away for treason. You're an honorable man, Captain Sloat. I don't want to do that."

Sloat had resigned himself to his fate, but why was the colonel holding out hope for him? "Sir, you just said that I was playing a dangerous game. Am I to understand that you wish to join me in that game?"

Muncie rocked back in his seat. "Things fall apart. The center cannot hold."

"Sir?"

"I'm confining you to quarters for the next thirty days to keep you out of sight and to allow this situation to cool down. I'll assign Sergeant Adams to Kettering's platoon. He'll be my eyes and ears and be an advocate for your men. You must know, however, that a small minority of them will be happy about this change. Men who are of like mind with Kettering."

Sloat suspected the opportunists among his men who might glom on to Halfjack. "Sir, what happens to me after thirty days?"

"I'm placing you in command of gate W3."

The distribution point with the civilians. By giving him this assignment, Colonel Muncie was providing tacit approval for him to continue. "That's Lieutenant Napoli's command. She's likely to resent my usurping her authority."

"Then you'll have to explain the situation to her," Muncie said, his tone severe.

His words meant that Muncie also suspected the extent of Napoli's involvement with the civilians. He was just formalizing what they had already been doing. "Thank you, sir."

"Watch your back at all times," Muncie said, "and bear in mind that my fate is now tied with yours."

"Yes, sir." Captain Sloat stood, saluted, and left the office. He wondered how many officers above Colonel Muncie felt the same way? Was the colonel a part of Mandible's cadre? How soon until President Kall's brave new world collapsed? Tomorrow wouldn't be soon enough.

Chapter 54

The clop clop of Tony's hooves against the pavement echoed as the buggy funneled through the tree lined narrows at the back end of Wineberry Hollow. The chill Thanksgiving wind stung Cooper's face making his eyes water. He pulled his collar up to shield his face and wished he had remembered to wear gloves.

Cove Road had been overdue for resurfacing even before the world went dark. Now any such maintenance would probably never happen. Fissures had opened in the macadam reminding Cooper of varicose veins, long runners where weeds had invaded. In some places, the pressure of those unwelcome wild plants heaved against the surface crumbling the pavement into chunks.

How many years would it take for nature to completely break down the road bed? Ignored, the macadam would continue to degrade until eventually only a muddy trail remained. Such was the fate of all things made by the hands of man. In time, even the mightiest of structures would dissolve to dust, reclaimed by God.

Ashes to ashes. Dust to dust.

Cooper contemplated the source of his depression. He had grown up with Timothy Foose, attended school with him, went to the Sunday meetings with him and his wife Grace. During that time, he had grown to admire their 4-year-old son, Lucas, the little boy known for his ever-present smile. Cooper helped the Fooses complete the processing of field corn into animal feed. Their family's harvest had been late, neglected because of the time Timothy and Grace had spent tending to Lucas. Their infant girl, Dinah, also required constant attention.

During the past few weeks, Cooper witnessed little Lucas slipping away. The boy constantly drank water and as a result had to always go to the bathroom. A few days ago, the little tyke collapsed while playing. Grace held a hand to his forehead and announced that he burned with fever. Since then, Lucas had been confined to bed. He couldn't keep food down and wouldn't drink.

The ordnung of his congregation seemed ridiculous to Cooper now. On the one hand they shunned automobiles, electricity, and all such English evils while on the other hand they had no problem accepting the English medicine. How could his elders reconcile the fact that these life saving drugs were manufactured in laboratories which sucked huge quantities of electricity and were distributed to all parts of the world by way of the internal combustion engine.

Hypocrites. All of them. Life had been easier in the before times when things such as medicine could be taken for granted. The misery and death he had witnessed during the past summer and autumn wore him down, caused him now to question his faith.

Yet Cooper held on to the hope of possibly one more miracle as he pulled on the reins, stopping Tony in front of Sheila Cunningham's home, now occupied by Dr. St. John and his family.

The man was a dentist, but didn't that mean he had at least some medical training? Coop had to try and convince Dr. St. John to help.

He stepped down from the buggy, tied Tony's reins to the mailbox and knocked on the door. Cooper recognized the doctor's wife, Heather, when she answered his knock.

"Your name's Cooper, right?" she asked.

Cooper removed his hat. "Coop, to you Ma'am."

"Have you come to see my husband? Do you have a toothache?"

"No, Mrs. St. John, it's nothing like that."

"For heaven's sake, call me Heather."

"I'm wondering if Dr. St. John could help…" He started explaining about Lucas.

Heather held out a hand. "Stop. Let me take you to see Blair right away." She led him to a back bedroom. "Wait here."

After Heather walked away, Coop examined the room which had been converted into an office. An overstuffed recliner served as a dentist's chair, and it appeared as if they used a five gallon bucket to spit into. Coop shuddered after seeing a set of Craftsman pliers laying on an end table.

The door opened and Dr. St. John entered. "What can I help you with, Cooper?"

Coop told him about little Lucas.

Dr. St. John raked a hand through his hair and sighed. "After we moved in, Dr. Hunt split his supplies and provided me with pain killers and antibiotics, things that I might need as a dentist. No insulin though. You'll have to walk across the road to see Nurse Vicky Clark or Katie Hunt. They still see patients, but as you are aware, most of the medicine is now used up."

Coop pressed him. "Don't you know anything about diabetes? Isn't there anything else we can do?"

Dr. St. John stared at the floor. "I don't think so. Look, Coop, I may be a doctor, but this is not my area of expertise. I'm not trying to pass the buck, but go see Vicky and Katie. They'll know better than me how to deal with your friend."

"I understand," Coop said. "Thank you for seeing me."

"I'm sorry I couldn't be more of a help."

Coop left, walked to the road and stared across at the Hunt's home.

Katie's house.

He hated intruding, knowing that he was probably the last person on Earth she wanted to see. But he was doing this for the Fooses, for little Lucas.

The last time Coop had knocked on their door, Sheila Cunningham answered and had been brutally attacked. This time, she eyed him warily and looked all around. Her eyes settled on his.

"I'm here for a neighbor who needs help," Coop said.

She held open the door and motioned with a nod for him to enter. When she finally spoke, she said, "I'll get Katie."

Coop suddenly found it difficult to breathe. What could he say to Katie? What did she think of him? Things had happened too fast, and Stan had shot Dr. Hunt before Coop could react. He hoped that Katie realized this. He also hoped that Katie had noticed how he had tried to stop Stan.

Coop hadn't seen her since the funeral. The few times she had come to pick up Wendy Godfrey and Sarah at the school, he avoided her, and she him. He supposed she hated him with every fiber of her being, his bringing Stan to her house that fateful day. She certainly had a right to those feelings.

The problem was, he still cared for Katie, deeply cared for her.

She appeared in the living room wearing jeans and an oversized sweat shirt, probably her father's. Her short haircut had grown back some. Dr. Hunt's nurse, Vicky Clark, stood behind Katie, arms folded across her chest, a stern look on her face like an Amish grandmother chaperoning two young courting teens.

Good, Coop thought. Katie had somebody watching out for her. It eased his mind some.

Coop read nothing in Katie's expression except for disinterest. All she said was, "Well?"

"It's Lucas Foose," Coop said. His mouth went dry.

"Oh," she said softly. "Has he…passed away?"

"No. I was hoping you could help."

Katie stared at him for a moment before shaking her head. "Nothing I can do for him. Nothing any of us can do." She turned to leave.

"Wait," Coop said. He looked between the two ladies. "Could one of you at least come and examine him. Maybe Tim and Grace aren't doing something right with his shots."

"You mean they're still giving him insulin injections?" Nurse Clark asked. "The medicine hasn't run out?"

"They still have some left," Coop said, "but it no longer seems to be working."

"Probably lost its potency," Nurse Clark said.

"Dad warned them about keeping it cold," Katie said.

"The Fooses have a root cellar," Coop told them, "but the summer was hot and the pond ice didn't last as long as in normal years."

"I suppose it wouldn't hurt to take a look. I'll go," Nurse Clark said.

"No." Katie pointed down the hall. "You should stay in case Cindy Berry's labor pains get worse. I'll do it."

Nurse Clark looked between Coop and Katie. "You sure?"

"I won't be long," Katie said.

After leaving the house, Coop said, "You can ride with me in the buggy."

She glared at him. "Not a chance. I'll take my car and meet you there."

Since the car was faster, by the time Coop arrived, Katie was in the process of examining Lucas. Coop waited in the kitchen with Timothy. After a few minutes, Grace appeared. Katie walked behind her holding some sort of medical instrument and wearing a stethoscope around her neck.

Coop smiled. The stethoscope suited Katie, made her look like a real pro.

After shooting a glance at Coop, Katie said, "You want him here? This is a private family matter."

Timothy raised an eyebrow. "Cooper is our friend. He can stay."

"Suit yourself. Please, let's sit."

They all sat at the kitchen table.

Katie cleared her throat and mumbled, "I'm not as good as my father at this. He had a way of compartmentalizing his feelings." She looked Tim and Grace in the eye trying to act detached, but Coop knew her better. She struggled to find the right words. She looked at the device in her hand and spoke, "Lucas's blood sugar is at 610. How long has it been that way?"

Tim and Grace exchanged glances. Tim spoke. "He's been over 200 and climbing for the past three weeks."

"How long has he been unconscious?"

Tim looked at Katie but couldn't speak. He just shook his head and squeezed shut his eyes. Grace laid a hand on his wrist.

Katie spoke again, her voice low. "Lucas has a fever of 103.5. His immune system is failing. His kidneys are failing. His body is shutting down. I'm afraid his situation is dire."

"How much longer does he have?" Tim asked.

Katie paused before saying, "His pulse is weak, his breathing shallow."

Grace sobbed. Tim embraced her and Katie stood. "I'll leave you folks to your privacy."

Just then, Lucas cried out for his mother.

Grace gasped and covered her mouth. "He hasn't spoken in days. The Lord has heard our prayers."

All of them rushed into the boy's bedroom.

Lucas lay in his bed wearing plain white pajamas. His eyes were closed, his face expressionless. Cooper stood there, shocked. Instead of the vibrant little boy that he had known, Lucas looked diminished, no more than a doll baby.

Grace knelt in front of Lucas and shook his arm, trying to rouse him. "Lucas, you called for me. I'm here. Your mama is here. Open your eyes. Please, open your eyes."

He didn't respond.

Coop's heart pounded. He whispered, "Katie?"

Katie knelt beside Grace. "Let me take him."

Grace stood aside while Katie picked up Lucas in her arms and stood. She tried to maneuver the stethoscope with her one hand while holding Lucas, but he was too heavy and she struggled.

Coop jumped to Katie's aid and slipped a hand under Lucas's back. With both of them supporting Lucas sandwiched between them, Katie was able to use her free hand to listen to his heart. Coop held the boy's little hand, and then he moved his fingers to Lucas's wrist and felt for a pulse. He barely felt it. Lucas's chest wasn't moving, but he had to be breathing. How could he feel a pulse if the lad had stopped breathing?

At that point, he realized that Lucas's pulse had faded away. Coop met Katie's eyes and read in them a confirmation. They stared at each other for a long moment. Coop felt Katie's arm twitch, the one holding Lucas. "Give him to me," he said.

Coop gently lowered Lucas onto his bed. He turned and wanted to say something to Tim and Grace, but he could find no words. He left them and walked out of the house.

Katie leaned on her car, both hands on the hood, hair hanging down and obscuring her face. Coop approached, but before he could speak, Katie uttered, "Damn you, Cooper Stover. That little boy just died in my arms."

And mine, he thought.

She whirled and looked as if she might strike him. "Goddamn you, for making me go through that."

Cooper struggled. What could he say? "It was never my intention to cause you pain. You have to know that."

He could barely see Katie's eyes from the way she narrowed them at him. Her entire body vibrated with anger, but she kept her voice down, Coop figured, so as not to further disturb the Fooses. "If you never intend to cause me pain, why does it always happen? Every time I see you, you bring me death. First your father, then my father, then this little boy." She raised both hands to the sky. "I was even with you when this whole world went to shit and died. You do nothing but cause me pain." Her voice broke. "Stay the hell away from me."

"Katie, please, don't cry."

"Don't you say that," she spoke with such vehemence that Coop stepped back. "I don't cry. I never cry. Not when my mother died, not when my father died, and I sure as hell am not going to cry now. Especially in front of you."

She regained her composure and glared at him, her jaw set, her posture statue still, as if she would tear him to pieces if he spoke.

Despite her hard look, he said, "I'm sorry. You are suffering because of my sin. I brought this down on you having asked you on that date. It's all my fault."

Katie's expression softened and she slouched against the door of her car. She looked away and lowered her voice. "Don't be such an ass. God wouldn't punish either of us for going out on a date." She hesitated, and then blurted, "I haven't cried since I was a baby.

I can't. I'm afraid that if I start I won't be able to stop. Oh god, I hurt so bad."

Coop chose his next words carefully. "Everyone in Wineberry Hollow cares about you. I care about you." He paused. "I love you."

She rolled her eyes, yanked open her car door, and threw herself into the driver's seat.

"I'm going to always be here for you, Katie Hunt, ready to take care of you. I can't help it, the way I feel about you."

"Don't waste your love on me, Cooper Stover. I don't need you or anyone else to take care of me." She twisted the key in the ignition, started the motor, and drove away.

Chapter 55

Cooper listened to the roar of the approaching wind as it tore through the woods. He faced it head on with outstretched arms and welcomed the assault. The gust exploded up the escarpment to where he sat on the Orr's property overlooking Wineberry Hollow. The burst of frigid air stole Coop's breath and made his eyes water. When the wave subsided, he shivered beneath his wool coat and yelled, "Woo wee, what a great day!"

Nate Orr who sat beside Coop gawked at him, the whites of his wide eyes contrasting against his dark brown face. "Man, you're crazy. I'm ready to go inside."

Coop inhaled. "The fresh mountain air of winter is always the purest. Go on, take a deep breath."

Nate sucked in a gulp of air and coughed. "Makes my lungs hurt."

"The view from here is spectacular. Now that all the leaves are off the trees, you can see almost the entire length of the hollow. Anyway, you can see farther now than in the summer when we camped out." Coop recalled that night. He eyed Katie's house sitting at the bottom of the mountain, the fresh blanket of snow covering her roof and lawn. A month had already passed since poor Lucas Foose passed away. Coop tried hard to put Katie out of his mind, but moments like these brought a pain to his heart like a pin prick.

"You ever been to the ocean?" Coop asked.

Nate's teeth chattered. "Sure, plenty of times when we lived at Fort Benning."

"Standing in the water, were the waves like this? Like how that wind just washed over us?"

"Sort of. When we used to go to Panama City on the gulf, the waves were gentle, but the surf in the Atlantic at Hilton Head would knock you down. But neither place was this cold."

Coop tried to imagine it. "I've never been."

"Really? How come?"

"Never had the chance."

From the valley below, they heard the roar of another approaching gust.

Nate stood. "Hurry. Let's go in."

"Race you to the house," Coop said and shot away. To Coop's surprise, the pre-teen easily beat him to the door. The two of them tumbled into the house, laughing, the wind blowing the door shut behind them.

Cooper's mother stood hands on her hips. "Act your age, son."

"Let them be," Chelsey Orr said. "It's been a long time since I heard laughter. It's sweet music to me."

Nate plopped onto a chair in the family room, the one closest to the fireplace. He held his hands toward the burning hearth and rubbed them together. Coop sat on the sofa beside his mother. Chelsey fussed with some ornaments hanging from the Christmas tree.

"We've been coping the best we can," Chelsey said, "and I want to thank you and Cooper for stopping by to check in on us. The holidays are difficult. Memories, you know?"

"Of course. I lost my husband this year and Coop his father. We appreciate what you must be going through and figured you might enjoy our visit."

But the Orrs also lost a son, Coop mused. How much greater was their suffering?

"It was kind of you to think of us," Chelsey said.

Coop's mother leaned forward on the sofa. "Please remember that if it gets too hard, there are plenty of neighbors who would be happy to take you in, you and Nate and Keisha. You don't have to live up here all by yourself."

Chelsey sighed and looked at the floor. "No. Declan bought this house for us. It was our dream, and this is our home."

Keisha walked into the room, her hair in pigtails. Hattie trailed behind her carrying a stuffed horse.

"Did you enjoy your playtime, sweetie?" Chelsey asked.

Keisha nodded but didn't say anything. Hattie crawled onto the sofa beside Coop.

"I worry about them, their future," Chelsey said. "Nate is so intelligent, such a whiz at computers, but that's no good any more. Keisha used to be so outgoing, but now she sits in her room or sleeps most of the time. She really misses her daddy. Misses the world the way it used to be."

What of Jamal? Coop wondered. He found it telling how their oldest son's name never came up in conversation, as if the family was too ashamed to speak of him. Maybe it pained them too much.

"It's almost noon. We should go." Mother stood. "Never hesitate to ask for help. We are all friends and neighbors."

Coop took his cue from his mother and also stood. "Any repairs you may need around the house, I'll be glad to work on them for you, especially this time of year when it's slow around the farm." He patted Keisha's head. "Just send word with one of your children when they come to our barn school and I'll come."

After bidding each other farewell, Coop and his mother walked the long driveway down the mountain, each of them holding onto one of Hattie's hands. His little cousin didn't seem to mind the cold and was mesmerized with the tread marks her boots made in the snow. She kicked a plume of snow and giggled.

"Stop that. We may never be able to buy you boots again so you'll need to make them last as long as you can fit into them," Mother said. She looked at Coop. "What'll we do when there are no more shoes?"

"I suppose we can make moccasins out of deer hide like the Indians used to," Coop answered. They still had plenty of things from the before times. It had only been six months since the world went dark. Mother was right, though. How would they make do when all of the many things they had taken for granted, like shoes, were depleted? Life had become a misery for the English without electricity, automobiles, and medicine, but their neighbors in Wineberry Hollow were fortunate to have food, water, and shelter. They were far better off than the rest of the world despite having suffered through the marauding raiders. Would the English be able to restore things back to the old ways before things got worse?

Tony waited patiently with the buggy and nickered when he saw them approach. Coop helped Mother and Hattie aboard. He checked the cinching and patted the beast's neck.

Coop climbed in and shut the door. He had boxed in the buggy for use in cold weather, but since it wasn't air tight like an automobile, chill air seeped in and they could see their breath.

"Go on home now," Coop said and gently slapped the reins across Tony's back.

The beast plodded along without complaint. Coop made a conscious effort not to look at Katie's house as they passed by.

Minutes later, as they approached the farm, Hattie pointed into the distance and said, "What's that?"

"Whatever it is, it's sitting in front of our home," Coop's mother said.

The object was a green automobile, one that he had never seen before, an oversized vehicle with a yellow light whirring on top of its cab. Coop's breath hitched. Was this another raid? Had another band of marauders broken through the defenses? They drew nearer and Coop noticed two tractor trailers parked on the other side of the vehicle. One of the rigs pulled an open trailer with high sides, a livestock trailer.

"Looks like the Army," Coop uttered.

"Thank God," his mother said holding a hand over her heart. "Perhaps they have news that the crisis is over."

Coop didn't think so. The scene seemed wrong to him.

As Tony pulled the buggy into the driveway, Gary Daw walked into their path and raised a hand, motioning for them to halt. Coop pulled back on the reins bringing Tony to a stop. Coop got out of the buggy. "What is this?"

"Trouble," Gary spoke in a low tone. "A hundred or so heavily armed troops are about to enter the hollow. Too many for us to stop."

Coop felt an anchor drop in his gut. "More marauders?"

"No. U.S. Army."

"What does the Army want of us? Why have they come here?"

Gary rubbed the back of his neck. "The man in charge, a Captain Kettering, wants to meet with all of the farmers living in the hollow. He's called a meeting for 1500 hours. Troops are going to come through and escort all farmers for a meeting here at your barn. The captain demanded a suitable place to meet, and since your barn is already made up and we've used it before for meetings, I chose it."

He looked into the sky and then met Coop's gaze. "Sorry about not asking for permission first. I had no choice."

"Where is Corporal Clark? I thought he was in charge of the militia now."

"They've taken him."

"Wha, what?" Coop stammered. "I don't understand."

Gary motioned for Coop to walk a few paces away from the buggy. From the entrance of the barn, Coop saw a gathering of soldiers, all of them holding weapons.

"Listen to me, Coop," Gary said. "These are regular Army troops. They have limitless manpower and resources. We cannot fight that. All of us are completely at their mercy, so do whatever they ask of you and your family, otherwise it will go badly for us all."

"Does this mean the crisis is over?" Coop asked. "Are they here to help us?"

Gary's lower jaw trembled. "The crisis is not over. You asked about Corporal Clark? About an hour ago, I witnessed Captain Kettering shoot him dead after finding out that he was active duty military. Kettering said he should have made his way back to Enclave 38 and that he was a deserter for not doing so."

He choked on his words. After composing himself, Gary continued. "Kettering shot him down in cold blood. Murdered him. You know what? I think he did it just to get our attention, to make us take him seriously, to spread the word that he means business. He really didn't care about Clark being a deserter, it was just an excuse. If it wouldn't have been Clark, he would've found a reason to murder someone else."

Coop wished he could lean against something. He felt like he would drop to the ground over the horror of this news.

Gary went on, "So, to answer your question, Cooper, no. These men are not here to help us. Not hardly."

Chapter 56

Coop said nothing to his mother about the murder of Corporal Clark, but she had seen in his face the danger. He persuaded her to take Hattie into the root cellar. She resisted at first, but Coop prevailed, insisting that as man of the house she should mind his instincts when it came to matters of the family safety. If not for her own safety, she needed to consider Hattie.

After securing his mother and cousin, Coop took a seat on one of the benches setup in his barn. The entire Wineberry Hollow militia sat in the back, disarmed and watched by a cluster of soldiers. More soldiers escorted his neighbors into the barn during the course of the next few hours. All of them wore shaken expressions.

Coop had never seen so many heavily armed men. Gary Daw had been right. They could not resist such a force. He saw Carl Miller and his wife enter his barn. Katie trailed behind them with a soldier pointing a gun at her back. Shocked, he jumped from his seat. "Katie."

"You, shut up and sit," the soldier nearest to him ordered.

Katie's eyes went wide, and she walked over to him. She spoke barely above a whisper. "I'm okay, Coop. Don't make a scene." She grabbed his hand and pulled him down onto the bench beside her. "Don't be a fool. One of these men already killed Jack Clark, or so I've been told."

Ordinarily, he would've welcomed holding her hand. Lately, it had been the stuff of fantasy, but a wave of sorrow washed over him. Coop pulled his hand free from hers. "Once again, I have brought you death."

"Yeah, it seems that way."

He eyed her. "What are you doing here? I thought they were only rounding up the farmers."

"Mr. Miller has a bad cough. I went there to listen to his chest. Make sure he doesn't have pneumonia. The good news is he doesn't. The bad news is the soldiers showed up while I was there. They scooped me up along with the Millers and made me come."

With a blink, Katie's bright eyes went dull. "They took my car, Coop. I don't think I'll get it back." She said it with such sadness that Coop wanted to gather her in his arms.

A large crowd of soldiers entered the barn and stationed themselves around the inside perimeter. One of them marched to the front and cleared his throat. On the front of his jacket, Coop read the name on the cloth tag over his pocket: Kettering.

"Everybody pay attention," Kettering said. "I'm going to make this short and sweet. The United States of America is under martial law, has been since June 21. We just haven't made it this far out in the country yet to pass the word."

One of Coop's neighbors, Joe Dewalt, stood and said, "What is the word? How long until the lights come back on?"

Kettering nodded to the soldier standing closest to Joe. The soldier punched Joe in the stomach and shoved him back down into his seat.

Coop gasped along with many of his neighbors. Katie whimpered and grabbed Coop's arm.

"There will be no questions." Kettering cleared his throat. "As I was saying, the country is in a state of martial law. I am the field commander for this area. That makes me god to you sod busters. It is at my sole discretion who gets to keep what they have, how much they get to keep, who lives, and who dies. Here is what you need to know. A lot of good people, important people, the best of humanity now live in military enclaves. The enclaves are self sufficient, but our reserves are low. It's my job to scour the countryside and procure food, grain, livestock, and whatever else I damn well please to build those reserves. Oh, yeah, anyone with the shakes I get to execute on the spot."

Coop and Katie exchanged glances. What did Captain Kettering mean?

"What about you, you are asking yourselves? According to the U.S. Government, you people do not matter. You do not exist. I don't give a rat's ass about your welfare or what is fair. That means my men and I are going to sweep through your farms and confiscate what we need. We have trucks to haul away what we take and we demand your cooperation.

"If any of you resist, we will shoot you and your family, starting with your children. Then we will take what we need anyway. It will all be perfectly legal, and I will not have a second thought about doing so. My roast beef and mashed potatoes will taste just as good after shooting you dead as they will taste if I let you live. I promise you that I won't lose a minute of sleep.

"So why not kill you all? Wouldn't bother me in the least, but get a clue people. If we kill you all then there won't be anything left when we come calling again next year. And make no mistake. We will come calling again. Unless, of course, you're all dead of CJD by next year."

Katie whispered, "I'm glad my father isn't alive to see this. It would've broken his heart."

"One more thing," Kettering said. "Effective immediately I'm disbanding your militia. I'll be collecting all of your weapons and all operating motor vehicles. Don't even think about any future insurrection or ambushes. That would not bode well for you."

From the corner of his eye, Coop saw Tomas Ortiz rise to his feet. He pulled a handgun from somewhere on his body, Coop didn't see where. He pointed the gun directly at Kettering. "You won't get my gun. You'll have to kill me first, but I'll take you with me."

Every soldier in the barn pointed their rifle at Ortiz and a collective snap resounded, the result of all their safeties being disengaged.

"Sergeant Adams, I thought I told you to search these sod busters," Kettering said in a strangely calm voice considering that Ortiz pointed a gun at his chest.

"I did, sir," Adams said from his station near the door. "Don't know how this man got by the search."

Ortiz smiled, his face glowed and appeared angelic. "This is for Jack Clark."

Coop heard pop, pop, pop as Ortiz pulled the trigger. Kettering's hand shot to his shoulder. He spun and dropped to the floor. An instant later, the world exploded as the soldiers opened fire on Tomas Ortiz.

Katie held her hands over her ears and screamed.

Coop wrapped his arms around Katie and threw her to the barn floor covering her body with his. Coop wasn't sure if he passed out, but his next conscious observation was Katie banging on him with her fists. "Get off of me."

He carefully got to his knees and looked around. Katie pushed him away and pulled herself into a sitting position. Both of them coughed from the smoke and stench of spent gunpowder.

Several soldiers lay on the floor bleeding. They had apparently shot each other in the crossfire. "Get me the medic," Kettering yelled.

"We didn't bring him on this trip," Sergeant Adams said.

Kettering cursed.

"I'm hit," Joe Hutmaker groaned. "Help me."

Katie got to her feet and brushed herself off. "Where are you, Joe?"

A hand shot up in the air. "Over here."

Coop followed Katie to where Joe lay. Joe held a hand over his ear. "Let me see," Katie said and pulled his hand away. Blood flowed from his mangled ear.

"I need a bandage," Katie yelled, "or a clean shirt."

Coop stripped out of his blue shirt and handed it to her. She folded and pressed it against Joe's ear.

"The bullet grazed you and you're going to be all right," Katie said. "Keep pressure on this bandage. Once the bleeding stops, I'll see what I can do to abrade your wound."

"Who is that? Are you a doctor?" Kettering yelled. They couldn't see the man because he was still down, but he must have overheard the words spoken between Katie and Joe.

Sergeant Adams walked over and took Katie's arm.

Reacting, Coop pushed the man away. "Don't touch her."

"No," Katie yelled. The sergeant narrowed his eyes and pointed his rifle at Coop. Katie shouted. "He's my assistant. I need him."

"Touch me again, you Amish piece of shit, and I'll drill you full of holes," the sergeant said.

Coop no longer cared about Gottes Wille. He had failed Katie too often. Not this time. Not again. Never again. With that decision, a strange sense of freedom flowed through him, as if he cast off iron shackles that had bound him.

The sergeant shoved both Katie and Coop toward Captain Kettering. The man sat up, a hand over his shoulder.

Kettering stared at Katie. "You look too young to be a doctor."

"I'm not a doctor, but I've had some training."

"Help me."

She inspected his wound. "It's a through and through. Lucky for you it was a small caliber. Probably a .22. From the way it's bleeding, I don't think it damaged any major arteries."

"Fix it."

Katie stood, hands on her hips and glanced around. "Later, dude. Due to the incompetence of your soldiers I see a lot of my neighbors that I need to tend." She shot him a wicked smile. "Good people, important people, the best of humanity now living in Wineberry Hollow."

Sergeant Adams slapped her face, knocking her to the ground. "You little bitch."

Cooper launched himself at Adams and pinned him against the wall with such a force that he felt the breath leave the man's lungs with an audible *ungh*. From the corner of his eye, Coop saw movement, the flash of a gun butt as it smashed into the side of his skull.

Hot white sparks exploded into Coop's field of vision before he passed out.

Chapter 57

Coop puzzled over his throbbing head, especially since he had never been prone to headaches before. The throb grew in intensity causing him to awaken from sleep. Mother stared down at him, a hand over her mouth.

"Thank God," she said. "Oh, thank God."

He found himself in his room, in bed. Raising a hand to the source of his pain, Coop found his head had been bandaged. He wasn't able to see clearly from his left eye. "What happened?"

Mother held a hand to her chest. "We were afraid you might never wake up."

"That's silly." He glanced at the window and could tell by the rays of the sun that it was mid-morning, maybe close to lunch. "Did I fall?"

"You don't remember?"

"I need to go, and I'm thirsty." Coop pushed back the covers and swung his legs over the side of the bed. When he tried to stand, he nearly fell to the floor, but Mother caught him by the elbow.

He felt dizzy and weak, his head on fire.

Mother steadied him as he shuffled into a small room they used as a bathroom. He used a pail. When done, he leaned over a washbowl and looked into a mirror. Someone had wrapped a white bandage around his head and over his left ear. He gently pressed the area which sent a bolt of pain through his skull.

It scared Coop that he couldn't remember anything.

Mother waited for him in his bedroom with a tall glass of water. Coop downed the water which eased his thirst but did nothing for his frustration. She wore an expectant look.

"What did we do yesterday?" Coop asked. "How did I get like this?"

She took his arm. "Let me help you back to bed."

"I've already slept away half the day. What is wrong?" He pulled his arm from her grasp but suddenly felt weak and on the verge of collapse. She took his arm again, and this time he didn't resist. After lowering him onto his pillow, she asked him, "What is the last thing you remember?"

Coop concentrated. "We visited Chelsey Orr and her children." He touched the sensitive wound to his head. "My memory is like a slice of Swiss cheese. It's not all there."

"Dr. St. John warned me that you might have memory loss but he said it should come back to you."

"Dr. St. John? The dentist? He bandaged me? What about Dr. Hunt?"

A pained look crossed her face. "You should rest. You'll remember it all later."

Coop wanted to fight it, but the effort from going to the bathroom exhausted him. He descended into a fitful sleep.

When he woke, the sun had gone down and a candle burned on his dresser. Coop sat up slowly. Mother wasn't there to help him this time, so he took it easy. He felt grimy and his own body odor repulsed him. He left his room and stood at the top of the staircase. "Hello?"

Mother appeared at the bottom of the staircase and looked up at him. "Let me help you come down."

"I think I should take a bath first."

"I'll bring you a bucket of hot water from the stove and then I'll heat up some soup for you."

While bathing, Coop tried harder to remember. There was a meeting in the barn, but the details were fuzzy. He pulled on fresh clothes and joined Mother at the kitchen table. Her soup tasted wonderful, canned vegetables from past summer with chicken chunks. He couldn't recall ever being as hungry as this. The entire time he ate, Mother studied him. When Coop could stand it no longer, he pushed away the soup bowl. "I'm frustrated trying to remember. How did I get this way? Who helped you get me upstairs and into bed?"

"Mr. Damroth and Mr. Miller brought you here. Dr. St. John cleaned and bandaged your wound."

"I can't remember any of it."

"You were unconscious the entire time. Oh, Cooper, we were all worried that you might die. You suffered a mighty blow."

At that statement, Coop's hand shot up to his wound, and he gently probed the bandages. He felt nothing through the thick material. Was she serious? The expression on her face suggested it hadn't been a joke. "Am I going to be okay?"

"Gottes Wille, now that you are awake."

"Did Bonnie or Tony kick me?"

"Nothing like that."

"Then what?"

She sighed. "The Army came and assembled all of the farmers in our barn."

Coop experienced wisps of memory. Violence had broken out. "Was I hurt in some sort of fight?"

"I was in the root cellar and didn't see it. There were shots. Mr. Damroth came to fetch me after it was all over."

"But how did I get hurt?"

"I don't know, Cooper, there was a lot of confusion."

Coop saw in her eyes that she was holding something back. "What else?"

She hesitated. "Four men are dead. Corporal Clark was shot when the Army first arrived. Tom Ortiz was shot down after he attempted to shoot an Army captain named Kettering. Two soldiers died during a gun battle. They shot each other in a crossfire. Many more of them and our neighbors were wounded."

Coop rested his forehead in his hand. It started coming back to him. Ortiz had pulled a gun and then the chaos had erupted. He still couldn't recall how he received his head wound. "What happened after that?"

"The Army confiscated all of the weapons held by our militia. They took a great deal of the hollow's grain stores and livestock…"

"…Bonnie and Tony?" he interrupted.

"No. They allowed us to keep our horses so that we could continue to work the fields." She paused. "For when they return."

Coop groaned. "What's the point of working the fields if they will continue taking everything from us?"

"Threats were made. They will do ugly things if there is no harvest next year. Mr. Hutmaker and Mr. DeWalt performed an inventory. The Army left us barely enough to survive this winter. We need to pray that God will provide wild animals like deer to supplement what remains."

The throb in Coop's head faded to a dull ache. It only hurt when he touched it, but he still suffered poor vision from his left eye. "How long have I been out?"

From across the table, Mother reached over and rested her hand on his wrist. "Cooper, you have been asleep for three days. The meeting was Wednesday afternoon. This is Saturday."

Coop's breath hitched. "Three days? No wonder I was so hungry."

"You'll need to take it slow until you recover. First thing tomorrow morning I'll send for Dr. St. John."

"I'm not that helpless. I'll take the buggy and go see him."

"No. That will be too much for you."

He would've argued but realized she was right. He was still weak and tired. "We'll see how I feel in the morning. I think I should rest again." Coop stood from his chair and slowly climbed the stairs clinging to the handrail. Mother trailed closely behind. She changed his bed linens and tucked him in.

"You gave me a fright," she said. "You're all I have left."

Coop motioned her closer and kissed her cheek. A few minutes later he dropped off to sleep.

During the middle of the night, Coop snapped awake and couldn't fall back to sleep. Having spent so much time in bed, he figured his body had enough rest. Coop glanced out his window into the black night. With no way of knowing the time, he decided to try and rest until morning. He tossed and turned, alternating between moments of fitful sleep and anxious wakefulness.

The horrors of the world had finally overtaken Wineberry Hollow. He and his neighbors had all been fools to think they could isolate themselves, live in relative peace and security. How presumptuous they had all been. Too many godless people seemed perfectly willing to destroy anything and anybody for selfish gain. The Army didn't need what the community possessed. They were acting out of pure meanness, wielding their power against defenseless people who meant them no harm. People they should be defending instead of exploiting.

Now it was Christmas, six months since the world went dark, and neither the English nor the Amish had anything left to celebrate. Everywhere there existed only cruelty, misery, and death.

Coop contemplated his existence. What was the point in being Amish? Try as he might to live a humble life, the outcome was the same. He was no better off than his English neighbors. His faith had not sheltered him.

That date with Katie had been the happiest moment of his life. Adhering to his Amish principles had cost him that happiness, Katie's friendship, and damaged her trust in him beyond repair.

Gottes Wille be damned. His life held more meaning and purpose during the times he tried protecting Katie. At her house when Stan had attacked her, Coop had finally felt like a man when that thing inside him had snapped and caused him to react. When the gunplay started in his barn, he never hesitated to protect her with his body. He would have died feeling no shame for acting the way he did. Then when Captain Kettering had demanded that Katie help him…

Coop jolted awake. The sun streamed through his bedroom window.

He remembered.

"Mother," he yelled. Throwing off the covers, he pushed himself into a sitting position and slammed the soles of his bare feet onto the cold floor. He stood and leaned into the wall after suffering a wave of dizziness.

"Mother," he shouted.

A moment later she stood at his side holding his arm.

He pulled away and faced her. "Where is Katie? I saw a soldier strike her. That's when I reacted and got beaten in the head. That's how this all happened. How badly has Katie been hurt?"

Mother's face softened. She tilted her head and laid the palm of her hand against his cheek. "My son."

Coop gently removed her hand from his face. "What happened to Katie?"

Her face pinched. "Cooper, you aren't healthy enough to bear this."

"What happened to Katie? Does she live?" he shouted. Dread filled his gut. He feared the answer to his question, and a wave of guilt displaced his fear. "Forgive me, Mother. I didn't mean to shout at you, but I must know."

"Cooper, please sit."

"No. Tell me now or I will run the length of Cove Road screaming until someone answers my question. If I have to I'll run barefoot in the snow all the way to the Hunt's house."

"She lives, Cooper."

He closed his eyes and stopped to catch his breath and wait for the pain in his skull to subside. He didn't realize until know how badly his infirmity had impacted his body. This little activity had drained all his strength.

"Cooper."

He met his mother's gaze and recognized from her expression that she was withholding something from him. Was she lying? Was Katie dead? Impossible. Mother never lied.

"Cooper, you need to be strong and consider with a calm heart what I must now tell you."

His racing heart was now anything but calm. "What is it?"

"My son. About Katie."

"What, Mother, what?" Coop felt as if he had to pull words from her throat.

"The soldiers. They have taken her."

Chapter 58

Kettering winced at the pain in his shoulder when he lifted the bottle and poured himself a shot of whiskey. Goddamn, it hurt like a son-of-a-bitch. In all the bloody battles he had lived through during the Middle East wars, he had never once suffered so much as a scratch. It angered him how a yokel, a mere sod buster had nearly ended it for him. A few inches to the left and he wouldn't be sitting at his kitchen table.

Out of the corner of his eye he regarded the girl sitting on the sofa, watching him, always staring. She had taken good care of his injury. Better than most field medics could have done. Forcing her to be his personal nurse had been a good move. She gave in easily after he figured out what button he needed to push, the thing he could hold over her.

She sat there staring at him. It made him uneasy, spooked him. She was uppity, had a smart mouth. But most of the time she remained quiet, eerily so. No emotion. No tears. He also had to admit the other reason he wanted her under his roof. She was a knockout. Pretty face. Hot body. Young. If it weren't for his preoccupation with the pain in his messed up shoulder, he would already have ravaged her.

Kettering met the girl's gaze. She didn't look away, but when he continued staring, she began chewing on her lower lip. He smiled. Yeah, she could read his thoughts. She knew what was coming. And he knew that if given an opportunity she'd kill him in his sleep. Except for one thing, the one detail he decided to remind her of.

"You know, of course, that if anything happens to me, your boyfriend dies." Kettering downed his whiskey and poured himself another drink.

"He's not my boyfriend," she snapped.

Kettering smacked a palm against his forehead. "Ah, yeah, that's right. How did you put it? He's your assistant." The girl's cold expression never faltered. "Stop that."

"What is it you want me to stop?" she asked. "I'm not doing anything."

Anger flushed his face. He got off on terrorizing women and despised having the tables turned on him. He stood and walked toward her.

She showed no sign of fear. Never even blinked. He took a seat on the sofa beside her and draped his undamaged arm around her shoulder. Only then did a look of concern flash into her eyes.

Better. He needed to regain control. "Your boyfriend, your assistant, whatever. The point is that you care for him, the way you begged Sergeant Adams not to shoot him." He needed to know for sure the extent of her feelings for the Amish boy. If he was just anyone to her, his hold on the girl would be only tentative at best.

"Cooper was defenseless and out cold," she said. "I'd have begged the sergeant to spare anyone in that condition."

From where his arm rested on her shoulder, he moved his hand to the back of her neck and squeezed.

Her look remained defiant as if saying, I'll not give you the satisfaction by reacting.

"If he really isn't someone special then I should just revisit Wineberry Hollow tomorrow during patrol. I know where your assistant lives. Maybe I should just finish the job."

There. Her eyes darted to the side, but she quickly recovered. Too late. He had seen the truth.

Kettering leaned in as if to kiss her, but it was a ploy. He enjoyed tormenting her. The girl screwed up her face and tried pulling away. He moved his lips to her ear and whispered, "I won't harm the boy. I'll just tell him how much you enjoy being with me and what a nice little whore you are."

"No," she said in a raised voice. Her face paled. Finally, she showed fear. "You can't do that. He'll react, and then you'll end up killing him."

"Then you'll stay here, won't you? You'll always do exactly what I ask of you. You won't try to run."

"Dude, I've been sleeping on your sofa for the past three nights. I haven't left yet."

His hand squeezed tighter around her neck. The girl's head bobbed as he shook her for emphasis while speaking each word. "Don't. Call. Me. Dude."

Her face turned red, and she coughed. Kettering released her, and she pulled away to the far end of the sofa. As if that could stop him from doing anything he wanted with her.

She wheezed. "Okay, I get it, captain."

"No need to be so formal. My friends call me Halfjack."

She shot him a dirty look and turned away.

"Look at me, girl."

"My name is Katie. Stop calling me girl, and I'll stop calling you dude. Deal?"

"Hey, Katie."

"What do you want?"

He inched down the sofa until his leg made contact with hers. She turned her face away. "You're doing a fine job as my nurse.

Another day or so and I'll be feeling well enough for you to give up this sofa. Admittedly, my BOQ isn't much, but I have a nice big bed."

"Touch me, and I'll kill you. I swear to god I'll do it. You know I will."

He believed her. The girl was stubborn and had real resolve. "No, you won't. My life is linked to your Amish friend's life. I've left word with my men. If I die, he dies."

Gone was the fire in her eyes, her expression now displaying resignation. This girl really did care about that Amish boy. Amazing. A knockout like her. A plain kid like him.

She hardened her expression. "You wouldn't like playing house with me. I'll make you as miserable as possible."

He snickered. "I don't think you appreciate how much I'm doing for you, how lucky you really are."

She rolled her eyes. "Yeah, my life is so charmed."

"Bet your little ass it's charmed. My men wanted to keep you, strip you naked, and chain you up in the back room of their barracks where they could take you over and over anytime they felt like it. You'd wish you were dead instead of having to suffer through that. I saved you from that indignity. You'll lay on your back for no man. No man except me."

The girl said nothing. She tilted her head as if mentally digesting what he had told her. Suddenly, she repositioned herself on the sofa pointing her knees toward him.

"My name is Katie Hunt," she stated. "I'm eighteen. I just graduated from high school this year. My plans were to go to college, to become a doctor. My mom died when I was just a kid. My dad was a doctor. He was a great man and a good father. He inspired me to study medicine. I like movies and pizza and loud music and driving my car real fast, and yes, I *do* care about Cooper. How could I not? The poor guy loves me unconditionally, and I've been so shitty to him. Halfjack, I'm just a typical girl, like any other girl, except maybe a little nerdier."

"Whoa," Kettering said. "That's the most I've heard from you in three days. Why do you suddenly feel the need to unload?"

"Because I don't believe that you're a soulless animal. I am a human being. Look at me and see me for *who* I am rather than *what* I am. You are a United States Army officer, a gentleman.

Someone sworn to protect people like me. Look, I understand. I don't hold it against you. When the world went dark, we all lost some of our humanity. You aren't yourself. Think about who you used to be, what you stood for. Would you have acted this way in the times before? Would you have even thought about abusing a young girl like me? Let me go, Halfjack, please. I'm just a kid. Don't hurt me."

The girl's hard façade softened. He saw it, her youth, the little girl she had been not so long ago, her innocence. Too bad her rant didn't affect him in the way she wanted. In fact, her pleading had the opposite impact. It turned him on. He wanted her badly now. If it weren't for the miserable shoulder pain, he'd take her, right there on the sofa.

Kettering got up. He stood in front of the girl, looking down on her. "Since you told me your life story, let me enlighten you about mine. I never respected women. Not before and certainly not now. My old man used to slap my mother around and call her a whore. I hated him for it until I got old enough to figure out that all those *uncles* she introduced me to weren't uncles at all. Her behavior taught me everything I need to know about women. Far as I'm concerned, God put women on Earth for only one purpose. To be the plaything of men."

She stiffened. Her hands balled into fists. "I'm not like your mother."

"What you're thinking about doing right now would not be wise," he said. "It doesn't matter how brave, determined, or mentally tough you are, what kind of physical shape you are in, or how intelligent you are. I'm bigger, faster, stronger, and definitely meaner. I will always dominate you. I will always have my way with you."

Her face displayed abject hate.

Kettering decided that he liked her facial expression. There was no bullshit in it. No deception. And it kept a nice, high wall between them. He didn't give a damn about *who* she was. Now that they finally understood each other, he was sure that they would get along just fine. He'd keep her alive.

Until, that is, he tired of her.

Chapter 59

Cooper Stover slipped his arms into the sleeves of his father's wool coat. It bore his scent, brought back memories of toiling alongside the man in the fields. Those were times of contentment. Times when the world made sense.

His own coat was too tight given all of the things he needed to stuff into his pockets. His father had been bigger around the girth, so now the coat suited his purpose.

He looked out the window. A heavy snow blanketed the ground and the grey sky promised more bad weather. The treetops swayed. The dial on the big round thermometer pointed to 20. He turned and faced his friends who had gathered in his kitchen. And Mother.

She lost her composure and burst into loud sobs. She got down on her knees in front of him and took his hand. No words. Just sobs.

Coop felt such sorrow for her. The guilt tore at his soul. The decision had consumed him during the past two months while he recovered from his head wound. He understood Mother's feelings. He might be killed. Chances were that he would. He might never see her again. The worst of it was that she would never know what happened to him. How many months would she wait up for him and jump at every noise thinking that he had finally returned? When would her agony become so intolerable that she would finally give up?

If Coop did happen to return, what would he find? Would Mother survive his absence? Would she pine away until she died? All those thoughts ate at Coop. He weighed everything, searched his soul, and had finally made up his mind.

Coop kneeled at her side and embraced her. "I don't expect you to understand, Mother. I only want you to hold on to the fact that Katie has no family to look out for her. She has nobody."

Mother balled her fists and banged them against his chest. "But when you leave I will no longer have my family. Your father is dead. You are my only son, Cooper. Without you, *I* have nobody."

Coop glanced at his neighbors standing in his living room and noticed their discomfort. They looked at the walls, ceiling, and floor. Everywhere but at Mother and him. They understood, but clearly, they did not approve. He pointed in their direction and said, "You have them. They pledged to look after you. They will work the farm. I've made arrangements with Mr. Damroth. He's a good man and will oversee the workers. You know that he won't take advantage of you. None of our friends will cheat you."

"I don't want them, and I don't want Mr. Damroth to look after my interests. I want you."

When her sobs subsided, Coop said, "You have neighbors who care about you. Katie is a stranger among strangers. She is truly alone. That is what finally swayed my decision. That is why I must do this."

"Cooper, you are lying to yourself about your motivation." Mother trembled. "You have an obsession over this English girl. Katie never cared for you in the way that you love her. She even mocked you. You are projecting your feelings onto her."

They had argued over these points ever since Coop made up his mind and had announced his intentions. It was of no use to argue again. Mother didn't want to hear what he had to say.

"You don't even know where to look. She might even be dead. You are seized with a madness, Cooper. Wait until next fall when the soldiers return. Please, they will bring you news of Katie."

Cooper helped Mother to her feet. "Maybe love is a form of madness. I don't care if she doesn't return my feelings. She needs me. I have to try. Somebody needs to care enough to try and find her."

Mother shook her head. "She's not even Amish."

Coop felt his face redden. He raised his voice. "Have you not noticed what has happened in the world?" He composed himself and lowered his voice. "Our Amish lifestyle doesn't matter anymore."

Shelia Cunningham stepped forward and hugged him. "I take your mother's side in this. Katie is tough. She can fend for herself." She wiped the back of her hand across her eyes. "Oh, Cooper, you're taking such a risk for Katie, and she doesn't even think much of you. She calls you Chicken Coop."

"It doesn't matter what she thinks of me. It only matters that I care for her."

"God bless you, Cooper. I hope you find her. I hope Katie finally sees you for the man you really are."

Coop glanced at his mother, at the pain remaining in her face.

"Thank you, Sheila, but the way I am hurting Mother, I don't feel much like a man right now."

Pete Damroth extended his hand. "No matter what you find out there, son, take comfort that we will care for your mother and your property as best as we can."

Coop shook his hand. "I appreciate that more than you can know."

Gary Daw handed Coop his shotgun. Coop slung it over his shoulder.

"You could wait a while longer," Gary said. "It's almost March. The weather will break soon."

"Then it will be time again to till the ground. I may lose my resolve."

Gary smiled, a sad smile. "Maybe that wouldn't be such a bad thing."

Coop swallowed. They all meant well, but he knew what he had to do. "What of Katie if I lose my resolve?"

Gary said, "What of Cooper if you don't?"

He chose to ignore the question.

"You know the way?" Gary asked.

"South."

"You'll want to hike over South Mountain. After a couple days of hiking, if it feels right, turn east. Eventually, you'll need to cross Pine Creek. It might take you another few days until you come across the four lane highway. That will be Route 15. Follow it south, but keep well away from the road and out of sight. In time, you'll reach the town of Milton. Enclave 38 is directly across the river from Milton.

"Remember. Avoid people. Those that remain alive will be desperate. Use that shotgun for food only when sure nobody is around to hear shots. Shoot only once. That way nobody will be able to get a fix on your location. Keep your campfires small and only during daylight. Above all else, don't go anywhere near any towns or developed areas. I can't stress enough how they are death traps."

"Thank you for your advice," Coop said. "I will remember."

Coop turned to hug Mother one final time, but she turned her back on him. He didn't blame her.

He looked around the living room and kitchen of his home

committing as much as he could to memory. He'd need to recall the warmth of this house in the times that lay ahead. Feeling that he could break down at any moment, Coop turned and walked out the door. He shuffled down the driveway under the weight of his pack and supplies, dried food, clothing, ammunition, all the things he would need to survive a long journey. He stopped at the edge of Cove Road and glanced east toward Katie's home and asked himself again. Was she worth it?

Coop resolved that would be the final time he would allow such negativity to enter his mind. With a clear sense of purpose, he stepped onto Cove Road and walked in the direction of the township road.

"Cooper." Mother's voice fluttered above the wind in his ears. She ran at him, no coat, arms outstretched and flung herself into his arms. This time, with no tears, she said, "I couldn't let you leave remembering my back to you."

He finally managed to say, "I love you."

"And I love you." She stepped back and wrapped her arms around herself. "May you find the peace in your heart that you seek, my son. Go with God."

Coop nodded and turned away. "Goodbye, Mother. Gottes Wille I will see you again."

He paced away counting his steps for no reason other than to fill his mind with some purpose. When he reached 100 Coop glanced over his shoulder. All of them stood there in the middle of the road, Pete Damroth, Sheila Cunningham, Gary Daw, and his mother. They waved. He returned their wave, turned, and soldiered on.

He didn't look back after that.

Nearing the entrance to Wineberry Hollow, he passed the Kroh farm and saw his friend Stephen hitching a horse to a buggy. "Pretty cold, isn't it, Coop?"

"Sure is."

"I'm going to fe, fe, fetch Rebekah. Otherwise I'd never be out on a day like this."

"Love," Coop muttered. "There is no better reason."

"Wha, wha, what did you say?"

"I know exactly how you feel. Goodbye, old friend."

"Goodbye, Coop. Say, where are you going?"

"For a walk."

Coop reached the end of Cove Road and glanced at the straw piles that had once made up part of the barricade maintained by the militia. Now abandoned. Torn down by the Army. The wind whistled through an old wagon wheel, a forlorn note in remembrance for what once had been, a determination to hold onto a piece of civilization, now degraded to anarchy.

The militia was no use against the might of the U.S. Army, and what remained of any raiding parties would still be holed up for the winter.

Coop sighed and turned south. A road to nowhere. He knew the township road ended a mile away at the base of South Mountain. A logging road led to the top. A few hours later, Coop found himself at the summit. He shrugged the pack off his shoulders to take a break. The wind howled at the peak unfettered by the trees. His eyes watered from the blast of air, his tears freezing against his cheeks. Coop took a final look at the valley below, all the fields in Wineberry Hollow blanketed in snow.

Despite the freezing temperatures, the sun emerged from overcast skies and hung high in the sky. Lunchtime, but it was too soon for him to stop and eat. If Coop didn't know better, he would think that all was well with the world. He stared at the homes of his neighbors below, wood smoke billowing from chimneys. A peaceful scene.

Coop picked up his pack, put his arms through the loops, and secured the belt around his waist. Looking south, trees lay in front of him all the way to the horizon. Skeletons without their leaves reaching for the sky. Here and there dark green splotches showed where conifers mixed in. A beautiful scene, all things considered.

In that moment, he was happy. Coop hoped that he would be able to string together many such moments and said a silent prayer asking to return someday to this place that he loved and to his mother.

He took his first step forward, down the other side of the mountain. Coop had never been here before. Then again, there were a lot of places he had never been.

Would he ever see the ocean? He doubted that now.

He started singing to himself, not one of the many church songs he knew so well, but a secular song, naughty. One that filled him with good cheer and a warm memory. A song that reminded him of his purpose. He didn't know the title. He didn't know the name of the musicians. He knew it only as Cooper and Katie's song. Marching on, he sang it:

"Tramps like us, baby we were born to run."

Chapter 60

Cooper followed Gary Daw's advice and walked south. Trudging up and down mountain ranges prevented him from making good time. He consulted a Pennsylvania road map that he kept in his back pack, the kind that folded up like an accordion. It wasn't much use because the scale was too small and there were no roads he could use as reference points, but around noon of the third day, he found a mountain stream. Looking at the map, Coop estimated his location and saw a stream depicted on the map flowing east into Pine Creek Gorge. He guessed it was the same stream and crossed where a log had fallen across the banks.

The water in the stream trickled which meant it was above freezing, but the banks were lined with ice. Coop refilled his water bottles. He'd boil the water later as a precaution. Probably nothing was wrong with the clear mountain stream, but he didn't want to risk being laid up with stomach cramps or diarrhea.

The act of hiking and bearing a load on his back kept Coop warm during the day. Being late February, the temperature dropped into the teens or even single digits at night. His father's coat and the many layers he slipped on underneath while he slept kept him relatively comfortable. The damp ground made a miserable mattress, but Coop learned that he could insulate himself against the dampness by using a thick layer of pine boughs as a mattress.

His first night, Coop found a hunter's tree stand and thought he'd be smart by taking advantage of it since the perch was high off the ground. Exposure to the chill wind had been worse than the damp earth, so he abandoned the platform and curled up against the leeward side of a large boulder.

The mountains had been lonely and desolate. This part of Pennsylvania remained a wilderness area. With the exception of a few farms that Coop spotted from higher elevations, he had no trouble avoiding people and took seriously what Gary Daw had told him. Anyone seeing Coop would likely assume him to be dangerous and would probably try to kill him on sight. Who other than an outlaw would have reason to wander around an isolated area in the middle of winter? Coop would make the same assumption about anyone he stumbled across out here, but he had no intention of harming anybody. He would simply avoid any confrontation.

Coop walked on following the water downstream. A year ago, he would've found this trip extraordinary, a real adventure. In this solitude, nature distracted Coop and he would hike long stretches forgetting his worries. Then, when he collected his thoughts, it concerned him how he might not be maintaining his focus. He needed to keep his wits about him. Coop realized that while daydreaming, he might inadvertently stumble onto other people. Then what would happen?

He made better time following the stream than he did hiking across mountain peaks and just as the sun started to go down, he reached Pine Creek. Coop studied the surrounding gorge. Void of leaves, he could see a distance both up and downstream. He took a moment to appreciate the spectacular scenery, the wall of mountains on both sides of the pristine creek. But then Coop realized he had a problem. Pine Creek was wider than he realized and the center of the creek beyond the ice lined edges ran deep and rapid.

How to get across?

He unfolded the map. Pine Creek stretched many miles before flowing into the Susquehanna River, and the map showed no nearby bridges. He could hike the length of the creek, but then how would he cross the Susquehanna? Coop wished he would've discussed this with Gary Daw or Pete Damroth. They were more familiar with the area and might have been able to suggest something.

Glancing into the sky, Coop saw that less than an hour of daylight remained. A bank of fog crept up the gorge from downstream. It would hide a small nighttime fire if he backtracked up the tributary a ways out of sight of anyone possibly watching the gorge. That thought nearly made him laugh. How many people still remained alive, and in the struggle to survive, who would have time or even care enough to be out in this wilderness.

Coop decided to heat up the last of the ham and bean soup that he had brought. After tonight, it would be cereal bars and jerky and any wild game he might be lucky enough to shoot. He found a large fir tree with large spreading boughs, a perfect spot to spend the night. He gathered firewood and dug for the lighter in his coat pocket. Coop never mastered the art of starting a fire Indian style by using friction, never had reason to. The lighter was his most valuable tool, probably more valuable than the shotgun. Without it, survival would be a great deal more challenging. He moved the nozzle close to the kindling with the intention of starting it quickly. The fuel in the lighter was precious, and he didn't want to waste a single drop.

Just as Coop was about to roll the friction wheel with his thumb, he heard a noise like rocks clopping together under someone's foot.

Coop froze and his heart rate accelerated. Had someone seen him?

He moved only his eyes toward the direction of the sound and breathed a sigh of relief. An old doe and two yearlings wandered into the tributary for a drink. Deer usually moved around just before sundown, but why hadn't they heard him? Probably because he was downwind and the gurgling stream had drowned out his activity.

They were about forty yards away. Could he shoot one?

The thought of discharging his shotgun made Coop nervous. One lone shot would echo off the mountains and carry a long way, but if anyone heard him, only one shot would be difficult to pinpoint. He might not have an opportunity like this again anytime soon and decided to take the gamble.

Slowly and deliberately, he reached down and picked up the shotgun. He pressed the butt end against his shoulder. His shells were loaded with number 6 shot, it was all he had, and Coop worried about the effectiveness of the small pellets at forty yards even at full choke. He aimed at one of the yearlings figuring the round to be more fatal to a smaller body.

When Coop disengaged the safety, it made a loud click. All three deer jerked their heads out of the water and looked straight at him. In an instant they would bolt.

Coop squeezed the trigger.

The thundering boom resounded through the peaceful woods like a shockwave.

The old doe and one of her yearlings bounded up the side of the mountain, their white tails waving in warning. The young deer Coop had shot lay flat in the middle of the stream. He chambered another round and approached the downed animal hoping that it wouldn't need a coup de gras shot.

Fortunately, the deer had died on the spot. The shotgun had been more effective than Coop imagined. The pellets spread to the size of a pie plate and had taken out a huge chunk of the animal's side. Heart and lung tissue washed away downstream along with blood. Field dressing the animal with a wound this big would be a messy affair. Coop got right to work.

An hour later, he had skewered the tenderloin on a stick and relaxed by his small fire. While the venison cooked, he chopped up needles from the fir tree and added them to the water boiling in the one pan he had brought. Plain tea and fresh venison. Not the greatest or tastiest of meals, but Coop was grateful.

The shot had him paranoid. Should he have moved away from the area and found a different spot to camp? He suffered from the uneasy feeling that someone watched him. Just now he thought he caught a whiff of what? Something sweet? Like perfume? It reminded him of Katie.

He must be hallucinating.

It also filled him with melancholy. He missed the farm, the warmth of the wood stove, and his mother. He felt another wave of guilt for having left her, but Katie had nobody to protect her. Nobody to love her enough to try and rescue her. She needed him, even though she despised him. Katie might never love him, but he hoped that someday, she would grow to appreciate his friendship.

At the very least he owed Dr. Hunt. The man had selflessly served Coop and his family every time they called him. Coop would never forget how hard Dr. Hunt had worked to save his father.

His father.

Coop stared into the fire.

His father had been harsh, but Coop understood now that it had been out of love. He should have tried harder to get along with him, to understand his ways.

Off to his right, a twig snapped.

Coop froze. Could the aroma of animal flesh and blood have drawn a predator animal? The cold weather meant that bears still hibernated. What about a big cat? They weren't supposed to exist in this area, but all his life Coop had heard rumors. He eyed his shotgun leaning against a tree and decided he'd be less anxious with it closer to his side. He walked over, retrieved the weapon, and scanned the darkness in the direction of the sound.

Again, Coop thought he caught a whiff of perfume. What was that?

He stood still and remained silent for several minutes.

Nothing. Must've been the wind.

Coop sat on the ground and began to eat the tenderloin which by now was well done. Having no utensils except for a hunting knife, he held the hot meat in his gloved hands and tore at it with his teeth.

He chuckled. Mother would not have approved of his table manners.

In mid chew, Coop heard another strange noise to his right, just beyond the sight of his campfire. A cough. He jerked his head and laid a hand on his shotgun. No deer. This was definitely human. Somebody was out there. Watching him.

If whoever it was had a weapon, they could've easily bushwhacked him by now. Most likely someone had heard his shooting, seen his fire, and hid. Probably alone and scared.

"Show yourself," Coop shouted. "I'm harmless and have plenty of food to share."

Branches rustled. Coop strained to see into the darkness and pulled the shotgun into his lap. Moving toward him, Coop recognized the shape, human. The shape moved tentatively into the light of Coop's campfire. Crawled in on hands and knees.

Chapter 61

The man appeared grizzled and gaunt. His scraggly beard and unkempt hair looked like it hadn't been cut since the before times. The grimy coat he wore sported cloth patches, his trousers shredded and frayed below the knees. Why did he crawl like that?

Coop stood and approached him. "Are you hurt?"

The man froze, wild eyed, and pulled a knife from somewhere inside his coat. He lay on his stomach, grasping the knife in both hands, and pointed the blade at Coop as if it were a handgun. He stared at the shotgun that Coop held.

Coop retreated a few paces from the fire and set the shotgun on the ground. He held his hands out in a conciliatory gesture. "I mean you no harm. My name is Cooper Stover."

The man's wild eyes moved between Coop and the meat lying beside the fire. Coop. Meat. Coop. Meat.

Coop stepped away a few more paces, the man's eyes still showing fear. "You hungry? I have plenty. In fact, I have too much. I won't be able to pack out this whole deer, and it would be sinful for God's bounty to go to waste."

The man regarded Coop's words and crawled closer to the fire, the one hand holding the nasty looking blade leading the way. Upon reaching the half eaten tenderloin, the man sat, legs crossed. Without taking his eyes from Coop, the man tore into the morsel like a starving wolf.

Coop marveled at the way he bolted the meat, barely chewing. When done, the man eyed the rest of the carcass.

"We can cook more," Coop said and moved toward him.

The man slashed the air with his knife in warning and growled. In a gravelly voice he said, "That's close 'nuff, sweetie."

Coop halted. "So, you can speak?"

The man hocked a glob of phlegm from the corner of his mouth.

"Do me a favor and use your knife to slice a hunk off the rear haunch. I'll cook it for us," Coop said.

The man narrowed his eyes and made a stabbing motion with his knife.

Although Coop considered himself to be understanding of his fellow man, this old timer had tested the limits of his patience. "Look, if I wanted to hurt you, I would've blasted you already with my shotgun."

The man eased up and Coop circled around him, holding his own knife. He went to work slicing off a couple of steaks. He skewered the meat and held the stick over the fire. "You have a name?"

The man kept his eyes on Coop and the shotgun. "Cletus."

"Pleased to meet you, Cletus. I'm Cooper Stover."

"Heard ye the first time. I'm not daft. Ain't no need to repeat."

Until now, Coop had wondered if Cletus did indeed have a mental disability. He had apparently been living in the wild for some time and had taken on feral-like qualities. So why did he smell so sweet? "Are you wearing men's after shave or some sort of cologne?"

The man raised his arms and sniffed his arm pits. "A woman's perfume."

"Why?"

"Draws in you sweeties like flies to honey." Cletus smiled. His top front teeth were missing and lower incisors protruded which gave him the appearance of a bulldog.

"What are you doing out here?"

The smile disappeared. Cletus's expression grew hard. "Survivin' best as I can. You got a problem with that?"

"Nope."

"You got no right to be judgin' me."

"Easy does it, Cletus. I'm just making conversation."

"What *you* doing out here?" Cletus asked.

"Just passing through on my way to Milton."

"Milton? Where's that?"

"South."

Cletus stared at the steaks on the end of the stick. "How'd you manage to find a deer? They've been cleaned out long time ago. Ain't no game anywhere. No deer, not even squirrels."

"Just lucky I guess." From the looks of him, Cletus hadn't had a decent meal in a long time. Or a bath.

"You don't look to be starvin' any," Cletus said. He eyed Coop like a man having been confined to prison for twenty years would leer at a pretty girl.

Coop winced. "I only left home three days ago."

"Home?" Cletus raised an eyebrow. "Where might'n that be?"

Coop felt uncomfortable. It would be a sin to lie, but he certainly didn't need to be specific with this stranger. "North and west of here."

"You got plenty to eat thar?"

Not wanting to provide this stranger with details about Wineberry Hollow, Coop redirected. "How long have you been wandering this area?"

Cletus eyed him with suspicion. "You out here alone? All by yerself?"

Coop realized that Cletus didn't want to be forthcoming with information either. "I'll make a deal with you, Cletus. You answer my questions, and I'll answer yours."

"Fair 'nuff, sweetie." Cletus flashed Coop another bulldog smile. "What ya wanna know?"

"Do you live around here? I mean do you have a cabin or some sort of place?"

"Sure, sure."

"You live alone?"

"Yeah, alone, ever since the world went dark. Got caught out on the highway. Too many bad people out there. Made my way into the woods. Been livin' off the land."

Made sense. Many such refugees probably sought solace in the wilderness away from treachery. How many, though, had made it through the harsh winter? Cletus had probably been more resourceful than most, but how much longer would he have been able to hold on? This venison might have saved him from starvation. Coop doubted that the man could walk. He had been reduced to crawling through the brush. "What's wrong with your legs?"

"Nothin'," Cletus said in a tone conveying it was none of Coop's business.

"Didn't mean anything by asking. Just trying to help you, if you need anything."

"Like a good Samar'tin."

"Yes, like the Good Samaritan."

Cletus's stern expression faded. "Are you a Christian?"

Coop didn't want to reveal to the man his Amish upbringing, didn't want Cletus to assume he was an easy mark. "I believe in the Lord. I can be charitable. Is there anything I can do for you?"

Cletus displayed his bulldog smile. "You can hand over that steak."

"It's not cooked through yet."

"Give it here," Cletus demanded.

Coop slid one of the steaks from the stick. "All right. Suit yourself."

Cletus tore into the meaty flesh, tearing, snarling like a dog. Despite the fact that the man had been starving, his behavior chilled Coop. After he finished, Cletus wiped his lips with his sleeve. "Got anything to drink?"

Coop handed over his canteen.

Cletus took a swig and spat it out. "Water? Hell, I can get that from yonder crick. You got anythin' better, like whiskey?"

"No." Coop wondered what diseases he might acquire drinking from the same canteen.

"You said you weren't gonna tote this deer carcass with you?"

"I'll take a few steaks," Coop said, "but I can't haul it all with me. I'm already burdened with my pack."

Cletus sneered. "Be glad to unburden you of that shotgun. Could use that."

"No," Coop said sternly. He didn't want Cletus to entertain any such notions.

"Can't blame a man for tryin'."

"You can have the deer."

"You help me get it back to my hovel. It'll keep me alive a while longer."

"How far is your camp?"

Cletus pointed north. "A short way up stream. I heard yer shot. Wanted to see what was going on."

"Lucky for you I'm a peaceable man," Coop said. "Curiosity killed the cat, you know?"

"Lucky for you, sweetie, that I figgered you to be peaceable. Otherwise, I'd a killt you right off."

"With what?" Coop said, amused. "That knife?"

"Slit your throat while you slept, mebbie. 'Sides, you don't know what I brought wif me back in them trees. Mebbie a rifle."

"Did you bring a rifle?"

Cletus cocked his head. "You tryin' to trick me?"

"Not at all. I just want to know if you had a weapon stashed out there."

"No worries, sweetie, I ain't got nothin' but this here toad sticker." He rubbed his knees. "Rheumatiz. Cain't walk long distances. That's why I had to crawl that last little bit to get here."

Coop now felt more than a little uneasy around this man. He had a sudden desire to be rid of him. "Can you find your way back in the dark? If it's only a little ways, I can drag what's left of the deer back to your place."

"Not in the dark," Cletus said. "Need to rest my bum knees. First light'l be soon enough."

No way did Coop want to fall asleep with Cletus by his side. The man made his skin crawl. "No offense, mister, but I'm going to move away some. I'll load up the campfire for you and sleep out there somewhere."

Cletus's lips formed a straight line. "You taking off fer good, ain't you? Gonna leave poor old Cletus behind."

"No. I'll see you at first light. I'll help you with that deer. I give you my word."

After snorting, Cletus spit a wad of snot onto the campfire. It hissed after landing on a burning log. "You think yer too good fer me, sweetie?"

"More like I don't know you enough to trust you."

Cletus sneered. "Trust? Yer the one wif that shotgun. I'm the one shouldn't be trustin' you."

"See you in the morning." Coop stood, picked up his shotgun and gear and walked a hundred paces west. Then, as quietly as possible, he turned south another hundred paces. If Cletus tried to follow Coop, he'd have trouble finding him.

Coop slept lightly, every little noise rousing him from sleep. When the sun finally crested the eastern rise, Coop woke grumpy. A steady breeze gave the air a crisp bite, but the skies were clear. A good day for hiking. He decided to make quick work of helping Cletus. Coop wanted to be gone from the area as quickly as possible. He found the old man standing, leaning against a tree.

"Where've ye been?" Cletus asked.

"Never mind." Coop looped a rope around the deer's neck. He kept the shotgun slung over his shoulder but handed Cletus his pack. "Can you carry this for me?"

"Sure, sweetie."

"I'm tired of you calling me sweetie. The name's Coop. Lead the way."

Cletus limped along. Coop followed him along the stream bank. When Cletus turned north into the gorge, uphill, Coop was happy with the slow pace. He panted while dragging the dead weight and they took lots of breaks. About an hour later, Cletus stopped and pointed into a ravine. "Up thar a ways."

A small canoe covered by a green plastic tarp lay on its side where the ravine met Pine Creek. "Yours?" Coop asked.

"Is now," Cletus said.

Coop was about to ask the old man to elaborate, but decided that would waste time. Instead, he had an idea. "How would you like to return the favor for me providing this deer for you? I need to get across the creek. Can I borrow your canoe?"

"How'd I get it back if'n you took it to the other side?"

"You come with me. Then you can paddle it back."

Cletus hocked a wad of phlegm into the creek and eyed Coop with suspicion. "Not me. Maybe I'll send Lulu Belle with you, that is if'n she's of a mind to agree to it."

"Lulu Belle?" Coop asked. "I thought you said you were alone."

Cletus raised his voice. "I am alone. Just me and the missus."

Coop liked this less and less. "And who else besides you and your missus?"

"Ain't nobody else."

Coop grunted and slogged on along the muddy banks of the ravine. They soon came upon a clearing with a dilapidated cabin. Probably somebody's old hunting camp from the before times.

Cletus doubled over and rubbed his knees. "Have to rest. Anyway, we're here. You kin go ahead and tote that deer over to that low hanging branch by the outhouse. See it?"

Coop looked to where the old man pointed and saw a poplar tree. He dragged the deer in that direction thinking that he'd waste no time in leaving. Before he reached the poplar, an old stump blocked his way. Coop circled around the obstruction and…

The sensation of falling.

Coop screamed and landed hard with his weight on his left ankle. It twisted, sending a searing wave of pain through his leg. He crumpled to the ground falling onto his back. The shotgun he carried lay under his back, jabbing into his shoulder. Coop rolled and freed the weapon from beneath him. He caressed his ankle and stared up through a tube into the sky.

It was then Coop realized that he had fallen into a pit.

Chapter 62

The pain forced Coop to suck air through gritted teeth. The old man must have deliberately led him onto this trap, a pit camouflaged with a covering of branches and leaves which now lay all around him. He looked up and yelled, "Cletus, where are you?"

Dirt fell from the rim above and landed in Coop's eyes. He wiped his face with his sleeve and saw the old man peering down at him. "You all in one piece, sweetie?"

"No thanks to you." Coop had lost the battle to control his temper. Angry and frightened, he yelled, "Get me out of here."

"You bleedin' anywhere?"

Coop tried standing. He put weight on his hurt ankle, but it was no good. He leaned against the side of the pit. "No, I'm not bleeding. Toss me a rope or get me a ladder."

Cletus ignored him and called out, "Lulu Belle, we got us another live one. Come on out here and have a lookie see."

This was ridiculous, the old man not helping him immediately. Coop reached up and discovered the rim to be a good four feet beyond the end of his fingertips. Too high for him to jump. The walls were earthen, slick with moisture, the base of the pit about six feet in diameter. He figured the pit to be the start of a hand dug well that had never been finished, now converted into a man trap and prison. "I'm no good to you down here," Coop yelled, aware of the panic in his voice. "Let me out."

A silhouette appeared at the edge of the rim. An old woman with short gray hair peered down. "Wee dawgs, Clete, he ain't as fleshy as the woman."

"Don't complain, he'll do just fine. 'Sides, we got us the rest of this deer to work on."

"Venison. Oh, Clete, you are such a good provider. How long's it been since we et deer meat?"

"Dunno. Lost track of it."

"What's in his pack?"

Coop heard them unbuckle and unsnap the compartments from his backpack.

"Is that jerky?" Lulu Belle asked.

"Sure as hell is."

"Wee dawgs!"

Coop balled his fists in frustration. "What are you doing? Get me out of here."

Lulu Belle looked over the rim.

"Careful, he's got his wits about him now so don't be stickin' yer nose out like that," Cletus said. "That sweetie's got a shotgun down there with him."

Lulu Belle covered her mouth, pointed down, and cackled. "That thing ain't no good anymore. Look at it, the barrel's all bent to hell."

Coop ran his hand along the length of gun and felt the crease in the barrel. He groaned in despair. How would he be able to continue his journey without a means for hunting food?

"Dammit, we could a used that."

"Why didn't you get it from him before leading him into the trap, dumb ass?"

"Don't you be callin' me a dumb ass. I'd like to see you go out there and lure anybody in wiff'n that ugly mug of yourns."

"Hush up, Clete. What else he gots in there?"

Coop couldn't see what they were doing with his pack, but he could imagine them pawing through his stuff. He concentrated. How could he convince them to free him?

"Think these clothes could fit me?" Lulu Belle asked.

Cletus snickered. "What, you a man now?"

"No more'n you fancy yerself as a girl wastin' all that perfume on yerself that the woman brought with her."

"I thought you liked the way it made me smelt."

"Covered up your stink, that's all. You coulda just taken a bath in the crick."

"I'll bathe in the spring when the water warms up."

Coop couldn't take it anymore. "Hey, I don't care what you do with my stuff, just get me out of here."

"All in good time, sweetie," Cletus said. "Are those boxers? I need me some new underwear."

"Uh, uh, them's mine. That woman's stuff wasn't my size. Too tight in the crease." She giggled. "These'l do."

"Look, Lulu Belle, a lighter, and it works."

"Wee dawgs!"

"A road map and a bible."

"A bible?"

Coop heard them rifling through pages. Lulu Belle looked down at him. "You believe in Jesus?"

Coop cleared his throat. "Yes, but I have to say that I'm not feeling very Christian at the moment. Please, let me out."

Cletus and Lulu Belle ignored Coop and continued fighting over his belongings. Eventually, their voices trailed off, and Coop guessed that they took their newly stolen booty into the old dilapidated cabin.

He slid against the side of the pit into a sitting position on the floor. Reaching forward, Coop cradled his damaged ankle. He could swivel his ankle around some which meant that it probably wasn't broken. He thanked God for that bit of good fortune. He could've been hurt a lot worse, maybe even broken his neck.

Not hardly good fortune, though. Coop realized that his predicament was dire. With no way to free himself, he was completely dependent on Cletus and Lulu Belle's charity. What did they want from him? Now that they had taken all his possessions, would they just leave him in this pit to die? He could scream all day and all night and nobody besides Cletus and Lulu Belle would hear him.

Coop closed his eyes and leaned the back of his head against the damp wall. This journey had been a risk, Coop knew that. There had always been a chance that he might be killed. But never had he envisioned dying like this, slow starvation at the hands of two deranged old timers.

Was this it? Had he failed Katie again for the last time?

* * *

Coop sighed and opened his eyes. He had dozed off. For how long? The sun shined directly overhead. His throat parched, Coop stood to stretch his legs. The ankle throbbed and had swollen. The wind howled above his head, but down here he remained sheltered. His heavy coat insulated him from the worst of the cold and dampness.

Now that the noon sun fully illuminated the pit floor, Coop spotted a small bag. He picked it up and recognized it as a purse made of leather, like an English woman would carry. Cletus and Lulu Belle had exchanged words earlier about a woman. Was it possible that he hadn't been the first prisoner held here?

Coop emptied the contents onto the ground hoping there might be something that he could use. He picked through a pen, a tube of lipstick, a pack of tissues, and a wallet. He opened the wallet and stared at the name and photo on the driver's license.

Candace Grove. She had a Jersey Shore, PA address. According to her birth date, she was 36. He rubbed his thumb over her picture. In her photo, Candace wore a pretty smile.

What had happened to this woman? What had they done to her? Had that been her canoe he had seen earlier? Probably. He slipped Candace's ID into his shirt pocket. When he got out of here, he would try to get word to someone who might know her, if any of her friends and kin still lived.

Coop also noticed a half dozen fist sized rocks. Bending over, he picked one up and hefted it. Could he use these rocks as weapons? The next time Cletus peered down at him could he smite the old man with a carefully tossed rock. Under the circumstances, would his conscience permit him to smash the skull of another human being. Besides, what good would it do him? Doing harm to Cletus or Lulu Belle still wouldn't get him out of the pit.

Coop inspected the rock more closely and noticed a smear of blood. Revolted, he let the rock drop like a hot potato and realized the truth. *They* were the ones who had used these rocks as weapons. Helplessly trapped, it would be easy. Had they killed Candace? Stoned her to death?

Coop pounded his fists against the earthen walls of his prison. "Help, help, get me out." He kept at it for a long time, pounding and yelling until he fell to the ground, exhausted.

His activity drew out his captors.

"Mebbie he's clusterfubbic," Lulu Belle said.

"Mebbie," Cletus said.

Coop struggled to his feet and looked up. The toes of their shoes stuck out over the rim, their faces gawking.

"Got something fer ye," Cletus said. He held Coop's canteen over the hole and let it drop. Coop caught it and twisted open the cap. Suspicious, he sniffed, tasted. The water seemed okay. He gulped it down and realized that they wouldn't kill him. At least not yet. Otherwise they wouldn't care about his thirst.

"Thank you," Coop said.

"Yer welcome," Lulu Belle responded.

How about that. Even savages could be polite. Could this be an opening that Coop could exploit? "The woman, Candace. What happened to her?"

Cletus and Lulu Belle exchanged glances. "She paddled up the crick in that canoe you saw. Told us she was lookin' fer herbs to use in medicine," Cletus said. "I got the woman to come to the cabin after telling her about how sick Lulu Belle was. Course, she wasn't really sick."

"What happened to her?" Coop repeated.

They backed away from the rim.

"Wait," Coop shouted. "How about some food?"

The two faces returned. Cletus said, "Cain't see no reason to share that deer or jerky wif him."

"Wee dawgs, no, but it wouldn't do us no good him wastin' away, neither."

Cletus looked at Coop. "We'll think on it some. Anything else we can get fer ye. Want yer bible?"

Coop raised his arms toward the rim. "Come on. You're good people. Let me out. Give me a hand."

"Hear that, Clete, we're good people."

"Hell, I knowed that, and good people wouldn't let a man starve, would they?"

"Wee dawgs, no."

"Got me an idear. I'll be right back."

It gave Coop the creeps, Lulu Belle staring down at him while waiting for Cletus to return from whatever errand he now performed. A few minutes later Lulu Belle gasped. "Hold it, Clete, I was savin' that."

"What fer?"

"I was plannin' to use it in soup."

"We got deer meat to hold us over. The sweetie needs this nourishment more than us." Cletus peered over the side and let something drop. "Here."

Coop wasn't ready and raised his hands to protect his face. The object struck Coop's shoulder and fell to the ground. He bent over and reached for it. After recognizing what it was, he shrank back. Laying in the mud, he saw a human bone, a forearm with gnawed teeth marks. Attached to the arm, a partially decomposed hand, small, with slender fingers. A woman's hand.

Candace Grove.

"Them fingers'll be tough," Cletus said, "but keep chewin on 'em like jerky and they'll 'ventually get soft 'nuff to swaller."

"Ye might try first fer that fleshy part 'round the base of the thumb," Lulu Belle suggested.

Coop gasped for air. "My god, what have you done."

Cletus looked at Lulu Belle and shrugged. "He asked me fer a hand. I just give him what he asked fer."

The two of them laughed. Coop put his hands over his ears unable to bear their cackling. Sick and deranged, they were. Animals.

A cloud passing over the sun cast a shadow and caught Coop's attention. He lowered his hands from his ears and looked up. Lulu Belle was no longer there, but Cletus eyed him while bouncing a rock in his hand. "That smallish deer of yours'll only last us a week, mebbie two."

"Then what?" Coop asked.

The old man looked at the rock in his hand. Then he eyed Coop and smiled, his bulldog lower teeth protruding over his top lip.

Chapter 63

Coop woke sometime during the night to a hissing sound. He had no idea what time it might be. He sat against the earthen wall of his pit hugging himself with his knees drawn to his chest. Heavy sleet fell from the sky - the source of the hissing noise - slapping the ground. It stung his face when he looked up. Coop shivered and his throat felt as if he had swallowed fire. Having suffered through bouts of strep throat as a child, he recognized the familiar symptoms, chills, high fever, difficulty in swallowing. The infection was difficult to cure without medication. Exposed to the elements and miserable, Coop realized that he might die before Cletus and Lulu Belle would come to finish him off. His stomach pinched with hunger, and he longed for a cup of hot tea laced with honey.

The longer he waited trying to figure a way out of his predicament, the weaker he would become. As it was, the pain from his swollen ankle and sore throat made it difficult for Coop to concentrate. He had to do something. And he had to do it now.

Coop forced himself up. He stood favoring his hurt ankle. The complete darkness made it difficult for him to get his bearings. He bent over and felt around the floor of the pit for his ruined shotgun. Coop's hand closed around a long object, and he thought he had found what he was looking for. Then it dawned on him that what he really had grasped was Candace Grove's arm bone. He gasped in horror and let the morbid object slip from his hand. He scrambled around on hands and knees until finally locating the cold metal barrel of the shotgun iced over from the sleet.

During the day, after Cletus and Lulu Belle had left him, Coop had the idea of using the shotgun as a shovel as it was no longer of use as a weapon. He dug the barrel end into the earthen wall attempting to hollow out a notch for a foothold. Immediately, the hard clay filled the end of his barrel rendering the broken gun ineffective as a digging tool. It was no better than ramming his fist into the wall. What he needed was something sharp and pointed that would penetrate the clay. Coop cursed himself for stowing his hunting knife in his pack instead of carrying it on his belt loop. He needed something like that.

He tried again using the shotgun, but it was no use. The barrel thudded against the clay on impact and compressed the wall tighter instead of chipping it away.

Could he use two of the blood stained rocks and smash them together, maybe break off a sharp shard to use as a tool? For the next hour Coop tried doing that, but the rocks were too hard, and he wasn't strong enough to break them using just his hands.

The physical pain, emotional anguish, damp, and cold threatened to break him. Let them kill him, eat him, throw his bones into this devil's hole for the next poor victim to find. That thought stirred his imagination, giving him a gruesome idea. Something that might work.

"No," he spoke trying to dismiss the thought from his mind, but even as he tried talking himself out of it, Coop knew it was his only remaining alternative. He squeezed shut his eyes and drew in a deep breath, the air crossing his throat burning like hell fire. "Forgive me, God, this desecration." He felt along the ground and found the mutilated body part.

Coop pictured in his mind how Cletus might have dismembered Candace's body. Most likely he had used an axe or a hatchet to separate her arm at the elbow. With Cletus and Lulu Belle having eaten away the flesh, what remained of both the radius and ulna bones had split into sharp points.

"I never knew you, Candace," Coop mumbled. "Don't hold me to account for this horror. Rest in peace knowing that even after death, you might be saving a stranger's life."

He took the arm and began to work the sharp end of the bone into the clay. Not too hard. Bone wasn't steel and could shatter if used too aggressively. Coop flicked away at a spot about three feet off the ground. He soon realized that he needed to gain better control and leverage by holding onto to the very end of the bone and taking Candace's hand. Coop's stomach roiled as he entwined the flesh from her dead fingers within his.

He thrust Candace's arm into the clay, but the force from his grip caused her flesh to squish as if he had squeezed an overripe tomato. Coop's fingers dug into Candace's skin and released the reek of decomposition.

Coop dropped the body part, collapsed to his knees, and retched. His hands and knees quivered at the fatigue of supporting his weight. He groaned. "I can't do this." He resigned himself to his fate and fell to the ground, curling himself into a ball.

He thought about his mother. What was she doing right now? Did she lay awake in her bed listening to the sound of sleet against the roof? Did she hear strange noises and wonder whether it was her son returning home? What of poor Katie? What anguishes did she suffer? Were his tribulations any worse than hers?

Ashamed of himself for having considered defeat, Coop struggled again to stand. Candace Grove had died, but Katie still needed him. His mother ached for his return. Instead of wallowing in selfish pity, he needed to focus on his mission.

With renewed determination, Coop picked up the arm bone and tried again holding onto the fleshy hand. Breathing from his mouth to avoid inhaling the malodorous stench, he dug. Concentrating on the task, he was able to ignore for periods of time his own discomfort, the pain, the fever. Only when he swallowed igniting the fire in his throat did Coop recall how ill he had become. This forced him to soldier on with a sense of urgency.

It took serious effort, but he managed to hollow out an indentation in the clay of about four inches. Coop stuck the toe of his boot into the hole.

It held.

Still pitch black, he had to rely on his memory. The top of the pit extended about four feet above his outstretched arms. This first indentation was waist high. The next one would need to be at shoulder level.

Coop resumed digging, gouging at the wall with the bone, trying to remain oblivious to the pounding sleet storm. Soon satisfied with the depth of this new indentation, Coop gave it a try. While standing with one foot secured into the new hole, Coop groped in the darkness trying to find the rim. It still remained out of his grasp. How much higher did he need to go? Unable to see, who knew? He might only be an inch away from his goal.

The third indentation required a lot more effort. He had to dig while standing in the notches and had to be careful not to fall. His sore, weak ankle threatened to give way while bearing his weight in the uncomfortable notch. Dead tired, his muscles ached under the exertion. Every time Coop swallowed, he yelped from the fire in his throat.

Thinking again of Katie, he persisted. After what seemed an insufferable length of time, Coop dropped the bone onto the ground and stuck a toe into the third notch. His knees ached as he pushed upward. His hand found the top of the pit. Using every ounce of strength, he hoisted himself up and over the top.

Coop rolled onto his back and lay on the ground. He let the sleet pummel his bare face.

Sweet freedom.

No longer sheltered from the wind, Coop quickly became cold, but he couldn't move. So weary. So much pain. He closed his eyes.

Adrenaline flooded through him and his eyes snapped open. If he slept now, he would freeze to death. Or worse, Cletus and Lulu Belle would discover him in the morning and push him back into the pit or stove in his skull.

Coop willed himself to a sitting position. He couldn't see a thing. How long until the dawn? Did he dare just wander blindly? Who knew what other unseen traps his captors may have used. He couldn't stand, his swollen ankle had reached its limit. He'd have to wait it out.

As a boy, he had hunted deer with his father. They often entered the woods before dawn, stood in the freezing cold, snow and rain. What he did now was no different, except he hadn't eaten in over 24 hours and was seriously ill to the point of collapsing. Coop pulled his hands inside the sleeves of his father's heavy coat. He yanked the collar up and around his ears.

Coop would periodically doze a few minutes at a time and then abruptly wake. He did this for what remained of the night until, at last, he was able to make out the outline of the cabin and tree line during the birth of the new day's sun.

Before leaving, he should kill them.

He could break in while they still slept and bash in their skulls with a rock. How many other innocents would Cletus and Lulu Belle lure into their trap? How many lives could he save by putting down these animals?

Coop tried standing and collapsed immediately after putting pressure on his bum ankle. He rolled up his trouser leg and found it to be horribly swollen when compared with his good ankle. Maybe it was broken after all? He'd have to hop or crawl until finding a suitable stick for a crutch. His pain and fever had him seeing double. He needed help, but his first order of business was to get away. Forget about his captors. In his weakened condition, he didn't doubt that even those old people could overpower him. He would settle for reporting them. Others would have to deal with the situation. He focused on what he needed to do next.

He needed Candace Grove's canoe.

Coop hobbled into the woods hoping that Cletus and Lulu Belle weren't early risers. The sleet storm had moved on, but the sky remained gray and overcast. It took him an hour to reach the canoe. Too long. By now they would know he was missing.

Laboring for breath and dead on his feet, Coop removed the tarp and struggled to drag the craft to the creek's edge. The paddle lay in the stern. Just as he was ready to push off, Coop heard a twig snap behind him.

"Goin' somewhere, sweetie? I think not."

Cletus and Lulu Belle stood on the bank, rocks in hand. Cletus hocked and spit a thick wad of green phlegm against the sleet covered ground.

Lulu Belle shook a fist. "Git him, Clete, tenderize him good."

The old man threw a rock with surprising accuracy. If Coop

wouldn't have ducked at the last moment, the missile would have hit him square in the face.

In a panic, Coop shoved the canoe across the ice lined bank and into the cold waters of Pine Creek. He broke through the thin ice and got soaked through up to his knees, the icy water burned his skin, but strangely soothed his swollen ankle.

A rock bounced off the side of the canoe. Coop jumped aboard and began to paddle, praying that a rock wouldn't find its mark on the back of his skull. The current here was swift and carried the canoe quickly away. Once in the middle of the stream, he didn't need to paddle.

Cletus and Lulu Belle shouted threats and curses after him, but he was soon out of range of their missiles.

Coop's frozen legs had gone numb, his vision clouded over. Looking back, he thought he saw Cletus crawling after him like a spider over the surface of the creek. The fever had made him delirious, and he was burning up. He had enough presence of mind to understand that despite his fever, he needed to stay warm and was probably actually suffering from hypothermia. Coop wrapped himself many times around in the green tarp and lay down in the bottom of the canoe.

If there were rapids ahead, he would be at their mercy. If the stream meandered, he may run aground. Either way, he was finished, and there was nothing more he could do but drift. At least he was pointed in the right direction.

He had resumed his quest.

"I'm on my way, Katie," he whispered, each syllable sending searing waves of pain through his throat. He closed his eyes and prayed, "Gottes Wille, into Thine hands I commit my safety."

His energy spent, Coop passed out.

Chapter 64

At the edge of awareness, Coop's throat still burned like hell fire. He heard raised voices.

"Kill him."

"No."

"Then let him die. It's not right to waste medicine on a murderer."

"We don't know that."

"He's alone and in Candy's canoe. He's got her ID in his pocket. That's all the proof I need."

"We need to at least give him a chance to explain."

Coop tried opening his eyes, but the effort proved to be too much. He lapsed back into unconsciousness.

*   *   *

He dreamed of a refreshing evening breeze, like the kind that comes after a thunderstorm at the end of a hot summer day. Coop woke and raised a hand to his brow. A soothing cool towel lay across his forehead. He glanced around and discovered that he was in bed, in a small room. Everything was dark except for a candle burning on a table in the corner.

"Hello?" he spoke. His throat still hurt, but not nearly as bad as before.

Footsteps approached from out of the shadows. Someone bent over, but it was too dark for Coop to see the person's face. Someone in a man's voice said, "How do you feel?"

"Thristy."

The man grunted and walked out of the room. Moments later he returned with a canteen and held it out. "Here."

Coop accepted the canteen and took a few sips. Plain water. His sore throat had eased some but his entire body was sore. It felt as if someone had deposited a hot coal into the Eustachian tube of his left ear. He realized that he was in poor shape. Vulnerable.

"Thank you," Coop said. "Where am I?"

"Owl Notch."

That meant nothing to him. "How far from Milton am I?"

"Milton? You're nowhere near Milton. Owl Notch is a settlement of a half dozen weekend bungalows along Pine Creek a few miles north of Jersey Shore. When the world went dark, my neighbors and I fled town and settled here. We're remote and out of the way. Nobody comes here. Nobody, that is, except for when we pulled you from the creek yesterday afternoon."

Coop tried to push himself up to sit on the side of the bed. "I have to get to Milton."

The man pushed a hand against Coop's chest pinning him to the mattress. Either he was unusually strong or the illness had robbed Coop of most of his strength.

"You're not going anywhere until you answer some questions," the man said in a threatening tone. "My neighbors and I have lots of questions."

"Like what?"

"You can start by telling me your name."

"Cooper Stover."

The man removed his hand from Coop's chest. "It's almost dawn, Mr. Stover. I'll heat water on the wood stove for you to wash up. You're a mess and you stink. While you're doing that, I'll find something for us to eat." He paused. "Let me make something clear. Don't leave this bungalow. It will not go well for you if you try leaving."

Why did this man want to keep him as a prisoner? Coop shuddered. He might be no better off now than with Cletus and Lulu Belle. So far, at least, this man had treated him decently and tended to him during his illness. Coop didn't believe that he was in any immediate danger, so he decided to play along. "How long have I been out?"

"You drifted past yesterday around lunchtime. We pulled you ashore and found you to be feverish and delirious."

Yesterday? He had passed out just after dawn yesterday which meant that he had slept for a whole day. "Thank you for helping me, mister."

"The name's Millen. Walt Millen."

His meal consisted of scrambled eggs and a piece of fish, not usual breakfast fare, but since he hadn't eaten in days, Coop was starving. It took all of Coop's will power to maintain his dignity and not bolt his food.

Walt served a cup of hot red liquid. From the aroma, Coop immediately recognized fresh sassafras. This was the perfect time of year to harvest the root bark.

"Ran out of coffee months ago," Walt explained. "Besides, this is better for your fever."

Coop figured Walt to be in his sixties. He had a medium build with wrinkled, leathery skin and white hair. He was clean shaven and had coal black eyes that displayed intelligence. He wore a stern expression and remained neutral, never smiling, never frowning.

"Are you a doctor?" Coop asked.

"I know a little about natural medicine, herbs, roots, and such, but I'm no doctor."

"Well, anyway, thank you for taking care of me."

"Don't thank me yet. You're not out of the woods. Not by a long shot."

"But I'm feeling a lot better."

"How you feel has nothing to do with it."

What did Walt mean? Having lost so much time, Coop wanted to be on his way. "You said you had questions. Please ask them."

"Listen to me, Mr. Stover…"

"…Call me Coop."

"Okay, Coop, in a little while we'll be getting company. Neighbors are coming to see you. Interrogate you…"

"…Interrogate?"

"That's right, and I'm going to be brutally honest with you. Your life depends on how well you answer their questions. I'd advise you to immediately tell the truth. If they detect any holes in your story or suspect any obfuscation at all, they'll likely tear you to pieces."

Coop's heart raced. "Am I to understand that your neighbors might kill me?"

"Depending on your answers, it could come to that. Everyone is upset and angry."

"But, why? What have I done to you folks?"

A knock at the door cut off their conversation. Coop's hands began to tremble and he labored to breathe. It didn't make sense. Why did Walt tend to him if his neighbors wanted him to die?

Five stone faced people entered, four men and a woman, all of them middle aged. They formed a semi circle around Coop, glaring at him. Coop tried to stand, but Walt pressed a hand to his shoulder, signaling that he should remain seated.

The woman spoke first. Her jaw trembled. "Dirty bastard. What have you done with my sister?"

Coop didn't know what to say. What did she want?

She tossed an object at him. Coop flinched as it bounced off his chest and into his lap. He picked up what she had tossed and noticed it was Candace Grove's drivers license.

"We found you in her canoe. You were carrying her ID in your shirt pocket," she said. "You sick bastard. What is it, some sort of trophy? You killed her, didn't you? Probably raped her first."

Suddenly, it all made sense. Candace had come from Owl Notch. Coop met the woman's gaze and noticed the resemblance to the ID photograph. His fear turned to sympathy. No wonder they were hostile toward him.

"I did not harm your sister, but I do know what happened to her."

"Tell me," she yelled. "Is she still alive?"

Coop squeezed shut his eyes and shook his head.

She swooned. The two men on either side steadied her.

"Talk," she said.

"What I have to say isn't pleasant. Maybe you'd better just let me tell my story to these men."

"He might have a point, Connie," Walt said. "Candy was your sister. You don't need to put yourself through this. We'll make sure we get the truth out of him."

"No chance in hell I'm leaving. I want to hear it all."

"Suit yourself," Walt said. He glanced at Coop. "Go ahead, Mr. Stover."

Coop cleared his throat. He didn't want to reveal that he had come from Wineberry Hollow, didn't know what danger these people might pose to his friends and neighbors, but then he recalled Walt's admonishment about telling the truth with no obfuscation. He started at the beginning, told them about the Army raid and Katie's capture and how he was on his way to find her. Coop looked all of them in the eye while relating his story, willing them to believe him, but when he got to the part about Cletus and Lulu Belle and how they had offered Candace's body part to him as food, he could no longer meet their gazes. It sickened him to tell about it.

After finishing his story, Walt, Connie, and their companions regarded him in a more relaxed manner. Did they now believe him?

Connie stared out the window. "I warned Candy about her foraging, begged her not to stray so far away, preached to her how she should never paddle the creek alone. Why didn't she ask me to come? I'd have gone."

"Your sister was a good provider to us all," Walt said.

Connie scoffed. "Yeah, and look where it got her."

"We can't let this stand," one of the men said.

"I agree," Walt said. "We won't tolerate eaters. We'll need to find them. Put them down."

One of the men who hadn't spoken yet nodded with his head toward Coop. "He ready to travel today?"

"It'll be too hard on him. We should give him another day to rest up, eat, regain his strength."

"I'm okay," Coop said. "I'd rather be on my way. I don't need another day to rest." An untruth. Coop knew he was still too sick to travel, but being here made him uneasy.

The way the men looked at him made Coop wonder if he had said something wrong.

Walt spoke. "Mr. Stover, we intend for you to take us to these eaters' nest. Your story rings true, but we need to make sure. None of us can allow you to go anywhere until we check it out for ourselves."

Coop felt the frustration build. More delay meant more suffering for Katie, more uncertainty. "I'm telling you the truth. I can give you directions how to find the old cabin. There are side streams, lots of landmarks, you don't need me."

"Mr. Stover, try to understand our position. We need to make sure of your story, and if true, we need to make sure no other poor souls fall victim to those animals. You wouldn't want the same thing to happen to someone else that happened to you. Would you?"

Coop groaned. He wanted to remind them that Candace was dead, but Katie was probably still alive and alone. These people were possessed with vengeance. They wouldn't have sympathy and wouldn't appreciate his comment about their dead friend.

"Look, I'm fine," Coop stood and took a few steps before slumping against a wall.

Walt helped him to a chair. "You're far from fine."

* * *

Coop remained in Owl Notch for three more days to recuperate. He pressed Walt about being able to leave.

Walt said, "Mr. Stover, since you're now fit enough to travel, we'll take care of those eaters tomorrow morning. Get it done and be back by sunset. You and I will take Candy's canoe. Ben, and Connie can follow us in another canoe, assuming Connie will want to come.

The next morning when Walt asked her, Connie replied, "Damn straight I want to come."

"Another delay," Coop grumbled. "I'm really concerned for my friend. Please, let me go."

Walt pulled a chair from the table and took a seat beside Coop. "Young man, we are decent folk and not without compassion. I understand your situation, and I hope you understand ours. I'm willing to make you an offer."

Coop perked up.

"Come with us today. Be our guide. In return, a few of us will escort you downstream and past town. I don't know how many poor souls survived the winter or what their state of mind might be, but if anybody means you harm, you won't stand a chance traveling alone. We'll have to travel past town under cover of night. Beyond town, Pine Creek dumps into the Susquehanna. I'll paddle you to the opposite shore and let you off. From there you can resume your hike over Bald Eagle Mountain to the enclave."

Coop quickly realized the advantage of an armed escort, but he didn't understand Walt's advice about hiking cross country. That would take him longer. "Doesn't the Susquehanna flow directly to Milton and the enclave? Shouldn't I follow the river?"

Walt smirked. "Sure it does, but the river also flows directly through the city of Williamsport. Only a fool would take that route."

Coop hung his head. "I've never been to a big city. The biggest place I've ever been is Wellsboro."

"You do not want to go there. The more remote you travel, the more likely you'll reach your destination. By the way, have you considered how to find your friend once you've reached the enclave? Have you even figured out how to get inside?"

"No. I haven't given it much thought. I've been focused on just getting there first."

Walt raised an eyebrow. "One does not simply march up to the gate and demand to be granted admittance. They'll likely shoot you dead, if you do that."

"What do you suggest?"

Walt sighed. "I have no suggestions. It's something I can't help you with. We can discuss that later."

Connie burst into the bungalow, rifle in hand, out of breath. "We're ready."

* * *

Walt and Connie and Ben believed Coop's story, but apparently they didn't completely trust him. Even though he told them that Walt and Lulu Belle never displayed firearms in his presence, when they arrived at the clearing, they made him walk toward the cabin. His skin crawled to be there again, but the others hid just inside the tree line covering him with their rifles. They planned for him to call them out.

Coop stopped about twenty paces in front of the door to the dilapidated cabin. Smoke rose from the chimney, so at least one of them was at home. He shuddered after contemplating what they might be cooking.

He had to get this over with. Had to get out of there.

Coop cupped his hands around his mouth and shouted, "Hey, you in there. Come on out."

Nothing happened.

"Cletus, Lulu Belle, I know you're in there. Come on out. I've come back."

Lulu Belle's face appeared at the window. It disappeared and then the front door creaked open. She stepped into the yard holding something behind her back. "Dat you, Sweetie?"

Whatever Lulu Belle held, it was too small to be a long gun. A handgun maybe? Most likely just a rock. "Where's Cletus?"

Lulu Belle tilted her head. "Step closer, Sweetie, these old ears ain't what they used to be."

"You heard me just fine. I asked you about Cletus."

"Poor ole Clete," she said. "Crippled up, he's no use to me anymore. Can't provide for me. He's no good anymore 'cept mebbie for one thing."

"Where is he?" Coop repeated.

Lulu Belle cackled. She sounded like an old witch. "Peasey porridge hot, Peasey porridge cold, poor ole Clete is in the pot, just a few hours old."

Coop felt bile rise in his throat. "God forgive you."

Lulu Belle revealed a blood streaked hatchet that she had been hiding behind her back. She shrieked, peeled back her lips in a rictus grin, and sprinted toward him waving the hatchet above her head.

Shots rang out. Coop closed his eyes and shuffled backwards. When he opened his eyes, Lulu Belle lay dead near his feet. Coop's legs turned to jelly. He fell to his knees.

Walt took him under his arm and helped him to his feet. "It's over, Cooper."

Coop gulped air. "You believe me now?"

"Every word."

"Burn it down," Connie ordered.

Nobody needed to ask her what she meant. Walt and Ben dragged what remained of Lulu Belle inside the cabin. The old structure went up like a pile of straw. All of them stood there, watching.

"We'll need to fill in the pit," Coop said. "Some innocent person may come upon this place and accidently fall in."

"Ben and I will handle that," Walt said. "You stay here with Connie."

Connie didn't argue.

While the two men worked, Connie looked at Coop and asked, "This friend of yours in the enclave. You care about her?"

Coop thought it to be a stupid question. Of course, he cared about Katie. Why else would he be risking his life to go to her. He was all she had left, probably the only person in the world who would risk his life for her. What came out of his mouth, though, was, "She's very special to me." He realized then how much of his feelings he was projecting onto her. He could only hope that at least she didn't hate him.

"You would've liked Candy," Connie said. "She was a caring person, just like you. Too caring for her own good. Too trusting."

"I would very much have liked to meet your sister."

"Just make sure you don't end up like her."

Burning the cabin and filling the pit took longer than anticipated. They didn't return to Owl Notch until after sundown.

Coop was dead tired. His throat stared bothering him again so he didn't want to push himself. "I may need to sleep in tomorrow. Is it okay if we don't leave too early?"

Walt smiled for the first time. "You're one of us now, Cooper. You can come and go as you please. Actually, to get the timing right for floating past town in the dark, we would have to leave late afternoon. Feel free to rest up as long as you need."

Grateful for his new friends, the idea of hanging around appealed to Coop, but his mind snapped back to his mission. "Tomorrow afternoon," he said. "I'll be ready."

Chapter 65

Captain Halfjack Kettering strutted up the walk to his BOQ. Having been out on wide area patrol for the past three days, he longed for a hot shower and a decent night's sleep. A beer would be great, too, except the enclave warehouses ran out last week. The supply sergeant had told him that alcohol was backordered indefinitely.

What a load of crap.

Halbert was supposed to be a logistical whiz, but what good was he if he couldn't even keep his own enclave supplied?

Halfjack's shoulder had healed, but the cold, damp air made it ache. His little bed warmer would heat it up for him tonight despite her continuing to be a pain in the ass.

He twisted the door knob and pushed his way into the living room. In a mocking tone, he announced, "Hey, Sugar, I'm home."

The girl sat on the sofa reading a paperback novel. "I'm not Sugar. When are you going to start calling me by my given name? I'm Katie."

Would never happen. She cared about her name, and he wasn't about to surrender even that much respect to her. Better to keep her in her place, subservient, "I much prefer calling you Sugar."

Glancing around, Halfjack noticed that she wore the same soiled shirt and baggy trousers that she had on the day he had left. Dirty dishes piled high in the kitchen sink, the place reeked of inattention. The girl smelled, too. "What's with this bullshit?"

"Bullshit?" She batted her eyes. "I'm sure I have no idea what you're talking about."

Halfjack felt the heat rise in his face. After three days in the field, he had little tolerance for dealing with attitude. "You look like shit. When's the last time you took a bath?"

"Since when have you cared about my personal hygiene? I thought I was only an object to you, a sex toy."

He picked up a dirty coffee mug from the counter and in

frustration tossed it into the sink. The mug shattered. "Get your ass off that sofa and clean this place up."

"I warned you that you wouldn't like playing house with me."

Halfjack grabbed her by the hair and pulled her off the sofa. The girl yelped. He marched her into the kitchen and slammed her into the sink. "You don't get to warn me about anything. I'll do the warning around here." He poked a finger into her chest. "Now, *I'm* warning *you*. I'm going to take a shower. By the time I come back, this kitchen better be spotless."

"Or what? What can you possibly do to me that you haven't already done? Kill me? Go ahead. It would put me out of my misery."

Cocky bitch. He grabbed her chin and tilted her face to his. "I've been too tolerant with you. Treated you too well."

She scoffed. "Yeah, kidnap and rape. You're a real prince."

He let go of her chin. "You could do a lot worse."

She rolled her eyes. "Let me guess, this is where you tell me about handing me over to your men and how they'd like to chain me up in the basement of their barracks and abuse me over and over. Yada, yada, yada, I heard it all before. Well, I don't believe it. I don't believe they're all as depraved as you. I'll bet at least a few of them are still decent human beings who would help me."

"Don't kid yourself, Sugar."

She held her wrists in front of her, as if waiting for him to slap on handcuffs. Her eyes blazed with defiance. "C'mon, take me to them. I'm willing to take my chances."

This girl was too smart, and he could see now that his threats had worn thin, but he still held his trump card. "I have something more amusing in mind. Like sending for your young man, bringing him here, tying him up, making him watch."

Her expression softened. She looked at the floor.

"That's more like it."

In a normal tone of voice, she asked, "Have you been back there? To Wineberry Hollow?"

"Sorry, Sugar, I can't tell you."

She stomped her foot. "Why not?"

He smirked. "Our patrols are classified need to know, and you don't need to know."

"Asshole," she mumbled.

"Hop to it," Halfjack said as he headed for the bathroom. "Remember what I told you. Spotless."

While showering, Halfjack pondered Sugar's continuing defiance and considered his situation. He realized that threats to people she cared about would someday also wear thin. He wouldn't be able to hold her much longer. Someday, he'd come home and she would simply be gone. Under normal circumstances, he'd consider it to be good riddance. God, she had a hot, young body and pretty face, but there were plenty of other girls outside the fence who would kill to be on the inside, have a man to protect her and feed her.

The problem was, when his little Sugar finally did work up the guts to leave, where would she go? If she headed for the gate, the sentries would never let her wander out alone. They'd ask questions, demand to know her business. He knew that the chain of command turned a blind eye toward soldiers bringing in girlfriends from the outside, because it was good for morale. They wouldn't believe allegations of her being held against her will, because even if it were true, what good-looking, sensible woman would consider the outside to be a better alternative? She wouldn't survive one day on her own out there.

At worst, she would be an embarrassment to him. After having put Sloat in his place, that freaking boy scout, he aimed to climb high. Plenty of opportunity existed under the new regime, and he intended to take full advantage. Especially tomorrow night. He couldn't afford any kind of embarrassment. Not now.

Halfjack toweled himself off and slipped into clean sweat pants. He strode into the kitchen bare-chested and found Sugar up to her elbows in the sink washing dishes. He said, "After you finish in the kitchen it's your turn for the tub."

"I'll think about it."

Resisting, always resisting, when would she learn? "You're going to take a bath willingly, or I'm going to give you one. How would you like that?"

"I wouldn't."

"Hurry up, then. There's something I need to tell you. A surprise. Something you'll like."

She snorted, "Like what?"

"If I tell you now it won't be much of a surprise. I'll keep you in suspense until you return." Halfjack stretched out on the sofa and picked up the novel she had been reading. He got bored after a few pages and put it down.

He almost dropped off to sleep before she finally emerged from the bathroom, wearing a robe, toweling off her hair. Her skin glowed. Instead of her pungent stench from earlier, she now smelled like lilacs. The sight of her aroused him. Halfjack patted the sofa cushion by his side. "Sit with me."

She curled her lip and sat on the chair across from him. A coffee table lay between them.

He sighed. "After we have our conversation, I'm going to take you to bed. Sitting over there isn't going change anything."

She narrowed her eyes. "You can force me to do things, but I don't ever want you to think that I enjoy it or that I'm a willing participant."

He decided to get to the point. "I'm taking you to the enclave shopping plaza tomorrow."

Her expression remained neutral.

"I thought all girls liked to shop. I'm buying you new clothes, new shoes even. I know all about women and shopping for shoes."

She yawned.

"You're a real hard case," he said.

"You wouldn't do something like that unless you had a good reason. What is it that you want."

Scary smart, Sugar was. The sooner he got rid of her the better, and he was resigned that he wouldn't be able to just let her go. The safest way to break up with Sugar would be to put a bullet in her brain.

He forced a smile. "I want to take you to a party tomorrow night, be my date, my arm candy, whatever. The point is I want you to look your best, and I'll get you whatever you need to look super model beautiful, a new cocktail dress, shoes, makeup, even a goddamned diamond necklace if that's what it takes."

Her jaw dropped. "Holy crap. Who are we meeting, the president?"

Halfjack's breath caught. Was the bitch a mind reader, too?

"You're serious," she said.

After regaining his composure, Halfjack said, "I want you to be noticed, as if you were the only woman in the room, because if you're noticed, then I'll be noticed. If you make an impression, I'll make an impression. I want everyone there to know who I am and to remember my name."

"I get it," she said. "A year from now when someone mentions your name to the prez, he'll scratch his head and say, 'Oh yeah, that was the guy with the hot, young babe in the short dress.'"

"You understand exactly where I'm coming from."

"Why don't I just go naked? They'll remember that."

"Affirmative, but they'd also remember me as the man who brought a slut. I want them to see you as classy, intelligent, and beautiful, so it reflects well on me."

"Uh huh," she said and sucked in her lower lip. She leaned forward in her chair and narrowed her eyes. "Dream on, asshole. First chance I get, I'll shout it out what you've done to me, done to my friends and neighbors, the atrocities you've committed. I'll never, never, ever, be a tool for your ambitions."

Halfjack felt relieved. If she had pretended to go along with his scheme, he would have known she was planning treachery. He had expected this negative response and was prepared for it. "I guess you're not as smart as I thought. You don't seem to realize that this is an opportunity for you, too. You hold the power now. You can finally get me to do whatever you want in exchange for play acting as my fawning sweetheart."

She sat back in the chair. "Are you suggesting that you want to make a deal with me?"

"Of course."

She squeezed shut her eyes and rubbed the bridge of her nose. "For the sake of argument, you know that there's only one thing that I want."

"Your freedom?"

She nodded.

Exactly as he had guessed. No problem. After tomorrow night, he'd personally escort her through the gate, take her down to the edge of the river and shoot her in the head. "I'll let you go. I give you my word."

Her eyes widened into a hopeful expression. "How do I know I can trust you to keep your word?"

"Katie," he said, purposefully using her name, allowing her to hear him say it, "By your way of thinking I've done bad things to you, but one thing I've never done is lie to you. Think about that. Haven't you always known where you stand with me."

Her eyes moistened. It's the closest he'd ever seen her come to crying, but he also knew that's as far as it would go. She wouldn't spill a single tear, wouldn't give him that satisfaction. "No tricks. I don't want you to just kick me outside. I want you to take me home and then never bother me or my neighbors again."

He could make that promise. No problem. He'd adjust his plan and drive her to the entrance of Wineberry Hollow, toss her out of the Jeep, and then put the bullet in her brain. "Agreed."

She eyed him with suspicion. "One more thing."

"Shoot."

"From this moment on, you don't get to touch me ever again."

He regarded her glistening, smooth skin, freshly shaven, silky legs, and her lilac scent. "That's asking a bit much. It's been three days, you know. That's a long time for a man like me."

She stood and pulled the robe tightly around her. "I mean it. You make one move toward me and the deal is off. I'm going into the bedroom and closing the door. If that door so much as drifts ajar one inch during the night, you can go to your party stag."

She drove a hard bargain. Halfjack nodded in capitulation. "Like I said earlier, you hold all the power now. I don't like it, but that's the way it has to be."

"Be sure to remember it," she said before retreating into the bedroom.

Again, not a problem. Tomorrow night, after the party, he'd rape her one final time. Really, that's one promise she couldn't expect him to keep. Then he'd drive her home. Then he'd blow her brains out.

Problem solved.

Chapter 66

Coop walked out of Walt Millen's bungalow and looked into the sky. A cold mist painted his face. Cold, but not icy. He wondered if the winter had finally lost its grip. Back home, he would soon be getting ready to cultivate the fields for spring planting. He thought about his horses, Bonnie and Tony, and hoped they were being well cared for in his absence. Guilt stabbed him after thinking about his mother. Had she finally accepted his decision? Could she see things from his perspective? He still thought of his journey as a duty-bound rescue. Everyone else considered it a suicide mission. After his experience with Cletus and Lulu Belle, they'd almost been proven right, but somehow he didn't believe he was going to die. The people of Owl Notch had held together and remained decent. Other groups probably had too. People who might help him.

Walt closed the door to his bungalow and stood beside Coop. "You ready?"

"I am," Coop said, "but are you sure you want to travel with me on such an ugly evening?"

"This weather is perfect, not ugly. The more uncomfortable the weather, the less likely others will be out and about, and the less likely we are to run into trouble."

Coop grabbed his pack which had been replenished with dried fruits and salted meat, as much as his Owl Notch friends could spare. What they couldn't provide for him was a firearm. Now that Coop's shotgun had been destroyed, he would be making the rest of the trip without a means to hunt game. That meant the food in his pack would have to last him until he got to Enclave 38. Then what? He put the thought out of his mind. One step at a time.

At the water's edge, Walt held the canoe as Coop settled in. Then Walt pushed off and climbed in with him. Connie and Ben already waited for them mid-stream.

"Thank you for helping me. Gottes Wille I will someday return to Owl Notch and find a way to repay you."

"You have it wrong, Cooper. This is us repaying our debt to you for letting us know about our friend, Candy," Walt told him.

"And for leading us to those murderous eaters," Connie added.

Ben dipped his paddle into the creek. "Besides, our helping you isn't completely altruistic."

Coop studied the man and wondered what altruistic meant.

"Every once in a while we need to scout downstream to assess the situation, determine if we need to prepare for any kind of threat from town. We'd be making this trip anyway, in spite of being your escort."

"He's right," Walt said. "We haven't had a chance to look around since the first snow fell back in December. Things were pretty bad then. Death everywhere. I suppose most everyone who hadn't already died probably starved this winter or died from exposure."

"You survived," Coop reminded them. "So have my neighbors back in Wineberry Hollow."

"Both your neighbors and our little community had the means to struggle on. We had skills and knowledge," Walt said. "The vast majority of folks, especially city dwellers think that food comes from grocery stores. Most of them have no idea how to survive in this new world."

"What remains are organized gangs of thugs," Connie said. "With any luck, they should all be dead by now."

Despite Coop's past misery with Stan Cox and the CCW, he wasn't convinced that all survivors were evil. "You folks managed to hang on to your humanity. Others must have, too. You can't assume that everyone you meet deserves to be killed on sight."

"Until the world returns to some semblance of normalcy, it's better to avoid all contact," Ben said. "Maybe you don't believe in killing people on sight, but there are people out there who would certainly kill us on sight while we float down Pine Creek. Four people traveling together would likely be interpreted as a huge threat."

"Which is why we need to slip past the town of Jersey Shore under cover of darkness," Walt added.

This was difficult for Coop to digest. A few bad people, like Stan Cox, probably existed, but to shoot someone dead without cause was unthinkable.

An hour later, Walt warned everyone to stop talking and to paddle softly. Darkness had descended and Coop couldn't see a thing. How did they know they remained in the middle of the channel? Where was the town? Apparently his escorts knew the creek very well.

Coop questioned whether he had misjudged after feeling the canoe lurch after scraping bottom. They stopped abruptly and Walt eased his way out, stepping into the creek while trying not to make a sound. Connie and Ben's canoe landed alongside. Coop looked in Walt's direction, although he couldn't see him. He whispered, "What are you doing?"

"Quiet," Walt snapped. He stepped away into the darkness.

Connie and Ben remained in their canoe. Coop could hear them breathing.

Sometime later, Coop recognized the sound of Walt's footfalls when he returned. In a soft voice he said, "All clear."

Connie and Ben got out of their canoe.

Walt spoke barely above a whisper. "We're near the middle of town, so keep quiet. There's a weir dam about fifty yards downstream of here. We'll need to carry the canoes over land to the other side."

Luckily, the canoes weren't heavy. Coop lifted the back end while Walt took the lead. He used a small flashlight to illuminate the way. A piece of red colored paper wrapped around the lens with a rubber band prevented reflection.

They proceeded at a slow, deliberate pace. Walt took a few steps and stopped, listened, and then took a few more steps. Connie and Ben followed behind with their canoe. After a few starts and stops they heard a noise. In the distance, someone smashed a glass bottle or maybe broke a window pane. This was followed by maniacal laughter.

The hair stood on the back of Coop's neck.

"Put 'em down," Walt whispered.

They set their canoes on the ground and waited in silence.

Minutes passed. They heard nothing. Coop felt the pounding of his heart in his chest.

"Let's go," Walt said. They picked up their canoes and walked on.

Soon, they were back in the creek. Shortly thereafter, Coop felt the current change, pushing them sideways.

"We're in the river now," Walt said. "Keep paddling across the current until we find the opposite bank."

The current was noticeably more swift here than it was while floating along on Pine Creek, so Coop grabbed a paddle and helped Walt pull through the water. Eventually it became easier after they left the main channel and soon they were beached on the other side. Coop got out and pulled the canoe onto shore.

Walt looked up into the dark, overcast sky. "Near as I can guess we probably have a few hours yet until dawn. Might as well get some sleep."

The mist and drizzle hadn't let up which left Coop feeling

miserable. He and Connie slept beneath the canoes. He didn't know where Ben and Walt bedded down.

Walt woke him at daybreak, reminding him to keep his voice low. Now that they could see, Coop and Connie dragged the canoes further into the brush. Ben glassed the opposite shore of the river.

"Anything?" Coop asked.

Ben handed the binoculars to Coop. "No sign of life."

Coop lifted them to his eyes. The town of Jersey Shore was a lot bigger than Wynot and reminded him of Wellsboro. From his vantage point, Coop saw church steeples, a water tower, the tops of a few buildings, but no activity. Everything looked peaceful and calm. He handed the binoculars back to Ben. "Maybe the residents all evacuated, just like you did."

"Not all of them," Walt said. "We definitely heard someone last night."

"Someone who didn't appear to be sound of mind," Connie added.

Walt sneaked in beside them with an armload of firewood. "Now that it stopped raining, we can build a low fire, make some tea."

Coop had grown to like these people and felt bad about having to leave them. A sudden thought struck him. "How are you going to get back to Owl Notch?"

"Same way we came," Walt said. "Today we'll scout around and observe. At sundown, we'll paddle across the river and back up Pine Creek. It'll take longer because we're heading upstream, but we should make it back by dawn tomorrow."

"Without me you'll have a tougher time paddling."

"Don't worry about it, Coop, we've done this before and know what we're doing. I'm more concerned about you. You still have your map?"

Coop reached into his pack and pulled out the highway map.

"Here we are," Walt said pointing to the spot. "After you cross the ridge behind us, you'll find yourself in a farming valley. I don't know what you'll find there, but you obviously want to stay out of sight. The valley is about three or four miles wide. After that you'll be isolated inside the relative safety of Bald Eagle State Forest. Keep heading southeast until you meet up with Interstate 80.

Parallel the interstate east until it emerges from the state forest. About that time you'll run into the fence for E38. As the crow flies, you have about twenty miles. If you don't run into trouble, you could make it in two days."

"Two days," Coop said. He could scarcely believe how close he now was.

Walt shook a finger. "Listen to me. That enclave is huge, maybe ten square miles, and the main gate at West Milton is located all the way around at the opposite end of where you will be. I don't know how you're going to talk your way in. In fact, I don't believe you will be able to, but I'd advise you to take the extra day and approach by the main gate. I wouldn't sneak around up on one of the auxiliary gates. That would be a good way to get yourself shot."

Another whole day, Coop thought. He'd see once he got there. "If it's all the same with you, I'll not hang around for tea. I'm anxious to be on my way. Maybe I can make it to the state forest by day's end."

Walt laid a hand on his shoulder. "That's your call, son. Be careful and good luck."

"God be with you," Coop replied. He picked up his gear, took a last look across the river and shook everyone's hand. He turned and faced the ridge looming in front of him. Other than the milder weather, it reminded him of the day he had set off down Cove Road in the snow and crossed his first mountain range. How many days ago had that been?

"Pray for an early spring," Coop said while walking away.

From over his shoulder, Coop heard Connie say, "Pray that all of us live long enough to see spring."

Chapter 67

Win Halbert stood in front of the mirror in his Sheridan Hall ready room knotting his tie. Until now, President Kall had left him alone to run Enclave 38, and he had done a damn good job of it, thank you very much. The crackdown on supplies leaking to the outside had met with considerable success, thanks to the special unit of soldiers under the leadership of Captain Kettering. The disease scare had worked. A random few civilians within the enclave had been infected with tainted inoculations. Anyone seeing those poor disease ravaged souls no longer wanted anything to do with the non-essentials.

The only thorn in his side was the resistance, that group of soldiers led by the mysterious unknown officer, Mandible.

He had kept President Kall advised as to his progress in his weekly communiqués, but played down the impact of Mandible's resistance. Apparently, Kall had been impressed with his reports. The president had suggested throwing a party as a thank you to Kettering's men for their efforts, and Kall wanted to personally appear to express his gratitude.

Or so he had said.

Did the president have a hidden agenda? One always had to consider all the angles when dealing with Kall. Although that man was now the king of the world, he did nothing unless it benefitted him.

Halbert pinched the base of the knot. Perfect. Turning sideways, he admired his profile in the mirror. He still looked damn good in a blue blazer, and he considered that despite his age, ladies might still find him handsome. He had been too busy to seek out opportunities to pursue his prurient interests. Sally remained tucked away at Enclave 2 in New England which suited him fine. The two of them exchanged letters every week and neither expressed any desire to see the other anytime soon.

Now that Halbert felt more in control of things, his longing for female companionship resurfaced.

He heard a knock on the door. "Enter."

His valet eased open the door and peaked into the room. "President Kall is ready for you."

"It's about time. Lead the way." The president's chopper was supposed to have been wheels down an hour ago.

A large contingent of heavily armed soldiers lined the hallway. No wonder Kall had showed up late. It looked like he brought along his entire Praetorian guard, a major logistical challenge. While they walked, he turned to his valet and muttered, "What's going on?"

The valet shrugged and spoke softly, "After landing, these men practically stormed Sheridan Hall and sealed it off."

Halbert grew anxious. Had he displeased Kall in some way?

When they approached the door to Kall's suite, one of the soldiers placed a hand on Halbert's shoulder. "Sorry, sir." With a firm grip he turned Halbert so that he faced the wall and frisked him.

Halbert's anxiety now turned to fear.

A guard at the president's door knocked, announcing their arrival.

The first lady pulled open the door and smiled. "Hello, Win." She extended a hand.

Shocked over having been frisked at his own facility, Halbert reacted by asking, "What the hell, Nika, after all we've been through together, don't you trust me?"

She motioned him into the room and closed the door behind them. "Don't take it personally."

He heard Kall's voice. "You speak of trust. What does that word mean? Is there such a thing anymore?" Halbert glanced around and found the president standing in a dark corner of the room. He puffed on a cigarette and swayed back and forth on his feet.

Halbert couldn't fathom Kall's suspicion. "I've made exemplary progress on your behalf, turned this facility around, followed every one of your directives. So, I'm sure that you can understand my indignity over being rough handled as if I were some sort of a threat."

"Are you," Kall snuffed out his cigarette, "a threat?"

Halbert wouldn't dignify the question with a response.

"I'll go fix us some drinks," Nika said.

"Excellent idea," Halbert said.

She stepped from the room.

"You're looking good, Win. This lifestyle suits you," Kall said.

Halbert turned his attention to Kall and noticed the man's rumpled suit and scuffed shoes. Bags under the president's eyes made it look as if he hadn't slept in days. "With all due respect, sir, you look like hell."

Kall chuckled. "Maybe I can trust you after all. Only a person who cares about me would presume to say that to my face. Have a seat."

The two men sat facing each other. Kall rested his forehead in his hand.

"What's bothering you?" Halbert asked.

Kall met Halbert's gaze and spoke. "We're politicians you and I. We're supposed to be expert at reading people and shaping public opinion. Throughout all of humankind's existence, men have sought to create a utopian society. Now that I have been able to provide them with the dream, I continue to meet with resistance. Why is that?"

Halbert wondered if he was supposed to answer Kall's ridiculous question.

Before he could speak, Kall ranted. "I've chosen the best and brightest Americans, leaders in their field, included their families, protected them with a highly trained and fully equipped military, implemented a sound plan to begin anew, repopulate the Earth, and this time do it right."

According to whom, Halbert wondered. Did it really surprise the president that not everyone had bought into the Gospel according to R.A. Kall?

Kall went on, "I provide this unique opportunity for mankind, my gift to them, and all I expect in return is loyalty."

Loyalty? Halbert considered the irony of Kall's statement. Those words from the man who committed genocide against the entire human race after swearing an oath to preserve, protect, and defend. "What's the nature and extent of the resistance?"

Kall scoffed and steepled his fingers together in front of him. "We've lost control of fly over country."

"What?"

Kall raised his voice. "The Midwest. All of the enclaves controlling Texas, Oklahoma, Kansas, and Nebraska have fallen."

"What exactly do you mean by fallen?"

"What do you think it means?" Kall snapped. "The military in those areas have ceded control to civilians, and they've opened all of the enclaves to the non-essentials. They've left us, Win. They're forming their own government, electing their own leaders. They've even been successful in effecting repairs. Civilian engineers have found a way to restore power to Austin and Wichita. Other cities will soon follow."

He paused and leveled his gaze at Halbert. "They'll soon be coming for us, Win. You and I and everyone else in a leadership role."

Where was Nika with those drinks? "As part of the planning process for Earthburst, I'm sure the mental health professionals advised you there would be some push back. You took that into consideration, right?"

Kall ignored the question. He stood and began pacing. He pounded his fist into his palm. "It's not too late. We can fix this. Cooler heads will prevail. We still have the time and the resources." He stopped abruptly and turned toward Halbert. "Win, I need your help."

Stupefied, all Halbert could say was, "What?"

"E38 is our most successful enclave. Under your leadership, the populace of this facility have adapted well. You have nearly achieved the utopia that I envisioned. More importantly, the military contingent stationed here have proven that they can be hard cases, do whatever they are told. All of this has not gone unnoticed."

Had Kall just complimented him? "I still don't understand what you want of me."

"The insurrection in the Midwest must be squashed before it spreads further. That area is the goddamned breadbasket of this country. Over the long haul, we'll starve without it. During my speech tonight to your officers, I'm going to ask for volunteers."

"To do what?"

"Invade, do whatever it takes."

"Whatever it takes?"

Kall narrowed his eyes. "I'll nuke their treasonous asses if I have to."

Halbert had no doubt the man meant what he said.

"Can I count on you to back me up?" Kall asked.

Some part of Halbert knew from that very first day in the Rose Garden when Kall had originally proposed his scheme that it would end badly. His choice then was to die sooner or die later. At the time, dying later seemed more appealing. What he hadn't counted on was that dying later meant dying harder. "I have no choice. Like you said. They'll be coming for us, and there will be no forgiveness."

His words seemed to encourage Kall. The man straightened his posture. "Let's go meet those brave soldiers of yours."

The first lady never did return with their drinks.

* * *

Halfjack kept Katie's arm within his as he escorted her through the reception line. The gesture appeared courteous and gentlemanly. Only he and Katie knew that his hold signified his control over her and served as a warning, a reminder for her to mind her manners and not to do anything that would make him look bad.

The fates had blessed him. In the before times, he would never have dreamed of shaking hands with the president. He resolved to make the most of this opportunity. He would stand above this crowd and be noticed. Looking around the room, he sneered. His nemesis, Captain Sloat, was nowhere to be seen. Banished to some insignificant gate, his former commanding officer could no longer stand in his way. Lately, he had wondered how he could tear down Colonel Muncie next, but that was no longer necessary. He planned to leapfrog over the entire command structure at E38 and land right in the president's lap.

Getting noticed would be easy with Katie at his side. He glanced around the room and saw quite a few of his fellow officers escorting good looking ladies, but none of them held a candle to the fine female specimen he had brought. Katie's brilliant red dress clung to her body, outlining her figure. Hemmed just above her knee, it fit her perfectly. The diamond necklace he had pillaged during one of his patrols sparkled as it lay against her bare skin, drawing attention to her cleavage.

Something about her neutral expression made it look as if she weren't enjoying herself. Bitch walked like a zombie. Halfjack leaned down and whispered into her ear. "You're about to shake hands with the most powerful man in the world. Smile. I want him to see your eyes sparkle like those diamonds."

Katie shot him a dirty look but then tried a smile. Sure, it was forced, but nobody else would know that. "Just remember our deal."

"That's better," he said.

The line moved slowly. Eventually, they reached Colonel Muncie and his wife. Halfjack introduced Katie and they all shook hands.

"I've never known you to keep such lovely company, Captain Kettering. Where have you been hiding her?" Muncie asked.

"Oh, locked away in his BOQ," Katie said.

Halfjack squeezed Katie's arm, a warning for her to keep her smart assed mouth shut.

"If he's a wise man, he won't remain a bachelor much longer," Muncie said. "We'll have to move the two of you out of the BOQ into family housing."

The colonel's wife met Halfjack's gaze in what could only be considered as a knowing look, somehow threatening, but she said nothing.

When the colonel and his wife greeted the next couple in line, Halfjack whispered in Katie's ear, "Another crack like that and you'll not live to see another day. Then I'll follow through on my threat to end the miserable life of your boyfriend, and while I'm at it, I'll torture and kill everyone living in that idyllic shithole of a valley where you came from. What happens tonight is important to me. I won't have you ruin it. Do you understand?"

Katie ignored him.

Damn it. He squeezed her arm tighter until she winced. "I said, do you understand?"

She bit her lower lip and nodded.

He relaxed his grip and reminded her, "Straighten your posture and smile."

Next up, they shook hands with a number of other dignitaries and a general, all of whose names Halfjack didn't care to remember. The prize awaited him at the end of the line.

Halbert stood next to the president. Halfjack wondered why the minister was alone. He'd heard rumors that his wife no longer lived with him, and now he supposed the rumors to be true. The man couldn't keep his eyes off Katie.

Halfjack cleared his throat. "Sweetheart, I'd like to introduce you to the man in charge of this entire enclave. This is Minister Winston Halbert. Sir, this is my lady friend, Katie Hunt."

To Katie's credit, she finally played her role. Her smile dazzled the minister. Halbert held onto her hand as if mesmerized, reluctant to let go. He uttered, "My god." Moments later, he regained his composure and said, "Forgive me, young lady, I didn't mean to stare. It's just that you remind me so much of someone I once knew."

"Someone you lost when the world went dark?" Katie asked.

"Yes, someone quite dear to me."

Katie touched his arm in a gesture of sympathy. "Don't be too sad. All of us have lost loved ones."

"Captain Kettering, she's a keeper," Halbert said while shaking his hand.

Halbert had called him by name. That meant he remembered it. What a home run! Halfjack's insides turned flip flops. The exchange couldn't have gone better if it were scripted. His gamble of bringing Katie here had worked. At least with Halbert. If they could only impress the president as thoroughly.

While celebrating to himself, it went even better for Halfjack when Halbert turned to President Kall and said, "Let me do the honors. First lady, Mr. President, this handsome couple is Captain Jack Kettering and Katie Hunt."

"Are you friends with this good-looking couple?" Nika asked Halbert.

"Friends, indeed," Halbert replied.

The first lady dipped her head. "Pleased to meet you."

President Kall extended his hand to them, "As am I. I understand Captain Kettering that you have played a pivotal role in the success of this enclave. You have my gratitude." Kall shook quickly and turned his attention to the next couple in line.

And just like that, it was over. An usher led them away to their table.

The exuberance Halfjack felt after having impressed Halbert vanished. The president hadn't connected with him at all. What had gone wrong?

Feigning chivalry, Halfjack held Katie's chair for her. He seated himself and glanced back at the reception line. Minister Halbert shook hands with someone, but his eyes remained fixed on Katie. Then the minister did something completely unexpected. He smiled at Halfjack and winked.

Halfjack's insides warmed. Maybe they hadn't impressed the president, but he still had a way in. Minister Halbert had been completely smitten by Katie. That was something Halfjack knew he could leverage. He felt Katie tug his sleeve. When he turned his attention to her, she asked, "Well? Did you get what you wanted out of me?"

Feeling beholden to a woman made Halfjack uncomfortable,

left him feeling less in control, a situation to be avoided. This time, he allowed himself to let down his guard. He took Katie's hand, wanting somehow to convey his gratitude. Putting up with her resistance to his advances and her silly teenager attitude had all been worth it for this one moment when it counted. He was glad that he hadn't killed her. All of these thoughts he tried to express but couldn't find the right words. In the end, he settled for a simple, "Thank you."

Chapter 68

President Kall's speech stunned Halfjack. Glancing around the room he noticed the pallor on the men's faces, the slack jawed expressions of the women. All of them had been caught completely by surprise, as if slapped.

Insurrection among the Midwestern enclaves? A call for men of strong will to join in an effort to put down the rebellion? Halfjack's mind spun. How could he take advantage of this?

From the head table, President Kall and the first lady stood followed by Halbert and the commanding officers. They were getting ready to leave.

Halfjack panicked. He couldn't let them get away. There was a good chance that he would never again be in a position to have an audience with these powerful men. If he were going to make a move, it had to now, it had to be bold, and it had to be decisive. "Stay here," he told Katie. "Play along a little while longer. It's almost over."

She grimaced. "Hurry up. You sleazy people make me feel dirty."

He jumped from his chair and hurried to catch up with the president's entourage. Kall and the first lady had already left the room. He caught sight of Halbert, his intended target about to slip away. "Minister," he shouted to be heard above the din.

Halbert glanced at him.

A burly guard jumped between them. "You'll have to return to your seat, sir."

Halfjack's heart raced. Now that he was so close, he couldn't let the opportunity slip away. "Minister, please, may I impose on you for a moment before you leave?"

Halbert stopped and said to the guard, "It's okay. Let him pass."

The guard stepped away. A sense of relief washed over Halfjack. The fates did indeed smile on him tonight. "Thank you, sir. I just want you to know that I'm appalled by the president's words. I feel duty bound to serve in a greater capacity. I want to be the first to volunteer to join you and President Kall in quelling this rebellion."

Halbert grinned and said, "The country is indebted to you, Captain Kettering. I'm proud of you, son."

"Sir, I need a small favor."

Halbert leaned back and eyed him suspiciously. "What kind of favor?"

"It's about Katie. You see, sir, she's alone. If I leave, I'm concerned about what will happen to her."

Halbert's expression changed to one of confusion. "She has rights. Whatever befalls you, Katie's future here is secure."

Halfjack took a deep breath. His entire future, his dream, rested on his judgment of this man's character. "I'm afraid, that's not the case. She's not on the official roles. She's here illegally."

"Captain, are you telling me that sweet, young girl is a non-essential?"

"Yes, sir. I admit my insubordination for smuggling her into the enclave, but how could I not? It would have been too great a waste for her to die out there. I felt sorry for her." Before the minister could respond, Halfjack went for the kill. "I'm willing to leave her here if you agree to take her in."

One of two things was about to happen. Either Minister Halbert would take the bait, or he would call for the guards to lead him off to the brig.

Several seconds passed while Halfjack held his breath.

Halbert didn't call for the guards. Instead, he said, "Perhaps we should speak about this privately in my ready room."

* * *

Win Halbert sat in his suite, drink in hand. Katie Hunt could be Lenore's kid sister, the two of them looked that much alike, but Katie had a softness about her, an innocence that Lenore could never have pulled off. The prospect of possessing this beautiful girl as his new mistress had his heart racing. He heard the knock at his foyer door. "Come in."

His valet peeked in. "Miss Hunt is here."

Halbert stood. "Show her in."

The valet held the door open and Katie entered. The valet closed the door leaving the two of them alone. She stood there, back to the door, clutching her handbag with both hands, staring at him, chewing her lower lip, her face a mask of confusion.

That red dress.

He had to remind himself to breathe.

Katie broke the silence. "Halfjack left me sitting at the party for over an hour. Alone. Twiddling my thumbs. What happened to him? Why have I been brought to this place?"

"Halfjack? Is that what you call Captain Kettering?"

"Uh huh, well anyway, that's what he prefers to be called. Where is he?"

Halbert walked over to the liquor cabinet. "Can I fix you a drink?"

"It's against the law. I'm underage."

Halbert smiled. "I don't think we have anything to worry about."

"Yeah, with you being the big Kahuna around here, I suppose we can bend the rules, right? Okay, a glass of wine to settle my nerves."

Halbert selected a bottle of Lambrusco, his last one. "To settle your nerves? You don't need to be nervous around me."

"That remains to be seen."

He poured her wine and made a gin and tonic for himself. He approached Katie and handed her the wineglass. "Please, have a seat."

Katie scanned the seating arrangements and chose a recliner. She crossed her legs and sipped her wine. Halbert sat across from her on the sofa. He studied her. God, he couldn't help staring at her.

"You still haven't told me about Halfjack," she said.

"I have good news," Halbert said. "You'll never see that man again."

Katie uncrossed her legs, set the wineglass on the table between them, and leaned forward. "Are you serious? I mean, please don't lie to me about something as important as that."

"I'm not lying."

She tilted her head. "Seriously?"

He held a hand over his heart. "I promise."

Katie slumped back into the chair and closed her eyes. "Thank you. Whatever you did to get that man out of my life, I thank you."

The sincerity of her gratitude touched Halbert's heart. At that instant, he was her hero. If only he could freeze the moment. He knew, though, this fantasy would be short lived. "Did he really treat you that badly?"

She opened her eyes and paused before answering. "I held a romantic notion that my first time would be with someone I really cared about. He took that from me."

Her trusting him enough to confide something that intimate touched him. Katie confused him. He was torn now between his longing to seduce her and his need to comfort her as a father.

"I mean, even in this day and age was that too much to hope for?"

"No. That was a wonderful dream, Katie. I admire you for having held onto it."

She rolled her eyes. "Yeah, well, that's that."

Halbert remembered his own drink and took a long gulp. He asked, "Aren't you even interested in what happened to Kettering?"

"I don't care. He's gone. That's all that matters." She looked at her wine glass but didn't pick it up. "I suppose you're going to tell me anyway. Pardon the cliché, but I sense the other shoe is about to drop. There *is* another shoe, right?"

"Yes." He wasn't going to lie. He could tell that Katie was too intelligent for him to try and fool her. He decided to be truthful. "Captain Kettering is an ambitious man, a real opportunist."

"Duh, tell me something I don't already know."

"The captain told me everything that he knew about you. He told me where you came from, about how you lost your whole family, about your Amish boyfriend, and about how you are an aspiring doctor."

Katie scoffed. "Another dream dashed."

"Not necessarily."

That got her attention. She met his gaze. "What do you mean by that?"

"Captain Kettering is now Colonel Kettering. I recommended

him as an aide-de-camp to President Kall. Kall promoted him on the spot. One hell of a field promotion. I must confess, however, that it was all Kettering's idea. Of course, President Kall accepted as part of a debt he owes me."

"Bully for both of you, but excuse me. Where does that leave me?"

"First of all, there is no need to excuse yourself. I enjoy hearing your voice."

Katie picked up her wineglass and took a sip. "Let me get this straight. You put in a good word for that degenerate scum?"

"I'm afraid I did."

"Why, what did *you* get out of the deal?"

Halbert sighed, but he didn't speak.

Katie looked at the floor. "Oh."

Halbert never felt more ashamed in his life than he did at that moment. But damn it, he was responsible for the operations of the country's most successful enclave and was enduring overwhelming stress. He was a man. He had needs. "I made a simple deal with Kettering, and I'm willing to make a deal with you."

She met his gaze. Moisture rimmed her eyes.

"Please, don't cry."

Katie got out of her chair. She stood, her fists balled at her sides, and shouted, "I don't cry. I never cry."

In the silence that followed, Halbert watched her facial expression fade from steely determination to a pout. "You know I'm young enough to be your daughter."

"I don't have a daughter."

"But you can imagine it, can't you? If you had a daughter like me, would you even be considering what you are now considering?"

"Katie, let's not make this more difficult than it has to be."

"That's easy for you to say." She slouched into the chair. "There has to be some decency remaining in you. You're still human. Please, let me go. I just want to go home."

How could any decent man turn down such a heartfelt plea from this helpless girl? He almost granted her her wish. Almost. Halbert realized he had abandoned his decency long ago. "Earlier I said that I was willing to make a deal with you."

"A deal? Look, mister, nothing you offer me is going to get me to willingly sleep with you. I'm not a *thing* to be bought and sold as part of any agreement between two men. Do you even realize how demeaning that is? Can you imagine how that makes me feel? You're no better than Halfjack."

"Katie, I am nothing like Halfjack. Forcible rape is repugnant to me. If it weren't, the deed would already be done. Now, are you ready to listen to what I have to say?"

She sat there trembling, taking shallow breaths.

He got up and made himself another gin and tonic, allowing some time to pass for Katie to settle down. When he returned to his seat, he noticed that she calmed some, but she still chewed her lower lip.

"I can't undo what's already been done. I can't give you back your father or the friends you lost. I can't give you back your innocence. But I do have it within my power to grant you a gift, return to you one of your dreams."

Katie wiped her eyes with the back of her hand. "What do you mean?"

"I can restore your dream of becoming a doctor. We have a world class med school right here at E38. I can enroll you tomorrow."

"And all I have to do is bargain away my dignity?"

Halbert ignored her remark. He was way out of her league when it came to negotiations. As a seasoned politician he was expert at it, and he already sensed victory. Katie would let go of her so called dignity easily enough if she were convinced the reason would be selfless. She was a kind-hearted girl. That was her weakness.

"Med school is my special gift to you, but I have so much more to give to Wineberry Hollow. Food, as much as the people who live there need. Free medicine and medical care. A big, honking generator to provide power. Transportation. Protection from marauders wandering around out there. Your neighbors would enjoy a life very similar to the way it was during the before times. Real peace. Real security. They would want for nothing."

Katie wore a far away look. "Cast yourself from the mountain top," she muttered, "God will send his angels to save you."

"What?"

"Never mind. I doubt you would understand."

"Schooling for the kids," he continued. "Trade school for your young adults. They could learn real skills, become whatever they want, just like before. And I'd let you go home. You could spend time there with your friends."

"No," she shouted.

That jarred Halbert. He thought he had won, he had seen it in her eyes.

"No," she repeated. "If I do this, I could never go back. I'd be too ashamed to ever show my face."

Halbert held back a smile of triumph. The deal was as good as done.

Katie looked at him. Her brow knit together. "You're asking me to be your whore. I'd be buying all of those things with my body."

"Whore is such an ugly word, and really what does that word mean? When a woman agrees to marry a man, isn't that the same thing? She's trading her body for the security her husband can provide for her and her children."

"That's twisted. You're just as much of a psycho as Halfjack."

"Some people think of marriage as nothing more than legal prostitution."

She scoffed. "Now you're proposing marriage?"

"Why don't we just call it a business deal."

"Why don't we just call it rape."

"It's only rape where there is no consent."

"Holy crap. You mean I have a choice? You'd just let me walk away?"

Halbert pointed, "There's the door."

Katie stood and straightened the wrinkles on her dress. "This has been a really nice conversation. *Not*. See you around. *Not*."

As she walked to the door, Halbert hated what he had to do next. Why couldn't she see reason? After all Katie had been through, why couldn't she be pragmatic? He didn't want to have to resort to breaking her spirit, but she left him no choice. "Of course, then you would just be another starving girl in Wineberry Hollow instead of a doctor who could continue in her father's footsteps. He loved his neighbors. Apparently, you don't. Kettering's squad has taken a real interest in Wineberry Hollow, too. They believe the people living there have been holding out on them. Especially the Amish families. You can't trust those tricky Amishmen."

Katie stood facing the door, her hand on the knob. "Coercion is coercion, be it physical or otherwise. This is still rape. I'm powerless, and you're forcing me to have sex with you."

"Powerless? Oh, Katie, you have it all wrong. You're so young, so beautiful. You have no idea the power you hold over me."

She turned and faced him. "Cut the bullshit. We both know exactly what this is."

They were interrupted by a knock at the door. Halbert's valet stuck in his head and dropped a large duffel bag. "A delivery."

"That'll be all," Halbert said.

The valet shut the door and left.

Katie shot him a questioning look.

"Your clothes," Halbert said. "I took the liberty of retrieving them from Kettering's BOQ. I figured you wouldn't want to go back there."

Katie stared at the duffle bag for a long moment. She sighed and picked up the bundle. "Where's the closet?"

Chapter 69

Trusting Walt's judgment, Coop avoided all possible human contact. With only twenty miles remaining to his goal, he wanted no more distractions. Crossing the ridge had been easy and quick. The sun had not yet reached its zenith as he stood just inside the tree line of a wide expanse. Coop judged the farming valley to be three or four miles wide, and he could easily make out the mountainous peaks of Bald Eagle State Forest on the other side of the valley. After crossing, he'd lose himself in the trees and be able to stay hidden. The crossing, though, would leave him vulnerable.

Fences, buildings, and lone trees lay widely scattered. Zigzagging between them would take too long and leave him frustrated. The valley lay still and quiet. Everyone had either moved out or died. Or they were holed up and watching him.

Not likely, Coop thought. He decided to take his chances and hike in a relatively straight line to the other side while giving dwellings a wide berth.

Coop stepped from the tress and glanced around. No sign of life.

By the time he reached the other side, Coop despaired. The

valley had once been well cared for and beautiful with rich soil and abundant water. This time of year, the fields should have been bustling with activity, men hard at work tilling the soil and getting ready for the new season, their wives turning their gardens or hanging out laundry, and children at play. Instead, Coop was greeted with utter silence. Not a soul, he saw. No cribs filled with corn, no silos full of grain, not even a single animal.

Pillaged, all of it. Marauders had found this place and had taken everything. Marauders or soldiers. Based on Coop's experience, there was no difference. Many homes had been badly vandalized, windows broken, doors smashed. Still, why hadn't the people who lived here stayed around? Where could they go where it was better? At least here the land was familiar to them. They could plant, live off the land, hunt for game in the mountains. If his Wineberry Hollow neighbors and the folks from Owl Notch were able to try and ride it out, why couldn't these people?

By mid-afternoon, Coop had made it across, unchallenged and unmolested. A small ranch lay near the edge of the forest surrounded by plowed fields. A farm that could sustain a family. Curiosity got the better of him, or more like a yearning to understand. He approached the house, slowly and cautiously. A pendant stuck in the yard read, *High Acre*. He stood in front of a two story structure with a wraparound porch. It reminded him of home. The front door stood ajar, gently swaying from the breeze as if beckoning him. The old door's hinges squeaked in need of oil.

"Hello," Coop tried, but not too loud. This was ill advised. He should head for the trees and keep moving. Then he rationalized that an extra five or ten minutes wouldn't make a difference.

Something about the front door spooked Coop so he walked around back. A wooden patio adorned with flower pots neatly hanging from the hand rails led to a large sliding glass door. Last summer, the pots would've been resplendent with blooms. Dead stalks were all that remained, their skeletons poking above the potting soil.

The door remained intact. Coop tried it, and it slid open. He wasn't surprised. Back home, he rarely locked his doors. He trusted his neighbors.

"Hello," Coop shouted into the house, but he would've been shocked to hear a response.

Just in case, he yelled, "My name's Cooper Stover. I'm alone and unarmed. I'm just checking to see if you folks are all right." He paused. "I'm coming in now. If you're here, please don't shoot. I mean you no harm."

He stepped into a carpeted family room. A large, flat screen TV hung from the wall crooked, one of its mounts having broken loose. He saw a sofa and two stuffed chairs. A sewing basket sat on an end table, several spools of colored thread scattered on the table beside the basket.

In a bookcase, Coop saw a trophy. He picked it up and read the inscription, "Little League District Champion - Clark Brewster," along with the name of a team and the year. Clark had been a baseball player - two years ago. Beside the trophy, a framed photo of a young couple and two children, both boys. Coop figured the oldest boy to be Clark, assuming it was a recent photo. The young boy appeared to only be about six, too young for serious baseball.

He wandered into the kitchen and dining room. Cupboards hung open, although nothing looked out of place. The refrigerator also hung open, but nothing remained inside. Looters would hurriedly open cupboards looking for easily accessed valuables, explaining the state in which he found this house.

The foyer and living room were filled with leaves and dirt that had blown in after the house was abandoned and the door so carelessly left open. Mold grew on the drywall and the carpeting looked a grimy mess.

Coop took a few tentative steps down the hallway toward the bedrooms. He peeked into a bathroom.

Nothing.

He eased open the door to one of the bedrooms and found that the area had been made into an office. A certificate hung on the wall naming, "Rich Brewster, Realtor of the year." On the desk lay a worn, tattered, "Field Guide to Edible Wild Plants."

Good. At least they were trying to survive.

In a second bedroom he found a small set of dressers and bunk beds. This had to be the boys' room. Fishing rods and a ball glove lay in the corner. It brought a smile to Coop's face. Although this was obviously an English family, these boys were no different from Amish, fishing and baseball, a passion for most boys regardless of religion.

After walking into the master bedroom, Coop wondered at what point in his life he had become jaded about death. He had seen so much of it during the past year, had witnessed gruesome violence. The bodies lying on the bed hadn't shocked him. Last year, he would've run from the house screaming. Now?

He slumped onto a footstool and stared at them. Beyond the point of smelling, the dried, partially mummified, partially skeletonized remains lay positioned, adults on each side of the bed, the two boys, he assumed, between them. It didn't look like they were murdered, the way they were posed. Coop assumed that one day during the hard winter, after the food ran out, after they had lost all hope, this family had just given up.

"God preserve their souls."

Is this how it was in all of the homes in this valley? English families, generations removed from tending the land, no longer possessing the skills to survive, not knowing how to feed themselves without buying food from a grocery store. What did a real estate agent know about a plow? What did a suburban housewife know about keeping a home without electricity? What did two young brothers know of hard work in the fields or checking trap lines or animal husbandry?

No wonder mankind was in the process of dying. Coop felt sorry for this once happy family. He choked back a sob in mourning for all of humanity.

Why had it come to this?

He got off the footstool and started to look for a blanket to cover the bodies. Then he reconsidered. What was the point? Coop shuffled into the family room and closed and locked the patio door. That much he could do for them. Allow them to rest in the privacy of their own home, their self-imposed tomb. He left by the front door and closed it as well.

The wind had picked up, chilling Coop. He hiked into the forest southeast and up a ridge pondering the fragility of life. He wasn't educated in the way of book learning like Rich Brewster obviously had been, but he knew how to survive. Unwilling to just lay down and die, Coop resolved that whatever happened next, he would fight with every fiber of his being against hopelessness, not only for himself, but for Katie, too, and for Mother, and for his Wineberry Hollow neighbors. He would be strong enough for all of them.

That night, deep within Bald Eagle State Forest, Coop built a small fire and unwrapped the few small scraps of dried fish that he carried. His stomach growled. He reckoned that he had traveled at least fifteen of the twenty miles to the enclave. He'd worry about food after reaching his destination.

In the distance, he heard a howling. This wasn't the yipping of coyotes, but something different. A wolf maybe? Wolves no longer existed in Pennsylvania, but who knew what happened in zoos after the world went dark? All manner of wild creatures may have escaped or been freed to roam the countryside.

That thought disturbed him and kept him from falling asleep. Sometime later, Coop heard another howl, closer this time. He jumped to his feet and kicked ashes over what remained of his small fire. Using a lighter to see, Coop left his pack on the ground and climbed a pine tree. When he judged that he was about fifteen feet off the ground, Coop sat on a stout branch facing the tree trunk. He wrapped his arms and legs around the trunk and tried to snooze.

The chill wind made him shiver, and he dozed fitfully.

Sometime during the night, Coop woke to the sound of rustling leaves. It sounded like a passing herd of deer except for the occasional yip and snarl. Looking down from his perch, Coop could see nothing in the darkness.

Not one wolf. A pack of wolves?

From directly beneath him, a creature unleashed an eerie howl.

Coop almost cried out. He reached into his pocket to retrieve his lighter. If some animal was coming up the tree after him, he wanted to see it coming. Terrified, Coop's hand trembled. He dropped the lighter, and he almost lost his grip on the tree trunk.

The creature howled again.

Coop squeezed the tree with his encircling arms and legs and mumbled, "Yea though I walk through the valley of the shadow of death, I will fear no evil, for Thou art with me."

He didn't know whether he had passed out or simply fallen asleep, but sometime later, Coop woke with the sun in his eyes. He squinted and looked all around. Had it been a dream?

Stiff, sore, his muscles aching from the insult of sleeping in a tree, Coop slowly unwound his limbs from around the trunk and lowered himself to the ground. Near where he stood, Coop found his lighter, or what remained of it. Two punctures perforated the plastic, all of the fluid had drained out.

It had not been a dream.

Coop's backpack had been pawed open, his jerky stolen, and his Bible chewed. The material making up the pack was not too badly molested. Coop grabbed it and couldn't think of any reason to delay. Still spooked, he tried making as little noise as possible while continuing his hike.

Shortly before noon, the forest ended and Coop faced a large, wide highway which he presumed to be Interstate 80. Remembering that this transportation route was used by both soldiers and what remained of marauders, Coop kept his distance and paralleled the highway walking east.

The wind eased and the sun disappeared behind the clouds. By mid-afternoon, the overcast sky looked ominous. Coop figured it wasn't cold enough to snow, but a front coming through would most likely bring with it an all day, heavy rain. He picked up his pace, ignoring his hunger pains, and crested a ridge. In the distance, he saw a ribbon of water. The river.

Hearing a noise from behind, Coop glanced around. Emerging from the woods, he saw a large framed dog, nose in the air. He wasn't too familiar with dogs but had once seen a picture book of exotic canines. This one, he recalled, appeared to be a Bullmastiff or something similar. Moments later, Coop and the dog met each other's gaze. More dogs emerged from the woods of all shapes and sizes, two dozen or so. They halted beside their leader.

In that instant, Coop admired them. These creatures lacking human intelligence innately had understood what it took to survive. They had reverted to a feral state, fallen in line behind a pack leader, and appeared to be thriving. How much easier would it have been for their former masters to have done the same thing? Cooperated. Held on their humanity and dignity. Worked together for the common good.

The lead dog tossed his head, pointed his snout into the sky and howled. His pack joined in, a cacophony of barks, yelps, and snarls.

Then they came for him.

The lead dog advanced in a slow lope, his pack members

trailing behind.

Coop dropped everything, his back pack, his walking stick, his maps, and sprinted. He glanced around for cover, for a fence he could scale, a tree, a hole in the ground, anything that could protect him from being eaten alive. Stopping to face them down was out of the question, there were too many of them. They would overwhelm him.

Running had also been a poor option. The dogs had been no more than a hundred yards behind at the start and would overtake him in seconds. He'd never make it to cover.

Lungs burning, Coop gasped for air and poured all of his strength into his legs. He heard them behind him closing the gap, snarling. In the distance, Coop saw soldiers, rifles pointing in his direction, muzzles flashing, the feel of bullets ripping by his head. Something pounded him in the back, knocking him to the ground, probably the lead dog, and Coop anticipated the pain of teeth being buried into the back of his neck.

Chapter 70

Coop wheezed and coughed. He rolled over onto his back and pushed the carcass of the dead dog off him. Strangers peered down at him, a man and woman, both in uniform.

"Wind's knocked out of him," the female soldier said. "Give him a minute to catch his breath."

While Coop lay there, the man said, "Those damn dogs. Somebody's going to get killed." He reached a hand down for Coop. "We should dispatch a party to hunt them down."

Coop grabbed the soldier's hand who then helped him to his feet.

Continuing his conversation, the man said, "This big mongrel must've been the pack leader. Now that we've taken him out, the rest of them will scatter for the time being."

"Thank you for helping me," Coop said, his voice noticeably scratchy. He glanced at the bloodied carcass of the dog that jumped on his back and wondered whose pet that animal might once have been.

"What's your name?" the man asked.

"Cooper Stover. Call me Coop."

"I'm Captain Douglas Sloat. Since you're a civilian, call me Sloat. I prefer being addressed by my last name." He motioned with his head toward the woman. "This is Lieutenant Napoli."

"Just plain Napoli," she said. "I take it you're with the MRC?"

"MRC?" Coop asked.

Sloat and Napoli exchanged glances. "Better come inside. I can see that you've got a story to tell."

"Inside?" Their talk confused him. Coop wondered if he suffered another blow to the head making him loopy.

Sloat pointed a thumb over his shoulder.

Coop looked up and spotted a series of buildings behind a high, wire topped fence that stretched as far as the eye could see. In front of him, a gate flanked by sentries. "Is this the enclave?"

"Number 38," Sloat said leading the way through the gate and into one of the buildings. They walked into a room that resembled a kitchen.

Napoli slid a chair out from a small table and commanded in a businesslike voice, "Sit."

Coop settled into the chair.

Sloat reached into a refrigerator and pulled out a bottle of water, handed it to Coop.

It had been almost a year since Coop saw bottled water. "Thank you." He screwed off the top and gulped, relishing the cool liquid against his parched throat. His stomach growled.

"You hungry?" Napoli asked.

"Other than some dried fish, I haven't eaten since yesterday morning."

She opened a cabinet. "I didn't bring anything back from mess, so I can't offer you anything substantial. I have a chocolate bar, though."

Coop's mouth watered. "A chocolate bar? Are you teasing me?"

She threw a long, flat object at Coop. He caught it in mid-air.

"Real chocolate." Coop marveled as he tore off the wrapper.

"Made right here at the E38 dairy," she said.

Coop closed his eyes at the sheer pleasure of experiencing the silky smooth, sweet treat. "This is so kind of you, but it makes no sense. Stories are told about the cruelty of the gatekeepers."

Sloat and Napoli exchanged another one of their glances.

"It's true that some of the personnel are pitiless," Sloat said, "but that's slowly changing. Anyway, you're damn lucky, Coop. We're wary of strangers. Fact is, we've mistaken you for someone else. You need to tell us what you're doing here. Start by telling me where you're from."

"I've traveled for many days on foot from a place in Tioga County called Wineberry Hollow."

Sloat perked up. "I remember meeting an old war horse of a soldier during one of my patrols who told me he hailed from Wineberry Hollow. An Army sergeant major, tough as nails. Can't seem to recall his name. He and his militiamen were in the process of rescuing some refugees stranded at a Route 15 underpass."

"Declan Orr," Coop responded. "He was a good friend of mine. A good friend to all his neighbors."

"Was?" Sloat asked.

"Killed by marauders," Coop said in a hushed voice.

"Sorry to hear that," Sloat said. After a pause, he continued. "Tell me, Coop, why would a young person from a self-sufficient community risk his life to come here?"

Coop told him the whole story, about the soldiers who plundered the hollow, the wanton violence, how he suffered a blow to the head, and the kidnap of Katie.

"You remember any of their names, these soldiers? Did you by chance hear the name Halfjack?"

"No. After I took that rifle butt to the head, my brain got scrambled. Even if I heard their names at the time, I wouldn't remember them now."

Sloat turned to Napoli. "Could've been Halfjack. Sounds like his style."

"Yeah, but he's gone now licking Kall's boots." To Coop she said, "Let me get this straight. You risked everything to come here to rescue your girlfriend?"

Coop muttered, "I have to find her."

"You're a saint," she said, "or maybe a fool. I can't decide."

Sloat leaned against the wall. "It's possible we know the man behind the troubles in your community. He's no longer assigned here, and his squad has been scattered to the winds on other assignments. You know how many thousands of people live inside this fence? Even if your girlfriend was taken by Halfjack, she could be anywhere. It's even possible that she's been discovered and turned out. I hate to tell you this, Coop, but if that's the case, her chances of survival would not be good."

"Nobody would be so cruel as to turn out a young lady like Katie," Coop said praying that his words were true. "Will you let me enter so I can find her?"

"I admire your can-do attitude, but you need to be reasonable. If she is here in E38, it could take years for you to find her. Hell, you may never find her. This place is a city, and a person can't just walk around freely poking his head into every building. You need clearances for most buildings. Meeting your girl would be serendipity, a chance encounter."

Napoli picked up the conversation. "If she's here, your girl has a better life than you do. She will want for nothing. She'll have food, shelter, and probably meaningful work. *If* she's here, that is."

"She's here," Coop insisted, but their words had an impact on him. He wasn't as hopeful now that he could quickly find her. The size and complexity of the facility was something Coop hadn't realized or considered.

Napoli drummed her fingers against the tabletop. To Sloat she asked, "Can you think of a way to help this young man?"

"You believe everything he's telling us?"

"He's no spy, and this is no trap," Napoli said. "Unless he's a very, very, good actor."

Sloat studied Coop and walked around him. "He's got the build of a soldier, and he doesn't look like he's sick or starving."

"But he doesn't have the demeanor of a soldier. He's too humble."

Sloat kneeled in front of Cooper to get eye level with him. "Look at me."

Coop met the captain's gaze.

"Do you work for military intelligence?"

Was this man teasing him? "I'm about as far from a soldier as a man can be." Coop went on to tell them about his Amish background.

Sloat got to his feet and walked away with Napoli. What if they didn't believe him? What would they do to him?

When Sloat and Napoli returned, they closed the door to the small room and sat at the table with Coop.

Lieutenant Napoli steepled her fingers on the tabletop and

leaned in toward Coop. "Both Captain Sloat and I believe your story, but on the off chance that you aren't who you say you are we need to tell you that we are not traitors. We swore an oath to protect the people of the United States of America, not do them harm. The actions of our commander-in-chief and those who follow him have proven to be despicable. The captain and I and a lot of good men can no longer follow Kall's policies on moral grounds."

The room fell silent.

"Why don't you just quit?" Coop asked.

Captain Sloat snickered. "Son, one does not just quit the military. You really don't know anything, do you?"

"Besides, we're in a position to help," Napoli added. "If we quit, a lot of civilians would starve."

Coop wondered what she meant. People were starving anyway.

"When we rescued you from those dogs, we expected you to be a contact from the MRC, the Milton Rescue Council," Sloat said. "A loose knit group of civilian volunteers from town who distribute food and supplies that we provide to them from the enclave."

"I see," Coop said. He gathered from their words that they were smuggling food away from the people living within the confines of the enclave. His instincts told him that if caught, Sloat and Napoli would probably face severe consequences. It sobered him, the trust they placed in him. But they didn't have to explain any of this. Why were they revealing these details to him?

"We may be in a position to help each other," Sloat said, "but what we have in mind would put you at risk. You're going to have to give it serious consideration."

Napoli picked up on the conversation. "Nobody knows who you are except us. Our plan is to pass you off as an authorized civilian resident of E38. A young agronomist-in-training, an agricultural expert."

"I'm no expert," Coop said.

"But you told Captain Sloat and I that you are an Amish farmer."

"I am."

"How good of a farmer are you? How much experience do you have?"

Coop wondered what they were getting at. "Since I've been a boy, I've planted, cared for, and harvested just about every crop that can be grown in this part of Pennsylvania."

"By hand and by horse drawn plow, right?" Sloat asked.

"Yes"

Sloat continued his line of questioning. "Without aid of power equipment?"

"That is correct. The ordnung forbids the use of gasoline engines."

"So you can read the soil pretty well, the weather, and are familiar with good farming practices?"

All of these things Sloat asked him were part of being a successful farmer. Coop had learned techniques from his father and neighbors, and now such things came naturally to him. But that didn't necessarily make him an expert, did it? He answered, "Yes."

"Then you can pass as an agronomist. You probably know as much about farming as anybody inside the fence," Sloat assured him.

"Whatever it takes," Coop said desperate for them to let him inside. "What do you want me to do?"

Chapter 71

Seven months ago, when Coop first departed from home on his journey to find Katie, he packed a Bible along with his other supplies. Along the way, the book had suffered considerable abuse. It had gotten grimy and damp after Cletus and Lulu Belle ransacked his belongings and left them out in the elements. The dogs shredded his pack to get to the dried fish he carried and ruined the Bible's binding. The cover separated and the first hundred pages or so were torn, yet it still remained readable.

The Christian congregations within the enclave passed out new Bibles to anyone who wanted one, but Coop preferred to hold on to his old copy. It had been given to him by a cousin. Too much had been lost after the world went dark, and he had been away from home now for nearly seven months. By handling it with care, Coop read his Bible at the end of every day. Life in the enclave was so far removed from his simple Amish upbringing that reading his tattered old Bible helped him stay grounded. He didn't want to forget who he was or the things he believed in.

Over time, however, Coop's religious views changed. He realized that tractors and gasoline engines and electricity were not of themselves evil, in fact, they were a source of great good. With the use of these machines, the vast fields that Coop worked within the enclave produced more food during this one season than he could in a lifetime on his small farm standing behind Bonnie's plow. How many more people could they save from starving by using these methods? He gained an appreciation for technology and how, if wisely used, would not become an unwholesome distraction.

Besides his work and Bible reading, he spent every minute of his free time searching for Katie. Coop was devastated the day that Captain Sloat had driven him into the enclave. Sloat had laughed after Coop told him how this must be the largest city in the world. He couldn't imagine the density of buildings and the thousands of people, soldiers and civilians. Sloat and Napoli had been right. It could take him years to find her.

Find her, though, he would.

Coop asked every place of business he visited, every new person he met, and all of his co-workers about a pretty young lady, she would be 19 now, just like him. As a result, he would often be shown or introduced to a lot of girls, but none of them were Katie. More often than not he was poked fun at. They would say, "You should be so lucky" or "We're all looking for a pretty girl" or something similar. A few of the soldiers he encountered were malicious and abusive, telling him to bug off or worse, but most of them acted sympathetic. He had been warned by Sloat to never reveal how he had entered the enclave and to stick to his cover story about how he had transferred in from a Kansas enclave.

Imagine, Kansas? He wouldn't even be able to find that state on a map, but the paperwork Sloat had provided was never questioned when he had to show it. This made Coop into a liar. He had no way to rationalize his way out of this sin, and that bothered him placing him in a moral dilemma. If he ever revealed the truth, harm could befall Captain Sloat, and Coop knew he might be forced to leave. Then how would he get back in? How would he ever resume his search?

All these months later, Coop lay on the cot in his dormitory room dejected and guilt-ridden, but God forgive him, he wasn't going to compromise his situation. He wasn't going to let anyone down.

Now that they were in the midst of harvest season, he wondered what was going on back home. He longed to be able to get word to his mother that he was alive and doing fine, and he wished he could find out how well she fared? Had the Army left his neighbors unmolested to plant and harvest? Was Wineberry Hollow still safe?

Given his experience with the military men who invaded his neighborhood, Coop had expected soldiers and civilians alike living here to be jaded and uncaring about the unfortunates living on the outside. With plenty to eat and their bellies full, it would be easy for the authorities to foment resentment about outsiders wanting to steal enclave food. To his surprise and delight, Coop realized that almost everyone felt compassion toward the outsiders. All of them had friends or family who had been left behind during Armed Forces Homecoming Day and the great cataclysm that followed, and all of them spoke about their feelings with reticence, fearing the hard core element that had set the great evil in motion.

A knock at the door interrupted Coop's thoughts. Expecting it to be one of his co-workers, Coop was surprised to see Captain Sloat at his threshold. He rarely had an opportunity to meet with the captain since their first encounter. After shaking hands, Coop invited him in.

Sloat closed the door behind him and eyeballed Coop's austere quarters.

"Anything wrong?" Coop asked.

Maintaining a stern expression, Sloat said, "You tell me. Does anyone suspect who you really are? Have you told anyone?"

"No and no," Coop answered. "I'm too grateful to you to get you into any kind of trouble."

"Good." Sloat took a seat in the one visitor's chair Coop had in his room. Coop sat on the edge of his cot. "I'm glad my judgment about your character has proven to be true, and you've built quite a reputation for yourself as a competent, hard worker."

"Who told you that?"

Sloat smiled. "My sources."

Coop wondered who among his co-workers had been reporting

to Sloat.

"How's the search going for your friend?" Sloat asked.

"I haven't found her yet."

"I'm sorry to hear that."

"I haven't stopped looking."

"Wouldn't expect you to." Sloat straightened in his seat. "Coop, I don't have a lot of time, so I'll get straight to the reason for my visit. Remember how when we first met, I told you that we could help each other? Also, that by helping our cause, it may put you at risk?"

"Yes, and I agreed to that. But after all these months you've never asked me for anything."

"The time has come."

Coop tugged at his shirt collar. "What do you need from me?"

"Until now there was nothing much you could do to help, but now that you're in the middle of harvest, I need you to divert some of your corn. People who are still alive and living in Milton and the surrounding towns are in desperate need."

"We're harvesting field corn right now. It's not for humans," Coop told him.

"Have you ever starved, Coop?"

"No."

"Starving people will give up everything they own for an ear of field corn."

"I understand that." Coop knew it could be ground into corn meal and baked into a bread, and it could be consumed if a person were hungry enough. "It's just that your request has taken me by surprise."

"Does that mean you won't help?"

"No, I mean, of course I will help. I owe you. Even if I didn't owe you, we have so much here. I don't understand why we can't share more of what we have." Coop ran a hand through his hair. "I don't understand. Why does there have to be an enclave full of privileged people? What gives us the right to keep others out? Why don't you soldiers tear down the fences and fan out into the countryside and help the survivors? Why couldn't you have done that from the start?"

Sloat stood and stepped in front of Coop. "You already know the answer to those questions. It's no longer a secret. I don't suppose it ever was. All of us suspected from the get go what had happened."

"Why doesn't anybody do something about it?"

Resting a hand on Coop's shoulder, Sloat said. "We *are* doing something about it. You, me, and a lot of good people all across the proverbial fruited plain."

Coop looked the man in the eye. "What do you mean?"

Sloat removed his hand from Coop's shoulder and took a step back. "Don't ask me about how I know this, but our country is reconstituting itself. It started out slow, but it's happening quickly now, state by state, the enclaves are falling. Kall and his minions are finished. Raven Rock and E38 and a few other surrounding areas are all that remain of this grotesque experiment."

Leaning his hand against the wall, Coop took a deep breath feeling a great weight lifting. "That's wonderful news."

Sloat creased his brow. "Even after the last enclave is dismantled, it'll take years, decades even to repair the damage, restore power everywhere, and rebuild the national infrastructure. In the meantime, there will still be great food shortages. That's why we need to proceed as planned."

Feeling better than he had since the before times, Coop asked, "How can I help, what is it specifically that you want me to do?"

"It's my understanding that the corn you harvest gets taken to a granary at the west side of the enclave for storage and processing. I'm also led to believe that you've learned how to drive a tractor?"

"That's right."

"Tomorrow, I need you to bring what gets harvested to Gate W3 instead of the granary. Lieutenant Napoli and my men will handle it from there."

"But...but," Coop sputtered. "They'll be expecting me at the granary. How will I explain when I don't show up?"

"The granary manager is one of us," Sloat said. "Our man will log your delivery as if you arrived there. Nobody will be able to tell a few wagon loads of corn missing from among the hundreds of wagon loads."

Coop wanted to ask about the identity of the granary manager but decided it was best if he didn't know. After thinking about Sloat's request, he said, "Sounds easy enough."

Sloat's eyes widened. He waved a finger. "Don't get

overconfident. It may seem easy, but it's also dangerous. A lot of lives are on the line. You need to be wary. If you suspect anything, abort and deliver your load to the granary as usual. We can always try again another day when it's safer."

The weight of Sloat's words sobered Coop. Here he was, an Amish man, and now a soldier. How had this transformation come to pass?

"In light of what I confided in you about the expected demise of the enclaves, I want to make something crystal clear to you," Sloat said. "I've been to war, Coop, fought many a battle. It's my experience that an enemy is always at his most vicious when he knows he is beaten. Ferocious as a cornered rat. That's the scenario Kall and his forces are now in. This couldn't be more serious, couldn't be more precarious for you."

Chapter 72

Combing his hand through a wagonload of husked corn, Coop allowed the kernels to pass through his fingers, an oddly soothing activity. He scooped up another handful from the back of the wagon and repeated the process, mentally counting all of the ways he was presently sinning. Lying, cheating, stealing. This harvest didn't belong to him. It belonged to the masters of this place, and albeit they were evil, he was stealing from them. There was no way to sugarcoat it.

Yet Coop felt great satisfaction about his sin.

The crisp October morning also contributed to Coop's good mood. He waited until the giant combine had reached the end of the field and far enough away so the driver wouldn't be able to see him before jumping onto the seat of his tractor. He glanced around and saw nobody out of the ordinary. Waving his hat to the man standing beside the next wagon in line – a signal that he would be on his way – Coop mashed down the starter pedal and fired up the diesel engine. As indifferently as possible, Coop drove away, slowly, so as not to attract any undue attention.

He reached the road for Gate W3 and slowed. Looking around, he saw nobody and turned down the road. Coop's heart raced. If he were stopped and questioned, he would have no excuse, no reason to be traveling this road. Coop supposed that he could say that he had gotten lost and taken the wrong road. That would be yet another lie.

Captain Sloat greeted him when he approached the gate and motioned for Coop to pull into a cutoff. After doing so, Coop noticed an empty wagon. He hopped off the tractor and fell in with the crew who were already scooping the kernels from his wagon into tubs for transport.

"We got it, Coop," Captain Sloat told him. "Your job is to hitch up to that empty wagon and return to the fields as usual. By the time you get back with the next load, this wagon will be empty, a sort of assembly line process where everyone has their part to play."

Coop walked back to the tractor. "Understood."

"You're doing fine," Sloat said, "but stay alert."

The second load also went well. On the third load, when Coop reached the gate, Captain Sloat didn't greet him. In fact, the area appeared to be deserted. He pulled into the cutoff and hesitated. Something seemed wrong. Should he turn around and drive to the granary? That's what he had been told to do in the event of trouble.

Instead, Coop cut the engine and dismounted from the tractor. He listened.

The cutoff where he parked was situated about an eighth mile from the gate and around a bend. Maybe the unload crew was running behind schedule and hadn't made it back yet. Coop started walking down the middle of the road toward the gate, but his instinct warned him to proceed with caution. He left the road and circled wide approaching the gate from the east.

He sneaked to within sight of the gatehouse and could see nothing unusual. He recognized Captain Sloat's men peering out through the gate, about a half-dozen of them. Of course, they wouldn't be looking his way. They were supposed to be guarding the entrance to the enclave and watching the outside.

What was going on?

He decided to risk it and stepped onto the road. "Hello."

They glanced his way. One of them beckoned for him to approach. The man spoke into a field radio.

"Are you Cooper Stover?"

"Yes." Coop was getting pretty good at recognizing insignias and their corresponding rank. The chevron on this man's shirt indicated that he was a corporal.

The corporal addressed him in a low voice. "Orders from Captain Sloat. You're to abort the delivery and take your shipment to the granary."

"What's wrong?"

"Trouble on the other side of the river. A skirmish."

Coop's breath caught. "Has anyone discovered what we have been doing?"

"Not exactly. Remnants of local brigands on the other side of the river are trying to hijack the corn from the MRC. One of the civilians has been shot. These outlaws have been plaguing us for some time. Captain Sloat and Lieutenant Napoli have crossed over with a squad of our men to put an end to it. About goddamned time if you ask me."

"They went alone with just a few men?" Coop asked. "With the thousands of soldiers at their disposal in this enclave, why haven't they asked for help?"

"How would they explain a fight over contraband enclave food?"

With a sinking feeling, Coop understood why the captain and his men would have to deal with this situation on their own.

"Besides," the corporal went on to say. "We're officially not to be concerned with the affairs of the non-essentials. You have to understand, Mr. Stover, the toadies following President Kall's orders would be delighted if all the civilians annihilated each other, the theory being the sooner they all die, the sooner we can leave these enclaves and repopulate."

"How can a human being be so cold toward his fellow man?" Coop asked.

"Yeah, well I didn't vote for the guy," the corporal said. "You need to get out of here. If this attracts attention, we would be hard pressed to explain a wagon full of corn sitting in our cutoff."

With that, Coop hurried back to the tractor and dropped off his load at the granary.

The rest of the day passed at a snail's pace. Coop was anxious to finish his shift and find out what happened. There were too few good people and Coop considered Sloat and Napoli and their men to be his friends.

When the day was done, Coop realized that he had no way to

contact Gate W3. He had no radio. Worse, he had no transportation and the gate was located about five miles away. He thought about it and decided that he could easily run five miles, so he set off in a slow jog. The cool autumn air made physical activity relatively easy and Coop lost himself in thought speculating about what occurred earlier in the day. Here it was, a year and a half after the world went dark and marauders still plagued decent people who were working hard to keep civilization going. Why didn't these brigands join up with the law abiding folk and work together?

He suspected that there would always be a few evil men, no matter what the circumstances. That got Coop to thinking about home. If bad things could happen so close to an enclave, what might be happening in Wineberry Hollow?

He wished he could've found Katie by now so that they could go home together. Coop felt anxious about his mother's safety and that of his neighbors. What a cruel joke it would be if Katie somehow had already returned home. If there were only some way to communicate with the outside world.

Having reached the cutoff for Gate W3, Coop slowed to a fast walk in order to catch his breath. A military vehicle approached from the direction of the gate traveling fast. The sun glinting from the windshield caused Coop to shield his eyes. The vehicle sped past. Coop thought he recognized Captain Sloat as the driver.

Why hadn't he stopped?

Coop didn't know what to do. Should he continue on toward the gate and find out from one of Sloat's men what was going on, or should he just return to his quarters?

In the distance he heard the drone of another approaching vehicle, this one traveling at a more leisurely pace. Coop waved his arms and the driver pulled even with him. It was the corporal that Coop had spoken with earlier. The man lowered his window.

"Was that Captain Sloat who just drove by?" Coop asked.

"Yes, get in."

Coop settled into the passenger seat and the corporal drove off. Coop waited for an explanation while the corporal keyed his mike and gave someone his position.

The corporal glanced at Coop. "Captain Sloat wanted me to tell you to discontinue the mission until further notice. The skirmish in Milton has drawn too much attention and Lieutenant Napoli has been hurt."

Coop gasped. "What happened?"

"I wasn't there, but from what I've been told she took a direct hit to the eye from a rock tossed by one of the marauders. It doesn't look good. She could lose that eye. The captain is rushing her to the medical center."

"That's why he didn't slow down when he saw me. This is awful. Are we on our way to catch up with them?"

"I need to be there to back up the captain's story. We're telling everyone that what happened to the lieutenant was a terrible accident. She slipped on the wet porch and rammed her eye into the porch post. Everyone in the unit is standing by that story."

"You will all lie?"

The corporal shot Coop a baleful look. "If the truth gets out, our entire unit will be in deep shit. Then what will happen to the people on the other side of the river who depend on us? Yeah, we're all going to lie, and that lie will save countless lives. You have a problem with that?"

"No," Coop said, "no problem at all." At one time, being part of this deception would have filled him with guilt. Now he didn't give it a second thought. He pondered the situation, how easy it had become to participate in one falsehood upon another.

"You ever been to the med center?" the corporal asked.

"No, is it far?"

"Not much farther. It's at the very center of the enclave near where all the honchos and big brass live. You're a civilian worker, so you don't have to salute anyone, but I'd advise you to keep on your toes. Watch what you say and do. When we meet up with Captain Sloat, I know you'll have lots of questions, but stay cool. Don't attract attention."

They pulled into the parking lot of a four story U-shaped building. He and the corporal entered through large glass doors located in the middle of the U.

The corporal addressed the attendant behind the main desk. "Can you point us in the direction of the E.R.?"

The bored looking woman never even met their gaze. She just muttered, "Through the double doors and turn left. Follow the signs."

Coop walked behind the corporal. He had visited a hospital

when doctors had treated his father's heart condition. This place smelled exactly the same. Everyone they passed walked the corridors seemingly preoccupied with a sense of purpose. Did they ever pause during the day to think about what was going on in the world? How large of a stockpile of medicine did this facility hoard? Did anyone here think about children like Lucas Foose who had suffered and died when the medicine on the outside ran out?

They passed through a door bearing a large sign with red letters labeled: EMERGENCY and stood in front of another desk behind which sat another bored looking attendant.

"A member of my squad, a Lieutenant Napoli has recently arrived. Can you tell me where I might be able to find her?"

The attendant consulted a computer display. Coop thought about young Nate Orr and how much he must miss his computer. When would the English living in the outside world ever enjoy such distractions again?

"Female?" the attendant asked.

"Yes, Ma'am."

"She's currently in the O.R. The waiting room is across the way." She pointed to a large open area filled with lounge chairs.

The corporal walked toward the lounge then veered off down the corridor.

"What are you doing?" Coop asked.

"Waiting is an unsatisfactory option. Let's find the captain. He's got to be around here someplace."

This made Coop uneasy. What if they were stopped and questioned? The corporal warned about not drawing attention to themselves. They peaked through windows and eventually found Captain Sloat in a side room standing in a corner. The corporal pushed through the door and strode toward the captain as if he owned the place.

Sloat spotted them and waved them over. "Corporal, it's about time you got here. Coop, I apologize for not stopping when I saw you on the road."

"No problem, I understand. How's Lieutenant Napoli?"

Sloat spoke in a hushed voice. "Still in the E.R., but I believe if we're stealthy we'll be able to monitor the situation."

"How so, sir?" the corporal asked.

"Follow me," Sloat responded.

They walked out of the side room and back into the corridor. Sloat led them through another set of doors and glanced around to see if anyone was watching.

Nobody paid them any attention.

They ducked into a staircase, climbed a flight of steps, and walked onto a balcony that resembled high school bleachers on a football field, although this balcony had only three tiers with room for only eight to ten people on each tier.

They all sat in the front row.

"There she is," Sloat said and pointed.

Coop looked through a windowpane onto the operating theater below. Was that really Lieutenant Napoli? The person lying on the gurney was draped in a white sheet with only her arms and head showing. A tube hung from one of her arms and one of the doctors – Coop presumed the people down there to be doctors wearing scrubs, masks, and headgear – held a clear mask over Napoli's nose. Two other doctors bent over their patient examining Napoli's face. The glass in front of them was soundproof.

"What are they doing?" Coop asked.

The corporal leaned forward and flipped a switch on a console. Voices carried through the balcony sound system.

The doctor holding the clear mask over Napoli's nose said, "BP 90 over 36. Pulse 110. I'm adjusting." He played with some knobs on a machine.

"Lot of damage here," a doctor wearing white scrubs said. He was the only one in white, the other two wore green. "Frontal bone is shattered for sure, and it looks like the Maxillary also suffered some damage. Can't tell for sure until we irrigate."

The third doctor looked around, "Speaking of which, who's assisting and where the hell is he?"

A woman's voice, Coop noticed. Maybe she was a nurse and not a doctor. With all of the gear they wore hiding their faces and bodies, he couldn't tell one from another.

"Whoever it is better get here fast. I don't want to keep this patient under any longer than I have to. Her vitals are difficult to control," the doctor holding the mask said.

A man burst into the theater by banging his butt against the swinging door and holding two gloved hands straight up in the air. Except Coop had once again misjudged. This person was definitely a lady, her pregnant belly protruding beneath her scrubs.

"Stand across from me and do as I say," the doctor wearing white ordered.

"What the hell," the nurse said, "what's *she* doing in here."

"We're short staffed," the doctor said. "There is nobody else right now."

"I will not allow this," the nurse protested. "This is an operating room; not a goddamn high school biology class."

The doctor raised his voice. "Stand aside. With the staff shortage, I'll take whomever I can get. She's proven to be competent, has a steady hand, and knows how to follow orders."

"Bullshit," the nurse blustered. "You wouldn't tolerate her either if it weren't for Halbert. The O.R. is no place for politics and back room deals."

"Hey, dudes," the pregnant lady shouted. After getting their attention she spoke in a normal tone. "I'm standing right here, you know? Now, are we going to help this patient or not?"

Coop couldn't recall exactly how it happened, but after hearing her speak, he suddenly found himself out of his seat, palms pressed against the glass, and staring wide-eyed. Her voice was unmistakable.

Katie, his Katie. He had finally found her.

But how could this be? How could she be…

…Pregnant?

Captain Sloat rested a hand on Coop's shoulder. "Are you okay? Don't be embarrassed if you're squeamish. Not everyone can handle seeing what goes on in an operating theater. I'd rather you left than have you puke all over this glass."

"I'm fine." Coop's palms remained glued to the glass. He gawked at Katie, trying to comprehend what he was seeing.

It dawned on him. Of course. Alone in this enclave and probably bewildered, Katie had found someone to take her in, to care for her, to fall in love with her, to marry her. As pretty as she was, as bright as she was, she would be noticed immediately and instantly pursued. Some young soldier, perhaps, or a doctor? That made more sense. Her new husband probably made it possible for her to continue her studies. Anyway, here there were plenty of handsome, eligible men. Why hadn't he considered that possibility? And now the happy couple had made a child together.

Coop sank back into his seat and buried his face in his hands. He had been a fool. Katie was intelligent, a lot smarter than he was. Of course, she would know how to take care of herself. What did she have to look forward to in Wineberry Hollow? Terrible memories, misery, and heartache. Her father had been taken from her. When the soldiers carried her off, it probably ended up being a blessing for her. Here Katie could start a new life, a happy one, where she could continue to pursue her dreams. As if nothing happened. As if it were the before times.

When Coop's father had passed away, he felt loss, but that feeling paled in comparison to the lead weight now anchored in his gut. He had abandoned his mother, risked his life, endured horrors to rescue Katie. And now, she was as good as dead to him. Disgusted with himself, Coop stood and went to the door.

"You sure you're not getting sick?" Sloat asked.

"I'm fine," Coop said. What was yet another lie when he had fallen so far?

"Where are you going?"

Coop glanced back at the captain. "Home."

Chapter 73

Unable to sleep, Win Halbert got out of bed and slipped into a robe. While tying the nylon sash around his waist, he walked to the liquor cabinet. He poured himself three fingers of scotch – the gin stock having now been totally depleted – and threw it down his gullet. He poured himself another. Although the weather outside was chilly, the air in his quarters seemed stuffy. He switched on the overhead ceiling fan and took a seat on the sofa.

Kall's disturbing phone call a few hours earlier stole his desire for sleep. More enclaves had fallen away. Everything west of the Mississippi and the South.

"Jesus," Halbert muttered. It was over now, the only question remaining was how long until the inhabitants of E38 revolted. From intel he had gathered, Halbert knew that the group of soldiers helping the non-essentials had become bolder and openly participated in distributing food outside the fence. Halbert made the tactical move of ignoring this minor insurrection. A draconian crackdown would only call further attention to the problem and possibly promote sympathy among the other units.

Kall and his minions, and Halbert included himself among those, had miscalculated the reaction of the enclavists. Fatally so. Their mistake? It seemed so clear to him now.

Men like he and Kall didn't think like decent human beings. Armed Forces Homecoming Day had been a joke. Did they really think that *all* families would blindly stream into the enclaves on that day? Did they really think that the enclavists would accept the death of their fellow countrymen, friends, neighbors, associates, and family left behind on the outside, the so-called non-essentials? Maybe that selfish bastard Kall didn't give a damn about those outside of his close circle, but decent human beings didn't think that way.

Halbert raised his glass and uttered a toast to himself. "To decent human beings." He downed his drink and stood, intending to pour himself another, but paused after hearing the wop wop of a helicopter engine. As a matter of fact, he realized, there had been quite a bit of aerial activity since dusk. Was the military performing some sort of drill? If so, he wondered why he hadn't been told. Tomorrow, he'd chew someone's ass about this.

That chopper seemed too close. Damn, he worried the noise might wake Katie.

He walked to the bedroom and leaned against the door frame, peering at their bed. Enough light trickled in from the kitchen so that he could see the rise and fall of her chest, one of her hands resting on her bulbous stomach.

He studied her as the noise from the helicopter faded away. She had been so tired that the noise hadn't disturbed her. Poor girl. She looked so peaceful and innocent sleeping there, and she had been so courageous, insisting on keeping her child despite the pressure he had put on her to get rid of it.

"It's not the baby's fault," she had told him. "This baby doesn't deserve to die because of the sins of its mother."

Reasoning with her that billions of people had already died during the past year who didn't deserve it hadn't swayed her resolve. God, she could be so stubborn.

Then again, it could be her way of getting back at him, a child being a constant reminder of what he had done to her. Of course, the baby might belong to Halfjack. Katie had gotten pregnant almost immediately after moving in with him. Could that be it? Was she trying to rub his nose in it by caring for another man's child under his roof?

In any event, Halbert didn't want a baby to deal with, but he couldn't bring himself to force her to abort the child. He had turned into a cold-hearted son-of-a-bitch, but even *he* wasn't that much of a monster. He had developed feelings for Katie. She had made the most of her unpleasant situation, not causing him too much trouble, pursuing her studies, not attempting to run. If this baby brought her some happiness, then so be it. He'd learn to live with it.

Someone banged at his door.

What the hell now?

Katie stirred. Halbert closed the bedroom door.

"Open up," someone shouted from the other side of the door followed by more pounding.

With anger rising in his chest, Halbert yanked open the door. He stood face to face with Colonel Kettering and a contingent of soldiers. "What's the meaning of this, Halfjack?"

The colonel and his men pushed past. Halfjack asked, "Anybody here with you?"

"Katie's in the bedroom. What's going on?"

The men fanned out and wandered through his quarters. Halbert moved in front of the bedroom door and stood there.

"Clear," came the shouts of men as they inspected each of his rooms. One of the men tried pushing past him to check the bedroom.

"Touch that door knob, and I'll personally toss you outside the enclave gate," Halbert said. In that moment he realized how much he really *did* care about Katie.

"I'll handle this," Halfjack said. He addressed his men. "Wait outside." After they exited, he said, "President Kall is here. I need to make sure your quarters are secure."

That news caught Halbert off guard. "Kall? Here? I just spoke with him by radio earlier this evening."

"He'll explain things himself. Right now, I need to go in there and verify that all is secure."

"What? You think Katie's hiding a gun under her pillow?"

"Wouldn't put it past her," Halfjack scoffed. "Don't make this difficult."

Knowing that he'd be powerless to stop Halfjack, Halbert said, "Give me a minute." He slipped through the bedroom door and shut it behind him. He flipped on the lights.

Katie stood beside the bed, wide-eyed and pale. She held a shoe in her hand like a weapon. She asked, "What's *he* doing here?"

"Shhh," he placed his hands on Katie's shoulders. She trembled under his touch. In a low voice he said, "I won't let anybody bother you. I promise. Get dressed and take the secret tunnel to the med center. Lock yourself in one of the rooms until I send for you."

A few minutes later, they both left the bedroom. Katie averted her eyes from Halfjack and walked directly out the door. Wasting no time, Halfjack searched the bedroom and master bath while Halbert poured himself another drink and waited. What did all of this mean? Why would Kall come here unannounced?

When Halfjack emerged, Halbert expected him to make some sort of crack about sharing Katie with him or about her being pregnant. Instead, Halfjack shot him a cold stare and left his quarters.

A minute later, President R.A. Kall walked in holding a briefcase. Alone. The man's eyes darted around the room. Crazy eyes.

"Can I get you something to drink?" Halbert asked. God knows the man looked like he needed one.

Kall ignored him. He set his briefcase on the coffee table and embraced Halbert. "I knew I made the right choice when I picked you. Win, my friend, you've managed to hold things together where everyone else has failed. How? How have you done this?"

"Begging your pardon, sir, I'm not sure I understand."

"The enemy," Kall shouted. It startled Halbert so badly that he nearly dropped his glass. Kall grabbed him by the collar of his robe and yelled into his face. "The enemy is at the gates."

Halbert set his drink on the bar and took Kall's wrists. He wrenched the man's hands free from his robe. "Get a hold of yourself, Mr. President. What enemy? Outsiders? Non-essentials? Nobody is coming through these enclave gates. Not on my watch."

Kall backed away and smiled, his lips peeling from his teeth. "It's not the outsiders who have come to kill me, Win. It's the enemy within." He paced the room, mumbling unintelligibly.

Halbert turned to the liquor cabinet and poured a stiff drink into a glass for the president. With a sigh, he drained the rest of the Scotch into his own glass. The last of it. Probably anywhere. Kall took the glass when Halbert offered it to him and sat on the sofa. Halbert joined him. Had Kall lost his mind? He tugged at the collar of his robe. Sweat rolled down his back despite the ceiling fan whirring overhead.

The president met his gaze. "They came just after we had our radio conversation. Wave after wave of insurgents. They breeched Raven Rock's perimeter."

"Non-essentials?"

"No, you fool, regular army troops. Organized by Mandible. We were completely surrounded. Your man, Halfjack, executed a bold plan for our escape. I owe you a debt of gratitude for your recommending him to me. He saved my life. We escaped by helicopter. Only one single helicopter made it out."

If Raven Rock had fallen, Halbert knew, then it was indeed over. How had the end come so soon? "One aircraft? You and Halfjack and who else?"

"The half dozen men you saw earlier, my most trusted guards. Everyone else has deserted us, Win. Everyone."

"My god. What about the first lady?"

"Nika?" Kall gazed vacantly at a spot behind Halbert. "House arrest, I suppose. I saw them march her away in handcuffs as we took off."

"The other ministers?"

"Taken."

The word echoed in Halbert's head. *Taken.* He inhaled and squeezed shut his eyes. "What other enclaves besides this one are still loyal?"

"New York and New England are all that remain." Kall waved his arms and raised his voice. "I will retreat no further. We are at the vanguard, Win. It is here where we will make our stand. You and I. Together. Standing as visionaries. Brothers. This is just a bump in the road. A winnowing of those who remain. We will prevail."

Leaning his forehead in his hand, Halbert kept his eyes closed. How long until the soldiers loyal to the citizens of the original

United States of America overran E38? Days? Hours? "This man, Mandible. Have you determined his identity yet?"

"If I knew, he'd be dead," Kall said.

"He appears to have considerable influence to rally the troops to his cause," Halbert probed, trying to measure if Kall would realize that all was lost.

"Traitors," Kall shouted. "Have they no vision? Can't they see how this new world order has reshaped civilization? Where is their gratitude for what I have done for humankind? How I have improved their lives? And now they want to throw me down? Where is their decency?"

Despite being in the presence of an unstable lunatic, Halbert couldn't help but laugh. He blurted, "Decency?"

Kall stared at him coldly.

Halbert stood. "I am a coward at heart. I'm a great businessman and accomplished politician, but when it comes to a threat against my own skin, I'll fold like a shrinking violet."

Kall's eyebrows knit together.

"Not very manly, I know, but give me credit, Mr. President, for knowing myself so well and for not being too egotistical to admit it. If we walk out that door together, chances are Mandible and his loyalists won't kill us. They'll want to put us on display in a showy trial, but they won't kill us." Halbert reconsidered. "At least not right away."

Kall narrowed his eyes and stood. "You're either with me or against me, Win. Choose."

"Mr. President, with all due respect, we have nothing left to fight with."

With a grin, Kall picked up his briefcase and gripped it with both hands. "As long as I control the football, we have leverage. I can still win this war. But I'll need a safe haven. Can you keep E38 safe for me, Win? Can you?"

Halbert eyed the briefcase and then Kall's face. The man would do it. He would actually unleash global nuclear annihilation rather than surrender. Thinking quickly, he said, "As you know, my office is on the ground floor of this building. It would make an excellent command center. Feel free to relocate your men there. I'm sure you'll find the facilities most accommodating. I'm going to shower, get dressed, and will join you shortly."

The corners of Kall's lips turned up. "Outstanding. I knew I could trust you." He gripped Halbert's hand and shook it vigorously. "I'll need all of your leadership skills for you to rally the citizenry and the troops right away. We'll need to prepare for what lies ahead. We can do this, Win. Put your faith in me."

"I always have, Mr. President."

"See you soon, my brother." Kall walked out the door.

Halbert's heart pounded. He walked to the liquor cabinet. No more gin, no more scotch, not even a bottle of cheap wine. Nothing. Now that he had sent Katie away, he couldn't even go to her for comfort.

His hand shook. Sweat poured from him.

Why was it so damned hot in here? He studied the ceiling fan and the whirling blades. He stripped out of his robe and let it drop to his feet. He stood naked under the fan letting the breeze bathe his body. "May the devil help me," he mumbled, knowing that God certainly wouldn't.

Lifting a kitchen chair with both hands, he smashed it into the fan. His first attempt had bent one of the blades, and the torque from the fan had torn the chair from his hands. The fan continued to spin in a wobble. He picked up the chair and swung it again and again until nothing remained of the fan but the housing which was attached to a ceiling stud. Nice and strong. It would do.

Halbert pulled the nylon sash free from his robe and set the chair under the broken fan. He stood on the chair and wrapped one end of the sash around the housing. He pulled the sash tight and tied the other end around his neck.

It was ironic, Halbert thought, how everyone would view what he was about to do as cowardly when in reality, it was the most courageous thing he ever did in his life. Pride filled him instead of shame.

Halbert kicked the chair out from beneath his feet.

Chapter 74

Cooper snapped awake to the sound of gunfire. He jumped from his bunk and looked out the window. Soldiers with guns streamed past his quarters running toward the center of the enclave. Some sort of disturbance?

The activity suited him. Maybe he'd be able to walk out of the enclave with nobody to question him. The night before, he had taken a long, soothing shower, stowed his belongings and as much food as he could carry into his back pack. He intended to leave after a good night's sleep. With any luck, he would make it back to *High Acre*, the Brewster's ranch at the base of Bald Eagle Mountain by nightfall. He knew the way well and already planned in his head the best route that would keep him clear of people. He'd see his mother again before the end of the week, Gottes Wille.

More gunfire. Men shouting. In the distance, an explosion.

Coop grabbed his pack and slung it onto his back. What was happening? He could care less. Without even a final glance, he exited his quarters and headed for gate W3.

As Coop rounded the corner of his building, a soldier collided with him. Both men fell to the ground. Coop recovered first, stood, and brushed himself off. He helped the soldier to his feet, a young man no older than he was. Coop bent down and picked up the man's weapon. Handed it to him. "What's your hurry?"

"Liberation!" the young soldier exclaimed trying to catch his breath. "President Kall and the last of his forces are holed up at the command center. We have him surrounded and are about to move in. The gates are coming down."

The young man ran off. Over his shoulder, he shouted, "They're coming down."

No concern of his, Coop thought. He paced in the opposite direction for a few steps and halted. The medical center was located adjacent to central command. If that's where the battle raged…"She's safe," he said. "Katie's husband will protect her. My priority now lies with my mother and my neighbors." Except he didn't know for sure if Katie would be safe. What if her husband was a soldier? On whose side did he fight? If the outcome went against him, would Katie suffer repercussions? Carrying a baby and being near term, she would be more vulnerable than ever.

He should have spoken with her, Coop realized, but he had been too stunned, too hurt last night to think rationally. If he went to the medical center looking for Katie now, he could get killed. Maybe for nothing.

Yet Katie was so close, and his mother so far away.

Coop took a deep breath, turned, and walked swiftly toward the sound of battle. It took him a half hour to reach the building. Expecting to be stopped, Coop was surprised that he was able to walk right up to the front door of the med center unhindered. The sound of gunfire echoed from the adjacent command center. Fortunately, the front door to the hospital lay on the protected side of the building, opposite the fire fight.

He approached the checkpoint setup at the med center's main entrance. Two men suddenly appeared from around the corner of the building carrying a stretcher, the limp form of a wounded soldier lay covered with a green blanket.

"Out of the way," one of the guards shouted.

Coop stepped aside while the guards ushered the wounded man and his bearers through the entrance. When they turned their attention back to him, one of them asked, "State your business."

"I'm here to help Katie Hunt. She's a doctor."

"You're on staff?" the guard asked.

"Well…I'm a helper. A volunteer." A stretch of the truth, Coop knew. He was here only to help Katie. If she needed it.

"You have an ID?"

"Sorry. I just jumped out of bed and got here as soon as I could. I didn't bring my ID."

The second guard said, "Let him pass, for Christ's sake. There's a lot of wounded men in there. You can see he's no threat."

The first guard searched his backpack and then waved him through.

Coop stood in the main lobby and witnessed utter chaos. With the front desk unattended, people raced back and forth barking orders. If Katie were here, she'd most likely be found in the surgical wing. He hurried down the hallway, retracing his steps from yesterday. He passed through the door labeled: EMERGENCY and was immediately confronted by an attendant dressed in a white lab coat.

"Who are you?" the attendant asked. "You don't look wounded."

"I'm not. I'm looking for Katie Hunt."

The attendant smirked. "Halbert's plaything. She's not here."

Coop wondered what the man meant by his statement. "If I can just have a look."

"She's not here, Pal. Beat it."

From the man's expression, Coop could see the attendant meant business. He wouldn't be able to talk his way past. He left and thought about finding the stairs to the observation area. Maybe he'd see her in one of the operating rooms. At least then he'd know where she was and could wait for her.

He found the door, tried opening it, but found it locked.

In a panic, Coop realized there was only one thing he could do. He walked the halls and approached everyone he saw. "Have you seen Katie Hunt? Do you know where I can find her?"

Most of the people he approached shook their heads and kept walking. A few sneered as if hearing her name was something repugnant to them. A few kind people took the time to tell him that they hadn't seen her or that they didn't know who she was.

At the end of the corridor, near the exit to the main lobby, Coop approached a man in a business suit and a woman wearing green scrubs having a conversation. He interrupted. "Excuse me. I'm looking for Katie Hunt. Have you seen her?"

The woman scoffed, "That little slut. Once the smoke clears from next door she'll get her comeuppance."

"No need to be rude," the man said, "whatever you think of Katie, one thing for sure is she's a damn good O.R. assistant."

Coop recognized these two by their voices. The doctor and the nurse he had seen yesterday in the operating theater attending to Lieutenant Napoli. He tugged the doctor's sleeve. "Please, sir, this is urgent. I have to find her. Is there anything you can tell me? Any idea where she might be? Or her husband?"

"Her husband?" The woman laughed. "That's a good one."

Why did so many people express such hostility toward Katie?

The doctor eyed him with a look of pity. "Who are you, son?"

Sensing that the unvarnished truth would be the only way to win over this man, Coop took a breath and said, "I'm Katie's friend from her hometown. I've known her since we were children. Look, I have no business being here except I really care about her. I need to make sure she's safe. Please, don't kick me out until I find her."

The woman stopped laughing and stared at him, her red face and downcast eyes displaying embarrassment. Or was it shame?

"I'm sorry, young man," the doctor said. "I haven't seen Katie today."

Dejected, Coop turned to leave.

"Wait," the woman said. "I saw her early this morning, before all the trouble. In the west wing, a room at the far end of the hall. I didn't know what she was doing, but I think she might have been resting on one of the beds."

"Thank God, she's not over there." The doctor nodded in the direction of the command center.

"Thank you." Coop pushed through the door into the lobby, found a sign for the west wing and ran down the long corridor.

"Katie," he shouted. "Katie, where are you?"

An orderly intercepted him. "Keep your voice down. There are sick and injured people here."

"Pardon me." Coop pushed by the man. Heeding the man's counsel, instead of yelling, he peeked into each room as he passed. Some of the rooms were vacant while some were occupied with patients. He didn't find her. Did he have the right wing? Could the woman have been mistaken about seeing her in the west wing? Had Katie been here earlier but now gone?

He glanced into the last room at the end of the hall. Empty. In desperation, he backed out and decided to check the other wings of the hospital.

Then he stopped. Something about that last room.

Coop peaked again into the room. On a hook, hung a long, black wool coat. He remembered the night of their date, how pretty she had looked bundled up in that coat. How her hair had smelled like...he removed the coat from the hook and brought the collar up to his nose...lilacs.

"Katie." He looked around the room. "Katie Hunt." Was she hiding from him? Feeling silly, he looked under both of the beds. He tried the bathroom door.

Locked.

"Katie, are you in there?"

"I was never a party to what went on," she said. "I'm a victim just like everyone else. Halbert kept me against my will."

The strength left Coop's legs. He sagged to the floor into a sitting position, relieved, thanking God.

"I'm pregnant," she said in a girlish voice. "For the sake of my baby, please don't hurt me. I had nothing to do with any of it."

Coop closed his eyes, rested his cheek against the door, and breathed. In a calm voice, he uttered, "Katie, I'm not going to hurt you. I would never hurt you. It's me, Cooper Stover."

From the other side of the door, silence. Then, "Coop?"

Pulling himself together, Coop stood. "Katie, please open the door."

A few more seconds passed. Then the door clicked and opened.

She looked tired, pale, washed out. But Coop had never seen a sight more beautiful. No words passed between them and she walked into his embrace.

Too soon, Katie pulled away. She shrank back against the far wall by the commode wide-eyed and hugging herself, trying to hide her belly. Red faced and looking at her feet she asked, "What are you doing here, Coop?"

"Katie, I apologize. I didn't mean to take the liberty of hugging you like that. I don't want to come between you and your husband. It's just that," he paused to catch his breath. "Katie, I've come from far away, searched for so long, and it's so good to see you."

She met his gaze and tilted her head. "What? What are you talking about?"

"You're safe," Coop said, "that's all that's important, but why are you so scared? Who do you think is going to hurt you?"

"God, Coop. I'm in shock. I mean, what are you doing here? How did you get here? How did you find me?"

"It's a long story."

She sighed and walked again into his arms, resting her head against his chest. "I can't believe this. Am I dreaming?"

"You're not dreaming."

"Crap, look at me. No don't. Don't look at me, at my shame. Close the door, Coop, lock it. They mustn't find me. I'm in such deep shit."

Why would she want to be locked in the bathroom with him? That wouldn't be proper. "Your husband wouldn't approve of this."

She brushed passed him, shut and locked the door herself. "You're confusing the hell out of me, and you haven't answered my question. What are you doing here?"

"Katie, I came here to rescue you, but now that you're married, well, I just wanted to make sure you were safe. There's a battle taking place in the next building."

She stared at him, her expression one of disbelief. "You came," she paused, "to rescue me?"

"Yeah, I feel like Job from the Bible, the trials and tribulations I've been through to find you."

Katie looked down at her stomach. "The trials and tribulations *you've* been through?"

"Please, let's not fight. Not now. Not after all this time."

"Holy crap. I can't believe it. I can't believe it's really you." She leaned in and kissed him on the cheek.

Coop pulled away. "Katie, your husband."

"God, Coop, you are so freaking clueless. There is no husband. I am not married."

Now it was his turn to be confused. "Well then, I guess we both have a lot to talk about."

She swallowed and stared at the door knob. "No talking. We don't have time to talk. Listen, Coop, you have to leave."

"Leave, what are you saying?"

"You can't be seen with me. It would be dangerous for you."

"That's ridiculous, Katie, I just found you. I'm not going to leave you."

"You have to, Coop. You have to leave now and forget about me."

"Forget you?" Coop said, "but Katie, I love you."

She held a hand over his mouth. "No. Don't say that. You don't get to say that." And then the girl who never cried leaked a single tear which tracked down the side of her face. She wiped it away quickly and sniffled. "I'm not the same girl you fell in love with. I've had to do things to survive."

"So have I. Since the world went dark, I suppose we've all had to do things we're not proud of."

Katie shrank back and pursed her lips. Another tear leaked from her eye. She wiped it. "Oh yeah? Well, try this on for size. You see this baby? Of course, you can't help but to see it. Guess what? I'm not even sure who the father is. What do you think of me now, Coop?"

"I know you, Katie Hunt. You would not sleep around. Terrible things must have happened to you, horrors I can't begin to understand." He took her hand. "In my heart, I know that you're still the same girl. And I still love you."

She sniffled and no longer tried to hold back her tears. "Damn you, Cooper Stover, for making me cry." She hammered his chest with the edge of her fists. "Damn you for loving me so unconditionally and making me feel so guilty for the way I've treated you."

He took her fists and squeezed them together in his hands. She buried her face in his chest and sobbed. Coop stroked her hair. "It's okay, Katie, you can let it out. You can finally let it all out."

She collapsed into him and wept. Coop supported all of her weight and said nothing. He just stroked her hair and allowed her to cry, happy that she trusted him enough to expose her raw emotion in such an intimate way.

After pulling herself together, she hiccupped and asked, "Does it always feel this good after crying?"

Coop didn't know how to answer and said nothing.

"Seriously, Coop, you need to go," Katie said. "This is going to be hard for you to believe, but by some cruel twist of fate, the people I've had to associate with are the very ones responsible for turning the world dark. It's over for them now, and the soldiers fighting to bring those evil people to justice will probably think I also played a part in it."

Coop straightened. "I don't care what the soldiers or anybody else thinks. You and I are walking out of here together. I'm taking you home."

She displayed a sad smile. "How?"

"Through the front door."

"Then what? Think it through, Coop. What you're planning is hopeless."

"I know of an abandoned ranch a couple days hike from here. It's isolated and a safe place for you to have your baby. We can winter there. In the spring, we'll return to Wineberry Hollow."

Katie touched his cheek. "You've become a man. So brave. I'm proud of you, Coop. What you're proposing sounds wonderful. I'd really like that, but how will we get out of the enclave? Security has this place locked down."

Proud? Her words warmed him. Coop opened the bathroom door. "Leave that to me. I know a few of the good guys." He picked up his pack and strapped it onto his back. After helping

Katie into her coat, Coop took her hand and led her into the hall. He turned toward the lobby.

The orderly who had chastised him earlier for making too much noise exited from a patient's room far down the corridor. He noticed Coop, stood in the middle of the hall, and folded his arms across his chest.

Chapter 75

Coop stared at the menacing man blocking their path. Katie tugged his hand. She said, "Not that way. Let me show you."

She led him in the opposite direction of the lobby toward the end of the corridor to a fire exit. They descended the stairs. Looking through the glass doors, Coop saw an armed soldier guarding the exit from the outside. Luckily, the man had his back turned to the door probably more concerned with keeping people out. Katie put a finger to her lips. Quietly as possible, they stepped onto the landing. He followed her to the backside of the staircase to an access door with a keypad. Katie punched in a series of numbers and the latch clicked. She eased open the door and led him into a long, dimly lit, narrow corridor, and closed the door behind them.

"What is this place?" Coop asked.

"It's supposed to be an electrical room. At least, that's the story everyone is told. Only the higher ups know that it's a secret tunnel."

They walked a few minutes until the corridor ended in a square room which Coop thought was about as large as his barn back home. A door was set in the middle of each of the four walls and the room furnished with a table, lounge chairs, a sink, and a refrigerator.

Katie sank into the one of the lounge chairs to catch her breath. She placed a hand over her protruding belly.

"Where do the other doors lead?" he asked.

"That one in the opposite wall leads to the command center and executive quarters. The one to the right leads to the enclave airstrip, but it's a long walk. At least two miles. I don't know where that one to the left leads. Someplace in the middle of the enclave, or so I've been told."

If Katie knew about these tunnels, why hadn't she simply escaped her situation? Probably because she would be unable to get past the enclave gates. Even if she did manage that, how could she have survived on the outside, especially carrying a child within her. He rummaged through the refrigerator and pulled out a six pack of bottled water. Removing his back pack, Coop stuffed as many bottles as he could in the spaces beside his spare clothing and canteen.

He handed a bottle to Katie. "When you're ready, we'll go left."

She stood. "We'll have to take it slow. I feel like I'm waddling like a duck."

Coop started to reach for his pack, but Katie threw her arms around him. "It's starting to sink in, what you've done for me, what you must have gone through." Her voice faded to a whisper. "Thank you."

A metallic clank sounded from the opposite wall. The door opened and a wide-eyed man strode forward carrying a shiny suitcase. Coop recognized the man from news photos. President Kall. A soldier entering the room behind Kall closed and latched the door.

Katie moved a hand to her mouth and whimpered.

The soldier who had secured the door turned and leered. "Well, lookie, lookie, here. If it isn't my old squeeze and her Amish boyfriend."

It dawned on Coop who he was, the man named Kettering who had ransacked Wineberry Hollow, murdered his neighbors, and kidnapped Katie. He stepped in front of Katie, shielding her.

"I don't give a damn who these non-essentials are," Kall yelled. "We have no time to spare. Our enemy is right behind us. Kill them and lead the way to the airstrip."

"Wait. If I may suggest," Kettering said quickly.

"What is it?" Kall snapped.

"A pregnant woman makes for an excellent hostage. During our escape, I doubt our enemy would shoot at you if you held her as a shield."

Kall arched an eyebrow. "Point taken. Bring her."

"No," Katie screamed.

Kettering walked up to Coop, his face so close their eyelashes almost touched. He whispered, "Besides, that bun in her oven just might be mine." He hammered his forehead into Coop's nose.

Coop heard the crunching of cartilage and felt a searing wave of pain as sparks exploded behind his field of vision. Both of his hands involuntarily shot to his face and warm blood flowed between his fingers. He moaned and dropped to his knees feeling consciousness slip from him.

He heard Katie screaming.

Coop took several deep breaths in an attempt to clear his head. As he regained his senses, he heard a banging noise and looked up. Soldiers began forcing their way through the closed door from the corridor leading to the command center.

Everything happened so quickly that Coop couldn't react.

Kall dropped the shiny suitcase he carried and pulled a handgun from the inside of his coat. He grabbed Katie, held her in front of him, and pressed the muzzle of the gun to her temple.

Kettering slipped in from the side, unnoticed by Kall, and grabbed the suitcase. He dove for the door on the left, the one Katie told Coop that she didn't know where it led. He disappeared behind the door. The latch clicked shut.

President Kall turned his back on Coop and faced the soldiers. "No closer. I'll kill this woman."

Coop's heart pounded in fear for Katie. He ignored the pain in his ruined nose.

"Stand aside," a familiar voice ordered from the hallway. To Coop's astonishment, Captain Sloat entered the room and pointed a handgun at Kall. A tall, lanky man wearing military fatigues followed behind Sloat.

Kall seemed confused. "Colonel Muncie?"

"Affirmative," Muncie answered, "but you can call me Mandible."

"You," Kall said. Coop could sense hatred in his tone. "We had it all. A utopia. You and your minions wrecked it. Why?"

Muncie stared at him grim faced. "If I have to explain that to you, then you'll never understand."

"Don't squeeze my waist so hard," Katie pleaded. "You're hurting me. My baby."

Coop had to get Katie away from Kall. On all fours, he slowly crawled toward Kall while trailing blood from his nose. He made eye contact with Sloat who gave him a barely perceptible nod of the head.

"How dare you obstruct me," Kall yelled. "I am the President of the United States and your commander-in-chief. I order you to lay down your arms."

"Not going to happen," Muncie held out his hand. "Give me that gun. Let the woman go."

Kall sneered. "Why would I do that when she's my ticket out of here? I'm going to walk through the door to the airfield, and you are *not* going to stop me. I have nothing to lose. I will kill her if I have to." Not realizing that Coop was getting ready to grab him from behind, Kall took a step backward and bumped into Coop losing his balance. He pin wheeled his arms reflexively and released his grasp on Katie.

Coop grabbed Kall's wrist, the one holding the gun, and rammed him into the wall. The force of it caused Kall to drop the gun. Stunned, Kall collapsed to the floor. Coop picked up the gun and pointed it at Kall's face.

The president shrank back and shielded his face with his hands.

"No," Katie shouted. "Don't do it, Coop. Don't kill him."

"Why not? This man hurt you. He would've killed you and your unborn child. This man is responsible for all of the hurt in the world, for all of the things that happened to you. He's killed billions. I'm in a position to stop him, to finally put an end to the madness. He doesn't deserve to live."

"Listen to me, Coop. Forget the terrible way I treated you in the past. Forget how I called you Chicken Coop. You have nothing more to prove to me, and if you pull that trigger it'll change you. You'll no longer be the kind, gentle man that I've come to love. You hear me, Coop? Don't ruin what we now finally have, what you've been struggling so hard to achieve."

Coop paused as he considered her words. In his moment of indecision, Colonel Muncie took hold of Coop's wrist and closed his hand over the gun. "Let go of the weapon, young man. This is my burden. Not yours." He rolled his eyes in Katie's direction and mumbled. "Go to her."

As they exchanged glances, Coop understood what the colonel was thinking. He released the handgun, stumbled to Katie's side, and made her face the wall. "Don't look."

"R.A. Kall," Colonel Muncie spoke with authority. "You once

swore an oath to preserve, protect, and defend the constitution of the United States of America. Your treasonous actions demonstrate your contempt for that oath you swore."

On the floor, Kall tried scrabbling away, but Muncie kicked him in the knee.

Kall cried out and quit moving.

Muncie pointed the gun at Kall's head and continued. "I also swore an oath. An oath to protect this nation from all enemies, both foreign," he worked the slide of the handgun to chamber a round, "and domestic."

The shot within the confines of the room roared with a deafening boom.

Chapter 76

The same doctor who had tended to Lieutenant Napoli repaired and dressed Coop's mashed nose. Katie demanded to assist, and of course, she got her way.

"You'll probably have a permanent crook in it," the doctor warned. "I'm no plastic surgeon, but I did the best I could."

Katie handed him a mirror.

Coop inspected his reflection, the white bandage wrapped around his nose all the way around to the back of his head. "Don't I look a sight."

She giggled. "It's enough to scare small children."

He looked at Katie's belly. "Speaking of which, you sure you're okay?"

"I'm fine, Coop," she said. "You saved me and my baby."

"Let's get out of here," he said.

"Yeah, right behind you."

They walked from the treatment room into a waiting area. Captain Sloat and a half dozen soldiers stood from their chairs.

Katie stiffened. She said, "So, the fairy tale ending wasn't meant to be. I'm so sorry, Coop." Turning to Sloat, she sighed. "I guess I have some explaining to do."

Sloat's eyebrows knit together. "You owe nobody an explanation. I know your story well. Your Cooper has bored me to death on countless occasions explaining his reason for showing up at my gate, about his feelings for you, and about how you were so rudely torn from your home." He took Katie's hand and stared at the ground. "I'm sorry for all you've been through, and your suffering at the hands of those who should have protected you."

Katie swallowed and wore a sad expression. "Halfjack got away, didn't he?"

"Only temporarily. He emerged from the tunnel and remains on the grounds somewhere. We'll soon have him in custody."

"Holy crap, what about the football? I saw him take it. He could…my god, I don't even want to think about that."

"No need to worry," Sloat said. "Kall wore the activation key around his neck. It's now safely in Colonel Muncie's possession. Besides, Halfjack doesn't know the launch codes. I'm sure Kall would never have shared those with anybody."

"You hope, but you don't know?" Katie asked.

Sloat didn't answer.

Coop didn't understand the nature of their conversation but realized from their tone that it was something serious. "I think we can trust Captain Sloat that whatever the situation is, it's under control."

"You heard the man," Sloat said.

Katie tilted her head. "Are we free to leave?"

"Democracy is in the process of being restored," Sloat said, "but we need to escort the two of you away of here. People are out for blood, and they aren't as familiar with your situation as I am."

Laying a hand on Coop's shoulder, Sloat said, "Is there anything I can do for you."

With no hesitation, Coop said, "You can let Katie and I climb aboard one of those helicopters and fly us home."

"That goes without saying. Anything else?"

Coop looked at Katie. "I have everything else that I could ever need."

"Wait a minute," Katie said, a mischievous glint in her eye. "There is one other thing…"

Chapter 77

Coop cuddled with Katie under a heavy wool blanket which shielded them against a relentless icy breeze. They sat, staring into the horizon. The helicopter along with the soldiers who accompanied them remained within sight, but at a respectable distance allowing them their privacy.

The air smelled foreign, not unpleasant, but unlike anything Coop had ever smelled before. He took a deep breath imprinting the first impression into his memory. He vowed never to forget these feelings, these sensations, this wondrous gift Katie had given him.

"Well, what do you think?" Katie asked.

He grabbed a handful of white sand and allowed the grains to trickle through his fingers. The powerful waves crashing against the beach thundered with unrivaled majesty, the water stretching into infinity awed him and made him feel small. Insignificant. He raised his voice over the sounds of the ocean. "How could anyone bearing witness to this display of nature deny the existence of God?"

Katie shrugged. "I don't know."

He strained his eyes looking into the distance. "What lies across this ocean?"

"England, I think."

"Do you think somewhere in England, someone might be sitting on a beach and looking in our direction."

"I hope so, Coop, I really do. Now that things are getting better, we'll probably soon find out."

The wind continued to sting Coop's eyes. He shut them for awhile and leaned his head against Katie's shoulder. "Does it ever get warm here?"

"In the summertime, it gets hot as an oven."

"Have you ever been here during the summer?"

"Of course."

"You think someday we'll be able to return to this spot during the summer?"

"Sure. Why do you ask?"

Coop opened his eyes and lifted his head from her shoulder. He made eye contact with her. "Because I'd like to see you in a bikini."

Katie pursed her lips and punched him in the shoulder. A love tap. "God, you are such a guy. Get your mind out of the gutter, Cooper Stover." She sighed and lowered her gaze. "Besides, how can you possibly think of me in that way after what I've done and now that I look like a beached whale?"

He held his hand above the blanket over her belly. "May I?"

She took his hand and moved it under the blanket, pressing his palm against her bulge.

Coop didn't feel anything.

"Here," Katie said and moved his fingers to just the right spot. "Feel it?"

A soft thud pressed against his fingertips. It occurred to Coop how much he didn't know about things and how much smarter Katie was than him. Still… "Your child is going to need a father."

Katie leaned away and stared at him with a shocked expression. "Holy crap, are you proposing to me?"

He looked into the ocean, an iron weight in his stomach. When he had held a gun to Kall's head, Katie had told him that she loved him. Was that just talk to prevent him from shooting Kall? He felt unsure now and didn't want to make a fool of himself. "Look, Katie, I know that I'm not what you want, that with me you would be settling for someone beneath your expectations."

"Cooper, don't presume to tell me what I want." She buried her face in the blanket. "God, you are so freaking bad at this."

Would he ever understand Katie's way of thinking? Now he was afraid to say anything, so he just stared at the horizon.

After an uncomfortable silence, she said, "What I *want* is a man to love me no matter how goofy I may act or how many mistakes I may make. A man who will tolerate me when I sometimes lose my temper and act out. A man who will keep me safe and look after me and my baby…even though the baby isn't his. A man who will accept me despite my history and all of the baggage I bring into a relationship. Do you know of anyone who fits those qualifications?"

Despite the chill wind, Coop felt his cheeks flush. He grinned and wondered how frightening that grin would look with the hideous bandage he wore. "I might be able to think of a dude who fits that description."

"I can think of a dude, too," she said. "Dude."

Beneath the blanket, he took her hand.

"However," she said, "I *still* wouldn't be caught dead riding in some buggy wearing a long black dress and a bonnet over my hair."

"I hate to say this, but we'll all be riding in buggies for a long time to come, or on horseback. And you can wear whatever you like while riding in my buggy."

"Damn straight, I will."

"Damn straight," he said, mimicking her.

Her expression turned somber. "Seriously, Coop, despite all of the changes, we're still from different planets. I mean, what of your faith? Can you be flexible enough to meet me half way?"

Considering the English clothes he had been wearing these many months and all of the compromises he had made during his mission to find her, it seemed a silly question to Coop. "Katie, I may no longer be Amish, but my faith is stronger than ever. It sustained me in my quest to find you. And look, I *did* find you." He had a further insight. "One good thing has come out of the world going dark, a lesson that should be plain to anyone with half a brain. The experience has taught all men, everywhere, that there is no more Amish, there is no more English, there is no more Jew or Muslim or tribes or nations or tongues. We are all just people now. Human beings. The incident has equalized us."

"Wow!" Katie exclaimed. "That's really deep, but maybe a bit naïve. You go on thinking that way, Coop. Maybe it'll rub off on other people."

Coop took a deep breath to still his beating heart. "So…"

"So, what?"

"You haven't given me a clear answer about you and me being together."

"That's because you haven't asked me a clear question."

His stomach fluttered with butterflies. "Okay, here goes." Coop looked her in the eye. "Katie Hunt, I love you more than anyone else in the world. I always will. And I will love your child that is a part of you."

She frowned when he stopped, but he was just teasing her now.

"I still haven't heard a clear question in all of those lovely words."

"Katie, will you be my wife? Will you marry me? Is that a clear enough question?"

She kept the frown on her face and turned her face to the ocean. Why was she doing this to him? Surely, she hadn't made him grovel just to be mean? Would she really make him into such a fool?

Katie's lips quivered and turned up into a big bright smile. Apparently, she was good at the teasing game, too. She wrapped her arms around his neck and touched her lips to his. So warm, soft, and sweet, and it occurred to Coop that this was his first ever kiss on the lips.

It had been worth the wait.

And Coop knew from her kiss that Katie had answered his question.

Clearly.

Author's Note

In 2001, the United States Congress established the "Commission to Assess the Threat to the United States from Electromagnetic Pulse (EMP) Attack" more commonly referred to as the "EMP Commission." A panel of experts studied the phenomenon of EMP and in 2008 published their findings in a 208 page comprehensive report. This report is available as a free PDF download from the official website at:

http://www.empcommission.org.

The premise behind this novel is not science fiction. The danger posed by both manmade and natural EMP is real and frightening. The dire consequences of an EMP event as portrayed in this book gives you some idea of what could happen. The immediate result of a collapsed electric grid would be mass starvation. Grocery stores carry only a three day inventory. When the delivery trucks stop rolling, there will be no more food.

Have doubts? Read the preface to the EMP report. That summary alone should be enough to convince you and sober you. Modern man wouldn't know how to survive. The protagonist of this story, Cooper Stover, said it best. "They have become too far removed from the Earth."

I confess that I am among those to whom Cooper is referring, because when it comes to living off the land, my knowledge and skills are woefully lacking.

Consider the sad state of affairs where it has now become necessary to teach American children that food does *not* come from grocery stores:

(Links accurate as of this printing.)

http://sciencenetlinks.com/lessons/crops-1-where-does-food-come-from/

http://urbanext.illinois.edu/food/

http://www2.kenyon.edu/projects/farmschool/food/foodhome.htm

http://tiki.oneworld.net/food/food2.html

The harnessing of electricity has improved our way of life in miraculous ways. Technology existing today would have been inconceivable to our ancestors living just a hundred years ago, but the price we pay for our standard of living is a highly specialized division of labor dependent on electric power.

I enjoy our modern lifestyle as well as anybody and have no desire to roll back what mankind has achieved, nor do I suggest that we all become expert at farming. Solving the problem involves preparedness and hardening of the electric grid in order to mitigate the impact from EMP. Of course, doing so will require a reprioritization of our financial resources and the will to make it happen.